CATCH A FALLING STAR

THE UNIVERSAL LINK SERIES: BOOK ONE

Lizzie Collins

ISBN: 9798819982808

DEDICATION

To my friend Caroline Miles
with grateful thanks for her encouragement, suggestions
and patient reading

ACKNOWLEDGEMENTS

Thanks to my husband Neil for his help in the fighting against my computer. It can't have been easy putting up with my black moods.

Prologue

The battered cases, hefted by three roadies, banged and clattered from the truck up the loading slide. In the background a cacophony of shouted instructions, voices layer on layer, rising and subsiding only to rise louder.

The cases landed with a bang which rattled a wooden gantry above the stage.

One voice, louder than the rest, shouted for calm. The whirlwind stopped.

This was unusual as the voice belonged to a young teen. Most of the men he was directing were at least ten years older than him, but they stopped what they were doing to listen.

"For chrissake stop banging those cases around. If you can't manage, get someone else to help. Here, Steve's free. He's unpacked."

Steve was one of the keyboard players, conservatory-trained and renowned in jazz circles as one of the world's best. It didn't matter to Gil. He needed someone to help shift cases of instruments. Steve would do.

Steve didn't argue. Gil had rolled up his sleeves and given him a hand to shift a heavy Wurlitzer before now.

Gradually the banging and clattering subsided and was replaced by discordant notes from a variety of instruments, from trumpets to flutes, guitars to electric pianos.

The dressing-room behind stage echoed with loud laughter, and the occasional shout of protest as someone was jostled or knocked out of the way of the bulb-lit mirrors. None of the band was over twenty-five so there was a fair amount of horseplay. Mostly from a slim, tanned boy with sun-streaked hair pushed back from his bronzed face. He raised on his toes and threw a baseball across the room to another band member who missed it. It hit one of the mirrors, cracking it across the middle.

"Oops!"

The oldest guy in the band was tall and spare with long hair, He pulled on an embroidered robe and, pushing one of the sidemen out of the way, picked up a beribboned tambourine and banged it experimentally against someone's music stand, Leaves of paper fluttered to the ground only to be scooped up by their owner and shoved back into their original portfolio.

By this time all the amplifiers were set up and the guitars plugged in. All the microphone stands were in place, wired up and screaming occasional feedback.

Gil strode from player to player, checking all were present, making sure they had everything they needed. Replacing a capo here, supplying missing guitar picks and broken strings. Fetching coffee to stressed-out musicians. Everything and anything he needed to be, he was.

And all the time the din continued until his head was aching.

The audience could be heard filing into their seats behind the curtain, their chatter and laughter mostly overwhelmed by the sounds on stage. Gil gestured for the band to keep the noise to a minimum then collapsed onto a packing case, lit a Marlboro and took a swallow of cold coffee. Someone shouted that a mic was repeatedly blowing a fuse and he was off again, cigarette butt dropped into his coffee dregs.

Slowly the discordant notes morphed into harmonies.

Gil ran for the dressing room, vaulting over instrument cases and coiled wiring. The other singers were dressed and ready in the greenroom, leaving the dressing room piled high with a detritus of hairspray, odd socks and discarded cigarette packs which hadn't quite reached the bin.

Gil stripped and threw on his stage clothes, combed his hair and applied a little stage makeup. He bolted into the greenroom just in time.

The MC was calling out:

"And now, THE CALIFORNIA CRYSTAL BAND"

Chapter One

Two boys stood backs to the living room wall.

The first was small, wiry and tough. The second boy, younger and his opposite in character and appearance, stood shaking next to him, his eye rapidly swelling – he was ten years old. Every so often he would give a sob and a nervous glance sideways at the menacing father who stood over them, fists clenched and red-faced.

Jamie looked mutinous, and his nose wrinkled in a sneer. He began to yell:

"You old bastard. Leave him alone. Just because you're a failure, no need to…."

His protest was cut short when his father lifted him by the collar and threw him bodily into his bedroom, which opened onto the living room in the tiny bungalow the Robson family called home in the Briarside suburb of Los Angeles. There was a muffled cry as Jamie hit the wall at the other side of the room.

Little Gil, throwing all thoughts of his own safety to the winds - bolted for the bedroom door after his brother.

"Jamie… Jamieee." There was silence in the living room before their father spoke into fresh air, since he was the only one left in the room:

"Jamie – the fucking idiot – brought that no-good son-of-a-bitch into my home. The brainless bastard! Him and his brother will be tarred with the same brush. That kid Ed Morris will walk all over them."

4

The boys' mother Nancy, who had disappeared out of the door in terror as the argument began, watched Jamie's schoolfriend run hell bent for leather up the road.

'Monty wasn't right about much,' she thought, "but he was spot-on with this' and summoned up the courage to go back into her home.

She was shaking and sick inside, but she'd need to defend her babies. She didn't doubt Monty could do serious harm.

When she got inside, Jamie, Gil and Monty had disappeared into the bedroom the boys shared, and Jamie was bawling at the beating he was taking.

Gil screamed – Nancy could hear the terror in his voice and ran for the door. It was locked. The screams ceased suddenly, and it seemed to Nancy that the next few moments happened in slow-motion.

There was a gasp from inside, the lock turned, and Monty emerged hauling a semi-conscious Jamie by the arm. He dragged him across the living room, opened the door into the garage, threw him inside and locked the door after him. There was no sign of Gil.

A grim Monty returned to the bedroom, dropped to his knees by Gil's bed and ground out:

"Come out, you little bastard. Come out and face the music."

"Monty - leave him be. None of this is his fault. He's only ten years old – he's not in High School yet. He doesn't even know Ed."

Monty dragged Gil from under the bed by the ankle. He was too terrified to speak, and the smell when he emerged was sickening. He'd messed himself in terror hiding under the bed.

Nancy took him to the bathroom. He hid his face against her arm and shook violently, although he made no sound.

Chapter Two

Nancy was a gentle, God-fearing woman of Danish stock who attended the local Presbyterian church every Sunday and arranged the flowers there each week. Her father had been a shoemaker in Cottonwood Falls in Kansas but struck out for California like so many others in the hope of a better life. He tried his hand at fruit picking but it paid next to nothing, so he went back to his old trade and set up shop in a back street of Venice, the beach-side of Los Angeles, where he did well.

Her husband was her complete opposite.

His whole family – he was the oldest of seven children - was displaced when their farm was destroyed in the Dust Bowl disaster which struck Oklahoma in the 1920s.

His father hauled his wife and kids to Los Angeles, to work on the citrus farms, but they had more job applicants than they could possibly cope with already.

So Jarrett Robson took part-time work on the huge oil derricks which pumped out black gold day and night on the sundrenched beaches of Southern California, their shafts creaking and groaning and slick with oil.

Monty's father was not afraid of hard work, but it seemed that the whole world made the decision to flee to the Promised Land of Orange County at the same time.

Jarrett determined to make his fortune in the oil business. His children were puzzled as to how that could be, since he had no experience, but they learned the hard way to keep their mouths shut once he started knocking their mother around. As his prospects lessened his drinking increased and soon his children felt his belt at the least provocation. Now with his son Monty, history was repeating itself.

Nancy's Christian values demanded she try to understand rather than condemn, but her children were the center of her world and there came a time Monty slapped baby Gil so hard he left a bruise on his face for a week, and that she couldn't condone. She prayed for guidance, but even the minister could offer her no consolation, so it was inevitable that she and Monty would grow apart.

Once he was cleaned up, Monty snatched Gil from Nancy's arms and locked him again in his bedroom still filled with the stench of his own excrement. He went without protest, terrified and sobbing.

Monty turned on the baseball and sat in front of the TV as if nothing had happened.

Such was Gil's distress for Jamie, he climbed out of the bedroom window, crept round the house, and opened the garage door from the outside. Jamie lay motionless on the concrete floor.

"Jamie... are you alright?" asked Gil, shaking his shoulder gently.

"Do you never stop with the dumb questions? Idiot! Of course I'm not," gasped Jamie, spitting out a broken tooth from a mouth black with blood.

"Go fetch Mr. Warren," he managed to whimper, collapsing back onto the floor.

Mr. Warren was a neighbor two doors up. His son John was a friend of Gil's. Terrified for Jamie's safety, Gil ran to the house and banged on it with his fist until Mrs. Warren answered.

"Hi there Gil. Come and have some lemonade – John's in the yard out back...."

Then she saw Jamie's blood all over Gill's t-shirt and dragged him inside.

"What's happened?" she demanded. "You just tell me what's happened."

Gil began to cry again.

"Please, Mrs. Warren – can Mr. Warren come and help Jamie? He can't move. He did something Dad didn't like, and he hit him. He's in our garage."

Ted Warren entered the hall, alerted by Gil's cries of distress. His wife turned:

"That bastard's been at it again. Gil says he's beaten Jamie and he can't move. He's on the floor in their garage. Go bring him back here and let me try and patch him up."

John's dad, trailed by his son and Gil, strode down the street to the Robson's garage and as gently and silently as he could, lifted Jamie from the ground. The measure of the child's distress came when he began to cry. This shook Gil to the core. Jamie was tough, Jamie never cried. Gil cried often – but Jamie never did.

Jamie had two broken ribs which Joan Warren bandaged, had lost a tooth and was bruised from the top of his head to the soles of his feet. He'd also lost a chunk of his prized long hair. Mrs. Warren said he was darn lucky but she tucked him up in John's bedroom – she'd run down and see Nancy later.

Gil hid behind a curtain in the Warren living room and waited for his father to leave for work, then he went home because he knew his mother would worry about Jamie and about him as well.

His heart was torn in two. He couldn't understand what

9

he'd done to make his Dad so angry. It had to be his fault. Jamie was the perfect brother. He could only assume his Dad was beating Jamie because he knew Gil loved him so much. It was very confusing when you were ten years old.

Chapter Three

Three years passed and things improved slowly. Jamie was now fifteen and into girls, cars, and music so cool no-one had ever heard of it.

He wasn't home much anymore since he started dating a girl in the year above him in school. He was still the family tough guy, too big for Monty to bully anymore, so he inherited Gil's share of his father's bile as well, which he only made worse by standing between his Dad and Gil when Monty lost his temper.

Gil and Jamie spent a lot of time fishing off Santa Monica pier when their father was on the rampage. Once they stayed out all night and found their bedroom window boarded up when they got home.

Their times together on the pier, with the bright sunlight reflecting on the waves, was as close to heaven as Gil ever came.

On Gil's fourteenth birthday Jamie and his mother presented him with his first guitar.

"Gee!" exclaimed Gil. "A guitar!"

"No shit – I thought it was a drum kit," said Jamie.

Their mother came in carrying a pot roast for their dinner and took Gil to task as she served it out.

"Jamie took a job tossing pizza at Venice Beach and helped deliver mail so he could save the money to help buy that for you. At least look grateful!" said an irritated Nancy. And as an afterthought, "Your Dad chipped in too."

Gil was contrite although he couldn't ever remember saying he wanted a guitar. He'd no idea which end was which but he knew forming a band was Jamie's dream.

John dropped by one evening and he and Gil went to check out some new girls from school over milkshake and fries – Gil was a 'fries with everything kind of kid' - at the local soda shop.

"How're you doing with the guitar?" asked John. "Learned anything yet?"

"Nope – no idea where to start."

Ed, Jamie's buddy from school so hated by their father, pulled up a chair unasked and helped himself to a handful of Gil's fries, stuffing them in his mouth until he looked as if he'd gag.

"Hey, how're you doing guys?" he said once he'd stopped choking. "Everything cool? Care to share a joint, man, before you go home to Mommy?"

He took a rollup out of his vest pocket and waved it under Gil's nose.

"Fuck off, Ed," Gill said, laconically.

Ed left with some guy whose grin was so wide it looked as if he'd a plate in his mouth.

Jamie and Gil sat on Santa Monica pier. Jamie with a black eye, was intent on his rod and line, Gil sat on the boards back to a bollard, plucking on the strings of his guitar and turning pages in a book called 'Guitar for Beginners' in an effort to tune his still-shiny instrument – still shiny as it had hardly been out of its case.

Jamie had this grandiose idea of forming a band. Ed was

all for it – well, he would be...he'd an ego the size of America. They'd knocked together a few basic tunes Gil thought were crap, but he might as well give it a go for Jamie's sake. He'd managed to get his fingers around a few chords but his guitar was so out of tune it was hard to tell if he was making progress.

Another of Jamie's school pals, Stevie Allen mosied along the pier, running his hands through his slicked back hair and pushing up the sleeves on a leather jacket he even wore in ninety-degree summer heat.

"Hi guys – how yer doin'?" He slapped Jamie on the back which, given his mood made him walk grim faced, several yards down the pier. Stevie shrugged.

"You do know you're doing that all wrong, don't you GilRo?" he said blowing a perfect smoke ring. "Here, hand it over."

He sat next to Gil and spent five minutes adjusting the pegs with his ear to the strings then handed it back. Gill tried a few of the chords he'd been attempting before and looked at Steve in amazement.

A perfect riff came out, although pathetic for want of an amplifier. Stevie threw his rollup over the rail.

"Do it again – do that again! I thought you said you couldn't play. I take it you meant you couldn't tune – which you can't - but goddamn, that was a riff Chuck Berry'd be proud of. We need to go plug it in an amp – loud!"

He grabbed Gil by the arm and hauled him along the pier to his rattle-trap of a Ford parked illegally on the ocean walk. Jamie managed to jump in just as Stevie's foot hit the gas.

They wound up at Stevie's house a couple of identical blocks from their own. Steve's dad had converted the garage into a den where he kept all his music gear. Gil and guitar were hauled inside and deposited in a chair while Steve leafed through a box of 45s. He plugged the guitar into a small, beat-up amp and turned the volume knob. Gil nearly hit the ceiling when he tried strumming. It was so loud his ears popped.

Steve put a copy of Buddy Holly's "Not Fade Away" on the turn-table.

"Here – try this. Just listen a few times to the lead - I'll play the same bars over once or twice - then copy it best you can."

Jamie stood in the doorway transfixed. He hadn't realized Gil had also inherited the Robson talent for pop music, the only apparent link between Jamie and his father.

Gil concentrated, head on one side, then copied Sonny Curtis's playing slower but precisely.

"Here – try this. It's harder," Steve said, excitement mounting. He put on a disc of 'La Bamba'.

This time Gil listened harder and plucked a few exploratory strings before he started painstakingly picking out the riff. Jamie coughed.

"Hey man. Where'd you learn that?" he asked, pulling his brother by the shoulder and staring into his eyes. Gil looked just as surprised.

"Didn't. Just copied it."

"Shit, kid!" said Stevie, "If you could sing, with a bit more practice the three of us could form a band."

Jamie ran his hand over his face.

"He can. Ma's made him sing in the church choir since he could stand up. He does all the solos now, and sometimes Pastor Frank lets him help with arrangements. He's not exactly Chuck Berry – damn he's a real square - but he can hold a tune and both of us play piano – Mom again. She plays 'Rock of Ages' but also a mean honky-tonk. I picked that up real easy."

Gil dropped his guitar into Jamie's arms, ran home and hid under the covers on his bed. He'd be on his case to join a band every moment of every day from now on, and he'd just found a cute new girl at school. He buried his head in his pillow.

And that was how 'the California Crystal Band' came into being, with the help of Stevie Allen, who joined the band rather than go to college much to his parent's disgust.

They still needed a bit of shifting around to fit together but the basic line-up was – Gil on guitar, lead vocals and common sense, John Warren, the friend Steve had coached along with Gil on guitar, Stevie on drums, because he was good at noise and had long hair, Jamie on keyboards and Ed who wrote a word or two of lyrics to sing himself and could wear weird clothes and dance.

But Ed's sidekick, Phil turned out to be a skilled keyboard player as well. Jamie – the overall musician of the band who wrote beautiful melodies he composed on their piano - was generally good at everything. Everyone but Ed recognized 'the California Crystal Band' was his creation.

Goddamn but they were awful and that was where little Gil came in. He made it his job to knock them into shape – if he was being dragged into a band against his will, it was going to be a good one. He made them rehearse until their throats were dry and their fingers on keyboard and guitar seized up. Then this little kid with a will of iron made them do it again, all the time his exquisite voice at first all 'Abide With Me', modulated and rose into a vocal wonder of the pop music age.

Then Monty got involved and kicked their butts up the professional ladder. Within a couple of years they were superstars and no one was more surprised than them - except perhaps Nancy.

Chapter Four

The doorbell chimed and footsteps echoed across the uncarpeted hall.

"Who's that? I hope it's parcels for me!"

Giulia bolted for the hall door and pulled up short. This tiny little girl full of joyous excitement was Giulia, youngest child and spoilt baby of the famous crooner Paul Giordano, who was at present sunning himself on the terrace at the pool side.

Sitting on stools at the kitchen counter in the clothes they'd fallen out of bed in, were Giulia's two brothers Larry and Tony, who were munching cereal and chatting away, totally oblivious to their excited sister.

"It's Gil! Hi, Gil. It's my birthday. I'm eight! "

"Too old for me, then," said Gil ruffling her dark hair. He fended her off as she threw her arms round his neck.

"Hey! Easy...you'll upset my present."

At eighteen, Gil was already a world-famous guitarist and matchless singer in 'The California Crystal Band', beloved of fans the world over from America to England, Germany to Japan and especially in Australia where people would turn out in their thousands just to hear the band play.

Gil carefully deposited the box he was carrying on the kitchen counter.

"For me? " said Giulia.

"No, stupid! For Lorenzo." Tony rolled his eyes and ducked as Larry took a swing at him for using the birthname he hated.

17

Giulia unfastened the pink bow on the box with infinite care and peeked inside. It was a chocolate cake with white chocolate frosting. Across it were piped the words

'Happy Birthday to us - Giulia and Gil.'

"Why?" she asked.

"Our birthdays are just one day and ten years apart – isn't that cool?"

"Wow. WOW! Isn't that boss? " she batted long silky eyelashes at him and pulled up her white knee socks. Larry and Tony laughed out loud at their baby sister's use of the latest hip expression.

"Shit, Gil. Don't encourage her. She's driving us crazy already. She'll pee her pants if she gets any more excited." said Larry, cereal spoon halfway to his mouth.

"C'mon, Larry. Get your jeans on and fetch your guitar," said Gil. "Time to get to work. Happy Birthday Titch!" he said to Giulia pinching her button nose.

On this particular day, as little Giulia sat sucking an icing-laden finger from her extravagant cake, and her brothers struck discordant notes from their guitars, Gil was relaxed and at peace with the world. He loved the Giordanos, so different from his own troubled family.

The Giordano house was a sprawling confection of add-ons. It was the most eccentric and oddly comfortable-looking house Gil had ever seen. To one side were a couple of tennis courts and a putting green – Paul Giordano loved golf - and behind them, tucked away on the far side of a hedge was a swimming pool.

The children of 1254 Sienna Circle were blessed with a kind father who listened to their every want, and if he deemed it suitable, provided it.

In Larry's case it was guitars. He had three Fenders and

a brand-new sunburst Rickenbacker – a gift from Gil, which sat gleaming in a rack away from the sun.

Just as Larry picked up his newest acquisition, and had begun to tune it, his school friend Bobby Meyer walked in, carrying his own guitar.

Bobby had also taken up piano at school, and Gil was showing him how to play, rattling the keys beyond anything his mother had ever taught him. Gil had to admit Bobby was doing very well.

The boys were so serious and beginning to learn the meaning of 'cool', that Gil had to hide a smile.

Had it only been two years since he had been sixteen too? His whole world had become a whirlwind of gigs, recording sessions and frenzied teenage girls in the meantime, and he still hadn't decided he wanted to be in a band at all. His Dad at least seemed impressed and had taken his decisions out of his hands. Sometimes he hated being the 'baby'.

Giulia poked her nose round the door, put out her tongue at her brothers and smiled winningly at Gil.

"Go away, pest" said Larry, "Dad! Come get Giulia. We can't practice."

Paul strode in, hoisted Giulia under his arm, and left, all in one smooth movement. They could hear her complaining all the way down the hall.

"I always wanted a sister," said Gil. "Perhaps brothers are a bit less demanding."

They all laughed at that. Jamie was notorious - he had remained the family renegade. His arguments with his father had become increasingly violent and were legendary amongst friends and neighbors alike, until

Jamie knocked Monty on his butt. Then things quieted down considerably.

Paul interrupted the rehearsal.

"A word, Gil."

They sat down on loungers on the grass by the pool, and Paul flipped open a couple of beers from the cooler. He handed one to Gil and said:

"How good are they? The boys. My songs are just a little bit different, so all that loud stuff sounds like junk to me."

"I have to level with you Mr. Giordano," said Gil, shaking his long fringe out of his eyes. "It sounds much the same to me. But they are very young, almost the same as me when I started, and I wasn't much better. But Dad gave me no option - I had to practice.

"When my parents and Jamie bought me my first guitar, I was thirteen. I used to check out my moves in front of the mirror. I didn't like the thought of looking a dork in front of all those girls," Gil finished with a grin.

Paul Giordano returned his smile and wiped the condensation off his beer bottle with his thumb before replying:

"Yes, they are young, and Giulia has the right of it when she says they're a pain in the neck, swaggering around like Elvis Presley. Even Tony does it and he can as much play guitar as I can – which is not at all. But as you say, Larry and Bobby are very young. Plenty of time to find out they're crap."

"Oh, I wouldn't say that. If they're prepared to put the work in, they'll improve. They could do with a drummer, though," said Gil thoughtfully.

Later that afternoon in the studio, the Robson dad Monty had started yelling instructions at everyone - again.

"Only a matter of time until the powder keg goes up," thought Gil glumly.

Gil, John, Stevie, Ed's pal Phil, the hated Ed and Jamie were for once in agreement. Monty would have to go – once someone summoned up the courage to tell him, and Gil suspected it would probably have to be him.

Monty Robson had used his bullying tactics on the entire musical establishment of Los Angeles in a failed quest for his own musical stardom. A&R men, who had had dealings with him before, would run for cover when he entered a building. Monty didn't care. His kids had talent. He knew this although he didn't understand the music personally. But he saw the effect Jamie and Gil's writing had on others and smiled with satisfaction, dollar signs writ large in his eyes.

As they grew out of childhood, his brother became Gil's hero. He knew the answer to everything Gil hadn't been able to teach himself. He seriously doubted anyone would ever take his place. In Gil's opinion he was the best there was, possibly the best there'd ever been.

The next time he called to see Larry, there was a girl sitting on the steps by the Giordano's front door. She had her face cupped in both hands studying a row of ants marching across the paving. She looked up at his approaching footsteps.

It wasn't like Gil to be stuck for words; in fact, he had the exuberance of youth by the bucketful. Suddenly, his tongue cleaved to the roof of his mouth.

She was exquisite, young and shy like a fawn, wild. Luminous dark eyes looked up at him through thick lashes. Her skin had the texture of rose petals but her most arresting feature was the cascade of raven hair, which fell over her shoulders to pool round her on the white steps.

"Are you waiting for someone?" he finally got out,

"I've been trying to make them hear me, but I can't." she whispered, blushing prettily.

"If they're in the TV room they wouldn't hear a hurricane. But we can get round the back. Come on."

Gil put out his hand to help her to her feet, but she ignored it and waited for him to walk on. He turned away and drew a deep breath.

There was a path round the side of the house. A thick black hose ran along it, providing constant water for the beautiful pink China roses climbing up a trellis on the wall. Their scent was almost overpowering in the enclosed space and would for the rest of his life, remind him of the lovely creature he'd found on the steps of the Giordano home when he was eighteen.

He moved the hose aside with one foot and looked to see that she was following. She bumped into him, and he put out a hand to steady her. This time, they both blushed, pink like the roses.

The reason the Giordanos hadn't heard her was immediately apparent. There was a raucous game of water polo going on in the pool. Larry and Bobby against Paul and Tony.

Little Giulia was sitting on a lounger wrapped in a towel, watching them.

"Oh, hi, Connie! And Gil - it's Gil, dad."

Giulia flung off her towel and launched herself at Gil, almost knocking Connie over. Gil put out a hand, but Connie stepped away and raised her voice over the boisterous play in the pool:

"Bob, Mom says to come back home. There's schoolwork and you've been gone all day,"

Ah, so Connie was Bobby's sister. Connie Meyer. Now that he thought about it, he could see the resemblance. They both had a very slight oriental cast to their features, and both had black hair.

Bobby grimaced.

"Okay, coming Connie. Great day, you guys" said Bobby, pulling himself out of the water and toweling his hair dry. "Science and math – lovely. See you later, Larry. Pick up my guitar then."

He ran down the path in his wet shorts, jumped on his bike and was gone.

"I'll give you a lift home, Connie." Said Gil shyly.

Chapter Five

Waves sparkled on an azure ocean and splashed against the salty bollards of the pier.

Since the day he first found her at the Giordano house, he had had eyes for no-one but Connie. Jamie, who knew about these things from frequent experience, said it was a crush and it would pass, but it hadn't.

She seemed to consume his every thought and going on tour was agony. He took her with him when he was working in the studio. The other guys weren't too pleased about the distraction, but he didn't care. She stayed out of the way, so he couldn't see what their problem was. The fact that he spent a large portion of their precious studio time gazing adoringly at her never entered his head.

Connie brushed the sand from her shins onto the towel she was sharing with Gil.

He lay on his stomach with his eyes closed. His t-shirt, obviously a gift from Jamie, read "Girls Rule!" across the back. She wished he would relax and take it off, but he was ridiculously sensitive about his weight. It didn't bother her that Gil wasn't fashionably thin. No-one else had the magical smile he reserved solely for her.

He raised his head and began to draw lines in the sand.

A young girl with retainers and a ponytail walked over and gazed at Gil speculatively. She offered her forearm and a pen.

"Can I have your autograph, Gil?" Gil smiled and signed her arm. She left.

"Will you marry me, Connie?" murmured Gil. He felt

24

his whole future rested on her reply. She smiled and the dimples in her cheeks showed momentarily.

"Gil, I'm seventeen. Papa would never allow it."

The same little girl came back with a couple of her friends.

"Can they have your autograph too, Gil?" He smiled up at them and signed a couple of napkins. They giggled and left.

"But will you Connie? You have to answer me first. If it's okay with your parents, when you're eighteen, will you marry me?" he pressed on earnestly.

The dimples disappeared.

"That's not fair, Gil. You can't demand an answer here and now. Please don't ask again. Not yet anyway," she said abruptly, and pulling the towel out from under him ran away up the beach.

He sank his head onto his folded arms and heaved a sigh.

"Blown it…" he muttered.

"Please can I have your autograph, Jamie?" said a small girl.

"It's Gil," he said but smiled anyway, although it was the last thing he felt like doing.

Gil went ahead anyway and bought her a truly beautiful Harry Winston engagement ring to ask her again to marry him when she turned eighteen but he was in an agony of uncertainty that she'd accept it. He had walked the floor over it, and still didn't know if it was the right one. If she didn't like it what would she do? Jamie told him not to be stupid. She wasn't going to turn him down because she didn't like the ring.

He had spoken seriously to her parents without her knowledge and asked them to keep it quiet, as she still hadn't given her consent.

They had been shocked when he, fretting with nerves, first broached the subject. They saw her as hardly more than a baby, but eventually they came round to the idea, although her father remained dubious. His only stipulation in the end, was that there would be no children until Connie was twenty-one. Gil readily agreed.

Connie did finally say yes, sobbing on his shoulder. He wasn't exactly sure why but thought it might be wise not to ask. The tears might well have been because he had asked her on one knee, in front of both families and she had been mortified. He'd think about that later.

Monty's reservations were quite different:

"I'd always thought you had more sense than the other one," he said in front of Connie's family, "but you don't. Just as stupid as your brother." Nancy tugged at his sleeve to quieten him. He shook her off.

Jamie pointed out to Monty the indisputable fact that he and Nancy had both been under twenty-one when they married. Jamie couldn't see a problem, so Monty was obliged to back down, as he'd been forced to do more and more now the boys were older. Unable to control himself, he turned on Jamie instead:

"Gil's in charge on stage. The band wouldn't function without him. You just wriite songs for him to sing. What'll the fans say when they find out he's married?"

Gil winced. This was so unfair. It worked the other way round too – without Jamie writing the music, he'd have nothing to sing.

But Gil would marry Connie whether his father liked it

or not. It surprised everyone he was so adamant. That wasn't his usual style at all.

In the end, a quiet civil ceremony was agreed upon. It took place in the first flush of an early Spring and was held in the garden of Connie's parent's home with only family present. Connie and Gil slipped quietly away at the first opportunity to spend their few final hours alone together.

The next day he left on a tour of Europe. Connie had been a bride for less than 24 hours, and Gil would be gone for a month.

Chapter Six

Gradually, over the next couple of years, Connie learned that being married to a rock star wasn't all it was cracked up to be. She was still only twenty. For the first year she had lived with her parents, who had come to know Gil and love him. Then, she decided to fill her solitary days making a home for her husband to return to.

She had made great friends with Jamie's wife of several months, Lizbeth, who full of fun and confidence, recognized her sister-in-law's standoffishness for shyness, and gave her every encouragement.

Lizbeth, blithe and spontaneous, helped her buy the first house for Gil and employ an interior decorator. It was Lizbeth who helped her choose the furnishings. It was fun and a surprise for Gil's return.

But then came the nights, when Lizbeth went home to Jamie and the new house was dark and empty and Connie was so alone.

The scent of jasmine hung heavy on the air, and an early summer moon shone down upon the still waters of the pool. Connie knelt, and her face wet with tears looked back at her from its mirrored surface.

The water looked so inviting. She put her finger into its warmth and moved it about in circles. On an impulse, she dropped forward, arms extended. The water rushed up her nose and bubbled past her ears, and she felt at peace with the world.

Lizbeth found Connie soaked to the skin and still in her clothes, semiconscious on the tiles at the pool side. She managed to get her inside, out of her dress and into bed. She was so relieved when Connie began to move, and her eyes fluttered open. She was whispering Gil's name over and over.

Lizbeth called home but Jamie didn't answer, so she tried her own father. Again, no reply. She didn't want to panic Connie's family until she knew what had happened, so she tucked her up securely, drove home and tried to shake Jamie awake.

"Jamie, JAMIE! Get up! I need you to help me. Jamie GET UP!"

The explosion of their world-wide fame had shaken them all to the core. To deaden his insecurities Jamie'd taken up with so-called friends who made Lizbeth shudder. Soon what he'd considered a fun way to relieve his stress was out of control. Convinced they would fire his creative imagination, he had become a bigger and bigger fish for their hook. They stole from him and drew him into their own circle of iniquity.

"Oh, for chrissake, Jamie! I don't have time for this crap!"

He put his head back on the pillow and resumed snoring.

Lizbeth tried calling her dad again – it was the only other thing she could think of. She rapped her knuckles on the telephone table impatiently. No reply. She called again. Thank God, this time her dad answered, his voice muffled from sleep. Jamie gave a grunt and a snore, turned over like a beached whale and went back to sleep.

"Dad, something's happened to Connie. I just found her laid out by the pool, soaked to the skin. She looks terrible. I don't know what to do." She burst into tears.

"I'm at home at the moment but I need to get back to Connie. Please come, Dad. I can't wake Jamie – he's out cold. I can't leave Connie any longer – I'll meet you at

Linden Reach."

Within the hour Ike, Lizbeth's father had arrived at Connie's house in the smart Linden Reach suburb of Los Angeles.

Ike stroked Connie's forehead while Lizbeth handed her a sleeping pill and glass of water.

"Sleep honey, and don't worry about a thing. We'll take care of any problems, and when you wake everything will look better," smiled Ike.

Father and daughter sat over coffee and discussed what to do, quickly coming to the conclusion that since they'd no idea how she'd got in that state to begin with, the only possible course of action was to call their doctor and get her checked over.

After a careful examination, the doctor took hold of Connie's hand and looked at her with serious eyes.

"Would you like to speak in confidence?" he asked Connie. She shrank back onto her pillows.

"N-no" faltered Connie, "I would like them to stay." She looked as terrified as Lizbeth felt.

"Did you know you were expecting a baby?"

Deathly silence. The doctor continued,

"Most women suffer from sickness, but early pregnancy can cause severe depression in some. Some unfortunates suffer from both."

Ike, relieved, barked out a laugh.

"Well, well Connie, you are a one for surprises."

Connie's mouth had dropped open, and she tugged at the sheet in agitation.

"What is Gil going to say?" she gasped, horrified.

"I would imagine he'll be over the moon," said Ike, with a sympathetic smile.

"But he promised my father there would be no babies until I was at least twenty-one and I'm .... not!"

"You will be by the time the baby comes, and if Gil's anything like I was, he'll have drunk himself under the table before he thinks of any problems. Anyway, he did have something to do with it."

He chuckled and the tension lifted.

No one told Gil about the incident at the pool. He would have been distraught with guilt, so what had happened remained a secret shared between Ike, Lizbeth and Connie. Even Edward and Kelani, Connie's parents didn't know.

Gil had been determined to be there for the birth, but the baby came two weeks early and he was still on tour in the mid-West. It was two days before he could get there, by which point all the excitement was over. Connie was at her parent's home, resting with the baby in her arms.

Gil fell to his knees at the bedside, and her simmering anger melted away.

"Come meet your son," she said, eyes alight, holding out the tiny bundle wrapped in an embroidered shawl. Gil stood and took the baby from his mother, his son's fingers curling around his own. He held him close and stroked a velvet cheek with his forefinger, while the infant gazed up at him through milky-blue eyes.

He returned their son softly to his mother's arms, then took Connie's face between his hands and gave her the tenderest of kisses, sweet and gentle.

"I can't tell you how bad I feel for not being here," he

whispered into her hair. He rubbed his cheek against her forehead and kissed her again.

Connie changed the subject.

"We didn't have a name picked out because you've been away so much, and I wouldn't do something so important without you. His grandparents will be so relieved when we name him. They'll be able to stop calling him 'the baby'.

"I'm so pleased you're back because Bobby's driving me insane. He drags Larry Giordano with him every time he visits, and once he brought Giulia too. She's twelve now, and very grown up! They've been here every hour on the hour. So far, Bobby's suggested Hugo, Jeremy and Richard for names," she pulled a face.

"Lizbeth's been wonderful. I haven't seen Jamie. He'll be along in his own good time I suppose," she said against all logic.

"Any ideas?" mused Gil still distracted by a name for the baby, "Something original. It has to be a unique name, a rare name. How's Jacob grab you?"

He'd obviously been giving it some thought.

"You don't think that's a bit old-fashioned? It's a bit.... biblical?"

"No, I don't... well perhaps just a little. But just you wait, every second baby in Los Angeles will be called Jacob in five years' time – but he'll have been the first, the original." Gil's eyes sparkled.

"Why don't you ask the family in and introduce them properly to Jacob?" smiled Connie, kissing the baby's fist.

There was no need to ask them in. The grandparents must have been listening. The door was flung open and little Jacob was whisked away to give Gil and Connie time together.

She snuggled into Gil's arms.

"I feel I might like to sit in the garden this afternoon. I could do with some fresh air. It would be good for us to spend time together. So the three of us can get acquainted."

She couldn't see the expression on his face had altered.

"I can't. I have to take the afternoon flight to Minneapolis." Gil said, aware he was walking a tightrope. "The guys have covered for me two nights in a row. I can't ask them again. I'll be back for a whole week like we planned week after next."

He tightened his hold on her, but she pulled away.

Less than two years later, Connie gave birth to a second son, Mylo. Two more different children it would have been difficult to imagine. Jacob was chubby and demanding with a shock of thick black hair, and Mylo was blonde, delicate and placid.

After Mylo was born, things were much easier for a while.

Gil loved their new home – especially the pool-house, which stood separate from the main building, and was surrounded by beautiful lawns and rose beds. He moved all his guitars there and he could often be heard humming to himself and strumming softly. It was where he went to be peaceful and alone. It was also where he went to work.

Then although he was back, his workload increased and he was only home to eat and sleep, then back to the studio again. The band had missed a deadline for the new album so everyone was working double time.

Gil felt deeply guilty for his absences but wouldn't or couldn't adjust his life to include his wife and children. He tried to explain his predicament to Connie, but she couldn't understand the pressure which was becoming progressively more difficult to cope with.

Gil had never been good with words and he didn't seem able to make her understand the drive just to keep going, always feeling as if he was swimming against the tide. So many people depended on him. Not only the band-members, but each sideman and the technicians relied on his leadership to feed their families.

Sometimes he was just so tired.

Chapter Seven

The band had managed four whole days off that Christmas, a situation almost unheard of. Mylo was just two months old, so this was Connie's first opportunity to hold a social event since his birth.

She loved family gatherings and had laid out a beautiful buffet with lobster and champagne.

Monty helped himself liberally to the buffet fare. His ability to make himself the center of any gathering put Gil's teeth on edge.

Nancy, mother of the Robson boys, was in her element entertaining her grandchildren.

Apart from Gil and Connie's boys, Mylo safely tucked up in the care of his nanny, and Jake who was running round in circles playing airplanes, Lizbeth had brought her two little girls Rosie and Carly. They pounced on their cousin Jacob to play. Jake took hold of each of them by the hand and swung them round, until all three fell laughing on the grass.

It wasn't often that the brothers could spend leisure time together, so there was sadness in Gil's heart that Liz and the girls had come without Jamie.

Jamie was a conundrum. By nature, he was the kindest, most loving person. On the other hand, he was an alcoholic and a serious drug user. When under the influence he was often abusive, even violent. People he didn't know tended to be nervous of his moods, which often made work, studio and on the road, difficult and demanding for everyone else.

Gil was the younger brother and took a lot of teasing

from Jamie. If it upset him, no-one ever knew.

'He lets him walk all over him,' thought Connie, irritated.

Nancy Robson had been terrified for her younger child as more and more responsibility passed to him. She was worried it would all be too much. If truth be told, Gil was worried it'd be too much for Gil as well.

Connie's family was open and loving. She had never known what it was to want for anything.

Gil had developed a grudging sympathy for his dad despite his obnoxious behavior and knew he had truly tried his best.

Afterall, he was only one generation away from oil wells on Long Beach where indolent surfers now lounged. He was bitter with the jealous realization he'd been born too soon.

His sons had it all. Jamie and Gil were the musician Monty had so ached to be. Gil? Monty would never comprehend that Gil was the lynch pin which held together not only his family, but the band too. Father and son were worlds apart in understanding.

So there were parts of Gil's persona Connie could never hope to fathom. One of these was his hero worship of the brother who had shielded him from his abusive father. Connie would never understand the indelible mark Monty's cruelty towards his boys had left on Gil. Jamie had been his life support - he would always be the center of his universe.

She had to accept that Gil's own little family would be lower down the list than his beloved Jamie, and the music they created together. Coming third was a bitter pill to swallow.

"Rosie, get in here — it's too cold out there without a sweater. ROSIEEE!"

Lovely, warm-hearted Lizbeth wasn't noted for her dulcet tones. Gil grabbed the woolly as he ran past her, whooping as loud as any of the kids. He grabbed Rosie and rolled over on the grass, tugging the sweater over her head.

"Uncle Gil. Let's play monsters!" yelled Rosie, bouncing up and down on his chest. All the other kids piled on top of him shrieking loudly.

His face turned from its usual smile into a lumpy, bug-eyed horror and his hands became claws to scratch them to bits. Little Carly began to cry. He wiped her tears away with his thumb.

"Scared of my monster, baby? I know... you can be the next one!"

Carly beamed and toddled after the other kids doing a pale imitation of her Uncle Gil.

Connie was passing round hors d'oeuvres to her guests when Gil walked back inside. She smiled at him across the room. The loveliest lady in California and she was married to Gil Robson. Any tension between them over his absences had receded with uninterrupted family time, and the joy of the Christmas season. He grabbed an open bottle of champagne and moved around, refilling glasses.

As the evening progressed, Gil picked up a guitar and began strumming one of their old songs. The children joined in the singing, and eventually the adults did too.

"Play one of mine, Gil. One of mine. They're better sing-alongs than Jamie's, they're too trendy," demanded Monty.

Gil humored him with a verse of one of his dad's better compositions, then morphed it seamlessly into the band's biggest hit. Monty seethed.

One by one the children dropped off to sleep in their parent's arms, as the sweet harmonies which were second nature to the Robson boys, swirled in the air about them.

It was early by rock stars standards when they left for home. They had a local gig the following afternoon, so an early night was a rare but welcome luxury.

Chapter Eight

It was the most beautiful day, a little cooler than of late and the garden sprinklers hummed in the background.

In fact, it was so lovely that Connie and the boys had a picnic tea on the lawn. She had invited their housekeeper Gloria to share the meal with them. Gloria loved the kids, particularly Jacob, who she spoiled shamelessly. Gil was in Japan and not expected back for another week.

So it came as a surprise when Connie saw a car pull up in front of the house and Gil step out. He ran across the lawn, lifted her in the air and kissed her on the mouth, swinging her round, her feet in mid-air.

"I met Giulia Giordano at the airport, and we shared a cab back. Her father was flying out to Vegas, and she'd been to see him off. Come and say hello, Giulia. You don't know Jacob and Mylo do you?"

Giulia walked across the lawn and sat down next to the boys.

"Only Jacob," she smiled down at him, "I saw when you were first born, but not since."

The sweet child with the claxon voice was now a trim and delicate teen. She had inherited her Italian father's midnight hair, which she wore tied in a high ponytail, and her mother's bright blue eyes. The combination was stunning.

"Hi Connie. Happy to see you again," she smiled, showing even white teeth.

"Hello Giulia. I hear about you often from my brother. He brings Larry and Tony along sometimes. Larry's given up the idea of fame and fortune in the entertainment business, so we haven't seen them quite so much, but Gil encourages them to get together to jam from time to time. You should come with them. We could have coffee and a gossip while they do their best to deafen us."

"I'd like that." smiled Giulia. "The coffee I mean, not being deaf!"

Gil had been playing piggyback with the boys, but he'd been a bit rough so poor Jacob was in tears. Gil put him down and he ran to Connie for comfort.

Giulia glanced at her watch.

"Got to dash. They'll all wonder where I've got to."

"I'll run you home," said Gil and he put his arm round her shoulders and gave her a quick squeeze.

"So good to see you after all this time. I haven't seen you since you could shatter glass with your voice."

Giulia giggled and leaned back against his shoulder.

They walked off together across the grass laughing and chatting. Connie watched them go, then shrugged and returned her attention to the children.

Gil was back within the hour. He ran across the lawn, scooped up little Mylo, and cuddled him. Connie kissed Gil over the baby's head, then put Mylo gently down on the blanket.

"I adore you," he whispered. The kiss he gave her took her breath away.

"Please tell me you're going to stay for a while this time. I get so lonely, Gil. Jacob and Mylo are not what you'd call chatty." She was suddenly serious. "I need someone to love and hold - in the evenings when we can be all alone. I love you so much."

The last sentence came out in a rush.

Gil handed her down to the blanket and wriggled between her and Mylo who had fallen asleep, thumb in his mouth. He glanced up. Jacob was busy pulling petals off the prize begonias.

"Why don't you come with me next time I go away? Grandmas can fight over who looks after the kids."

"I might do that" she said thoughtfully. "I just might. It'll need to be before September though because Jacob starts kindergarten then."

"I'm sure we can figure something out. I'll look into the schedule."

He made to kiss her again, but she only laughed and said:

"Damn, Gil, cut your hair! And your beard is rubbing my face raw!" He grinned back at her.

"We rock stars have to keep up appearances!"

"You might want to lose the kaftan then," she said with a grin.

Gloria took the children back to the house and Gil and Connie moved to the peace of the pool-house.

The explanation he gave of the tour was the same old routine. She could have chanted it by heart. She was surprised to realize that not only was she lonely, but she was bored too.

Gil sat on the edge of her sun-lounger and bent and kissed her. The seat tipped sideways, and they both ended up on the grass. The ecstasy of their lovemaking emptied her mind of everything but Gil.

Afterwards, as the sun sank and fireflies danced amongst the flowers, he took a small gold pendant from round his neck and fastened it around hers, kissing her shoulder. She rubbed it between her fingers.

"What's this?"

"It's a symbol of true love. Because I do truly love you with all my soul," Gil said gravely. "Do you remember my friend Harry Forster? When we were teens before you and I met, he introduced me to a man called Daniel Jones. He began a movement he called the Union of Souls. Harry is a devout Catholic but this sect appealed to him. It encourages peace through meditation and personal example. Not like those money-spinner oriental sects Ed's taken a shine to.."

"Go on," said Connie, for the moment intrigued.

"I spent a whole weekend talking to him. I loved his ideas, but found I was already doing most of them. You know – candlelight, music, incense – except I prefer rosewater. Just the set-up I have here. He gestured to the pool-house, its door ajar.

"This is the group's symbol. See? It's a representation of the soul as the sun. The lines are the many ways to get there, Their intersection is meant to represent the wearer.

"When I was at Harry's place later, he told me Daniel said he thought for the first time ever, he had met someone he couldn't help. Still not quite sure what he meant by that. I can't be such a hopeless case. Can I?"

He looked at Connie for reassurance. She ran her fingers through his hair and kissed his cheek.

"Anyway, he goes by the name of the Teacher now. But I have been with Harry to see him a few times. He is a 'go-to' person for a chat. You know. None-judgmental."

Connie kissed his neck and lay back in his arms.

Chapter Nine

Gil and Connie poured heads together over the schedule

for the next trip. They were opening in London mid-month followed by a few dates in other English cities, then home. Gil suggested she might like to go and spend some time shopping and sightseeing in London. There'd be other wives and girlfriends there to keep her company.

"What do you think?" he asked. "Think you can bear Ed for that long?"

Ed had decided to be frontman for the band – mostly because he could neither sing nor play any instrument. He was mostly there because he'd bullied the Robsons into including him. Gil had to concede he did serve a purpose, because his strutting allowed the real musicians to concentrate on their playing.

Ed often reminded Gil of his father in that he was consumed by jealousy and wanted in on the act any way he could. He was aggressive with or without discernable cause.

Jamie teased Ed unmercifully as a defense mechanism and to protect his brother, another parallel with Monty. Gil suffered him in silence but had become his victim.

"Sounds good! And yes, it'll be a pleasure to stay away from the delightful Ed," said Connie.

"I take it Liz'll be going? I'd like to spend some time with her."

"Probably."

He became suddenly serious and the look he gave her was apprehensive.

44

"It's years since you came on tour with me, and some things have changed. Some I know you won't like. You might think about it a while before you finally decide.

"Like what?"

"Well... some of the guys are not always as honest as they might be."

He chose his words with care, even then he realizing they were wrong.

"They're all as rich as Croesus. Why wouldn't they be?"

"I don't mean money......" His face had gone crimson.

He watched as realization dawned.

"But who?" then answered her own question. "Jamie - surely not if Lizbeth's there!"

"Doesn't seem to bother either of them. He's not the only one. Ed. usually. And.... guilty myself but...."

He looked as if he could crawl under the table.

"When?" she choked.

"Not since the kids were born, I promise," and earnestly, "I had to tell you now. I don't know how I'd handle anyone else telling you."

"You mean if I hadn't chosen to come with you to England, you wouldn't have said anything? How do you think I feel about *that*, you BASTARD!" she yelled, her voice crackling with suppressed rage.

She lashed out and slapped him hard across the face.

"You bastard!" she repeated, her voice dropping to a menacing growl.

Gil didn't retaliate though his face carried her palm print. He'd never seen her so angry. He'd never once seen this side of her – he'd always thought she'd be more like Liz. On the few times she'd been with him before the kids came, the question hadn't arisen – they were together all the time.

"Please, Connie, don't. It was stupid and it meant nothing at all."

"And that makes it better, how? I'm horrified you could even think like that!"

She dragged off her beautiful engagement ring – the wedding ring wouldn't shift - and threw it in his face, flouncing out of the room. She slammed and locked the door behind her. Gil could hear her sobbing on the other side. He flopped into an armchair. The man who had said honesty was the best policy had obviously not been married.

It had been his idea to take Connie with him. It was all his fault. But what if she had found out? He should have known this would happen one day. She wouldn't understand, that when he'd been away from home for weeks, and a groupie targeted him as often happened, he was sometimes too needy to resist. But Connie was his life. How could he have been so weak?

Connie's sobbing had stopped. He waited, but nothing happened. The hours ticked slowly by. He tried going down to the pool-house and picking up one of his guitars, but the notes wouldn't stay still in his head. So he walked back into the kitchen and made some coffee, which an hour later he realized he hadn't drunk.

The lock clicked but the door didn't open. He walked over and checked. Propped against the hall wall next to their bedroom door was a leather sports bag. It didn't take a genius to get the message.

Gil left it where it was, and ran from the house too

furious, too devastated to pick it up. He swung his car round in a spray of gravel and sped down the drive.

He instinctively headed for Jamie's LA home, given over to Lizabeth and the girls since she had thrown him out. Lizbeth answered the door and he practically fell inside.

"Liz... she's thrown me out! Tell me what to do. What do I do?" he yelled in despair.

For a moment, Liz couldn't put together the sense of his question. It was so bizarre. What on earth was he talking about? Connie was absolutely devoted to him.

"What did you do?" asked Lizbeth.

"Nothing!"

She looked at him suspiciously, arms folded.

"Come on, spill," she said. No-one knew the Robson boys better than Lizbeth. She'd a good idea of what was coming so she preempted his reply.

"No... don't tell me. Let me guess! You told her about the rock star life-style and how you came to be a part of it."

The expression on his face told her she'd hit the jackpot.

"You prize idiot! What did you expect? And I suppose you confessed all?"

He nodded, distraught.

"What do I do, Liz?"

"Damned if I know," she snapped. "I'm sick of digging you boys out of the shit." But she relented, as she always did with Gil.

"Whatever you do, don't buy her anything expensive. It smacks of desperation."

"But I am desperate," he said,

"Yes, but she doesn't know that. At least she probably does, but it wouldn't be a good idea to admit it."

The silence lasted longer than Gil could bear as Lizbeth eyed him quizzically.

"All you can do is try and convince her you really are sorry – I take it you are sorry? Nothing else is going to work. But first I would give her some time to think things through, to work out she's going to miss you."

"What if she doesn't?"

"Give me a break, Gil. She thinks the sun shines out of your ass. That's why she's so mad!"

Chapter Ten

The road back to normality was a rocky one, but Connie did decide to go to England.

They were still uneasy with each other, but they'd be apart for a few days while Gil flew out ahead, busy with last minute arrangements.

The tour consisted of three days in London. Then they would play a couple of dates in other UK cities before heading home. Connie would go home after the last London show to look after the boys.

She had lots of company should she want it. Lizbeth asked Nancy to take the girls and check on the house a couple of times to stop her home being invaded by Jamie's disreputable friends in her absence. So Nana Nancy, to her delight, had not only Jacob and Mylo to spoil, but Jamie and Lizbeth's daughters Rosie and Carly as well.

The following day, Lizbeth picked Connie up and they went to the airport. There they met up with a small crowd of other wives and girlfriends, who clearly for the most part knew each other well. Hugs and greetings were exchanged, and news and insider jokes shared.

Connie stood back feeling completely at sea, until Lizbeth dragged her by the arm into the middle of the group and introduced her. Then she was the center of attention. Shy by nature, she smiled tightly and spoke sparingly. Sometimes she wished she was more like Liz.

Most of the wives and girlfriends where old hands at touring. They were aware of the mind-numbing boredom of sitting around in cold grubby halls, watching endless sound checks and the unpacking and setting up of equipment and instruments.

Dressing-rooms were cleaner, but they were usually too small to hold many other than the band members. There was a green room for guests at most of the venues, but they smelt awful, so they were little used. Most of the girls just wanted to be somewhere else until show-time – some weren't even bothered about the shows themselves. Most were less concerned than Connie about what their guys were up to – it was par for the course. It was a fraught and confusing day.

When they arrived at Heathrow Airport, limos were waiting for them. The first they saw of their partners would be at their hotels. Safer, quicker, easier.

Gil had come down to the foyer, informed by the front desk Connie had arrived, and saw that her luggage was dealt with. He kissed her briefly on the cheek. Connie was relieved to be in the quiet of their Mayfair hotel suite.

It was furnished with antiques and full of vases of scented white roses and lilies. There was even a baby grand in front of a large picture window in the sitting room. She could see that Gil had been playing. There was a beer glass and ash tray on the piano top and the bench was askew.

"I feel filthy. Where do I take a shower?" she said abruptly.

"I've had a bottle of champagne brought up. I thought perhaps you might like that."

"Yes, I would. But I'd like to shower and change first." She put all her attention into digging around in her purse for a pack of tissues and made no move to greet him.

He slid closer. She didn't move away, but that was the

50

best that could be said of her response. Although he'd apologized a thousand times in the meantime he said again:

"Connie...won't you please forgive me? I don't know how else to tell you how sorry I am."

Connie was not unkind, and no matter how hurt and angry she had been, her anger had slowly worn off. Now she felt lonely again, and she couldn't bear to have him feel the same.

She put her arms around him and felt him shudder.

"Oh God, Gil. Please don't do that! This can't be fixed like that," she said more sharply than she'd intended. "I have to trust you and that's the part that's missing. We have to try and get it back."

He sat up and wiped moist eyes with the heel of his hand.

"I'll do my best to be what you want me to be. I promise, I do promise."

They lay on the bed in each other's arms, too shattered by emotion to speak.

There was a loud rapping at the door and when Gil opened it, Jamie was standing there grinning in his usual easy manner, a bottle of vodka in one hand and a couple of glasses in the other.

"Hey there, bro." Jamie's elbow slipped on the door jamb, and he took an involuntary step forward. "I brought us a little light relief." He grinned engagingly.

"Not now Jamie. Not the right time."

Gil tried subtly to remind Jamie of Connie's presence in the room behind him. Jamie winked too broadly.

"Gotcha, bro!" And he wandered off down the empty corridor hushing loudly at every door.

He wasn't gone long and when he returned, he was dragging a grinning sideman by the arm. Clearly, Jamie had been at the vodka some more in the meantime, since when he got to the door and Gil opened it, ready to get seriously annoyed, Jamie crumpled at his feet spluttering a loud "Oops."

"Oh, shit Jamie, go and sleep it off or at least go somewhere else. I don't have time for this right now."

Jamie peered round Gil's arm and gave Connie a cheeky little wave.

"Yo, Conn! Comin' out to play?"

"That's it!" spluttered Gil, "Out...OUT!" and he dragged Jamie bodily into the hall and slammed and locked the door. There were several loud protests from the hall, but eventually his brother tottered away to create havoc elsewhere.

"Something has to be done about Jamie. His drinking is out of control," warned Connie.

Gil shrugged. There was nothing to be done. Jamie was a force of nature.

The following morning, they breakfasted together early in their rooms, and Gil set off for the Crystal Palace Bowl, where the first two concerts were to be held. He needed an early start to see all the musicians and their equipment and instruments had arrived. It wasn't unusual for one or two of the guys to be missing, especially on trips abroad.

It was a good forty minutes' drive through heavy traffic, so Gil took a cab. The first show was scheduled for three o'clock that afternoon.

Connie had arranged to meet Lizbeth and Suzy, wife of the bass player John Warren, in the hotel foyer.

Before she left her room, Connie checked her makeup in the mirror and gave her long hair a quick flick. She was a little late, but it didn't matter as Lizbeth and Suzy were drinking coffee and catching up on each other's news.

"Great.... Hi Connie. Let's go hit the shops!" beamed Lizbeth.

They walked to Harrods, past the beautiful marble-fronted houses that lined Berkley Square, and past little alleys with small exclusive boutiques. Harrods itself was absolutely vast and so luxurious Connie hardly dare touch anything. There was stained glass and carved wooden panels everywhere. It was old expensive, luxurious like the best hotels in New York.

"Oh, you'll get used to it!" said Lizbeth, grinning at the expression on Connie's face. "Come on, let's check it out."

They wandered from department to department, past names like Ives St Laurent and Gucci, Dior and Chanel, and ended up in the jewelry section where Lizbeth bought a small but devastatingly expensive watch.

"Come on girls. Quick coffee then a cab to the theatre."

The Crystal Palace Bowl was a huge open-air theatre, and the stage was fronted by a crescent-shaped lake, with wide grassy banks for the audience to sit on.

Gil had tucked a pass into her purse before he left.

It wasn't a conventional theatre – there were no dressing rooms or formal seating, and it took them a while to get backstage. Behind the auditorium was a veritable village of trailers. The principal musicians had their own with their names on the doors. Someone had lit a barbeque nearby, and the smell of roasting meat permeated the air. Laid out on trestles were plates of food, covered from the sun, and here and there, coolers full of sodas and beer.

Gil, with a towel round his neck ran over, lifted Connie off her feet and swung her round.

"C'mon babe. Let's check out our trailer."

He gave her a resounding kiss and carried her off. Connie was too overwhelmed to object, so she wrapped her arms around his neck, her long hair draping his shoulders, Perhaps things were improving, thought Lizbeth.

"Good job!" she shouted and laughed as Gil carried Connie into the trailer like a caveman.

The show was a blast. For once absolutely everything went to plan. All the players turned up, including Jamie who from his coordination, had been smoking something rather than drinking or injecting it. Rehearsals went well with nothing broken and no blown fuses, electric or human. Gil closed his eyes and prayed for the same for the evening show.

Nobody knew where Jamie and Ed were, which was a bit disconcerting. It was always wise to have some idea of Jamie's whereabouts.

On the other hand, Ed could be a nasty piece of work, but one thing was for sure, he would always be there to open the show. He loved to strut his stuff and check out the pretty girls in the first couple of rows, although he might have a bit of difficulty tonight across the lake and through the spotlights.

Catch a Falling Star

The evening show began at seven-thirty. That gave Connie and the girls just an hour's free time. Lizbeth suggested the three of them should sit in the audience.

It was still light when the show began, but as it got darker the spotlights got brighter. Ed, resplendent in a sequined gold jacket, pranced across the stage front picking out of the crowd girls he couldn't see. He was a hoot on stage. Pity he was such a jerk the rest of the time.

Gil quietly counted in the backing band, then turned to his mic and started to sing the first number. His glorious voice soared through the scented evening air. The audience was enraptured, lost in the beauty of the moment.

"Gil's voice is a miracle Connie – truly gorgeous," said Lizbeth.

Then she clapped and jumped up and down to the next song, which was loud and raucous.

The crowd became more and more enthusiastic as the evening wore on. By the end, the whole audience was dancing and singing along with the band. It was a wonderful evening.

"Gil loves his fans," Suzy said thoughtfully. "He connects with them so completely. Jamie too, although I think perhaps his attachment is more superficial. John loves the music more than anything else, but I don't think Gil would get the same buzz without the audience. He needs people."

Connie knew this was true. The music was number two in the list after his brother. But after watching him on stage she often wondered if it wasn't the other way round. The fans came first.. But, whichever, she and the boys definitely came third.

Back at the hotel Gil, exhausted, slept like a log. Connie lay next to him mulling over the events of the day, until she too fell into a deep slumber.

The next day was more relaxed as there was no afternoon show, but Gil took the time to put in some extra rehearsals. The band members were mostly not amused, but they went along with it simply because every one of them wanted to do their best for Gil. He was a hard task master but praise from Gil was an accolade. There was no show the following afternoon so he gave them time off.

Connie, Lizbeth and Suzy decided to take a boat from Westminster Bridge up the Thames to Hampton Court Palace. It was a three-hour journey but fascinating. They saw fashionable Chelsea. The city buildings thinned, and they passed the wonderful gardens at Kew and Richmond Park. Gradually, the gloriously green English countryside took over.

Hampton Court itself was just beautiful. Built of Tudor red brick, it stood alone on the riverbank surrounded by its own formal gardens, at this time of year in full flower.

Suzy and Lizbeth couldn't wait to see inside the house which was famed for its tapestries and paintings. Not that they were into 'old' especially, but it was quite thrilling that some of the items inside were twice as old as the United States.

Connie decided to spend some quiet time alone amongst the box hedges and thyme and lavender and it was peaceful standing by the river, watching rowboats ply back and forth, leaving a gentle swell in their wake. The peace was blissful.

"Mrs.. Robson, isn't it?"

Connie turned to see a man of about her own age eyeing her speculatively. She didn't recognize him.

"Yes," she replied tentatively. "Should I know you?"

"Perhaps you wouldn't remember me. My name is Oliver Maxwell. I own a car dealership in Los Angeles. Your husband bought a car from me last year – Aston Martin as I recall," he said thoughtfully. "All this way to meet someone from Los Angeles, what a coincidence!"

Connie didn't recall having met him, but Gil had bought an Aston Martin about then. This man seemed harmless enough, so she smiled.

He was rather an engaging character and clearly wealthy. His well-cut blond hair was beginning to thin a little, but he was bronzed and smooth-skinned and very well spoken.

"May I buy you a coffee? My wife is inside and likely to be some time yet. She loves antiques but I'm not enthralled by dusty old houses," he smiled.

Connie followed him to a little teashop, half-hidden by overhanging honeysuckle. Pots of bright geraniums lined the path.

He held a chair for her to sit and ordered coffee from a waitress in a crisp white apron. After it arrived, he continued:

"I hope you don't mind me speaking to you. It's nice to see a face from back home. Rachel hasn't been well, but she was determined to see London." He smiled.

"What do you do back home? Oh, I already asked that, didn't I?" Connie said, flustered. He chuckled.

"As I say, I own a car dealership – mostly imports particularly from Europe. But apart from that I am an absolute nut for Nascar. Racing, watching – anything really. I even sponsor now and then. Ah, here's Rachel now.

"Hello darling. This is Connie Robson, also from L.A., Isn't that a coincidence? Her husband is Gil Robson. You know, the singer?"

"Pleased to meet you Connie" said Rachel, holding out a slender, blue-veined hand for her to shake.

She had eyes of an unusually deep blue, and while her husband appeared to be brimming with health, she seemed drawn and pale in the warm English sunshine.

"Are you here for long?" she enquired politely.

"No just a couple more days. Gil and the band are playing at Crystal Palace. They have two more shows, tonight and tomorrow, then are going to Manchester and Leeds. I'll be leaving after London. I have two boys at home I need to see"

"Two boys? If you don't mind me saying so, you don't look old enough," said Rachel.

They indulged in small talk for a while before Connie saw Lizbeth and Suzy walking across the lawns looking for her.

"If you will excuse me, I can see my friends. It was very nice to speak to you. Perhaps I will see you again in California." She smiled her goodbyes.

Oliver stood politely as she left the table.

They caught the boat from the landing stage. The journey back seemed quicker, as they discussed their afternoon. Suzy, who was a gardening fanatic, had bought packets of flower seeds from the palace garden shop.

"Probably won't survive a California summer, but I'll give it a shot."

They took a cab to the hotel from Westminster Bridge. By the time they'd got to Crystal Palace they would have missed the start of the show in any case.

After a shower and change of clothes they met in the restaurant and had dinner together.

Then Suzy said goodbye and Connie and Lizbeth headed back upstairs.

"Come and see what I've got. You'll need to come to my room!"

Connie was intrigued.

Lizbeth led the way, and shut and locked the door behind them, then she opened the window as far as it would go.

Pulling out her suitcase from the wardrobe, she scrabbled about inside for a few minutes before triumphantly extracting a small, battered tin box.

"Connie," she grinned. "You're going to roll your first joint!"

Connie nearly fell off the bed. "WHAT?"

"Aw c'mon. You'll love it – it's fun. You must have seen Gil and the others smoke pot. Everyone does it. It's not a serious drug. Just a bit of fun like drinking a little too much."

Connie knew about smoking pot of course. She'd been to parties often enough with Gil. He never smoked when he was with her, but she knew he did when she wasn't there.

She was dubious but she liked and trusted Lizbeth so

59

when she said: "It need only be this once," Connie decided to give it a go.

Sitting cross-legged on the floor, Liz showed Connie how to roll the joint, took a cigarette lighter out of her jeans pocket and lit it. The smell was horrible.

She handed it to Connie and invited her to try for herself. Connie copied her, but almost choked as the smoke hit the back of her throat. Red-faced, she spluttered:

"Euk! I could never get used to this. It's horrible!"

"Try it again – just once more." A dubious Connie sucked in more smoke and this time didn't cough quite so much. The third toke had her smiling.

It was rather pleasant. She took another puff.

"Good, isn't it?" said Lizbeth, drawing deeply and nearly losing her balance.

Twenty minutes later they were giggling together helplessly.

Lizbeth took another drag and leant her head on Connie's shoulder. She spluttered on the smoke and handed the joint to Connie. Both of them were glassy-eyed and pleasantly drowsy.

Connie had never smoked – anything – so before long she began to feel very sleepy. Lizbeth hoisted her to her feet, unlocked the door and supported her, rather unsteadily, down the hall to her suite.

Connie dropped to her knees on a small rug next to the sofa, and went to sleep, smiling.

She was still asleep when Gil returned. He shook her by the shoulder. She opened drowsy eyes and smiled up at him, suppressing an involuntary giggle.

"What have you been up to?"

Connie stretched, smiled and promptly fell asleep again.

Smoking a little weed was okay but that wasn't the problem – it was the pariahs who used it to hook innocents like Connie onto the more expensive stuff. He'd carefully shielded her from the seedier side of his life. After married life with Jamie and all the difficulties that had entailed, Liz should have known better.

He looked down at Connie sleeping peacefully with a smile on her dimpled mouth and leaned and kissed her. He'd need to have a serious word with Liz.

When the shows in London were complete, Connie packed for home. The band had gone down so well that everyone was glowing from the adulation.

The rest of the girls, including Liz who clearly intended to spin out her time away from home as long as possible, were accompanying the band on the other dates. Connie had had a better time than she'd expected and wished she could have gone with them. But she had her boys to look after so that wasn't an option.

Gil dropped Connie off at Heath Row in his cab, then set off back to join the tour bus. She watched the car as it rounded the corner, and alone dragged her suitcase through the sliding doors.

It was late when she got home, but once she'd dropped her keys into the china bowl next to the door, she called Nancy to see the boys were okay, then promised to pick them up the following morning.

The following afternoon was spent at the beach, with the kids covered in ice cream and sun block. It was a beautifully relaxing day but very hot. The beach was full of boys and girls, mostly young teenagers, jumping on and off surf boards in smooth water. Older more experienced teens had travelled to Newport, Malibu, and dozens of other beaches along the Southern Californian coast, where the waves curled high before pounding on the sand.

Connie's mother had a holiday apartment in Santa Monica just yards from the beach. They wound up there so the kids could get cleaned up and fed burgers and fries by a doting grandma. Then home to bed very tired, but happy to have Mommy home again.

Once home again, Gil had his serious chat to his wife and showed Liz he was not happy she'd introduced Connie to a drug, however mild. She was very abashed and apologized profusely. Then she hugged Connie and said:

"You know I love you. It was a bit of misguided fun and for that I'm sorry. But Gil's right. Jamie's a prime example of why it mustn't go any further."

"All I ask is that you do nothing unless I'm there," said Gil. "You don't know these bastard dealers. You have no idea how manipulative they can be."

"Scout's honor," said Connie giving the salute. Gil hugged her and whispered in her ear:

"You are my life. If anything happened to you, I wouldn't survive."

Connie wondered cynically if he ever used that as a pickup line.

Party time became a regular Friday night date for Lizbeth, Connie and other invited friends who dropped by to have fun and get high on the pool-house terrace.

She had discovered a new-found confidence, relaxed with the drug and with a circle of friends of her own.

They'd light the barbeque and splash in the pool, getting gradually higher and higher in the sunny autumn afternoons. Then they'd lay out on the lawns to sunbathe and relax, some to sleep, some chattering like magpies.

Gil was always there.

She glanced at his grim expression and wondered if she wasn't there, he'd have been with the guys doing something stronger, and decided he wouldn't. He'd warned her often enough of the consequences.

In innocence, she and her girlfriends wound flowers from the garden around their wrists and set coronets on their hair. These were Halcyon days of sunshine.

Chapter Eleven

November of that year saw a spate of unusually wet weather. The loungers on the beach front were packed away in canvas bags and the detritus from burgers and disposable coffee cups skittered across the Ocean Walk and floated out to sea.

It was a city day.

Connie and her friend Jean dashed from boutique to perfumery to shoe-shop, splashing through puddles with logo'ed shopping bags held over their heads.

They looked like a couple of drowned rats by the time they were seated in their favorite cafe.

"Its past time I grew up," said Connie with annoyance, trying without success to run her fingers through the knots in her long hair. Come on, drink up, we have another stop to make."

More rain, more splashing and they stood before the coolest hairdressing salon in L.A.

"No way, Connie. You've to wait a month for an appointment here!" exclaimed Jean.

"Watch this!" said Connie and marched confidently through the swing door to the reception desk.

"I'd like my hair cut and styled, please. And blow-dried."

The receptionist took out a shiny appointments book from a shelf under her desk.

"When would be convenient, madame?"

"Now would be best," said Connie confidently.

"I'm afraid we have nothing until Friday. Would that be

suitable?"

"No, I have an urgent appointment this afternoon at five, so it'd be great if you could do it in the next half hour."

"I'm afraid that's out of the question, madame," said the receptionist whose face had started to flush.

At that moment, a fey gentleman with long black hair, plucked eyebrows and just a hint of makeup, walked through the salon door.

"What seems to be the problem?"

"I'd like my hair cutting now," Connie was emphatic. Jean was thinking this might be the last time she went shopping with Connie.

"I'm afraid we can't do that, madame. We are booked solid for the next couple of days."

"If you cut my hair now" said Connie, "I won't charge you for keeping it."

Connie's hair from shoulder to beyond her waist was over three feet long, in beautiful condition and as black as ebony – an absolute godsend for expensive hair pieces. The hairdresser's eyes took on an acquisitive glint and Connie knew she had him.

"One moment please. Sarah, get madam and her friend some coffee," and to Connie, "I can't promise anything, but I'll see what I can do."

He floated back through the door he'd entered from.

He returned within minutes, gesticulating in their direction to a little man with good skin and a black suit. He smiled depreciatingly at Connie.

"Would madame mind if I examine her hair?" he asked in an unmistakably British accent. "Perhaps you'd like to follow me," and he led them into a small sitting area behind the reception.

He looked at Connie's hair strand by strand.

"If you can have your best stylist cut it now, I'll make you a gift of it."

It had finally dawned on Jean that her friend wasn't joking. When the truth sank in, she was horrified.

"Connie! Your beautiful hair! Gil will have a heart attack!"

"He'll get over it." said Connie with more bravado than she felt. I need to grow up sometime. Might as well be now."

Both hairdressers disappeared into the salon and the small man, who appeared to be the owner, returned almost immediately and led Connie inside.

It seemed an age until Connie re-emerged looking so different Jean hardly recognized her. She no longer looked a gauche twenty-one. Before Jean stood a confident, shapely young woman with enormous brown eyes fringed by thick, black lashes. Her hair swung to just below shoulder length, softly curled and held high at the sides with tortoiseshell combs. She gave a side-ways glance at the little man, who actually blushed.

Gil was stunned.

"What in God's name have you done, Connie?" he spluttered. "What the hell were you thinking? Will it grow back?"

"It's not growing back because I don't want it to grow back. I can't stay eighteen forever. Surely you knew I had to grow up sometime."

That evening he disappeared down to the pool-house, and she knew he'd lit candles and was playing softly on his guitar, as he often did when he was troubled or tired, and needed to think things through. She thought he was over-reacting, and she wasn't the only one who should grow up.

Chapter Twelve

The next day, Gil had to go to a business meeting. There were contracts to sign for another tour.

In the office block he ran into Larry Giordano who was there with his dad and sister Giulia.

Paul gave him a friendly hug, took his daughter's arm and wandered off down the corridor towards an elevator at the end.

"Hi, it's been an age! How're you all doing?" Gil smiled at his friend Larry.

"Cool," said Larry. "Dad's just been signing a contract for a show…. somewhere. Can't remember where exactly. He does the same act wherever it is."

"Connie cut off her hair yesterday," said Gil abruptly. He looked so shattered Larry instinctively put a comforting hand on his arm.

Paul and Giulia had walked on ahead, but Giulia came back when she recognized Gil.

"Wow, Giulia," Gil smiled at the glowing teenager, and made a monumental effort to control his anxious expression. "Looking good!" He gave her a peck on the cheek.

She hadn't seen Gil for a while and was a little surprised at the change in him. He seemed to have altered since the previous summer, or perhaps she just hadn't noticed. Although the mischief in his gentle eyes danced just the same, the once rotund boy with smooth chestnut locks had been replaced by a very attractive man with long hair and a full, thick beard. He'd lost a little weight too and spoke with a new-found confidence.

"'Well, bye, Gil. See you soon I hope," Giulia said and

ran off after her dad, tucking her arm through his and smiling up at him engagingly.

"God-damn daddy's girl!" remarked Larry, wryly.

Gil grinned and watched them disappear down the corridor.

His haggard expression returned.

"Gotta go." His shoulders sagged. "My dad could be blowing a fuse. If Jamie's there, he'll certainly be blowing a fuse." There was a certain amount of trepidation in his voice. "Give me a call. We'll have a beer."

Larry gave a quick salute and strode off after the other members of the Giordano clan.

In the meeting, as usual Monty was holding forth. Jamie was to all intents and purposes asleep, his head supported on his hand and his expression half-hidden by long hair. Gil knew he was very much awake and taking it all in. He wondered if Monty had noticed the half-bottle of booze sticking out of the jacket pocket Jamie had slung across the back of his chair. He supposed not or the fur would be flying by now.

Also there, was John, serious and sensible if a bit bored, Phil, grinning in his usual way, Steve paring his nails with a pocketknife and Ed a complete bastard whatever the situation.

Gil sat in the only spare chair which happened to be next to his dad.

Monty drummed his fingertips on the tabletop and cursed the promoters' executives for being late.

"Bastards couldn't organize an orgy in a brothel. Good of you to join us by the way, Gil. Hope we didn't dig into your social life. Hate to have inconvenienced you."

He cast Gil an evil glare.

Jamie snorted but turned it into a pretty good imitation of a snore.

The door opened and in walked a young man wearing a sharp suit and gold pin in his narrow tie, and an older man with greying hair who had an air of authority. The former had a sheaf of papers under one arm which he dropped in a neat pile on the table. He passed them to Monty to hand out.

Jamie, sitting up straight, flicked back his hair and with a very theatrical display of surprise said:

"Have I missed anything? Where's the pen? Where do I sign?"

Monty sneered at him.

"Useless shit, pay attention."

Jamie, hands clasped, did a reasonable impression of the dutiful son. Everyone but Monty, who was distracted by the prospect of the paperwork, and Ed whose face showed its usual distain, dropped their heads to hide a grin.

Four copies of a three-page document were passed round for them to sign – one for the promoter, one for the band's lawyer, one for the promoter's lawyers and one for Monty's personal files. Nobody bothered reading them. Monty would have bullied copies out of the promoters' secretary and combed through them beforehand, until he knew them by heart.

"The itinerary is attached to the back. Fifteen shows in the eastern states starting in Florida and ending in New York. Fairly easy travel."

They all winced. When a promoter made a point of

saying it was easy travel it usually meant the opposite. 'Fairly easy' was worse.

"Let's hope the frickin' dressing-rooms are an improvement on the last tour. There were rats in the walls at one of the Indianapolis shows. You could hear them skittering about."

Ed glowered at everyone, as if they had deliberately made his life uncomfortable.

"Well, if that's all I'll be on my way. Things to do!"

"Things to do?" said Jamie, "Which one – do I know her?"

Ed left.

It was all they could do to be civil to each other, and mostly they fell short of that.

"Enough! Out!" ordered Monty. There was something in his tone which always made his sons feel ten years old, and Gil ducked automatically.

There was a scraping of chairs and they all trooped out, leaving the contracts on the table. They were collected by the younger man, who did a quick check that Jamie hadn't written Monty Robson instead of his own name, as he had the time before.

Monty nodded tersely at them on the way out.

Once outside, Gil excused himself and headed across the road to Rick's Bar, a place he knew well. It was only three-thirty. Connie wouldn't be expecting him home for a couple of hours yet. After a beer, the meeting with Monty might not seem quite so bad.

Alone, Gil's thoughts returned to Connie. He pictured her fall of midnight hair as it used to be, and her deep loving eyes.

The bartender brought his beer

He downed it thoughtfully, then ordered another, with a bourbon chaser.

Gil was kneeling on the large white rug beside the coffee table with Jacob, turning over the pieces of a jigsaw puzzle. It was a picture of Popeye and Olive Oil. The very sight of Popeye made Jacob roar with laughter. He had before now, reduced a family party to tears with his hysterics. But at this moment he was serious. Minutes spent with Daddy were precious and he wanted to enjoy every one.

Connie smiled fondly as Jake pressed his forehead to his dad's in concentration. She rocked little Mylo on her knee.

The idyll was interrupted by the phone.

"Yes? Oh hi, Ed." Gil listened for some time, his expression increasingly strained.

"Oh for chrissake, Ed. You can't do that. How the hell will they learn the arrangements in time?"

Although Connie couldn't hear the words, the voice on the other end of the line became louder and the speech faster.

"Don't you fucking dare." Gil had become so red in the face Connie was alarmed. She grabbed his arm. He shook her off and continued yelling down the phone.

"We've five new band members. You can't just go on a jaunt to Switzerland. They need rehearsals – shit, they don't even know the notes and I can't do your job as well as mine.

"The hell you don't," he was incandescent with rage by now. "We all need rehearsals. You're not getting on that stage without knowing what you're doing." He paused to take a breath. "Shit, Ed. I don't care if you've sung the song a million times. The arrangements and players change so they have to be rehearsed over again. Make sure you're on that stage and ready to go tomorrow."

He slammed down the phone and clutched his head in his hands in frustration.

Connie by this time was truly worried, and little Mylo began squirming and fidgeting in her arms. This was so out of character for Gil. He was the mildest of men and patiently mended fences between band members time and time again. His was always the calming voice, the voice of reason. He sat back on the floor and Jacob climbed on his knee and kissed his cheek.

"I'll take care of you Daddy. If that was Uncle Ed, I'll…. I'll give him a smack in the mouth." He clapped his hands over his own mouth, eye's wide with dismay.

Gil was contrite. He lifted Jacob gently in his arms and stroked his curls. Then he pulled the toddler towards him and hugged him fiercely. Jacob hugged him back and was disappointed when Gil handed him to his mother and stood up.

"I have a storming headache. I'm going to the pool-house for a while. He left, head bowed.

Connie used to be able to comfort Gil, but recently he had become increasingly reserved. She called Gloria and together they bathed the children and readied them for bed.

The rehearsals did go ahead as planned and Ed did turn up, although he spent the afternoon sulking and being generally obnoxious.

"Hey, Ed – what's the deal? Thought you were going to...." Jamie considered mockingly, finger pressed to his cheek. "Where was it now.... oh I remember, Berlin? No? Oh, well...one of those places in Europe."

Jamie was nothing if not predictable. Gil slapped him across the back of the head as he walked past his chair. Jamie laughed aloud.

Gil worked hard with the new musicians, playing through their parts until he was sure they had them. He played most keyboard instruments and guitars by ear himself and could follow written music but not write it. The band now comprised thirty plus musicians. Some of them had classical training and could take up the slack. He was always careful to show his appreciation.

One of the new guys just didn't measure up – he was neither skilled nor quick enough. So, Gil paid him generously and quietly let him go.

Later, after their evening meal and while the kids were still covered in tomato sauce from the pasta, Connie said:

"Can I bring the boys down to see the rehearsal tomorrow? They would love to watch what you do, and we would stay out of the way. You could all see a little more of each other before you go off on tour again."

She didn't seem to understand, he thought. He was stretched to the limit. He was now a man down for the band, Ed was threatening to be elsewhere. He couldn't do with any distractions.

"No. I don't think that would work. I'd be sidetracked

and wouldn't be able to give them any attention anyway. No, I don't think so."

Connie was livid. It was one thing to not want them there, but quite another to be so dismissive. The kids saw him so rarely, but he seemed to go off for weeks at a time with no thought for them at all – or her either come to that.

She stacked the crockery in the dishwasher with a clatter, breaking a plate in the process, then slammed the door shut, not caring if he noticed or not. He didn't.

The following morning, Connie made sure she was busy with the kids before he left for the studio. He came and kissed her absentmindedly, so taken up with the day's work he hadn't even noticed how upset she'd been. Her resentment increased.

Connie drove to downtown LA at a speed likely to get her a ticket if she was pulled over. She turned into a back street and killed the engine, considering her next move.

She was mulling it over, when a beautiful girl in a bright blue custom Mustang pulled up in front of her. Another car - something to make him sit up and take notice – something that would break through the effort of preparing for yet another tour.

The more she thought of it, the more appealing the idea became. He could hardly ignore an automobile if it was pulled up outside the front door. It would have to be something eye-catching and stylish – foreign, perhaps.

Connie had no idea where or how to buy a car – that had always been Gil's domain – but she wasn't stupid – she would learn.

Chapter Thirteen

There were usually staff to take care of the bulk of the work now. But preparing to go on tour had always been a major job and took a couple of days. First were the instruments which had to be locked in trunks with the owner's name stenciled on the side. Gil usually took at least half a dozen guitars, plus numerous boxes of strings and spares.

Next came the stage costumes. In their band, they were fairly every-day. Nonetheless, they all had to be pressed and packed on hangers into travel cases along with towels and toiletries. The whole assemblage became a mobile city, loaded onto trucks and *en route* this time, for Fort Lauderdale in Florida.

Before he left for the airport, there was just time to kiss the children – Jacob sobbed – and Connie. Then he was gone. Once again, as always, she felt deserted and bereft.

After the flurry of activity, the house seemed to echo, bare and silent. The children played listlessly with toy cars on the marble tiles. Every so often Mylo would hiccough, and a stray tear would track down a grubby cheek.

This time Gil wouldn't be back until Christmas Eve and would have to leave again on the twenty-sixth.

She was so disappointed in Gil. They had had such a special, loving relationship and it all seemed to be turning to ashes.

Watching other girls throw themselves at your husband, even when he was as true and faithful as Gil – and what a disillusion that had turned out to be - was a nightmare. Some of the groupies looked like super-models, all long tanned legs and flawless make-up. Some could hold conversations in other languages. It had never stopped being intimidating.

Was that her problem? Was he so bored with her availability he looked elsewhere for stimulation? Whatever it was, Gil needed a shock to get him to even notice her existence.

Next day when the kids were taking a nap, Connie dragged the huge White Pages tome from the cupboard under the phone and slammed it down on the breakfast bar. She leafed through it until she found the entries for LA car dealerships.

Connie ran a neatly manicured finger down the entries. One stood out from the rest. The bordered, deco-style design jumped out of the page. 'Windham Luxury Car Dealership' on Beverly Boulevard. She must have driven past it a hundred times.

A couple of hours later, she pulled into the forecourt of a rectangular concrete building with floor to ceiling windows, and 'Windham Autos', written in sage green letters picked out in silver, over a swing door.

What caught her eye, was a revolving display stand behind the plate-glass window. On top, gleamed the most beautiful car Connie had ever seen. It was a silver blue Porsche, slowly revolving and displaying its unique elegance to prospective buyers. It had the added advantage of being German-made. Gil always went for English automobiles – he'd be double sure to notice it.

She pushed her hair back behind her Gucci sunglasses and breezed through the glass door.

Inside, were perhaps a half dozen gleaming motors. No prices of course, since the people who bought this kind of vehicle required no other motivation than an urge to possess. Money was no object.

Connie walked directly to the stand to take a closer look. The car door was open to show its plush black leather and chrome interior.

"It only arrived this morning," said a smiling salesman. "Would you like to take a closer look?"

He flipped a switch on the wall to the side of the stand and it stopped.

A smart looking man in a blue suit and tie entered the showroom through a rear door.

"Fetch the ramp from the back store, Jess. Then the lady can get a proper look and perhaps we could…..."

He paused, uncertain.

"Haven't we met before?"

Connie was puzzled - he really did look familiar.

He snapped his fingers,

"Now I remember. Mrs. Robson, isn't it – and I think we met in London? I didn't recognize you at first - you've cut your hair!"

"Of course," she smiled. "Hampton Court! I'm Connie Robson but I'm sorry I don't recall your name."

"We only met once in passing. You called with Mr. Robson before that, but it was a brief visit and we didn't speak."

He had a quiet way of talking which sounded confident and capable without seeming overbearing, and he looked her directly in the eye, which felt disconcerting.

"My name is Oliver Maxwell, and this is my little enterprise."

His gesture encompassed the whole of the large showroom.

"Last time we met I was with my wife Rachel, if you recall."

"Yes, of course I do."

He glanced at his watch. "I'm about to go to lunch. Would you join me for something to eat, a glass of wine perhaps?"

What could be the harm in that - especially as she was a prospective customer.

"Thank you, yes," she said, not altogether comfortable with the idea.

"And while we're out, I'll get the guys to take the Porsche down so you can test drive it when we come back?"

"I'd like that," said Connie, smiling.

Oliver knew of a fashionable little bistro nearby, and they sat and chatted over pastries and wine.

He was such a gentleman, and when it came time to leave, held her chair for her as she rose. If he'd meant to charm her, he'd certainly succeeded.

When they got back to the dealership, the car was waiting as he'd promised. But it was far later than Connie had realized – they must have talked for a couple of hours, and she'd totally lost track of time.

"I am so sorry Oliver. I had no intention of wasting your time, but I won't be able to test the car this afternoon. It's much later than I thought, and my boys will wonder where I am."

This was an excuse. She was feeling uncomfortable –

she hadn't had lunch with another man before – she'd been so young when she and Gil first met, the situation had never arisen. That she'd enjoyed herself was unnerving.

"Think nothing of it," said Oliver smiling, "Another time perhaps?"

It clearly was a question requiring an answer.

"I'll call you – perhaps Gil should look it over," she said hurriedly over her shoulder as she left.

Oliver smiled at her in his usual confident manner.

Once home, Connie hurried into the kitchen flustered, but the children were sitting at the counter eating cookies, still rosy-cheeked from their bath, safe in Gloria's care. Connie smiled her thanks and picked Mylo up. Chubby little arms wrapped around her neck, and she hugged him close.

"No need to carry me, Mom," said grown-up Jacob, clambering down off his stool. "I'm four now so I can walk on my own," he grabbed hold of her skirt.

"Give them some time in the playroom Gloria, then call me. What story shall I read you tonight, angels?"

"Gee, Ma. Popeye – I want Popeye."

"That's a comic book, Jacob – and don't call me that. It's not a story. How about 'The Giving Tree'?"

"S'pose so," answered a grumpy Jacob.

The next day was Thursday. Connie was delighted when the doorbell chimed, and a delivery boy left a dozen red roses. Gil's card held sentiments indisputably his, but the message was typewritten. She knew she was being unfair but seeing his familiar writing would have been such a comfort. It seemed life was littered with small disappointments these days.

Chapter Fourteen

Christmas came round in a flurry of activity. Jacob had asked Connie if they could help decorate the huge tree she'd bought in a downtown mall. It had been delivered that afternoon. It was so big they had had to trim the top off so the star would fit.

The three of them spent an hour hanging lights and decorations – Mylo trod on a plastic Santa and Connie had to put a band aid on his foot - and then it came time for the official lighting.

"Tar-ah! Come one, come all. I present the switching on of the Robson Family Tree!" announced Connie in her best fairground voice.

She gave Jacob the switch and picked up the baby.

"At the count of three, Christmas will begin. Jacob Robson is in charge of the count down."

As he finished counting, Jacob pressed the button, and the lights began to sparkle and twinkle in the reflective baubles. Two little faces, with eyes like saucers, stared in wonder at the glorious tree.

Gil was expected back from Pennsylvania in the early afternoon of Christmas Eve. He had rung Connie from back-stage after the show. The cacophony in the background was deafening, so their conversation was necessarily short.

She was picking him up from the airport. He'd be exhausted she thought, depressed. She just hoped he'd be fit to deal with a family Christmas.

"Please," she whispered. "Please let him have some time for us."

Gil fell asleep in the car on the way home, his face grey with fatigue. He left his luggage in the car and, kissing the kids in passing, went straight to bed. He was asleep, fully clothed, in seconds.

Connie tugged off his shoes and socks – my God they stank – and undressed him as best she could. He was a dead weight, completely unconscious. This did not look good.

"Where's Daddy gone?" asked Jacob, confused by Gil's sudden appearance and just as rapid departure.

"Dad's been working very hard and is very tired. You'll see him in the morning."

"Will he be there when we open our presents?"

"Of course he will."

But he wasn't. He wasn't there for Christmas Dinner either. When he finally emerged, it was five o'clock Christmas Day afternoon. He'd slept the clock round.

"Hi, kids – did I miss anything?" Gil said with forced cheeriness, his hair still messy from sleep.

"You missed everything," accused Jacob, refusing to look at him.

Little Mylo nodded sagely in support of his older brother.

"You missed Dinner," accused Jacob. "Mom made us wait until after dinner to open our presents and you still hadn't woken up."

"I am so sorry, Jake," said Gil. "Would it help that I got you some presents to open now?"

But Jacob was inconsolable and ran off to his room.

Gil had forgotten Connie. She stood stony-faced, propped against the breakfast bar.

"Not much of a homecoming, was it?" he said to her, ruefully.

"What did you expect?" Connie ground out, "Bells and whistles? You've ruined their Christmas – mine too. I've spent the whole of Christmas Day making excuses for you."

He went over to kiss her, but she turned her face away.

Gil showered, dressed, unpacked his cases from the car trunk leaving the few gifts he'd had one of the roadies buy for the kids under the tree. With no further conversation, he jumped in his car and left. Where he was going, he had no idea, but he was drawn to Rick's again. It was completely empty at this time on Christmas Day. The bar tender was stacking the glasses he'd been drying on a shelf over the bar.

"Gil... This is a surprise. What can I get for you?"

"Give me a Bud... no, make that two." He ran his hand through his hair and spoke with no thought whatever for the poor barman,

By ten o'clock he was maudlin drunk. The beer had long given way to whisky.

"Closing up now, Gil. I've a wife and kids to go home to if you haven't."

This chance remark almost shocked Gil into sobriety. He sat up straight and for a moment his eyes focused.

"Gotta get home," he slurred, and pulling himself to his feet, furniture-surfed to the swing-door.

The chill air outside was like walking into a brick wall. Gil fell over untidily on the sidewalk and pulled himself upright against the bar door. The effort made him dizzy and he stumbled and fell again.

Catch a Falling Star

A short time later, the bartender came out of the door, and turning to lock it, saw Gil collapsed on the ground.

He was making a concentrated effort to untangle his car keys from his jacket pocket.

"Want me to call you a cab?" said the barman.

"No, it'll be fine," muttered an unsteady Gil.

"Wouldn't be much of a Christmas for your family scraping you up off the road. C'mon, I'll give you a lift home. You can collect your wheels in the morning."

"That's so kind.... sooo kind," said Gil and promptly burst into tears.

Pete the bartender, hoisted Gil to his feet and tipped him into the passenger seat of a Chevy parked next to the curb.

He managed to decipher, not without difficulty, the address Gil gave him. His inebriated passenger sat with his head tipped back and spent the journey dozing or mumbling incoherently.

Once home, Pete dropped him unceremoniously onto the doorsteps, and sped off to his own family gathering.

Gil hauled himself to his hands and knees and promptly vomited into a flowerpot. He wiped a dirty hand down his jacket. It had just started to rain.

He managed to reach the bell and pressed it repeatedly. Within seconds the door was flung open by an irate Connie, who loudly whispered:

"What the hell are you doing? You'll wake the kids."

Until that point, she hadn't taken in his appearance. He was standing swaying in the doorway, his clothing in disarray, and rain mixed with the tears coursing down his face.

"Get in here and shut up or you'll wake everyone. Where the hell have you been? You smell worse than a brewery." She took his arm and helped him inside. "How could you Gil? How could you?"

Gil made a sudden dive for the bathroom.

By the time he reemerged, Connie was fixing a pot of black coffee. She handed him a cup and he took a scalding mouthful.

"I was just so worn out and so longing to be home," he said, still shaky from the alcohol.

She looked skeptical so he took her hand in his – this time she didn't pull back. There was no way she could stay annoyed with the pathetic creature before her.

"Please help me to put this right. Anything I say will sound like an excuse and that isn't what I want to do at all."

"Just talk. We'll sort out blame later."

"It was a nightmare." He paused to wipe a hand over his face and take another drink. Then he kissed her hand and continued:

"Stevie – this time - was out of it most of the time. At one point he fell off the riser in front of the audience and knocked himself out. I don't know what to do about him. Gil's face became haggard with worry as he went on:

"Ed has been even more of a bastard than usual. He sat in the middle of the stage cross-legged like some stick-insect, making weird noises, and refused point blank to shift. Then he stomped about until show time spitting abuse at everyone."

Gil went to the sink and swilled his hands and face with cold water.

"Someone stood on my 12-string and snapped the neck. I never found out who. One of the horn players went off sick at the end of the second show."

Gil stood, steadier now. "I need to shower and get into some clean clothes. Can you wait?"

Connie nodded. The litany of problems he'd had to deal with made her sorry for him, but she was still smarting from the ruined Christmas. Jacob and Mylo couldn't be allowed to see their father in the state he'd been in when she first opened the door.

But when he returned all he said was:

"Would you mind if we went to bed, Connie?"

So much between them was left unsaid as he had to leave the following day.

"Only another four shows and I'll be back for a month."

She didn't believe it. There was always something. And there was this time, too.

They extended the tour by another four dates, which meant Gil would miss New Year as well.

And Jamie was now in rehab and had to be replaced for the extra gigs. He had been arrested for being drunk and disorderly and ordered to pay a $500 fine and attend a rehabilitation clinic. Things were going from bad to worse.

Relations between herself and Gil – already shaky - were made even more frosty by his late return.

Although Connie knew it wasn't his fault, and although she knew he was bound hand and foot by signed contracts and personal obligations, it didn't make any difference to the way she felt.

Although she still loved him, and always would, she was not foolish enough to pretend that things were going to get better.

But despite all they'd been through, Gil still cared for her so much he would never bring himself to hurt her. If they were to get some workable plan, she would have to take control. She had absolutely no idea how she should go about that, but she knew a parting of the ways was slowly but surely becoming inevitable..

Chapter Fifteen

Somehow, they managed to limp on through January and February. Nothing much was said, but both children picked up on the bad feeling, and were fractious and tearful. Friends and relatives were aware of the awful atmosphere in the house, but it was clear that neither Connie nor Gil wanted to talk about it, especially to each other. The children felt Mommy and Daddy no longer wanted them. In their little minds, what else would account for their coldness?

Gil was working in the studio during the Easter holidays, but as usual his working days seemed to be getting longer. Sometimes he'd be there until midnight, long after everyone else had gone home. He had deep shadows under his eyes, and a permanently worried expression. Everyone saw. Nobody felt it was their business to comment... except Jamie.

"Fuck, little bro' – what in God's name's gotten into you? If you lose it, the rest of we'll follow."

He took a pack of Marlboro from his shirt pocket and shook a couple out.

"Here. For fuck's sake, unwind. You're going to snap if you don't."

Gil lit the cigarette and continued to work the slides on the console. He didn't speak and the expression on his face didn't lighten.

"Gil!" yelled Jamie. "What the hell is going on?"

Jamie pulled a bottle of hooch out of his jacket.

"Here – it'll help you relax. Does wonders for me!"

"I'd noticed," said Gil without expression, but he took the bottle anyway, wiped the lip and took a good long swallow. He continued working with the console, but Jamie could tell his mind was a million miles away.

"What's going on, Gil?" said Jamie, more gently this time.

Gil finally looked at him. Jamie was shocked by the pain behind his eyes. Why hadn't he noticed it before? This was his little brother who no matter what stupid situation he got himself into, was always there to bail him out. Yet the first time Gil needed him, he hadn't even noticed.

"What's happened?"

"My marriage is crumbling and there doesn't seem to be a damn thing I can do about it."

Gil's expression of grief had deepened. Jamie handed him the bottle again.

Gil passed out first – he didn't have Jamie's capacity for alcohol. Jamie lowered him gently to the floor. He curled himself round Gil for comfort as he had in their Briarside days when Monty was rampaging round the house, threatening to kill them.

But Gil had been little more than a baby then, and now he was a grown man. Jamie tightened his hold, then fell asleep too.

When they woke, cramped from the cold floor, Jamie upended the empty bottle ruefully:

"Guess we're out of juice. First job, a refill. Then do you want me to come home with you? Y'know... in case there are any problems?"

"If you come home with me, you will *be* the problem," said Gil, then in a sudden panic: "What's the time? The cleaning staff will be in soon and look at the god-damn mess in here!"

Gil busied himself picking up burger wrappers and drinks cans and throwing them in a bin. Jamie sat slouched in his chair, idly spinning the bottle round in his fingers, and watched him.

"You need serious help, you know? That's what cleaning staff are for," Jamie said. "C'mon, I'll drive you. Perfectly safe - not late enough, and too early for me not to be sober." Pause. "That was crap, wasn't it? Bottle definitely needs topping up."

They picked up jackets, turned off the lights and locked the door.

Jamie dropped Gil at Rick's to collect his car, and a dog-tired Gil drove up the hill home, When he turned into the drive, the first thing he noticed was that Connie's car wasn't in its accustomed spot.

He looked at his watch. It was early, only nine-thirty. Perhaps she was running the kids to school – no, too late for that. Gil put his hand out to open the door only to find it locked. He scrabbled about in his pocket for his keys. Inside, all the windows were shut, and the air conditioning turned off. Big as the room was, it still managed to feel stuffy. Silence. No Connie, no boys, no Gloria. He ventured further in, feeling more trepidation by the second.

"Stupid…. this is stupid," he muttered to himself suddenly realizing he was tip-toeing around in his own home. He strode across the kitchen and flung opened the sliding glass doors as wide as they would go. The scent of roses flooded in.

On the breakfast bar was a folded sheet of paper. It read:

"You've really excelled yourself this time, Gil. You've been

missing all night and not even thought to call. We've gone to Mom's house in Santa Monica. You and I both need time and space to think things through and we won't get that here. There's plenty of food in the freezer to keep you going. Please give it a couple of days, then call if you want to. Until then, leave us alone."

He stared at the paper. He shook his head as if the action might sort his jumbled thoughts. He had to speak to her. But the note said don't call. What if he called and she wouldn't speak to him? What would he do then?

He made himself a cup of coffee and sat on a lounger on the terrace.

All at once, it was too much. He flung the cup across the Italian tiles, and smashed glass and steaming coffee flew everywhere.

He couldn't think about this now - he'd calm down and put everything in perspective. Everything would fall into place once he'd sorted himself out.

A half bottle of Jack Daniels sent Gil into an uneasy sleep, from which he was awakened by the door-chimes. He smoothed his hair and tightened the belt of his robe as he crossed the hall. It wouldn't be Jamie – he'd be sleeping it off somewhere. Who then? Connie? Please God let it be Connie.

It turned out to be Stevie, high as a kite.

"You cool man? Saw your old lady was out – no car - so thought I'd call in to smoke a joint or two. You okay? You look a bit peaky."

'Just what I need,' thought Gil – getting high with Steve, but he took a toke anyway.

They sat and chatted for a while until Steve mentally and physically shook himself.

"Gotta go see a new guy across town. Does good stuff." He waved the stub of his roll-up under Gil's nose. "Good to see ya!"

He drifted out of the door, forgetting to close it behind him.

Chapter Sixteen

Once Steve had gone as mysteriously as he had arrived, Gil was again faced with the deafening silence of the empty house. He put music on the deck, but the words only brought Connie's face to mind.

Gil had never felt so disconnected from everything in the world he loved as he did at that moment.

He jumped in his car. At least he wouldn't need to face the empty house at night. He'd book into an airport hotel until he needed to leave for Chicago in a couple of days. The road-crew would have everything covered. He packed a suitcase, locked up the house and left without a backward glance.

A couple of days later, when she'd heard nothing, Connie called the house.

She rang periodically for the rest of the day, then decided she may as well go home. She'd thought Gil wouldn't be leaving again until the weekend. Apparently, she was wrong.

If Gil was back on tour, he would be away for at least a week. What would happen then, she had no idea.

She rang Gloria and got her to open the house and fix a meal for the kids.

When the boys were asleep, Connie felt as overwhelmed by the emptiness of the house as Gil had. She sat on the terrace with a magazine, but she couldn't concentrate. Putting her head back on the lounger she closed her eyes and tried to conjure up the sweetness of her husband's expression, but to her bewilderment his face morphed into another. She sat up in shock. Oliver! But she hadn't thought of him in weeks. The more she tried to put him out of her mind, the more his face intruded.

Connie slept fitfully that night and woke up early. It was not quite six o'clock. She pulled on a silk kimono. and rifled through her purse for her wallet and Oliver's business card. She ran her thumb against its silver edging then slotted it back again.

It was still too early to call. What the hell was she thinking?

Gloria arrived at seven-thirty and busied herself with the boys' breakfast pancakes. The clatter and chatter of a new day erupted in the kitchen.

"Mommy, can we go to the sea today?" yelled Mylo, his mouth full of pancake and syrup.

"Oh yeah! Can we Ma?"

"We'll see…and don't call me Ma, Jacob."

"Why not? I like calling you Ma - all the kids on TV call their Mas Ma."

"Well you're not on TV." she said.

Connie stood by full of admiration as Gloria wiped the pancake syrup from her children's faces and hands. She had her own very efficient way of doing it, which involved grabbing the hair over their foreheads, tipping their heads back and scrubbing every inch hard with a soapy cloth. For some reason, neither of them objected to this rough treatment. They just walked off with shiny faces and clean hands.

Later that day, strollers folded and stored in the car, and one of Gloria's picnic baskets, including towels to sit on, also packed, Connie lathered the boys in sun block, pulled on beanies and all three set off for the beach.

In the huge parking lot, Connie shook out Mylo's stroller and stuck him complaining loudly, into it. Why the hell hadn't she asked Gloria to send her niece to help out? Lana was always glad of a bit of pocket money. By the time Connie finally got two fractious toddlers to the beach she was hot, bothered and short-tempered.

She lifted a screaming Mylo from the stroller. Instantly the deafening noise ceased, and a huge grin spread across his face.

Meanwhile, Jacob was rifling through the picnic basket for his favorite peanut butter and jelly sandwiches. As sandwiches came out, sand went in. She grabbed his wrist.

"Oh no you don't! You'll have to wait like the rest of us."

"Aww! Ma"

"And don't call me that!"

"Need some help there?" said an amused voice.

Connie blew a strand of hair away from her sweating forehead as she turned round.

Damn, it was Oliver.

Holding onto each hand were two children: a brown-haired boy with bright blue eyes a little bit older than Jacob, and a little girl with pretty blonde curls held in a neat ponytail, a year or two younger. They had clearly already been in the sea because their hair was damp and beginning to stiffen with salt.

"Say hello to Simeon and Deborah. My own little sea monsters," he growled at Jacob and Mylo. "They're not much for playing but...."

At that, all four children began running round in circles hollering and kicking sand in the air.

"Well, that's that sorted. Mind if I grab a corner of your towel?"

Connie shifted across and Oliver sat down. Looking for the safest subject she said:

"I didn't ask you about Rachel when I was looking at the car. How is she?"

Oliver looked taken-aback.

"She left almost immediately we got back from London – I thought I'd told you. It was a shock at the time but I understand it in a way. She hadn't been well since Deborah was born. She's always found looking after them a strain. Rachel's back with her parents but I can't see us getting back together – too much water under the bridge."

This was not the safe ground Connie had anticipated.

"I'm so sorry. She seemed a nice lady when I met her in London."

He was quiet for a while gazing out to sea.

"Would you have dinner with me?" he asked softly

"Oliver, you know my situation. That wouldn't be right."

"Lunch then? Between friends. Like we did last time. I saved the car for you. It's in my garage at home. We could go afterwards, and you could see it you still wanted it."

That seemed innocuous enough. No harm in lunch in public and she did like the car.

Oliver said: "Well, what do you think? Better you look at the car first, then you can leave the boys to play with my two and pick them up afterwards."

Oh, what the hell…. she didn't exactly have other pressing engagements.

"Saturday morning okay?"

Connie suddenly realized their quiet conversation had drawn them so close together they were touching. She was looking into eyes so different from Gil's gentle blue-grey. She drew away.

That Saturday, as Gil brooded on his plane to Houston, Connie and the boys arrived at Oliver's beautiful Bel Air mansion. In an area of gorgeous houses, this one stood out. She drove passed emerald lawns shaded by graceful palms and studded with rose beds. Wisteria twisted over the roof of a pagoda surrounded by a small moat. Fountains splashed and sparkled in the sunshine.

Oliver waited, smiling, by the front door. Deborah watched Mylo as he climbed precariously out of the car. Jacob, as befitted the older brother, walked solemnly into the house behind Simeon.

"Let's have a quick look at the car before we leave. Then if you like it, we can take it downtown. That'd be as good a way as any to give it a test-drive, don't you think?"

He led the way across the lawn to a large garage complex. He'd said he was keen on cars but she wasn't prepared for the array of motors, including what was clearly a racing car on a gantry. 'Her' car was parked to the side of the main door. It looked newly polished and perfect – still as lovely as she remembered.

Oliver opened the door for her, and she slid inside.

He began to speak about the controls and leaned across

to demonstrate the air-conditioning. He smelled of lemongrass and musk.

He handed her out of the car, then as she straightened, he didn't stand back. He pulled her roughly to him and kissed her. Her knees gave way. If he hadn't been holding her so tightly, she would have fallen. Without conscious thought she raised up on her toes and kissed him back.

"Just say stop and I will," he breathed against her lips.

Children's voices chimed distantly and there was a loud splash as one of them leapt into the swimming pool. Connie and Oliver jumped apart.

She was furious with him. Connie smoothed her hair and picked up her sunglasses which had been knocked to the floor.

"I have to go home. Please.... I have to leave now."

Connie was flustered. She packed two very confused and damp little boys in the back seat and drove home, swerving to a stop before her own front door.

"Out!" she yelled at Jacob and Mylo who obeyed instantly but just stood there frozen.

She drew in a slow breath and counted to ten.

"I'm sorry. Come on, get back in the car and we'll go check out MacDonalds." The past hours were instantly forgotten. But not by Connie.

Chapter Seventeen

When Gil arrived in Houston and had taken a cab from his hotel to the venue, he was confronted with mayhem. If he wasn't there, everything appeared to fall to bits. One of the amps had blown and the backup had fallen off the truck and broken a roadie's leg. So, now no amp and no roadie who was in hospital. Jamie was high as a kite. Ed was unreachable as he was in deep meditation. John was distraught but he was okay and had shut himself in a dressing room because the panic was making him crazy. Stevie sat three rows back staring at the ceiling while all hell broke loose around him.

On the upside, all members of the backing band had turned up and were doing their best to set up. The furore meant that they were behind with the sound checks.

Gil would have liked to get straight back on the plane and get out of there. Instead, he yelled for quiet, and the hubbub instantly subsided.

"Get those mics set up now. Coil the wires properly - I don't want to fall on my ass. We'll have to make do with the amps. Damnation, you should be able to sort that out! Which roadie is in hospital? Jeff? Bobby – find out the situation. I'll sort out Jamie and Ed. Anything I've forgotten?"

"Me, man," said a disembodied voice from the auditorium. Gil ignored him – he'd no time for Stevie's shit now.

"Get everything set up and get the soundchecks started now."

Everything began to move as if on oiled wheels. Panic changed to order.

Gil strode backstage and found Jamie who was laying on this back staring at the ceiling.

"Oh shit, Jamie – not now. Drink or drugs? Which?"

Jamie pointed unsteadily to a large, empty vodka bottle on a nearby chair. Gil breathed a sigh of relief.

"Right...up," and Gil hauled a happy Jamie to his feet and supported him to the nearest dressing room. He turned on the shower, set the temperature to cold, pushed Jamie inside clothes and all, and shut the door. He grabbed the nearest available arm and instructed its owner not to let Jamie out until he was halfway sober. Then organize him getting into his stage clothes.

Ed was another matter. He could be belligerent under the best of circumstances. Gil's idea of meditation was being alone with his guitar, candlelight, the scent of roses and the occasional joint. Ed seemed to go out of his way to try and annoy and inconvenience as many people as possible with his relaxation techniques. Gil grimaced and looked heavenward. Round two coming up.

"Ed, time to check out if all your costumes have arrived. I only noticed one case in the truck. If they're not all here, you may have to make do with what you have until we can get them replaced."

The one thing Ed couldn't do without was his stage costumes. And replacing them would be damn near impossible.

He dashed past Gil almost knocking him over. Gil grinned at his disappearing back. No one had easier buttons to push than Ed – except perhaps Jamie.

As Gil was giving his guitars a final check over, and plugging in his amp, he took a few quiet moments to himself to light a meditation candle and restore his own peace of mind. The surrounding whirlwind receded. If there was a way to fix things with Connie he surely would. He sighed, and picking up a soft cloth, began polishing his beautiful guitar.

There was a new sax player so, when he wasn't singing Gil's attention was fixed on him, giving him small, prearranged signals for his parts. At the same time his own voice soared to the rafters, bolstered by exquisite harmonies from the other band members.

The audience knew their songs and sang along, Dancing and laughing. Gil always felt a special connection with his fans, and there was a particular song he sang at every concert, which was just for them. The interaction lifted his spirit in a way nothing else could. He supposed that was why he put up with all the shit from the rest of them.

When they came off stage, reaching for towels to dry off the sweat, a theatre official handed Gil an envelope.

It was a note to say the next couple of shows were cancelled. There had been a small electrical fire. The hall was intact, but the power had had to be turned off for a few days.

Gil always felt spent and emotional after a big show like that night's – tired to the bone – but this time he didn't know what to expect when he actually did make it back to LA, which made it so much worse.

He managed to get a seat on the next flight out. There had only been three, so even some of the principal singers had had to reschedule.

Catch a Falling Star

The lights in the house were off when he arrived home, but the pool-house was candle-lit. It was his special place. His own little haven filled with his guitars, his music. He smiled to himself. He loved candlelight. It was beautiful and gentle and relaxed him like nothing else.

Gil tiptoed to the French windows, hoping to surprise Connie. She was sitting on the chaise longue, laughing, with a glass of wine in her hand. He hadn't seen her laugh like that in a long time. She was talking to someone just out of view who, as he watched, walked forward and sat next to her, kissing her fondly on the cheek. Connie turned her head and kissed him in return, gently, affectionately on the lips.

Gil backed away not knowing what to think.

When he had calmed down a little, he climbed in his car and drove it to the side of the house, out of sight. He had to give her another chance. He took a swig of brandy from a half-bottle in his flight bag. It calmed him a little.

There was a peel of laughter and Connie and her 'friend' skirted the corner of the pool-house and walked up the drive. She was clearly tipsy from the wine, and clung to the stranger's arm, giggling. They stopped, and he kissed her long and hard. She moved against him.

Gil leapt from the car and stood in the driveway, silent.

The smile melted from Connie's face. The vaguely familiar man with her froze, stunned.

"Oliver, leave," ordered Connie. She turned her head and said, "NOW!"

He looked between Connie and her husband, hesitated as if to stay, then walked to his car and drove off.

Connie strode into the house, head held high and a defiant expression on her face. She was defensive, but her fists were balled as if for a fight.

Gil said nothing. He just followed, his heart pounding

"You knew it was always going to come to this!" spat Connie. "I've warned you over and over."

"Just tell me...what do you expect me to do about it? You know I would fix it if I could, but you won't come with me on tour and I can't stop here because I have to travel." said Gil. "You've come with me in the past but now the boys are older you can't – you won't – come."

Connie could feel the pent-up rage rising.

"First it was the band, the band, the band. Then it was that waster Jamie. They all treat you like a doormat. Your kids wonder who the hell you are when you do finally come home. Shit, they know Oliver better than you!"

Her hand flew to her mouth. She'd thought the last sentence but hadn't meant to say it aloud.

Gil felt as if his heart had stopped. This was his Connie who he loved desperately. How could she not know that? He began to beg forgiveness, but she cut him off.

"It's long past okay, Gil. I can't live like this, and it isn't fair on Jacob and Mylo."

She walked out of the door, slamming it behind her. Gil, rooted to the spot, heard her start her car, heard the tires screech on the drive.

She'd gone.

It was eleven in the morning when Gil came to. He was laying on the floor, still in the clothes he'd travelled home from Houston in. His mouth felt sour, and he had to work to open gummed eyes.

As he slowly came back to consciousness, he realized he was still hugging the brandy bottle from the car. Near his head was a quarter full bottle of Jack Daniels, tipped on its side, its contents spilled across the floor and soaking the ends of his hair.

Still threequarters drunk, he couldn't quite put his finger on what had happened. Then, as reality dawned, still laid out flat on the tiles, he began to weep. Sobs from the bottom of his soul shook him from head to foot. All of a sudden, his stomach heaved, and he vomited on the floor. He couldn't sit, never mind stand. A combination of alcohol and grief held him motionless. Blessed unconsciousness returned.

An hour on, the door was rattling and someone was shouting.

"Gil – get your ass out here. What the fuck are you doing? When I have to teach you responsibility, we're scraping the bottom of the barrel!"

Gil raised himself to his hands and knees, shook his head and crawled across the hall to the door. He dragged himself upright on the handle.

"Come on, Gil. You should have been at the studio two hours ago. What the hell are you doing?"

Gil reeled backwards and had to grab hold of the handle to steady himself, as he concentrated on turning the key. Jamie shoved the door open and knocked Gil flat. He fell with a thud.

"For fucking hell's sake, Gil, what's that smell?" He looked down at Gil, struggling to regain his feet without much success, then at the debris besmirching the once pristine room. Gil was notoriously tidy. This bombsite was an illustration of the seriousness of the situation.

"What's happened?" Jamie got hold of Gil by the

shoulders, hoisted him to his feet and shook him until his eyes refocused. His head fell forward onto Jamie's shoulder. He continued to tremble, but he made no sound.

"Gil! Oh Christ... Connie's gone for real this time?"

Gil looked up at him, his whole face puffy, his eyes raw.

"Let's get you cleaned up. Then we can sort this."

"Can't," muttered Gil. "It's done - there's nothing left to undo...there's nothing left,"

Amazingly, it was the unreliable Jamie who fetched a mop and bucket and cleaned up the mess. Gil sat on the sofa and stared unmoving into the distance. It was Jamie who stripped him out of his soiled clothes... it was Jamie who lovingly washed the whisky and vomit from his hair... it was Jamie who returned him to some measure of order. It was Jamie who sat quietly and held him until his shaking ceased.

The phone rang.

"Oh Christ. I forgot. They're still waiting to find out where you are. Quick, quick... what shall I tell them? What do I say?"

Gil shook his head to clear it. Even in this state he had to sort out problems.

"Say Mom's been sick, and I've had to go stop with her. Then call Mom and tell her she has to lie."

Jamie returned a minute or two later.

"Fixed. Now what do I do with you?"

"Nothing. Just go back to the studio. I'll be in again tomorrow. I'll cope- I have to."

Jamie sat with him for another ten or fifteen minutes while they smoked a joint together. By the time he left,

Catch a Falling Star

Gil had calmed down enough to sit outside the pool-house and play his guitar. But the weight of depression didn't lift. He slept in the sunshine, with tears seeping from his eyes.

The following morning, he was first at the studio and tuning his guitar as the others arrived, not only the band, but the sidemen.

Gil looked terrible. His face was white and drawn, and his crashing headache made it difficult to hear, never mind play. His clothes were creased. His hands shook.

Ed looked at him and sneered. He didn't really care about this session. He'd be flying out to Paris in the morning on a meditation course. In fact, these days he didn't care about any of the sessions. They'd played the songs a thousand times. Gil couldn't possibly find a reason why he needed to be there.

Gil didn't want to be there either, but professionalism was in his bones. Terrible as he felt, he still couldn't turn in a bad day's work.

They plodded on with the rehearsal, which obviously wasn't very successful. Then one of the mics broke, the harmonies just wouldn't gel. People were noticing Gil was not himself.

"Go home, Gil. This isn't working. We'll try again tomorrow," said John, "Houston was tough. We could all use a couple of days break."

"Yeah," said Phil with a sympathetic smile. "Today's already been a waste. Do you want me to see if we can rebook the studio for Thursday?"

Gil waved a tired hand.

The musicians packed up and left, and within twenty

minutes the studio was empty.

"You want to stay at mine tonight?" Jamie asked, concerned.

"That'd be great, man," Gil said and put his arm round his shoulder.

Jamie drove them at a dangerous speed to his ranch-style house in Pacific Bay. It was rented as most of his money had been spent on a magnificent yacht moored at the Marina there. Gil knew Jamie would end up living on his boat. He also knew nothing would please him more.

Jamie crashed through the door and threw his keys down on the sofa, but Gil stood on the threshold too weary to take another step. Jamie dragged him inside and dumped him into a big easy chair.

"Come and sit down before you fall down."

"I'm spent Jamie. Completely fucked. I have no idea what to do or where to go next."

"Well, your second problem is fixed. You can stay here as long as you like, and if you think it would help, we'll see if Connie's at this Oliver's. Do you know where he lives?"

"No idea. He'll be in the book I guess, but I don't know his second name."

"Gloria'll know. She's part of the Mexican housekeeper network. If she doesn't, she'll know someone who does," said Jamie with a grin.

Gil suddenly looked more hopeful, and a little color had returned to his face. If he could find Connie…if he could just talk to her, perhaps this time he could persuade her to stay. He had to at least try.

Gil slept better that night. The bed was comfortable and there was a little more hope in his heart. The following morning, he even managed to eat eggs and toast and drink a large mug of steaming coffee. With the food came renewed energy. He'd find Connie and somehow persuade her to come home.

Gil borrowed a clean t-shirt and jumped into Jamie's Corvette. Jamie keyed the engine which roared into life and he swerved onto the Pacific Highway to Los Angeles.

The wind was dry and hot on their faces and the surf surged on a glittering sea. Jamie dug a pair of shades from the glovebox and handed them to Gil.

"Start of a brand-new day, brother. A new day!"

Gil grinned for the first time in days.

Chapter Eighteen

As they turned away from the ocean and drove into the dusty outskirts of Los Angeles, Gil said:

"We'll have to go to my house first. Connie'll probably have the address in her desk somewhere. She does all that kind of thing. I've no idea where the staff live."

"Why the hell can't you have live-in staff like everybody else?" said Jamie

"No idea." Gil shrugged his shoulders. "Connie doesn't like it."

Once home, Gil was only gone a couple of minutes and came out with paper torn from a notepad.

They checked the map and pulled into the parking lot of an apartment building on an unremarkable street in an unremarkable part of the city.

Gil checked the note against the numbers on the security entry system and pressed the buzzer.

"Yes?" said a muffled voice.

"It's me, Gloria. Gil."

There was a pause and the intercom crackled.

"I'll come down Mr. Gil."

"You don't need to do that. Do you know where Connie's Mr. Oliver lives?"

"Sure do. He's in Bel Air – Elton something or other…. Way, I think. Don't know the number though. I'll call Maria. She's his housekeeper."

Jamie grinned an 'I told you so' at Gil. Two minutes later she was back:

"1025. Although Mr. Oliver and Mrs. Connie are not there."

Like the good tactful housekeeper she was, her voice betrayed no opinion.

Gil's heart sank, and when he didn't reply Jamie spoke over his shoulder.

"Thanks, Gloria. See you later," said Jamie in the tone he always used to her, because he knew it made her go weak at the knees. "C'mon Gil, Maria might know where they've gone. For all we know they're still in LA"

But Maria didn't know where they were. They'd left for the airport, but she had no idea where they'd gone. Would they like to leave a message in case Mr. Oliver called?

Gil was just on the point of saying an enthusiastic yes when Jamie grabbed his arm.

"No, that's okay. We'll call back in a couple of days."

He pulled out a diary from his pocket as if to note an appointment and leafed through it.

"Dang...I've forgotten to take his last name."

He turned the pages again, supposedly searching for it.

"It's Maxwell."

Maria smiled tightly and shut the door.

"Don't make a big deal of it," Jamie advised seriously. "She knows where they are. She'll have a number so she can get back to them. For the kids, if nothing else. At least you know his full name now, but Maria realized she was being questioned."

Gil was feeling sick again.

"Let's go. You shouldn't be in that house alone. Come back with me again." said Jamie.

That evening, a morose Gil sat in front of the TV without seeing a single thing.

"A smoke?" asked Jamie with a raised eyebrow. "Best stuff. Nepalese. Cost a fortune."

Gil shook his head tiredly.

"Keep it - does no good anyway. The last one I had just brought me down even further – if that was possible." He returned dull eyes to the TV.

Jamie picked up his jacket and slung it over his shoulder.

"Back in ten."

It was half an hour before he came back but he was grinning from ear to ear.

"If this doesn't fix you, nothing will."

He threw two tiny bags of white powder down on a low table near Gil's chair.

"Fuck, Jamie. I'm not doing coke. I might be near-suicidal, but I don't have a death wish yet."

"Oh, come on. It's not as if its heroin. It's gone in an hour or two. Just might give you a bit of a lift."

He knelt and lined up the white powder on the table with a credit card. Then he took a $20 bill from his pocketbook and rolled it up.

"Here… you've seen me do it often enough."

Gil dubiously took the note and rolled it between his fingers. Why not – he needed something to lift him.

He dropped to the floor at the other side of the table and sniffed the cocaine as he'd often seen Jamie do - one nostril, then the other.

The high shocked him. His body jerked and he sank sideways onto the floor. Jamie dragged him back into his chair, and Gil convulsed with laughter, his heart racing ten to the dozen. His agitation increased and Jamie laughed along with him.

"I told you it'd give you a lift! How do you feel?"

Gil opened his eyes, hooded and unfocused, and looked around the room.

"Fuck, brother... why didn't you tell me it was this good?"

He sat up unsteadily and held onto Jamie's arm to stop from keeling over again. He laughed, this time more of a nervous giggle.

By the small hours when the effects began to recede, his spirits slowly sank lower and lower, until he wasn't laughing any more.

"What am I going to do about Connie? We have to go find Connie now or I'll lose her for good. Where's my jacket?" He was in a real panic.

"It's the middle of the night, Gil. Come on, let's get some air. There's an all-night bar about twenty minutes from here. We'll start again in the morning."

As they walked along the beach, Gil's head cleared and his mood began to come back to normal – not happy because of Connie, but not depressed from the drug.

"You're looking better – let's go for a drink," encouraged Jamie.

At a bar overlooking the ocean, Jamie ordered bourbon, and the brothers got very drunk together. They ended up singing loudly to the dismay of the management. When Jamie saw a couple of girls he knew, he called them over.

One of them obviously knew Jamie well, and before long was sitting on his lap. He staggered to his feet and dragged her down a flight of steps onto the beach.

The other girl sat down next to Gil and began running her hand up his thigh. He wasn't so drunk his body didn't respond, but he really couldn't cope with the groupie thing right now.

Gil stumbled down the steps and made his way unsteadily along the sands to Jamie's house.

When Jamie arrived home, it was late. He swung himself up the steps to the front door and fell on his face. He couldn't find Gil, who was asleep on a garden bench.

The following morning, battling hangovers they sat in the sun for a while.

"Come on Jamie. I've got to go and find my wife. I have to know what's going on for better or worse. Damn, I feel shit. I hope you feel as bad as I do. I never want a night like that again."

"Just the name of the game, Gil."

For one fleeting moment Jamie looked ineffably sad.

Chapter Nineteen

Jamie ran Gil home.

The house was dark, the blinds were closed, and it was eerily quiet. It used to be full of children's laughter and Connie's perfume and gentle smile. Now there was nothing, not even an echo of what had been.

He opened some of the blinds and found one of Mylo's teddy bears which had fallen behind a chair. It smelled of baby powder and candy. He hugged it to his chest for a moment before walking to the piano and running the tips of his fingers across the keys. The sweet notes sounded unnaturally loud.

Sitting on the bench, he put his head in his hands for a moment, then lit up a cigarette. Perhaps if he could just play for a while the intricacies of a song might occupy his mind. He would write it for Connie. Gil put the cigarette out and began to concentrate.

The song came with such ease that he had the bare bones of it down within a half hour. It was sweet and sad, and told of his longing to be with her again. The song allowed for no doubt – it was when, not if, she came back to him.

He poured into it all his grief and longing. He spent another half hour polishing the words and putting the final touches to the music. He'd never been good with lyrics. Perhaps his difficulty with words was the root of his problem with Connie.

Softly closing the piano lid, he sat in thought for a minute or two. Then he folded the paper the music and words were written on and put it carefully on top of the piano beneath the ashtray. Perhaps he would see her tomorrow.

That afternoon, unable to stay away, he went to Oliver's house. It looked even more unoccupied than before. All the blinds were closed this time, and there were no cars parked outside.

This put Gil in a quandary since he'd have to be back in the studio tomorrow and wouldn't finish until late. There would be no opportunity to find her today, and maybe not for the next couple of days either.

He hung about the gate at the end of the drive, until a cop car started taking particular interest in him loitering outside an expensive house, with no apparent reason for being there.

Lighting a cigarette, Gil had begun his walk home, when a car stopped and the occupant lowered the driver's side window.

"Good to see you again. Where are you going? Can I drop you?"

Bright blue eyes crinkled at the corners when she smiled. Black hair but not like Connie's - softer and with a slight curl. She had it drawn up in a messy ponytail and wore sunglasses perched on her head.

"Well, are you going to get in?"

Then an awful truth dawned on her, and she cringed with embarrassment.

"You don't remember me, do you?" She blushed to the roots of her hair. "I'm sorry. Damn, that wasn't supposed to be a pick-up line! Its Giulia, Giulia Giordano. Please say you remember me now."

It was Gil's turn to look mortified. With all his recent problems he had failed to recognize Larry's sister. He flicked his spent cigarette onto the sidewalk and crushed it against the concrete with his heel.

"Of course I know you - I've known you forever. And yes, I would like a ride but I'm only going home - just a few miles," he paused, "but I'd be happy to fix you coffee if you'd like. I make the world's worst coffee, but if you're open to a life-threatening experience, I'll be happy to provide it."

She checked her watch.

"I've about an hour - I'm meeting Larry and Tony downtown. Larry's playing at Pandora's this evening, but Mom wants to go, so I have to collect her first. Is an hour okay?"

The house, dark empty and none too fragrant, should have needed explanation. If Giulia noticed, she was too polite to comment.

He drew the blinds and sunlight flooded in, leaving bands of light across the floor. The brightness only served to emphasize the dismal appearance of the room. There were smears on the floor he noticed, where Jamie hadn't cleaned it properly.

Gil escorted her quickly to the kitchen and opened the glass sliders onto the terrace. The remnants of the coffee and the pieces of broken glass he had flung across it, were still visible. He drew a couple of recliners from the terrace to the window.

"Here, sit down. I'll be right out with the coffee."

Gil returned to the kitchen and surreptitiously tipped the grounds from the coffee machine into the half-full bin. He recoiled at the smell and quickly closed the lid.

Then the percolator was stuck fast.

"Shit, this would have to happen now!" he muttered under his breath.

He tried to tap it gently on the countertop to loosen it. No deal. Then he heard a badly suppressed chuckle from the door.

"Oh give it here. In our house its Larry, Tony and Dad in that order who can handle making coffee. Dad's a disaster – no matter how you tried you couldn't be worse!"

Gil grinned, halfway between amused and embarrassed. Although Giulia had to stand on her toes to reach the top of the coffee maker, she deftly reassembled it and switched it on. Within minutes they were sitting on the terrace enjoying their drink.

"Cream? Sugar? Oh, sorry – no cream."

She shook her head, smiling. "Neither thanks."

They sat in companiable silence for a few minutes. After the past few days, it was such a relief.

"What time are you picking up your mother?"

"Oh, my goodness. I'd forgotten all about her! What's the time?"

"Half five."

"Gotta dash, I'm supposed to be there at half six. I'm sorry to be so rude but I really do have to go. Perhaps we could have coffee some other time. Call me?"

She sped away in her car, and Gil closed the door behind her, returning to the kitchen.

He tried to remember what it was like to be so young, so impulsive. He'd been doing a man's work since he was sixteen and run California Crystal's tours from nineteen.

Had he ever been like her? Or had he always been carrying this crippling weight?

Giulia stopped out of sight of the house until she'd cooled down and her heart stopped racing. She rested her head against the steering wheel and drew a couple of deep breaths, before restarting the car and heading home.

Early the following morning, Lizbeth rang and asked Gil if he and Connie would like to come for something to eat. They were having a barbeque that evening.

"That'd be great, but I can't be definite as we're in the studio all day tomorrow and I don't know if we'll finish in time....and anyway Connie's out of town – with her mother, I think."

Odd...Lizbeth had only seen Kelani in a shopping mall in LA that morning. She shrugged.

"Doesn't matter. It's only a yard barbie.

She was disappointed that Connie wouldn't be there. She always thought of herself as Connie's mentor. Her sister-in-law was no longer the timid little mouse she'd been when Gil had first known her, but Lizbeth still felt protective.

Jamie and Gil arrived at the studio together, a fact which wasn't usual and didn't go unnoticed.

Of course, Jamie couldn't care less, and could be seen through the glass of the recording booth, swigging from a large bottle of something alcoholic.

Gil, looking even more drawn and tired, put on headphones and began to check out the tapes from the last session. He looked about to drop and seemed a little unsteady on his feet.

"Gil's usually more dependable than any of us. There'll

119

be a reason." John said confidently to the sound engineer.

Ed sneered. "They're a bad lot – all of them from that prick Monty to little baby Gil. Oh, possibly not Nancy. She's okay," he conceded.

"Oh..... go meditate yourself," snapped Gil, raising his voice for the first time. It wasn't until that moment that anyone realized he'd been drinking. A gentle, considerate, and kindly soul as a rule, Gil was a mean drunk. In fact, neither of the Robson boys did well with stimulants. Jamie got fighting mad and Gil lost his temper.

"Gil. A word please," said Jamie, beckoning.

"Can't it wait?" snapped Gil.

"Nope, don't think so."

Gil followed Jamie impatiently into a small room that served as storage for extra chairs and trestles. Jamie jammed a chair under the handle and took a couple of packets of cocaine from his pocket, arranging lines on one of the tables. He handed Gil a rolled-up bill and bowed slightly.

"After you. But get a move on. I need this as much as you do."

Gil paused but shrugged and took the note. He snorted good and hard and felt the immediate rush - Jamie, who was more of an adept, only seemed a little more cheerful than usual and laughed at is brother's glassy eyes and heavy head. Gil tried to stand but staggered.

"Just give it a moment. When we go back you might actually get some work done, then we can all go home."

It was another half hour before they returned and the

change in Gil's demeanor was noted by the others, who looked at each other nervously.

"Come on, let's try it again," said Gil with more fervor than he'd shown all morning. "This time, John a little higher and watch that second note. You're not getting it. Ed, headphones please."

They resumed, and this time everything went to plan, and they managed to get something on tape.

Before the session's end, Gil's mood began to drop away with the drug, and he was asking Jamie for more. Jamie had none so Gil gave him a hundred bucks. He left. Gil owed him after all.

Gil went back to work but felt increasingly bad tempered. He became short with everyone and chewed them out for nothing at all.

They all felt shocked and dismayed. The band without a functioning Robson was an unimaginable thing, and no-one could rely on Jamie anymore.

Ed's jealousy was understandable when you considered just how musically adept the Robson brothers were. In Gil's case, he could turn his hand to most instruments, even drums, although he loved his guitars with a passion. Jamie composed and often produced their albums, played keyboards and drums. Ed wrote sporadically, usually parts for himself but had no other musical abilities.

Gil waited Jamie's return impatiently, chewing on his nails and walking distractedly back and forth.

When Jamie finally did show up, taking the packets from his jacket pocket, Gil grabbed one from his hand and ran into the back room. He tore into the little plastic envelope and lined up the cocaine, snorting it before

Jamie had even got through the door.

"Whoa, my child. Be cool," said Jamie who was usually anything but.

Gil leaned back on the table, his eyes unfocused and relief clear on his face.

"This can be fun or a chain. Make sure it's fun," said Jamie, momentarily surprised by Gil's impatience. "I'll keep a couple back for the other times, okay?"

"Sure. Anything you like. Let's go eat. I'm starving." Jamie laughed out loud. Gil was always starving.

Gil was not a diet eater. His idea of a meal was burger and fries with cola – any salad accompaniment was tossed to one side - and his capacity for putting it away was legendary. Jamie looked on in amazement but also with concern. Gil's state of mind could be determined by his waistline and things were not looking good. Once he'd eaten his fill they moved to Ricks. Gil ordered beer then joined Jamie in his usual vodka.

A couple of hours later Gil, high and drunk, wanted to see Connie. Jamie decided to bale. He'd some girl he wanted to see across town, so he ran Gil as close to Oliver's as he was going, then left.

Gil walked unsteadily to Oliver's house and yelled for Connie to come out.

There was no response, so he walked closer and yelled again. Oliver ran down the steps with Connie close behind.

"You do that again and I'll flatten you! There are kids in the house who are not accustomed to filth like you. Connie doesn't want to see you so go before I call the cops." Oliver hissed.

Gil stood swaying and looked belligerent.

Connie was appalled. She'd never seen Gil in this state before. Gil, always the soul of discretion; Gil, always considerate and kind. She gently moved Oliver aside and took Gil by the arm to a garden seat.

"Let me talk to him for a minute alone, Oliver," and at Oliver's dubious look, "Don't worry. I'll be perfectly safe."

Connie watched him walk through the door then turned to Gil. He couldn't speak for a moment, in his befuddled state bereft of words.

"Please, please come home," he finally managed.

"I can never come back Gil. I have to build a new life and so should you. What we had is gone. I think you should leave now. Oliver's right. His two kids are asleep in the house and you're making enough noise to wake the whole neighborhood. Go home and I promise we'll talk again in the morning."

"I can't. I'm flying to Denver in the morning. I'll be gone for a couple of weeks. I'll phone from the hotel. Do you have a number?"

Connie threw up her hands in despair.

"Gil, you can't call me here!"

In his right mind, which was what Connie was used to, it would never have occurred to him even to ask. But he wasn't in his right mind, so he pleaded with her.

"Please, Connie, please."

Connie thought for a moment.

"Ring home tomorrow around six. I'll go to the house. Six...will you remember?" She shook his arm to make him concentrate.

Gil nodded, stood shakily and headed back down the drive.

At the end of the drive, he sank down by the gatepost and pulled out a half-bottle of bourbon. He took a good long swig, pulled himself to his feet and set off on the walk home.

Connie watched him go and would not be comforted.

The following afternoon, she sat on the terrace of the house in Linden Reach and nervously sipped a glass of wine, awaiting Gil's call. Connie'd turned up early to compose herself for what she suspected was going to be a heart-breaking conversation. She checked her watch again. Five thirty. The minutes were dragging by.

Then quite unexpectedly the doorbell rang. Connie went to answer it and Giulia Giordano was standing on the doorstep. They looked equally surprised.

"Erm, is Gil there?" asked Giulia, not quite knowing what to say.

"No,"

Connie realized she didn't feel inclined to be helpful, so she waited. Out of nowhere, came the realization she was jealous. How could she be jealous after last night? Hadn't she wanted Gil to leave her alone? Now here was this bright, pretty little livewire asking after her husband.

"I.. I just came to ask if he still had Larry's guitar – Larry's my brother."

"Don't be ridiculous – I know who Larry is," Connie said tartly. "Gil's in Denver so I don't suppose he has it, but you can come in and see if you can find it."

Giulia was put on the back foot. She couldn't go searching Connie's house for a guitar she knew Gil didn't have.

"No. It's okay. I'll get Larry to call. I was just passing so I thought I'd save him the trouble."

Connie couldn't see how she could be just passing in a gated community – Gill must have given her a key.

"Well, nice to see you," and a very embarrassed Giulia walked back to her car.

Five minutes later the phone rang.

"Connie? How are you?"

"Good."

It seemed to be her day for short responses.

"Please apologize to Oliver for me. The way I acted was out of line, but I meant absolutely every single word I said to you….," he suddenly became aware of the silence at the other end of the line. "Connie? You still there?"

"Damn Gil, what a mess. You have to understand that I really have left. Oh, and if you're interested, you might want to call the boys. They're still with your mother."

In the midst of this tragedy, he hadn't thought of them once.

"If you don't want me to come there, will you at least call in when I get back? Do that for me. Will you?" he pleaded.

"My feeling guilty – which I would unless I did come - wouldn't be helpful to either of us so yes, I will - but I don't want to hear from you again in the meantime," and as an afterthought, "By the way, Giulia Giordano has just been here. She was passing and stopped to pick up Larry's guitar."

"I don't have Larry's guitar. Why would she do that?"

"You tell me."

.

.

Chapter Twenty

The Denver gig, and those following, went by in an alternate haze of coke and alcohol for Gil. At times he wished he'd never called because now he had two weeks to find out his fate.

He wasn't like Jamie who had always been feckless. He realized he had to be there primarily for his audiences, and the backing band who so loved and respected him.

But the nights were long, and he couldn't wipe Connie's face from his mind. And then he gave into temptation and often drank himself to sleep.

On the night they were due to arrive back in LA, Jamie bought a further five-hundred dollars-worth of cocaine and gave half to Gil 'just in case'. Where the hell Jamie, who was permanently broke, got $500, Gil refused to consider. But he took it 'just in case'.

He arrived back at the dark and empty house. It was time he sold it - all it held were sad memories.

Gil strolled down to the pool-house. He picked up an acoustic guitar, replaced a broken string and sat down to tune it. There was a box of ready-rolled joints on the table. He lit one, took a couple of deep drags and picked up his guitar. He sat cross-legged on the tiles at the pool's edge and began to strum.

The weed was beginning to relax him. He was calmed by the gentle ripple of the water in the pool, and the scent of dew-sprinkled roses in the garden. Their perfume suddenly brought back Connie's face, and his peace was shattered.

He sat by the pool, occasionally smoking another joint

and trying to leave the coke in his jacket alone. But he couldn't face her high in the morning and he couldn't be sure once he started, he'd be able to stop. She knew him so well she would notice at once.

So, he went back to the house and lay down on their bed. After three or four hours spent staring at the ceiling, he did eventually drift off, but woke with a start when he couldn't remember when he'd arranged for her call – or even if he had at all.

He cleaned the place up then went and took a long cool shower and changed. He had to wash off the smell of hash, but he gave in and sniffed a line of coke to steady his nerves.

Connie phoned in the late afternoon and said she'd be there about seven, but when she hadn't arrived by eight thirty his nerves started to get the better of him. He became agitated and began to nervously pace back and forth across the hall. Twice he went to search out the cocaine and twice he put it back in his pocket. He poured himself a large glass of vodka – at least that had no smell – and sat out on the terrace to drink it. He drank a quarter bottle and still his foot was tapping, uncontrolled, against the tiles. He could stand it no longer.

He broke out the coke, sniffed it and almost collapsed with relief, but the rush was starting to subside quicker now. An hour later, despite his determination to stay clean, he was doing another line.

Connie arrived at the house at ten o'clock ready to apologize profusely for her lateness. She doubted he'd believe her car wouldn't start but that had been the truth of the matter.

The lights in the pool-house were still on, and the hall

light in the house. There was no-one near the pool, so she crossed the lawn to the house and notice the door was unlocked. Everything was as it should be, but although the lights were burning, there was no noise and no indication that anyone was about.

Connie saw a note on the piano and on examination it turned out to be the words and Gil's musical notation for a song. She spread it and wept when she realized with shock it was a love-song. She knew it was for her - it described their situation so perfectly. Usually, he was lousy with lyrics but there was no mistaking the song's meaning. She read it once then twice.

"It's just impossible for me to live with you," she whispered aloud.

Connie headed for the kitchen. As she went round the corner from the hall, she nearly fell over him. He was laying on the floor, with his head turned to the side and his hair half-covering his face. Connie dropped to her knees next to him. He was deeply unconscious. She shook him hard, but he didn't respond, his face chalk white. She snatched up the phone from the kitchen counter and rang 911.

"Come now.... NOW...my husband's unconscious and I can't wake him."

Connie took several deep breaths, and finally managed to give the controller the address before she covered her face with shaking hands and sobbed. She shook Gil again and finally succeeded in turning him over on his side. He was as unresponsive as a rag doll.

The ambulance when it arrived made enough noise to be heard in the next county. The worst thing about being married to a celebrity was you had to be so careful about drawing attention to yourself.

So, as Gil was placed on a gurney and hoisted into the waiting ambulance, lights flashing bright blue, she instructed the driver to turn off the siren until they were well away from the house, or very soon the whole of the western world would know Gil Robson had over-dosed, and it wasn't known if he'd survive. Whether it was true or not was immaterial.

Gil still wasn't conscious, and his color hadn't recovered, but he was now hooked up to a drip and was being given oxygen. When he began to stir Connie sighed with relief, but he only flopped over the gurney guards and vomited noisily on the floor. He then collapsed, waxy skinned and sweat-streaked back onto the pillows.

"He still looks bad but he's stabilized," said the paramedic.

"What do you think will happen to him? This is the first time I've seen him like this," said Connie.

"You sure about that?" asked the paramedic. "Cocaine by the look of it."

Connie was shocked into silence. She was still numb when they were led to a room bedecked with tubes, flashing displays and switches. It was frighteningly sterile.

Gil's unresponsive body was lifted on to the bed and he was linked up to various machines. Thank God he was showing signs of recovery. Some of his color had returned and he was tossing his head restlessly from side to side.

The doctor checked out his pupils and shook his head.

"He's been taking cocaine for weeks, if not months, on a regular basis. But for the past twenty-four hours he's been on a bender of cocaine mixed with alcohol. That's the only thing which would result in such a severe breakdown. He's lucky to be alive."

Connie had always assumed he was drunk or happy on hashish. Had it been cocaine? She didn't have the experience to know the difference.

"This is all my fault! It's all my fault!" She began to rock back and forth convulsively.

"You'll do him no good like that," the doctor almost snapped.

Drug addiction was the bane of his life – it was becoming increasingly difficult for him to summon up much sympathy.

"I'd like to keep him here for a day or two, just to check there's no permanent damage. His heart rate is off the scale, so we need to clear the drug from his system. Withdrawal can be nasty and there's no medication to help cocaine users. Then we need to decide what kind of treatment he needs. It could be rehab - it could be a psychiatric clinic. I won't know that until I've spoken to him."

Connie, looking over the doctor's shoulder, suddenly realized that Gil was conscious, his eyes open and his attention concentrated on what the doctor was saying. Connie stood abruptly.

"I could fucking kill you, Gil Robson!"

If he wasn't fully awake before, he was now – she only ever swore under duress. She pulled a pillow from behind his head and made to hit him with it, but the doctor took it out of her hand. Weak as he was, Gil began to laugh.

"And I don't see what's so fucking funny. You nearly killed yourself, you idiot."

"Mrs. Robson, control yourself," said the doctor firmly.

Connie rounded on him – if she'd had sleeves, she'd have been pushing them up.

"I'd like a few words alone with my husband. I promise on this occasion, I won't stove his stupid head in – but that's a temporary arrangement." She glowered at Gil.

He was loving this. Her anger was a measure of her distress. He loved her so much - if she would help him, he could kick this in days. If she'd help him, there'd be no need for the drugs or alcohol at all.

The doctor left.

Connie stalked across the room, her fists clenched and tears running down her cheeks.

"So, what do we do now?" she screamed. "You heard what the doctor said - rehab or psych ward, A psychiatric unit, Gil! They could be treating you as a basket case!"

"As long as I have you, I can do anything," he emoted.

"Oh no! You can't do that – that's blackmail!"

He freely admitted to himself that's exactly what it was. But this was no holds barred, life or death, so he looked at her and shrugged.

"However you want to play it I'll be here. As long as you are too."

"I don't believe this!" Connie groaned. "You *are* a fucking basket case!"

He dragged her to him, his kiss was searing.

He was in the hospital for three days before the doctor okayed his move to a rehabilitation unit.

Security and nurses were instructed that under no circumstances, was his brother even permitted in the clinic.

Connie tackled Jamie. She threatened him with hired violence if he came within five miles of the clinic. And he could see she meant every word.

She returned to Oliver, but all the time Gil was in the clinic, she couldn't settle – didn't sleep, couldn't eat, couldn't abide conversation. She spent all her time in the garden, pulling up weeds and planting begonias like the ones at her old home.

On the day before she would be permitted a short visit to the clinic, Oliver finally lost his temper.

That morning, Connie had found Deborah trying to copy her, but instead of pulling up the weeds, she was carefully pulling up the begonias Connie had just planted. Connie, nerves finally snapping, slapped her. And Oliver saw.

"I think you'd better go back to Gil. You clearly don't belong here if you've taken to hitting my daughter," he snapped.

This was the second time Connie had experienced his temper.

She was mortified but knew her behavior had been entirely irrational. She was completely obsessed with Gil's welfare - she could think of nothing else.

She packed a bag, slung it on the back seat of her convertible and drove home.

Once there, she flung open the blinds, opened all the doors and windows and stripped naked. She spent the next hours in the pool until her fingers and toes began to wrinkle.

After taking a joint from Gil's box, she strode with determination back to the house where she drank coffee and smoked. Only then did she feel marginally better.

In this situation, Oliver was a secondary consideration. She'd see to Gil first then call Oliver and try to patch things up.

She crushed out the joint and frowned with annoyance. She always seemed to be choosing between Gil and something or somebody else, and damn him, Gil always won.

Connie took a shower, dressed in an expensive silk dress, and put on the most extravagant jewelry she could find, including the Harry Winston engagement ring she'd thrown at Gil in temper before she left. She drove to Nancy's house to see the kids.

She'd abandoned them to Nancy's care when she went to live with Oliver. How could she have done that? And Gil, as usual, had forgotten they even existed.

She'd take them home. But it would have to be after tomorrow when she'd checked their father out. She wouldn't like to think his actions would let them down again. She'd behaved badly enough for the two of them.

Chapter Twenty-one

Gil had inherited his nature from his mother. When Nancy opened the door to her, instead of doing what any normal person would do, and lay into her for abandoning her children, she said:

"Oh, Connie my love, are you okay? We haven't seen you in an age and I've been so worried about you."

Connie found herself wrapped in a warm and comforting embrace.

"Come on out, boys. Mommy's here – isn't that great?"

Connie was aghast at how they'd grown. She'd missed Jacob's first day at school and Mylo, brown and with sun-bleached hair, had grown inches and lost his baby chubbiness. They launched themselves into her arms, laughing and crying at the same time.

"Oh, Ma, we've missed you. Where have you been?" wept Jacob, and Connie's guilty heart sank.

"I love you Ma," said little Mylo quietly. Then with more emphasis. "You went away, and I didn't know where you went." His eyes, wide as saucers, held no trace of condemnation.

"Off you go now," said Nancy. "Finish your pictures so you can show Mommy what good artists you've become since she's been away."

They pushed and shoved each other out of the way as they went through the door.

Connie and Nancy sat on a sofa so soft Connie had to sit forward to stop it engulfing her. Nancy's house was typical of Nancy. There was a small electric organ next to the window. It was covered in framed pictures of her sons, mostly as children. A large bunch of iris stood in a lusterware vase on the hearth.

"Now," said Nancy firmly, "before you say anything, I know about Gil. After Jamie's behavior I can't say I blame you one bit for leaving. It's a real pity the kids had to be in the middle of it but that can't be helped now. I know what it is to have a difficult home situation with a wrong-thinking husband, believe me."

"I am allowed my first visit since he was admitted to rehab tomorrow, and I have absolutely no idea what's going to happen," worried Connie, biting her lip.

"Gil is my baby," said Nancy, "and always the closest to me. He would never intentionally hurt you. But he's in a vice here. He has you and the boys who he loves, and a job which takes him all over the world, with people who rely on him. When Jamie lost all sense of responsibility, a lot of his work fell on Gil's shoulders.

"I honestly never thought he'd cope but because he has a soft heart, he was determined to give Jamie all the support he could. It has cost him. As a child he had the sunniest disposition. Now he is worn and tired. It's there more every time I see him. He needs you for support Connie."

Connie opened her mouth to speak but Nancy held up her hand and continued:

"I know this isn't what you want to hear but it's the truth. If you don't love him anymore the only thing to do would be to tell him and hope he gets over it.

"My three sons grew up with their father to contend with. Gil may have a different outlook on family life to you, although that is absolutely no excuse. Monty terrified them – Lord knows, he terrified me – to the point where they would hide. I've seen him slapped Gil so hard across the face that he had a bruise on his cheek for days. He'll have been about six, I think."

Connie regarded Nancy, wide-eyed. She'd been married to Gil for eight years – how could she not have known this? Monty was a bastard but she hadn't realized he'd beaten them.

"Gil never, ever mentioned it. Why didn't you stop him?"

She winced. She'd slapped little Deborah. How could she say that? It brought home to her just why Oliver had done what he did.

"Gil got the best of it because he was a child. When he was fourteen, and Jamie roped him into the band by helping buy him his first guitar, Jamie was already seventeen, a young man. Jamie got the worst of it I think because he naturally had a lot of what Monty so badly wanted. Talent and a cool attitude – people plain liked him. Monty had so badly wanted both he was eaten up with envy. He then listened as Gil's voice became one of the best in the world. He'd never even thought of Gil as competition – like a lot of the rest of the world, I suspect. He came as a shock to a lot of people who'd always thought of him as 'the kid'".

Nancy pulled up short.

"I really shouldn't be talking like this about my own husband, and if things had been different, I never would have. But you have to understand Gil if you want to help him. His life has been so hard, and he has taken on so much just simply because he loves us – and his wife and children too. Although it might not feel like that to you at the moment."

A sudden small movement in the corner of the room caught Connie's eye.

"Don't you want Daddy anymore, Mommy?" It was Mylo, who looked so crest-fallen. "I know he can't come home like most daddies because he works so hard."

137

He walked over to Connie and climbed on her knee, crushing the silk of her dress and smearing yellow paint in her hair.

"But he does it for us, Mommy. He really does." He gazed into her eyes seriously.

Nancy smiled proudly.

"Of course he does, sweetheart – Mommy knows that." Connie smiled wryly at Nancy.

"You've been coaching him."

"Of course. He's growing up. This is when the questions begin because that's when the answers start to make sense. I've been through it three times." Nancy laughed.

The outside door slammed, and Mylo shot off his mother's knee and back to his painting.

"Nancy – NANCY.... get the iron out and press me this shirt!"

Monty stopped dead, shirt dangling from his fingers.

"What the hell are you doing here? Get off home and fix your husband's dinner."

"He's not at home, Monty. He's in hospital as you well know," said Nancy, the patience in her tone palpable.

"Don't give me that shit! He's drying out like the other two before him."

"If you hadn't pushed them so hard it might have been different," said Nancy.

He turned back to Connie. "Well, what are you still doing here? Collect your brats and go home."

"May I remind you Monty, this is my house and I say who goes or stays. At this moment, it's you who should leave. Please go home." Nancy's face and manner were

138

determined, unusual for her.

Nancy and Monty had been living apart for several years now. The day came when she just couldn't put up with him anymore. She couldn't be bothered with divorce – she was tired like Gil. She rarely agreed with him but on this they were of one mind, they'd disagree in separate homes.

Nancy couldn't hide a sly smile as Monty dumped the shirt on the table and walked out, slamming the door again.

"I do enjoy my little bit of power," chuckled Nancy, "Now, what are we going to do about your situation?"

"I really am sorry to impose on you further Nancy, but would you please keep the boys for another couple of days? I need to see how Gil is and how he's coping. If he's in a bad state still, I'd rather they didn't see him. And he was bad, Nancy."

Tears marred her mascara, and she took a tissue from her bag and wiped away the smudge.

"I have to go back. Even if it's just for a while until he gets on his feet again."

Nancy looked dubious but said:

"You were both babies when you married but I always looked at you and saw how much you loved each other. Of course I'll look after Jacob and Mylo. They're darlings, no trouble at all."

Connie breathed a sigh of relief, but she really hadn't thought Nancy would turn her down. Loving his sons was part of loving Gil, and that she would always do.

"I'll call you tomorrow and let you know what shape Gil's in. If he's good and he can come home, give me twenty-four hours to settle him in, then I'll come for the boys."

"Don't worry about it. You just let me know when to bring them back and I'll run them over. If it's okay with you, I'd like to see Gil."

"Oh Nancy, you don't need my permission to see your own son!" said Connie standing to give her a hug. The boys came racing in.

"Is Grandpa gone?" asked an anxious Mylo.

"Yes, my darling," said Nancy. Then to Connie. "As you can see, he's made his usual impression." She looked heavenwards, which made Connie laugh.

"Thank you, Nancy. You always have been kind to me." She kissed each child and told them she'd be back soon. They clung to her but smiled bravely as she waved from the car

Chapter Twenty-two

The following day, Connie drove down the Pacific Highway to the clinic, and was shown to Gil's room by a smartly uniformed nurse.

He was sitting on the balcony when she walked through the door, and didn't see her at first, so she had time to observe him for a moment. He was gazing out over the ocean, deep in thought, with one hand clutching the chair arm.

Connie put her purse down and walked as quietly as possible, so as not to startle him, over to the sliding window. She bent and kissed his forehead. He looked up at her with a glowing smile.

"Gil, you must promise me you will never, never do that again. I thought you were dying.... you *were* dying. If I hadn't found you when I did....," she turned to him and said with determination. "I want your solemn promise never to do that again."

For the first time Connie noticed the haunted look in his eyes. He really had been through the mill.

"It must have been hell in here. Tell me about it. Share it."

He told her how they'd locked the screen door the first night and tied him to the bed when he was alone. He'd screamed. She looked so distraught, even though she was pleading, he refused to say more. What was the use anyway? It was over now.

"There's no medication for cocaine addiction – only 'cold turkey'. Fortunately, it takes days not weeks. But then the real problem comes. You need help staying off the stuff. If you get down or depressed it's just so easy to say just once more, it'll only be this once. Then the next time you hit a problem, you're back on the roller-coaster again." His voice became almost inaudible.

"Please stay. Please help me."

Connie walked back into his room and sat down in the wing chair next to the bed. The restraints were still hanging from its rails. This was the first time she'd really faced up to what he'd done. The silence between them lengthened.

"I'll come back. But it's on condition that you treat us as a family again. I knew what your life was, even though I was so young when we got married. I have no right to complain. But you have to promise to make some time for us. We have to matter to you."

Gil was bewildered.

"But you mean the world to me. How could you not know that?"

"Consider my life Gil. There was no one in it but two babies. I'm a young woman still. Sometimes my whole body aches for yours. You're not here – you're never here. How is it unreasonable I should look elsewhere?"

Gil knelt at her feet and brushed the hair from her cheek.

She went on: "Can we speak to the doctor now and see what he says? Are you fit to come home? Truth now. How do you feel?"

"Truth? I feel awful. I feel as if my brain's been ripped out through my nostrils. Will I survive? Yes, I think so – no, I know so."

The doctor on his daily rounds entered, took Gil's pulse and temperature, and wrote the results on a clipboard, seemingly satisfied.

"Home today Doc?" Gil said hopefully, holding tightly to Connie's hand.

"No, sorry. Not today. Maybe tomorrow."

Gil pulled a face, but Connie knew he understood. The doctor left.

"I need some answers, Gil. First and biggest question is what you intend to do about Jamie? You know he won't stop trying to give you the stuff."

Gil stood and began to pace. He loved his brother – he had always been his protector and they worked together as a team. Could he live in a world that didn't have him in it? He'd never even had to consider it before.

How would he be able to work? The one thing he absolutely couldn't do was give up his music – it was the blood in his veins. He would cease to exist without it. But then, it had become forcibly clear to him he couldn't live without Connie either.

"Why don't you come on the road with me." The circle had to be squared somehow.

"Be sensible. You know I can't do that. Jacob's at school now. I have to stay home."

It felt as if he was making her choose between himself and the children, but that had always been the case, he realized.

"Mom'll help out. Just do a couple of months until I get straight."

"I can't do that Gil. One of us has to be there for them. I can't believe I left them with Nancy all that time. It can't go on."

"Is Oliver the reason you won't come?"

He realized his mistake before he'd even stopped talking. She had paled but stood and faced him.

"There is no point in avoiding this. Oliver has been so good to me. When I just couldn't cope, he gave me a home. He shared his family with me. Without him, I couldn't have survived. You can't ask me to give him up altogether. Perhaps you might come to know him as well? If he'll have me I'll be going back eventually. I have to."

All Gil's carefully constructed façade shattered.

"How can you ask me to be a friend to a man who's screwed my wife!"

"If you don't feel able to do that, we'll have to find another way."

Neither of them, privately, knew how that could be made to work. He drew a deep breath.

"Can we talk about this tomorrow? I've had about all I can take for now." She knew this – he looked exhausted.

"Will you be okay until then? We will work this out between us. Try to put it out of your mind for now."

His expression told her he would chew on it until he saw her again. He couldn't give it up.

She hugged him tightly.

As she walked away, he couldn't help the unwanted thought, 'If one of us wants it more than the other, then what?' He knew he'd be the loser.

Paul was a handsome man of a certain age. He'd been a fool. He could see that now. He'd behaved like some half-wit wanna-be teenager and got himself into this stupid fix. Cocaine was not a drug to be trifled with – he knew.

He gazed out of the open window across an ocean as blue as a peacock's tail. The sunlight was blinding on the chrome window surround, so he moved back into the room.

He was edgy and fidgeting. The drug did that to you. But it wasn't as bad as it was yesterday and a darn sight better than the day before.

There was a tentative tap at the door which slowly opened, and a small dark-haired sprite in her late teens crept in and closed the door behind her.

"Hi, Poppa. Can I come in?"

He waved her in then stood to hug her tightly and twirl her round.

"Poppa don't do that! I'm not ten years old anymore," said Giulia Giordano, straightening her skirt.

"You're as old as I say you are, Poppet. And right now you're…hmm.. how's six sound?"

"Not good," she pouted.

He turned away to take a pack of cigarettes from the coffee table and lit one with a gold lighter.

"You'll always be my little girl," he said through a haze of smoke.

Giulia loved her dad more than anyone on earth, and he spoiled her in every way possible. She was the youngest of all his children, those of Paul's first wife now mostly married. She would never grow up in his eyes.

"How are you today? You look better. When can you come home?" asked Giulia.

"You know I have to get this stuff out of my system. I

don't want you to remember your old man as stupid."

"I'll never think of you like that Pop." That she so clearly meant it did little for his self-respect.

She bounced down on the sofa and looked up at him, her dark curls tied up in a pony-tail which showed off her delicate cheek-bones and bright blue eyes.

He smiled at her – he always did.

"I'll be home before you know it, don't worry. Then we'll put all this behind us and start again. Drugs are a bad scene, darling. And cocaine is one of the worst of all because you think it's so much fun. Which it is, until you try to do without it. Be warned. Never go down this road."

He wagged a finger at her.

"Too serious. Change of subject. Will either of your brothers be here today?" His teeth looked white against his bronzed skin.

"Tony has football practice, but Larry should be here sometime soon. He won't be long."

As she spoke, a handsome young man with shining blond hair and the same bright blue eyes as Giulia, stomped through the door dragging a man slightly smaller, slightly rounder and with what Paul had to admit, was an entirely impressive beard.

"Come on in, Gil – so great to see you. How long has it been? No, perhaps I shouldn't ask that. It'll reflect worse on me than you."

Paul laughed out loud. Damn, being cheerful for everyone else was frickin hard work!

Giulia was trying to be as inconspicuous as possible cuddled up into a corner of the sofa.

146

"Hey Giulia. Look - it's your old crush," said Larry. "You loved Gil to bits when you were ten. He's changed a bit since then. Cool beard, Gil."

Gil loved the Giordanos and he never in a million years would have expected to meet Paul in a place like this. Clinics were for losers which Paul certainly was not.

Paul's smile faded.

"I'm sorry. I take it you're not visiting - I hadn't realized. Here sit down. How're you doing?"

"Not bad now but it's been a while since I could say that." Gil looked embarrassed and rubbed a hand over his eyes.

The mood of the conversation had plummeted.

"So what sent you over the edge?"

"Connie left me," said Gil. There just didn't seem to be a better way to put it. You could have heard a pin drop.

"Well done, Pops," said Larry. "That's a good one even for you."

Gil's smile was tight-lipped.

"Well, the only way is up," Gil said, without conviction.

"Absolutely right," agreed Larry, "Give me a call when you get out. We'll have the beer I skipped out on last time."

"That'd be good," said Gil. "But if you'll excuse me, I have to go......," he could think of no excuse. "I have to go now," he said, moving backwards to the door before turning and running up the hall to his own room.

He closed the door, panting. Oh God, he just wasn't ready to face the world yet. He had some hardening up to do first.

When the doctor called to check him out in the early afternoon, Gil told him what had happened, and the doctor agreed another day was definitely needed.

Gil called Connie.

"Do you want me to come? I can be there in a couple of hours," she said. "How odd that you should bump into Paul. I would have thought he was past that sort of thing."

"I wouldn't have known he was here at all if I hadn't bumped into Larry. He pretty much dragged me in. Giulia was there which surprised me a bit. I wouldn't have thought her mother would let her come to a place like this. Perhaps Larry brought her without saying."

Connie was quiet for a heartbeat. Giulia seemed to be cropping up a lot recently. Silly thought – she was such a baby.

"I'll come see you tomorrow then. Be there about three."

"Sure, if that's okay," said Gil. "It'll mean two trips unless the doc says I'm fit to leave tomorrow."

"It's no bother." said Connie. I'll call your mom - she still has the boys. I'll get her to bring them over Friday - that'll give you a couple of days to settle in."

"Can you find out how the guys are doing? We were due to do a couple of dates in Ohio yesterday. Then we'd booked studio time for two weeks from Friday afternoon. They'll never cope. I've let them down again."

This had been nagging at Gil ever since he'd been in rehab. Always the band, always his brother. Always someone who couldn't function without him.

"Don't worry about them. I called Jamie as soon as I got

home. They know what's happening, but I won't tell them where you are, or let them anywhere near until you have a handle on this."

He was distracted by a soft tap at the door.

"Gotta go now. I'll see you tomorrow. I love you. Please never forget that for one second." He blew a kiss softly down the phone and replaced the handset.

The tap came again, and he called to come in. To his surprise Giulia edged into the room.

"I've come to apologize for my dad. He can be such an insensitive clod at times – but he means well," she said shyly.

She walked over and reached for his hand.

"Are you going to be okay?" she asked looking deep into his eyes. He found himself momentarily distracted.

"Sure. But you'll know how it is with your dad - he'll be fine but he'll need all your support. It was sweet of you to think of me too, and I appreciate it."

He smiled at her and kissed her on the cheek. She smelled of flowers he noticed. She blushed then excused herself and returned to her father.

Gil watched her leave and raised an eyebrow. When had she grown up?

Her visit had restored some of his confidence, so he decided to eat his next meal in the dining room rather than alone.

It turned out to be a good decision. By the time he went back, he was feeling much better, and sat out on his balcony for a couple of hours enjoying the fresh air and sunshine. He'd get Connie to fetch one of his guitars tomorrow. He slept better that night than he had in months.

When Connie arrived the following afternoon, she was amazed at the improvement in his looks. He actually smiled at her when she came through the door and beamed when he saw his guitar.

"Are you alright, Gil?" she asked, puzzled. "Have they put you on medication?"

"No. Do I look that different?"

"You do. Much better."

"Paul's going home tomorrow - the doc has okayed me too."

He picked her up and twirled her round. He was so cheerful that after yesterday, Connie was lost for words.

"Giulia's a cute little thing. She came to check on me before she left. I felt well enough afterwards to go downstairs to eat."

"Why? Because Giulia came to check on you?"

"No – well, not really. The Giordanos always cheer me up. They make me laugh. They are all so affectionate with each other."

His face fell when his own father came to mind, but he quickly recovered.

"It makes you happy to see it, and feel a bit left out at the same time."

Gil smiled broadly.

"Thanks for this," he picked up his guitar and ran his fingers lovingly over the strings.

They had a lovely dinner together on a flower-decked terrace overlooking the ocean. It was years since they'd held hands over a candle-lit table. All the tension between them melted away. They even slow-danced to some old-fashioned love songs playing through the sound system. Very un-rock star but so romantic.

It was late when Connie finally left. She felt elated, like she used to when they were first married, before the boys came and work intervened. Then there had been only the two of them.

Gil grinned at himself in the bathroom mirror as he cleaned his teeth. It had been a good day. Things were looking up.

Connie returned mid-afternoon the following day. Gil was waiting with his bag packed and the room tidied apart from the cigarette butts in an ashtray.

The door to the balcony was ajar. Gil had arranged for a cafetiere to be placed on the table, and they sat gazing across the bay and relaxed, with little conversation

He chain-smoked while they waited for the doctor. He was still bright but a bit more nervous than the day before, which Connie attributed to leaving the safety of the clinic.

The minutes ticked by, and finally the doctor arrived and greeted them both with a smile, then became serious.

"Mr. and Mrs. Robson. I just wanted a quick word before you left. Routine advice. Absolutely no drugs of any description – even pain relievers - in or around the house. That really should go for cigarettes too. But I can accept them Mr. Robson, unless it leads to cannabis or anything similar. Then it stops immediately. Please don't go anywhere or with anyone who might have access to narcotics, especially cocaine and alcohol. Alcohol impairs your judgement. Don't drink at all, at least until you have everything under control.

"So far as is possible, please stay in the company of close family, especially supervised children, as they will make you control the way you think and behave.

"Chew gum and get into the habit of counting to ten before you make decisions."

He smiled at their disbelieving expressions. "Anything that makes you pause and think before you act is good.

"I apologize Mr. Robson, if this makes it appear you are being treated as a child, although in fact you are. Addicts are like unruly children. They are irresponsible and untrustworthy and need constant supervision."

Gil felt humiliated. The majority of the time, the doctor had been talking to Connie over his head as if he wasn't there at all.

The medic smiled and shook their hands.

"I really do wish you the very best. You've been given another chance. Use it well."

He went, leaving the door ajar.

Gil watched him go. The onus was now on him. He lit another cigarette with shaky hands.

"Oh, come on Gil – you've got this," said Connie. "You control a whole band and every instrument in it. Kicking something like this should be a piece of cake by comparison,"

"That's true. But music has been my life since I was a kid. This is new and I'm scared." He shook himself. "But a long journey begins with the first step so let's go."

Chapter Twenty-three

Gloria was sweeping the front steps when they drove up to the house.

Connie had called her the day before to see if she was still available to work - she had always shied away from having live-in staff. It always felt to her as if her private space was being invaded, but this was a special situation.

She had helped Gloria move her belongings into a small suite of rooms at the rear of the house. Gloria was delighted.

"Welcome home, Mr. Gil. Can I get you something to eat or drink?" she said, then a little more unsure, "Or would you like to go rest first?"

"I'm fine, Gloria. I've done nothing but rest for four days. But coffee would be great. A steak sandwich would be good too if you could rustle one up."

Gloria beamed. Looking after Mr. Gil was one of her favorite things – he was always so appreciative. She bustled off to the kitchen.

Once Gloria was out of sight, Gil's shoulders sagged. Connie kissed his forehead, maternal in her concern.

"I keep saying 'we', but it's you who needs to have the strength. All I can do is hold your hand and wait for you to tell me what to do."

"Right now I want to drink my coffee, eat my sandwich then hold you in bed – and that'll be a disappointment too, because all I'll want to do is crash."

He tipped back his head and closed his eyes. Connie leant over to take his arm, but he stood abruptly and walked to the window.

153

"Tomorrow we have to sort out this mess with Oliver. It's for you to tell me what you want this time and not what you think I want to hear. I will try not to be pathetic, but I can't make any promises. I'm going to bed now." He left the room abruptly.

Connie covered her face with both hands and shook her head in despair.

She didn't have to wait to contact Oliver because he was on the doorstep first thing the following morning.

He appeared anxious and harassed, which was completely out of character – he was usually composed, even urbane, and clearly used to being in charge.

This morning his usually immaculate hair was slightly ruffled, and he had perspiration on his upper lip. He was carrying the biggest bunch of red roses she'd ever seen.

"How can I ever apologize enough, Connie? I behaved like a lout. It was totally unwarranted, and I am so sorry."

He handed over the flowers, and his view of her was momentarily obscured by the sheer size of the bouquet. She put it on the hall table.

"I fully understand why you were so angry. I will come and talk to Deborah myself. She didn't deserve what I did."

"Will you please come home?" he asked earnestly.

There was a long awkward silence.

"Don't you want to come back?" He looked aghast.

"I can't. Gil is here and very unwell. I picked him up from hospital yesterday afternoon. I will have to stay at least until he's back on his feet again."

"But.... but you left Gil. He has no right to ask you to come back."

"He hasn't asked me to come back - it's my decision. I am utterly and completely confused. If you love me, you will have to give me space to think things through."

Oliver's demeanor altered in a split second when he noticed Gill walk across the hall behind her.

"You piece of shit, Robson," he shouted. "I should wipe the floor with you. You've come back and already two lives are on the point of being ruined, not to mention your kids and mine. Why don't you fuck off back to Briarside where you belong?"

Connie's mouth dropped open. Gil was unable to move, frozen to the spot with shock. Connie shut the door behind her, remaining on the steps.

"You can come back Oliver, with a suitable apology," she said through her teeth. "Or don't bother coming back at all. Gil can be thoughtless at times, but he has never – never – spoken like that in my hearing in all the time I've known him. He and I are not good together. I don't know what will happen. But I do know I don't want to spend the rest of my life with someone who can be so without feelings. It might be me you're using that language on next."

She turned and went back inside, shutting the door with a bang. Immediately it flew open again and the thorns on the expensive bouquet caught Oliver across the face.

Gil was standing in the middle of the hall, white as a sheet.

"Get a hold of yourself, Gil. This has to stop now," said Connie. She grabbed his jacket and threw it at him.

"Pull yourself together, put that on."

Connie drove them up the coast to a tiny beach. The only people for miles appeared to be a family with two small children. Their parents were deep in conversation and the children had lagged behind.

"Get out. We're going skinny dipping," ordered Connie.

"Oh, no." He brushed her hand away, "What about the kids?"

"Their parents can continue to ignore them or take them away. I don't care."

She got out of the car and started stripping her clothes off. Gil was still gazing at the horizon.

"You can either strip or go in fully clothed – your choice. Oh, c'mon Gil. Don't be such a drag."

He smiled and waved her off:

"I'll get a better view from here." He sounded regretful.

'His life would be so much easier if he could only get over his obsession with his weight', she thought. Jamie's childhood teasing, and their father's bullying had damaged Gil's life beyond repair.

She plonked her sunglasses on his nose and ran off into the surf. Gil admired her retreating ass. Pretty good for a woman with two children.

He got out of the car and pulled off his shoes and socks, wiggling his toes in the warm sand. There was a popsicle stick half-buried next to his right foot. He picked it up and began to idly doodle in the sand. Every so often, he looked up to catch Connie bathing amongst the waves. He knew she would rather he had been there with her, laughing, playing, maybe making love. He wished he could have been there too.

There was a scream. Gil's head jerked up and he scanned the beach. The older little girl of the distant family was standing at the water's edge jumping up and down and crying inconsolably. The parents were nowhere to be seen. Gil and Connie were too far away to hear what the child was saying.

Connie dragged her sundress over her wet body and the two of them pelted down the beach.

The little girl was by now almost hysterical. Gil picked her up, holding her firmly against his chest and stroking her hair."

"Now, my little sunbeam, what's the matter?" The warmth of his body was calming her.

"My...my sister...," she pointed across the waves to a tiny speck just visible yards from the shore.

Connie ran into the sea, dived and swam with all her might towards the baby, who was crawling along a sandbank just inches below the surface. She grabbed her just before she dropped off the edge into deep water and dragged her back by her sodden diaper.

Gil held her sister gently, stroking her hair, rocking her and making hushing noises until her crying stopped. Then he began to sing:

"You are my sunshine, my only sunshine,

You make me happy when skies are grey...."

Her eyes, large and china blue, gazed trustingly into his, as his beautiful voice wove its magic.

Connie waved from the sea, holding the tiny bundle in her arms and slowly wading back to shore.

The little one Gil held had stuck her thumb in her mouth

and her eyelids fluttered.

Still several yards away Connie suddenly shouted frantically:

"Gil, look out. Quick – behind you!"

He half-turned, the child slack in his arms.

From behind, the little girl was grabbed and swung upwards. As he turned to look back, a muscular arm wrapped around his throat squeezing until he could no longer breathe.

"Let go," screamed Connie. "LET GO!"

She dumped the baby with the woman and throwing modesty to the winds, launched herself on Gil's attacker, kicking up sand and accidentally kneeing Gil in the face.

Gil was knocked over and a left hook caught him squarely on the jaw. Connie was grappling with the children's father who was doing his best to fend her off and get at Gil again.

He raised himself on all-fours, gasping for breath with blood running from his nose.

"You pervert! What kind of filth picks kids up on a beach? You dirty bastard!" The man kicked out and caught Gil in the ribs.

"You ungrateful idiot. If it wasn't for him, your daughter would be halfway to Hawaii by now!" yelled Connie. "Why the hell weren't you watching them?"

By this time both children were screaming and wriggling to get away from all the shouting. The mother was having difficulty holding them.

Nevertheless, she managed to grab her red-faced husband by the arm.

"Quit, Ray. Stop it! This guy wasn't harming the kids.

He was holding Janey while the lady grabbed the baby! She was in the sea."

The man pulled up short and looked from Gil to his wife and back again.

"Oh man, I'm so sorry. Here...." He held his hand out to help Gil to his feet. Gil stood, still gasping.

"Forget it, man. I'd probably have done the same if it was my kid."

Connie snorted – she doubted he'd have been there to notice.

"Can we get you something to eat...or a drink? There's a little coffee shop just over the headland. Then maybe you could dry off a bit."

Connie took Gil by the arm and felt his muscles tense.

"No, it's okay. We really have to be getting home, Gil," said Connie.

Gil gently removed her hand and turning to Ray said:

"May I?" and while her father stood protectively by Gil kissed Janey on the cheek and gave her a half-dollar coin to get both of the little ones an ice cream."

"Fifty cents?" Janey looked questioningly at her dad who smiled and nodded.

Once she'd said his name, Connie saw the woman start to eye Gil curiously. She was beginning to realize who he was. Connie didn't think he'd be up to signing autographs at the moment, so she said:

"Come on. We need to be heading back. These children have had enough excitement for one day."

She took his hand and cuddled up to his arm, like a

newlywed. "Let's go."

By the time they got back home, Gil's nerves were getting the better of him. He hugged Connie tightly until he started to unwind again, then sank into an armchair, ashen faced, knuckles white against the dark fabric.

"I'll be okay in a minute," he lit a cigarette, inhaled deeply, and very gradually some color began to come back into his face.

But the afternoon's sunshine was already a memory.

Giulia had brought her dad a cup of coffee. He was due in rehearsal at ten and it was now nine-thirty. He just about had time to drink it. He tied a sweater round his waist and checked his immaculate hair in the mirror.

"Thank you, darlin'; thoughtful is your middle name," he said, taking the coffee from her.

"When'll you be home, Poppa?"

"Don't know. Depends if the boys all show up on time and what mood they're in."

He winked and she laughed. 'The boys' were her dad's best pals and some of the most famous entertainers in the world. But Giulia knew them as uncles. She became serious.

"How're you doing, Pops?" she asked. At his raised eyebrow she continued.

"You know very well what I mean. Don't try to play it down."

"Well, thanks for your concern darlin', but as you can see I'm doing great."

He sniffed and wiped his nose on the pristine handkerchief he pulled from his pants pocket. "Have to watch that. Can't have a cold. Playing Nevada next week."

He pressed his lips to her forehead then, whistling, gave a skip and disappeared out of the door.

Giulia went to her room to dress. She was meeting up with Lucy, sister of one of her brothers' friends. They got on well together and would drive out to the beach today, maybe have a little lunch. She sang softly to herself as she put the finishing touches to her makeup and added a towel and sun cream to her beach bag.

Lucy was sitting on the wall at the bottom of her drive when Giulia arrived. She was sturdily built with thick auburn hair. As the fashion in LA was dictated by Hollywood, she wasn't a beauty, but she had such vitality that people were drawn to her. Where Giulia was a little on the reserved side, Lucy was outgoing and full of fun.

"Hi Gules! You good?" Instead of opening the door, she vaulted over the side of Giulia's imported convertible and shuffled into the passenger seat. Giulia shook her head and smiled, put the stick-shift into gear and took off down the road.

They parked on the headland above a small bay. After they'd changed into bikinis, they followed the little path down to the beach, which was deserted apart from a couple with a little girl and carrying a baby, who were halfway up the corresponding path at the bay's other side.

"Good. They've gone." said Lucy. "We've got the beach to ourselves."

She threw her towel down on the sand and whooping ran into the sea, kicking up a rainbow of droplets.

161

Catch a Falling Star

Giulia's tan was fading, so she chose to sit on her own towel on the sand. With her arms wrapped round her knees she watched Lucy cavort in the waves.

She turned onto her stomach, chin on her hands. Someone had stuck a popsicle stick in the sand, and she picked it up, idly twirling it between her fingers before throwing it away and settling down for some serious sun-bathing.

They spent the whole afternoon on the beach, and rather than look for somewhere to eat, they decided to go back to Giulia's.

It was early evening when they arrived. The gardenias near the front door perfumed a gentle breeze blowing in from the ocean.

Giulia pushed open the door and dropped her damp bag on the floor-tiles.

"Cindy! Please fix us some pasta and pour a couple of glasses of Cabernet. Just going to shower and change."

The girls walked arm in arm to Giulia's room.

"There's another bathroom next door. Why don't you use that? Did you bring a change of clothes?"

Lucy reached into her bag, pulled out a creased bit of material and wafted it in Giulia's face.

"What on earth is that?" laughed Giulia. "It looks like something I'd use to polish fingerprints off the car!"

"What do you mean?!" said Lucy in mock horror. "This is a Gucci!"

Giulia raised an eyebrow. Knowing Lucy, it probably was used for cleaning her car, and it probably was a Gucci.

162

Chapter Twenty-four

Deborah stood in the middle of the foyer, stamped her foot and cried. She had on a little blue and white spotted swimsuit which was her favorite, but by now a bit on the small side.

Mary Jane, the children's' nanny crouched to put her face on a level with Deborah's and asked her kindly if she would like an ice cream. Deborah stopped crying, glowered and hit her hard across the face. It brought tears to Mary Jane's eyes, and she stood and went back to the kitchen. Deborah looked smug.

"You know, I saw that," said a voice from the top of the stairs. "That was a horrible thing to do. Mary Jane can't hit you back so its bullying. I think I should let Dad know what you did."

Deborah turned to see her brother Simm watching her, one hand on the stair-rail. She tossed her white-blond curls and smiled sweetly at him.

"Go ahead, you know he won't believe you."

This was true. Deborah had her daddy wrapped round her little finger. If this wasn't so, she wouldn't have been able to get rid of Connie so easily – did they think she didn't know the difference between flowers and weeds? Did Simm know? She didn't think so, or she probably wouldn't have been able to wriggle out of that one. Daddy was soft about Connie. She'd got rid of Mommy, hadn't she? So, she was fair game.

But she had gone too far with Simm this time. He did know about Connie, and he truly loved his Dad, and hated to see him look so unhappy. In fact, he didn't recall seeing him smile since Connie left. He would fix this but how? The word of an eight-year-old didn't carry

163

much weight. He'd have to think about it.

That Friday, Nancy brought the boys back home. It had been decided between her and Connie that they would see how Gil reacted to their presence. Of course, this was kept from Gil. In a long phone conversation, Nancy said that if he couldn't cope with the noisy play, Jacob and Mylo could go home with her for a few days.

Gil had been playing his guitar in the peace of the poolhouse when his mother brought the boys back. He saw her car pull into the drive and walked across to greet her. He helped her lift the boys out, and all their belongings from the trunk. The minute they saw him, a fight began as to who could get out of the car first, which Jacob won simply because he was bigger and more determined.

"Daddy!" Gil bent and picked him up and Jacob flung his arms round his neck. All Mylo could manage was to attach himself limpet-like to Gil's right leg. Gil limped along, Jacob in his arms and Mylo giggling, still holding tight to his leg. Once they reached the grass on the far side of the drive, Gil dropped to the knee that didn't have Mylo attached and holding tight to the kids, rolled onto his back.

"Aghhhh! You got me, you got me, I surrender." He pretended to lose consciousness, and didn't get up, though both kids started shaking him with increasing panic.

"Mommy! Daddy's dead," yelled Jacob.

"Yeah, dead," echoed Mylo with a blood-thirsty expression.

Gil jumped to his feet, grabbed a child under each arm and dumped them in a nearby fishpond. Then he stood back, drying his hands on his jeans, and roaring with laughter at two drenched kids with green waterweed hanging from their clothes and hair. Mylo launched back in with both fists flying, but it had all been too much for Jacob, who stood dripping and tearful.

Nancy, alerted by the noise, came running from the house, and confronted by three of her boys in various stages of dampness, burst out laughing.

"Oh my God Gil. Will you never grow up?" she scolded.

Connie stood behind her in the doorway, delighted to see the old Gil back again. She ran inside and returned with a pile of towels and began to dry the kids, removing pond weed as she did so.

"Come on, Mom," said Gil to Nancy, hugging her as they walked into the house. "I'll fix you a maitai. Where's the rum, Connie?"

Connie pulled a face. Besides the fact he wasn't allowed alcohol, they'd never, ever had a bottle of rum in the house.

Connie called Gloria to strip the boys off and put them in dry clothes.

"Want a coffee…or a cola?" asked Gil.

"Oh. Anything cold will do," Nancy replied.

Gil left his mother alone in the living room and came to help Connie with the tray of drinks she had placed on the breakfast bar. One of the glasses wasn't quite level, and as he lifted the tray, it fell and shattered on the marble floor. His nerves gave way. Connie dropped the tray back on the bar, grabbed him by the arm and dragged him into their bedroom.

"Where's Daddy gone," asked a confused Mylo. "He promised me we'd look for bugs in the pool. Look, I've got my jar and everything."

"I can do that with you. That's if you don't mind," said Nancy. Mylo really didn't care who looked at bugs with him as long as he got to handle them.

His Nana led him into the garden, where he was soon distracted trying to drown beetles while Nancy did her best to stop him. Jacob joined in. The beetles lost.

In the house, Connie sat Gil on the bed, brought him some water and held his hand tightly.

"Don't let go," he gasped.

"The intervals between are getting longer and the effects milder," Connie observed. "Come on. We'd better get back before your mother notices."

At that moment the door chimed, and Gloria opened it to a small boy, standing politely on the doorstep.

"Hello, is Mrs.. Robson home?" he asked. Gloria stood back so Connie could see this unknown child.

On the doorstep stood little Simeon Maxwell. His face and hair were damp with sweat and his hands grubby. There was a dirty smudge under one eye.

"Please may I speak to you Connie....er, Mrs. Robson?" he asked.

"How on earth did you get here, Simm?" asked Connie. "Does your dad know where you are?"

"No," said Simeon proudly. "I walked."

"But it's nearly six miles!"

"I know." His smile was weary but triumphant.

Connie took him by the hand and walked him to the garden where they could speak, careful that they

166

couldn't be overheard.

They sat down on a garden seat and he was suddenly overcome with shyness. Connie had begun to love this old-fashioned little boy and took his hand in both of hers.

"Come on Simm. What's wrong? It must be something serious to bring you here."

"Please come home, Connie," he blurted. "Pa is so miserable without you. And...and I miss you so much." He slid sideways into her arms and hid his face against her breast. "Please come home." Connie hugged him.

Suddenly, he shot to his feet and wiped his eyes with the back of his hand. His misery had turned to terror in a split second. Gil stood several feet away, looking blankly on. Clearly, he'd heard the entire conversation.

"I'll see you back at the house later," he said to Connie. "Good to see you, Simeon."

He turned and walked back to the house and disappeared inside.

Gil pulled out one of the seats at the breakfast bar and rested his head in his hands. He was shaking again but this time it had nothing to do with cocaine. He knew she was going to go. Why would she stay?

Jacob climbed onto the seat next to him and put a hand on his shoulder.

"Don't cry, Dad. It'll be okay. Mommy won't leave us. I know Simm - he's a good guy."

Gil pulled him onto his knee and buried his head in the boy's hair. How was he to explain this situation to his child? How could he explain something he didn't understand himself?

At that moment, Mylo came flying round the corner

holding a jam jar with a huge beetle trying to climb its way out.

"Look, Dad. Look what me and Nana found. Isn't it great?" He banged it down on the bar in front of Gil.

Sometimes Jacob was wise beyond his years. He climbed down from Gil's knee and, taking his brother by the hand, he started to pull him towards their playroom.

"Daddy wants to talk to Nana. Let's go build a castle with your bricks." Mylo was always up for that. The beetle was instantly forgotten.

Nancy bustled in, picked up the jar and went and shook it outside in the garden.

"Poor thing deserves another chance."

She pulled up short when she saw Gil, head in hands. He looked weary beyond bearing.

"Come on, son. Sit over here."

She tugged one of the easy chairs closer and helped Gil sit. Then she pushed him gently forward and began massaging his neck and shoulders.

"She gave me a second chance, Mom but I can feel her slipping away from me. Why would she stay? What has she to stay for? I'm no good. I drink. I snort cocaine – sometimes worse than that. I leave her alone with the kids for months on end. I cheat on her with other women and she knows about it. Why would she stay?"

Nancy put her arms round her precious son's neck. She didn't tell him he should pull himself together and put his mind to fixing at least some of his problems. She felt that would be unkind, so she only said:

"Things will work out, baby. One way or another, things

will work out. They always do." He leaned his head back on her shoulder.

"Not this time." He sounded so drained. Nancy walked round the chair and knelt at his feet.

"One thing I know you do understand, Gil. When God closes a door, he always opens a window. You just have to find it."

Gil wandered down to the pool-house. He could see Connie still sitting with Simm on the garden seat. The little boy had his head in her lap.

He took out a lighter and lit a dozen white candles, some with drips of wax hanging from the sides, and sitting cross-legged on the floor, picked up his guitar and began strumming. The scent of the burning wax, mixed with the aroma of rosewater, usually calmed him. He stared into the closest flame, as his fingers found chords he didn't need to see.

He laid aside his guitar and jumped, fully clothed, into the pool. The water bubbled from his nose and mouth and echoed loud in his ears.

What if he were to stay here? All his problems would be solved. Beneath the surface was peace. Beneath the water was calm. But the water wouldn't take him. It threw him back and his lungs filled with air, so he pulled himself up and lay on his back on the pool surround, until his chest recovered. It was peaceful here too.

If he turned his head, he could see the candle flames flickering in the draft from the open door. He closed his eyes.

Connie took Simm by the hand and led him indoors to call his father. Nancy was sitting in the chair Gil had vacated. She looked sad.

"Where's Gil?" asked Connie.

"He went down to the pool-house."

Connie picked up the phone, gave the receiver to Simm and dialed Oliver's number. She could hear police sirens and an irate voice said:

"Where the hell have you been, Simm. I've had half the LA police force out looking for you. Where are you?"

Simm's lip began to tremble, so Connie snatched the receiver out of his hand.

"Hello Oliver? He's with me. He walked six miles to find me. How in hell he didn't get lost I've no clue. Come and get him please. I can't bring him now – I've got a problem that needs sorting here."

"Don't tell me! The problem's name is Gil Robson," sneered Oliver. "Be there in an hour - I've the police to sort out first. God knows what I'm going to tell them. My son ran off to be with some woman who dumped his father. Sounds good, doesn't it?"

He slammed down the phone.

Connie took Simm to play with her boys.

"Shall I come with you to see Gil?" asked Nancy with raised eyebrows. Connie shook her head.

"No need. He'll be knee deep in candle wax by now."

When she got to the pool the door was ajar, some of the candles had blown out and the smell of cannabis was thick in the air. Gil was lying flat on his back, unmoving and soaked to the skin, by the pool.

"Gil!" she breathed. She knelt beside him and slapped his face.

"Come on, Gil…. Come on. You can't do this twice, you son-of-a-bitch!"

Gil, woken from a deep slumber, wondered what the hell was going on.

"Ow!" he yelled, rubbing his cheek.

"What the hell are you playing at?" shouted Connie, "Cannabis? CANNABIS! Have you lost your mind? Do you want to end up in an asylum? This time she slapped him for real.

"Goddam, Gil. You're a nightmare," she fetched a toweling robe from the pool-house and dragged him up by the arm.

"Get out of those wet clothes. Then get back to the house - Oliver's coming to pick Simm up."

Just the sound of his name on Connie's lips was painful.

Connie was beginning to feel a deal of sympathy for Lizbeth, who had rescued her from a similar poolside situation.

Oliver arrived, picked up Simm and left. No words were exchanged, but Simm looked pleadingly out of the window at Connie as they drove away.

"Yet another peaceful day at the Robson ranch," said Nancy, then dashed inside to break up a noisy fight which had broken out in the playroom. Jacob had stomped on Mylo's castle.

After Nancy had helped put the boys to bed, kissed both kids and grandkids and gone home, Connie and Gil sat out on the kitchen terrace. The silence was blissfully relaxing after a tiring day.

"How are you feeling now…," and at his expression,

"That's not a loaded question."

"Okay, I guess. Doing better. What will you do about Oliver? It took guts to do what that kid did. He must have been desperate."

"Yes. Poor child doesn't have much of a life. Deborah gets away with murder and Simm suffers for it. He takes the blame for practically everything."

She paused, then said:

"My grandmother has asked me to go to Honolulu to see Uncle Noa. I thought I might take the boys for a couple of weeks holiday. They've never met my side of their family. It might be good for them. What do you think? Could you cope?"

"If that's what you want, go ahead," said Gil. At least Oliver would be out of the picture for a while.

"You don't mind me taking Jake and Mylo?"

"No. As you say it'll be a change for them."

He lit another cigarette from the stub of the one he'd been smoking.

"I'll go back to my first question – damn, this is hard work Gil – will you cope okay do you think? You didn't do too well on your own last time."

"I'll cope. Take the boys and have a great time – this has been hard on you too."

"Okay, I'll call Grannie and give you some details."

There was a flurry of packing toys and boxes of sandwiches in a carry-on bag. Then they were gone.

The quiet of the house took on a different tone this time. Gil had nothing to worry him, so the silence felt restful.

He drew a bath and put in some of Connie's essential oil. Candles suffused a soft glow, deepening shadows, blurring edges. Then he climbed in and let the warmth spread through his body and loosen his muscles.

Gil couldn't remember the last time he'd felt so relaxed. He shampooed his hair then closed his eyes and lay his head back on the edge of the bath. The scent and warmth were sensuous - it felt so good. He wouldn't think about tomorrow now.

Chapter Twenty-five

The following day at the studio was a complete shambles. Gil had missed so much that he had completely lost control of the session. He was forced to backtrack to a point that everyone could identify, which put them back an additional few days' work. He apologized over and over, until he was so sick of being sorry, he almost threw in the towel and went home.

On top of that, Jamie turned up stoned.

But there was no denying his brilliance. He staggered over to the piano and began playing nonsense, which gradually morphed into a beautiful love song, custom-built for Gil's voice. The whole process took little more than an hour, although it would require polishing. Gil made sure it was recorded.

Four packs a day had put paid to Jamie's voice. Gil also habitually smoked cigarettes but his God-given voice seemed to be just that. It never lost the sweetness or clarity of pitch. Occasionally, if he overdid it, his voice would roughen almost imperceptibly to all but himself. Then he would cut down on the tobacco for a few days for it to recover.

"John, take it from the fourth bar. Steve, you need to come in on the third beat."

It was a shambles of mistiming. They did it again and again, and finally got it right at the eleventh attempt. That was the basis for the harmonies.

'Oh, shit,' thought Gil. 'Why do we need to do harmonies? Why can't we just sing straightforward R and B like everyone else? What's wrong with a bit of improvisation?'

All pointless argument, of course, since harmonies were what they were known for and what their audiences demanded.

Eventually, they at least reached a place Gil could pick up and move forward from. Things got easier from then on. Or at least they did temporarily.

These were just the vocals. There were the arrangements to sort with the backing musicians. They'd be at East End Studios tomorrow. Perhaps if Jamie could hold on to reality until then he might be able to help. He just seemed able to take all the musical strands and hold them in his hands, weaving and intertwining them. Gil had watched him so closely and learned all he could, but Jamie was the master and Gil was often in awe of his abilities.

They worked on until it became obvious voices were beginning to give out.

That night Gil slept soundly until his alarm woke him at eight a.m. A shower, a beard-trim later – he must check out the barber – and he was on his way to East End.

Jamie did make it to the next session and his involvement, often minimal, was total. The music seemed to pour out of him, but Gil wasn't fooled. What Jamie began with enthusiasm he could just as easily dump in the trash.

Gil and Jamie were back at work together and he knew Connie would not have understood – she'd forbidden Jamie from visiting the clinic, so the possible repercussions filled him with dread.

About three o'clock, Jamie decided he'd had enough and

went home. Gil hid the tapes in case he decided to come in when he wasn't there and wipe them.

By now, the session musicians were used to Jamie. So, they sat around waiting for the nod from Gil, drinking coffee for a while and chewing the fat, before on his say-so they packed up their instruments and left.

Gil and Jamie locked up and stood chatting for a few minutes, then Jamie who had remained nervous of Connie's threat, left.

"See ya.... whenever," said Jamie, revving up his latest acquisition, a brand-new silver Kawasaki. Then he was gone, weaving dangerously through the traffic.

Gil headed out. He was stopped just outside by a group of autograph hunters. He knew their type well – two gigglers and one so shy she could hardly speak. He signed their albums and stroked the hair of the dumb-struck teen. The other two swooned. It was all part of the scene and he really didn't mind. These were basically nice kids, and a pleasant relief from some 'musicians' who thought they owned a piece of him simply because he paid them. He'd never been able to figure that out.

It would be ten days before Connie was back. Maybe a trip to the mountains with Jamie would be good, He loved the sparkling, icy air, so different from the dusty heat of Los Angeles with its gas fumes and deafening traffic. It had an otherworldly silence which always drew him in. He never wanted to leave.

He would have to be available for work though. They had a gig at Anaheim on Saturday – he'd have to be with Jamie again - then he had some business odds and ends to tie up before more studio work over the rest of the weekend. That gave him a couple of days – not enough time to go. There never seemed to be enough time.

He finally decided to stop with his mom for a couple of days. It would do them both good. She loved to spoil him and she was a superb cook – her specialty was pot-roast and no-one made it quite like his mom. He looked down at his burgeoning waistline and sighed. He may as well face it, he was never going to be fit and muscular like Jamie. For him it was effortless, for Gil an endless battle he repeatedly lost. In a profession where appearance was all, it made him feel very insecure.

Still, he must have something he supposed, because he had very loyal fans, some of whom he had been recognizing in the audience since he was a teen himself. Their faces had become so familiar he found himself looking out for them, peering through the spotlights.

"Hi there, Ma!" He banged on the door then barged straight in. Mom's home would always be his own. Thankfully Monty wasn't there.

Nancy looked in from the kitchen and her face lit up. Since their teens, she had been a mother to her sons first and a wife to Monty second. She and the boys had joined forces early on to combat his aggression.

"Can I stay for a couple of days? Connie's out of town with the boys and I'm rattling around in that big empty house. It'll only be until Saturday when we play Anaheim."

The words were hardly out of his mouth before she enfolded him in a warm hug. He leaned into it, happy in the moment to feel her warmth.

"Do you have a bag? Go unpack it. The front spare room would be best I think. It gets sun in the morning. I'll make you something to eat."

He spent a whole evening watching TV with his mom like he used to do as a kid, and the following morning Nancy cooked him pancakes with bacon and maple syrup for breakfast..

Then Monty turned up and the day began to go downhill fast.

"Where the hell is Jamie? Damn no good fuck-up. "

Gil cringed. He was sure his father couldn't know how distraught Jamie became when Monty made such remarks. Monty was totally without any sympathy, which wracked Gil with pity.

When you knew Jamie as well as Gil did you could see the heartache in his eyes. But then he would react by baiting Monty until he was so angry his hands were fists at his sides, and his face had turned beet red.

Gil had had enough. He'd had such a peaceful evening with his mom, he didn't want it spoilt.

"Why do you want Jamie?" There was a warning edge to his voice.

"None of your goddamn business. Now, where the hell is he?" then completely ignoring his own statement he continued, "The entire Morris family is harassing me because Ed says he's due some money from the record company. I don't believe a damn word of it. Jamie writes with him so he must know. I'd rather string that poncing excuse for a Christmas tree, Ed, up by the balls, than pay him a red cent."

Nancy looked from Gil to her husband and left the room. Monty followed her and Gil could hear his strident voice in the kitchen:

"Get over it, Nancy. Ed would screw his own

grandmother unless someone stopped him, What the hell would the band do without me?" He stomped back into the living room.

"Well, where is Jamie?" he demanded of Gil.

Gil actually had no idea where Jamie was. He couldn't have been at home because that would have been the first place Monty would look.

"Did you try any of his friends? They would be more likely to know than me."

"Which leeches has he taken up with now?"

"Can't help you there Pops. No idea." Gil made no attempt to hide his smugness.

Monty scowled and left.

His fuck-up son came bowling into his mother's living room later that afternoon. He'd been looking for Gil all over town so, by process of elimination, had ended up in the right spot.

After picking up his mother and waltzing her round the room, he flopped down on a chair, one leg over the arm.

"Hi, Ma! How come Gil's always here before me? Has he left any food?"

Nancy disappeared into the kitchen, delighted at the thought of feeding two-thirds of her brood and Jamie turned to Gil:

"Gil, my man. I'm flying out to Anasazi after the gig. Wanna come? We can be back Monday morning. Jeff'll put us up for a couple of nights."

Jeff owned an entire village of cabins and studios – high in the mountains in Colorado. It was purposely designed to be away from the distractions of Los Angeles. A constantly rotating number of bands and singers spent time up there in what mostly turned out to be very productive jam and recording sessions. Gil, and Jamie too, had made good friends there from all over the world. It had a great vibe.

Nancy called them to the kitchen.

"Well, are you coming?" said Jamie shoveling food into his mouth then talking round it.

"I can't really. Got some paperwork to finish. Then I have to call in to the accountants," said Gil in an attempt to extricate himself from a dangerous situation.

"What... on a Sunday? How'd you manage that?"

"Double time," grinned Gil, wryly.

"Aw! Come on. Life's not exactly been a gas lately. Getting out of LA and breathing that great mountain air" – he took a deep lung-full – "will do you a power of good, even if it's just a few hours."

Gil reached in his pocketbook and thumbed out a business card. He cancelled his appointment.

"Sounds like a great idea," said Nancy, hugging first Gil then Jamie as she walked past. "Will you stop here tonight?"

Jamie dropped his knife and fork on his empty plate with a clatter.

"Yeah, if that's okay."

"What'll happen about packing away the gear after the gig?" asked Gil, practical as always.

"I'll slip Freddie a grand. He'll take care of it."

Gil shook his head. If it were anyone else but Jamie,

he'd know they were joking about that amount of cash.

There were very few members of the road crew he would trust with his precious guitars, but there were one or two. He could make arrangements for the rest of the gear. Why not? Why shouldn't he feel free for a few hours?

"Okay," he replied, "but we'll have to fly back first thing Monday to be in the studio for noon. I can't lose any more time."

Jamie whooped and did a cartwheel back into the living-room. Gil wondered why he needed stimulants at all. But Jamie was mercurial and could go from high to low in minutes. Gil wasn't sure how much of that was coke and alcohol, but he suspected a large part was just natural Jamie.

Jamie sniffed and wiped his nose surreptitiously on his t-shirt sleeve. Then he grinned knowingly at Gil.

"Oh no, Jamie. If that's your intention, I'm not going."

"Why not, dear?" asked Nancy, completely at odds with the conversation. "Jamie's right, it would be good for you."

Gil rolled his eyes at Jamie behind her back and mouthed "Now see what you've done!"

Chapter Twenty-six

After the Saturday show, when both boys had spent two blissful days being spoilt by their mom, that night they took a plane from LA to Denver, picked up a hire car and drove up to Anasazi, high in the Colorado mountains. Occasional rushing mountain streams skirted the highway and produced intermittent sound. Apart from that, the silence was palpable, the three-a.m. darkness absolute.

The studio complex was still and deserted at such an early hour. An occasional light did glimmer but that was the only indication of habitation.

Gil drove slowly across the rutted path to the cabin Jamie had booked with Jeff. It was plain stripped wood and a bit claustrophobic, but someone had lit a banked-down fire and it was warm and cozy. There was coffee, and beers in a small cooler in the kitchenette, and a pizza in a box sitting on top of a microwave.

But both were too whacked to eat. Jamie lay down fully clothed on the sofa and Gil fell across the bed. Both were asleep in seconds. Neither had yet noticed the clean air or the surrounding peaks faintly visible in waxing moonlight.

They were awakened by thumping on the door at eight a.m.. Jamie curled up and buried his face in the sofa, instantly asleep again. Gil, bleary-eyed, fought through a fog of fatigue to consciousness, lurched to his feet and opened the door. Freezing cold air hit him in the face and brought everything into sharp focus.

There was a woman on the doorstep holding a tray with already cold coffee and toasted waffles. Gil took the tray from her and put it on the dinette counter.

"Jeff thought you might like some refreshment after your late night," she announced in a broad Kentucky accent.

Gil thanked her and slipped her ten bucks. She left and he closed the door quickly.

He reheated the food in the microwave and the smell brought Jamie to his feet.

"Oh God, heaven!" he enthused, coffee in one hand, two syrup covered waffles in the other.

Gil stirred the fire to life and scrabbled about in his bag for a fleece. The door had only been open a couple of minutes and already the heat had gone.

"I'll go find Jeff and see who else is here," said Gil.

Jamie had started on the pizza. Gil felt sick just looking at him. Sometimes life was so unfair.

It was a good half mile from the cabin to the studio complex. Gil stood for a few moments taking in the peaks of the Continental Divide which crossed Colorado. Layer on retreating layer of snow-capped mountains reaching to an impossibly blue, cloudless sky. He'd heard of a place not too far away which had a reputation as the largest crystal deposit in the world, and crystals Harry's teacher Daniel Jones taught, were transmitters of spiritual strength. He could do with a deal of that. He promised himself he would check it out sometime, although it sounded more like Shangri La than a real place.

Gil turned and walked towards the studio complex. There were some picnic-style tables outside and already there were figures standing or lounging around talking, some strumming on or tuning acoustic guitars.

It felt to Gil that these small insignificant creatures were somehow impinging on the majestic serenity of this place. They didn't fit.

As he drew closer, he recognized members he knew from other bands. Gil was a well- respected musician and people just plain liked him. He was a number one nice guy.

He saw Jack Thorpe and Mickey Stone from Snakeroot. They'd known each other from their teens when they were all babes in the business. And there was guitarist John Layton from the Pen – which was an in-joke since his band was Pennsylvania Jam. Gil had taught him some licks he'd used on their early albums. There was the whole of one of Gil's favorite bands Flyte, with Harry Forster – they'd been great friends once but work had intervened. Also there were the members of India for whom he had sung backing so many times for the sheer joy of it. The list went on. Gee! He hadn't realized how many there were who came up to Anasazi.

He was patted on the back as he walked past and occasionally pulled into a hug. He smiled warmly and hugged back.

"Anyone seen Jeff?"

"Hey, man! he's run into Riverside for pizzas – apparently you and Jamie took the last one."

"Nope, it was beer. He knew the Robsons were on the way and was worried the county could be drunk dry. He'll be back when he's restocked."

Gil grinned and there was more back-slapping.

"Is Todd here?" Todd Benson was Jeff's chief engineer and right-hand man.

"Yeah, man. He's in the box."

Catch a Falling Star

Gil ducked inside the studio door and waited a moment for his eyesight to adjust after the brilliance outside. The studio was one large room, with a glass booth at one end, and dustsheet-covered keyboards and drum kits, and guitar stands, for the moment empty, stacked near the rear wall. Around the edges of the room were easy chairs and low tables, currently clean, but by the day's end they'd be littered with empty beer cans, discarded Styrofoam cups, and overflowing ashtrays.

Todd was setting up the sound booth ready for the day's work.

"Hey, Gil," he smiled grasping Gil's outstretched hand. "You here with the boys?"

"No, just Jamie. And it's a flying visit - he'd to come see Jeff about something. Y'know, I forgot to ask what."

Gil shook his head.

"Jeez - I must be losing it! Anyway, it's been pretty bad in LA recently, so a day out of the city seemed a good move."

"Here, plug this in over there," said Todd. "Did you see your pal Harry Forster? He's cutting an album with Flyte. Lots of folks here at the moment.

"Yes, saw him. It'd be good to catch up, but I doubt it'll happen this time round. We're leaving early tomorrow. We have to be in Denver for a nine-fifty-five flight."

Gil looked around. He'd had some happy times in this studio. He pulled down his cuff and affectionately wiped fingerprints off the chrome surround of the console.

"Tell Jeff I'm around, eh? I'm just going to soak up the peace and quiet. Be back soon."

As Gil started to walk back to the cabin, he met Jamie

coming from the other direction.

"Anything to score down there?"

"No there isn't, and don't say that in front of Jeff. He hates drugs at Anasazi, which is why I'm here at all. I like this place. Don't fuck it up for me – and you too, come to that."

They turned together and walked up a wide path which took them above the snow line. It was great throwing snowballs and rubbing icy handfuls in each other's faces until they were red and raw. Then crying with laughter as they had at home in Briarside a lifetime ago. Brothers always.

"What did you want to see Jeff about anyway?" Gil asked on the way back down.

"I'll tell you," said Jamie, uncharacteristically serious, "but you have to swear to me you won't discuss it with anyone else. I don't want Ed involved in any way at all. Ever and for whatever reason. Not at all!"

"Okay – I get it – you don't want Ed to know. Go on."

"I've five or six halfway decent songs ready for a solo album. They still need work and I have to come up with more." Gil flung an arm over his brother's shoulder.

"Wow! When can I hear them? Now?"

"I wanted to ask Jeff if there would be any down-time when I could work alone – well, you can come if you like," Jamie conceded. "I may need to do some fast talking to bring him round. That's why I brought you. You're good at that kind of thing. Even Ed'd be better than me."

"We need a way to get him on his own. The cabin would be best. No ears. What do we tell him? How about an overdose? He'd come on his own for that. He wouldn't want anyone else to know. As for the acting – what do you mean? I can't act to save my life!" chuckled Gil.

Jeff had a two-week slot in October when most bands were on the road. Gil always tried to be back then in any case as it was Mylo's birthday mid-month.

The place would be empty, and Jeff had planned a holiday for his family. He gave the keys to Gil on the express instruction he would never leave them with Jamie unsupervised. Jamie was a bit put out. Gil completely understood.

It was given to Gil to get support musicians and backing singers up there - of course it was. That's what Gil did. It gave him no pleasure at all, but he was good at it. If he couldn't find anyone who was willing to make the journey, they would have to resort to the LA studios which Jamie wanted to avoid.

There were a few good guys he could think of off the top of his head, but he didn't know if they'd be available. Most of the sidemen of the quality Gil needed were in high demand, sometimes for weeks, even months, in advance. He'd put the word out and see if he got any takers.

Jamie wandered off to find female company, and left Gil alone, making notes on a pad, and leafing through the pocket diary that accompanied him everywhere.

It sure felt good to be busy again.

Chapter Twenty-seven

The return to LA was uneventful and they were back in the city by noon as planned.

East End Studios were buzzing when they got there. Of the four units, three were in use. They had to finish laying the tracks and complete the mixing. There were odds and ends to perfect with the backing musicians, but it wouldn't be a long session. Ed, who had elected himself the leader when Gil was in rehab, was furious that he was again pushed into the background as work progressed. Gil ignored him and dug Jamie in the ribs when he started to open his mouth.

The album was set for delivery to the record company mid-September, and they were running on time. He should be able to disappear to Anasazi with Jamie, at least for a few days, Connie permitting. Nancy wouldn't mind taking the boys again, he was sure. Nancy wouldn't mind but Connie might have a deal to say about it.

He turned out to be right about Connie.

"This is typical. You can't just swan off with Jamie – goddam, especially Jamie, have you lost the will to live? - whenever you feel like it. You have kids and a wife. What about Jacob and Mylo and….and what about me!" the last a crescendo ending in a shout. "You are just about the limit, Gil. Dammit, grow up."

"But going to Honolulu was your idea!"

"You've been to your mother's. You've been to Anasazi already!"

"Those weren't holidays. The first was two days with

my mother and the other was business."

Gil held his breath but thankfully Connie didn't notice his gaff. Jamie would not have been pleased he'd broken his confidence – even if it wasn't Ed.

"Go…go, then. I've other places I can be. And the kids will be with me. So, you needn't give them another thought."

Gil didn't appreciate being threatened.

"You must do what you think is right. But you can leave the kids out of this. I don't intend putting them in the center of a fight. Your argument is with me, not them." said Gil.

"And how do you propose I do that, Gil? I'm sick and tired of all this… we're talking divorce here. There – I've said it. It's no longer the elephant in the room. This is where it ends. Go think about how you want to do this. It can be hard or easy. Right this minute I couldn't care less which. Your call."

It was like listening to somebody else. He could hear the words, but it was as if they were coming from somewhere far away, as if he was a third party listening to someone else's anger. He was dizzy with fury.

He went to see Jamie.

Afterwards, he wondered if he had realized what would happen with Jamie. Clearly, he hadn't thought the situation through but surely, he must have realized.

Chapter Twenty-Eight

Connie's tears were not of sadness but pure, unadulterated fury. She'd let this situation go on far too long. At this moment in time, she hated Gil with the same passion with which as a teenager, she had worshipped him. She hated his selfishness, his thoughtlessness and his self-absorption. But most of all she hated that she didn't believe he loved her anymore, and probably hadn't in years. It didn't matter a jot that her own feelings were just as confused.

She took the boys to Nancy's, dumped them on the doorstep and rang the bell, never even checking to see if the door opened. Mylo began to run down the path after her and grabbed hold of her skirt.

"Mom...Mommeeee! Don't leave me. Please don't go. Please don't...," and he collapsed sobbing in a heap on the sidewalk. Connie's car pulled away. Nancy picked Mylo up and took both children inside.

Once out of sight of the house, Connie pulled into the side of the road, turned off the ignition, banged her fist on the steering wheel and gave way to her grief. Then she pulled herself together, sat up straight and started the car. This time, whatever, she would not give in. This time the bastard could throw himself off a cliff and she wouldn't give him a thought. She went to see Oliver.

At Jamie's seaside house Gil's car screeched to a halt and he bolted through the door.

"Jamie.... JAMIE!," he yelled. "Where the hell are you?" Silence, but for distant waves on the beach. Nothing. Empty.

He sank into an armchair. It was worse than last time since it felt so cold. No rage or heartbreak, not even self-pity. Nothing. Empty like Jamie's silent house.

Ten minutes later, Jamie found him slumped over the chair. He'd lurched through the door, a girl giggling on each arm. Usually so quick on the uptake, Jamie was too wasted to react quickly. It took him a few swaying moments to register Gil's presence, and then the state he was in. Then he sobered up instantly.

"Girls. Get outa here – wait outside. Go…GO!" and he slapped them both on the ass, pushed them outside and slammed the door.

The noise brought Gil's attention back.

"Oh, go to hell Jamie. Just go. I can't talk now."

Jamie shrugged and left with the girls in tow. If Gil wanted to be a pain in the ass, that was a problem he'd deal with in his own good time – not Gil's.

It had started to rain, a sharp, short torrential downpour. Between the car and Oliver's front door Connie was soaked to the skin. Maria answered her knock.

"Good day, Mrs. Robson, how may I help you?"

Connie pushed past her and called Oliver's name. But it was Simm who came skidding out of the diner and wrapped his arms round her. She disentangled herself gently.

"Where's your Dad?"

"He's helping the pool man…. with something. Would you like me to call him?"

"No, that's okay. I'll go find him myself. Stay here - I'll be back in a minute."

Oliver was surprised and dismayed to see her. She had invaded his home before, and that had been a disaster.

She'd have to do some fast talking to get his trust back. But he'd forgotten how exquisitely desirable she was, now especially since her drenched clothing was clinging so provocatively.

He quickly dismissed the pool man, then wiped his hands on a towel, passing it to Connie. She dried her face and rubbed her hair.

"Hello Connie. Something you need?"

His expression held no trace of warmth. Fear made Connie more forthright than perhaps she'd intended.

"I want to come back. I made a stupid mistake and I regret it. I'm sorry."

"And what happens next time Gil crooks his little finger?"

Connie felt insulted. Gil had never crooked his little finger at her. It was just a thing he would never think of doing.

"We've both agreed, face to face, that we need to separate - permanently."

Slow tears began to run down her cheeks and she wiped them angrily away.

"What you did was cruel and unfair," said Oliver. "You said repeatedly that you loved me then as soon as I needed you, you were gone. It isn't an exaggeration to say you broke my heart, but even worse, you made my little boy so unhappy. I won't let you do that again. If you come back you have to swear it's for good, and you won't run out on us again the next time things get awkward."

Not usually so thoughtful of Simm's feelings, Connie thought.

Oliver paused and pulled her to him. He could feel the

192

rain from her clothes soaking through his chinos and shirt. She rested her head on his shoulder and snuggled closer. He drew a steadying breath.

"Then there's your own children to consider. What will happen to them? You'll have to sort all this out with Gil."

"Could Jacob and Mylo live with us? I think Simm would like it, but Deborah would absolutely hate it. Do you think she would come round?"

"Seriously? No I don't, at least not without a great deal of effort on your part. It'll be a long, slow up-hill slog with Deborah. Can you be patient with her?"

"We – I – just have to accept that some things won't come easy." This was terrifying!

"We're all, including Gil and Rachel, going to have a lot of growing up to do to make this work, Connie. I won't ask you for any kind of undertaking now. I think you should go home and think about what you want to do and how. Then we can talk about it seriously and try to work out a plan of action."

It was hard but at least he hadn't turned her away. She could figure this out. She turned her head and gazed up into his eyes. Oliver had no resistance when she looked at him like that. He turned away while he still could.

Simm was standing in the center of the foyer. A curved oak stair-rail led to an upper floor, and a huge elaborate crystal chandelier hung through two stories from the high ceiling.

He was a stoic child, mature for his age. Naturally tanned from his love of outdoor living, and with his father's fine blonde hair, he was a real child of California. He swam and played tennis with the skill of an adult. No surfer yet, his father had nevertheless bought him a board of his own, and he practiced in the shallows most weekends. Connie loved him.

Deborah was another matter. a natural white blonde with her father's arresting sapphire eyes.

She blamed Oliver, and more particularly Connie for her mother's leaving - her mouth would twist with distain at the mere sight of her. Was this fixable? Connie doubted it.

After much discussion, Oliver and Connie decided the only way forward was to contact Gil and Rachel and arrange a meeting to thrash things out. Both regarded the prospect with horror.

They called Rachel first.

"She could blow either way," said Oliver. "Either she'd ignore what I say totally or have a fit of hysterics."

Oliver called her and Rachel could be heard loudly sobbing on the other end of the line.

He motioned Connie to quickly take Simm away. The boy had been standing in the doorway, seriously attentive when she put her arm around him and led him away. The noise from the phone abruptly stopped and Connie turned.

"Where's Deborah?" she mouthed over Simeon's head, to Oliver who was standing with his hand over the receiver.

"Oh, damn! She's with Rachel's sister. Let me finish here, and I'll call Ella. See if she can keep her occupied for a few hours."

Connie took Simeon out. They walked by the sea and ate pizza out of a box. All the time, the question of what she was going to say to Gil was pounding in her brain. She'd called Oliver within the hour.

He told her the conversation had been harrowing, but Rachel had agreed to a meeting.

Now it was Connie's turn to tackle Gil.

She drove Simm back home.

"You have to promise me you won't see him – he can play you like a tin whistle. Swear it'll just be a phone call," said a worried Oliver.

"I promise. I'll call him from a booth - that way he won't be able to find me. I hope and pray it's not a long conversation. Rachel's the picture of calm and composure compared to Gil when he's upset."

Connie drove round until she found a public phone booth, then called home. No reply. So she tried Lizbeth. He wasn't there, and Lizbeth had no idea where he might be. Connie didn't dare call Nancy. So lastly she called Jamie. Gil answered.

Gil was alone when the phone rang. He'd been sitting on the decking gazing out morosely across the ocean. He'd no idea where Jamie was.

He didn't much care – right that minute, he didn't much care about anything. He picked up a beer bottle from the ground near his lounger and took a good long swig. It was his sixth since arriving. He finished off the bottle and picked up another from the cooler. The worst of it was, he didn't feel even remotely drunk.

"Yeah?" he asked, without the slightest interest.

"Gil?" He ricocheted to his feet. Oh, shit!

"Connie, where are you?"

"I'm with Oliver. We've had a long discussion and come

to the conclusion, if you and Rachel are agreeable the four of us – you, me, Oliver and Rachel - should sit down together and decide where we go from here."

"Who's Rachel?" asked Gil. Connie rolled her eyes.

"You know damn well Rachel is Oliver's wife. If ever in your life you loved me Gil, you have to be helpful, or there's going to be one almighty mess before we're through."

The last thing Gil felt was helpful, but he loved Connie and always had, from the time on the Giordano's doorstep when he first set eyes on her. That was never going to change.

"Okay, okay. So what happens now?"

"Our marriages are done – yours and mine for sure – you know that. We've already discussed it, and Oliver's spoken to Rachel now too. She is not about to be helpful. She had a fit over the phone when Oliver broached the subject."

"Well, what did you expect her to do? Put out the flags?"

"No, of course not. Don't be ridiculous."

"I didn't think I was being ridiculous."

Connie bit her tongue in irritation. He was being obtuse.

"Oliver and I wanted to suggest a meeting on neutral ground – your choice – to thrash things out and figure where we go from here. But I want to be clear with you, this is not going away, and it will be resolved."

Gil hated the 'Oliver and I' part. It was the bare truth that he was now excluded from Connie's life. He didn't know if he could survive that.

Gil didn't feel he had anything useful to add. His pride was in tatters, but it was still there. The small part of his marriage that was left was about to disappear down the drain. He'd be alone; alone with Ed, with his father; alone with a drug-addled brother. And alone in his own solitary life. No Connie to come home to and cuddle when he was feeling small. No playing 'boys' with his sons. None of a thousand little, inconsequential things which make up a happy marriage. All gone. How? Why? But he couldn't claim he didn't know the answers.

He had sold his soul to music before he'd left childhood. The roar of the audience when he came on stage took away the self-doubt he carried with him continually, and made him glow with love, received and returned. He was a very good musician gifted with an exceptionally beautiful voice, but he was no Jamie. Jamie was a genius, Jamie had had no other thought but music either until he'd discovered cocaine - Jamie, beautiful and willful, with his flowing hair and tanned skin, who could take any woman he wanted simply by smiling at her. How could Gil compare with that? So, he was just little Gil, the baby brother, who did what he could. Here too, he would do what he could; he would do what he could for Connie for the last time. So he said:

"Give me some time to think and I'll call you. I'd rather not chat about it - I have no heart for that. I promise I'll try to give you what you want."

So, both Oliver and Connie were left in limbo, dependent on the people they had hurt most to make the decisions. No timeline. Just waiting.

Chapter Twenty-nine

Gil needed to be alone, so he packed a bag and hopped the first flight back to Denver. He'd go to Anasazi to try and get what was happening into perspective. Then he'd call Connie.

The plane arrived at 12.45am, so by the time Gil had cleared the airport it was nearly two. He decided to stay in Denver overnight and resume his journey the following day.

Checking into the Westin Hotel, and despite thinking he wouldn't be able to close his eyes, he was deeply asleep within minutes.

The following morning, he showered changed and took breakfast in the restaurant. He was hungry. He was always hungry when he was depressed. Perhaps if he wasn't so depressed, and so often, he wouldn't have such a problem with his weight.

He was just wading into his ham and eggs when he felt a tap on his shoulder and turned.

"I thought it was you! What a co-incidence - again!"

"Giulia? Jeez, what are you doing here at...," he checked his watch, "eight-ten a.m?"

"Come to meet Larry and Diana. They're staying for a few days."

"Staying where?"

She laughed, and her eyes crinkled at the corners. She was such a breath of fresh air after the past 24 hours.

"I didn't know you had a home so far from Los Angeles."

"Well, I do now. Sort of. I was twenty-one in December

– of course you know when my birthday is – and Pops decided it was time I was independent and learned to be a businesswoman."

She giggled at the sheer stupidity of such a notion.

"So, he bought me an apartment building in Denver, so I got to...hmm...practice a bit."

"Here, sit down and have some coffee." – he waved the waiter over – "Want something to eat?"

She shook her head to the food. Gil ordered a large cafetiere and sat back. Once the waiter had gone, she sipped at her coffee and said:

"I'm meeting Larry and Diana off the LA flight. Better to meet here than in the airport, don't you think? They're helping me with the interior decoration. I'm amazed to say Larry is as good as Diana. I've grown up thinking my brothers are useless, so it comes as a shock that he actually has an aptitude. So that's me! What are you doing here?"

There was a tense silence.

"I haven't said the wrong thing again, have I?" asked Giulia, biting her lip.

Gil sighed and tapped the coffee spoon nervously against his cup. How did he broach this? The chances of a reconciliation were zero. If he admitted it out loud to Giulia, he'd have to believe it himself. He'd been purposely blocking it from his mind. At least he could be reasonably confident Giulia'd be sympathetic. He didn't doubt she'd see him as an abject failure, but she would believe he'd at least tried. So, he gritted his teeth and looked her straight in the face.

"We are separating, Connie and I. I'm meeting with her, her boyfriend and his soon-to-be ex-wife so we can sort out the details when I get back home."

That he felt his chest was caving in must have shown in his face, because Giulia grabbed his hand and held tight to it, although he tried to pull away. He tried again. She held tighter and her face filled with concern. She drew him closer and whispered:

"I am so sorry, Gil. I know how much you have always loved her. But you have other people who love you too. You must know you are not alone. You will never be."

"You're wrong," he said simply. "She is the only one – only one - who ever loved me unconditionally, never wanted anything in return. Now she's gone, and my sons with her, there's nothing left."

Giulia was distressed that he had so misconstrued her meaning. He really didn't see her at all.

His hand in hers lay still and clammy. Giulia laid her palm softly against his cheek, turning him to face her.

"Please promise me if you can't cope you will call me. I can listen when you need to talk if nothing else."

She tucked a business card into his shirt pocket.

"One of Pop's better ideas - to go with the apartment block."

He placed his own hand over hers, momentarily closed his eyes and nodded, although he couldn't imagine discussing with anyone else what he felt for his wife. No-one could even begin to understand.

"You're driving up to Anasazi, I take it," said Giulia changing the subject. She pulled her tote bag from the floor at her side, so the waiter could clear their table.

As she started to straighten in her seat, and Gil was about to reply, Giulia's elbow caught the edge of the waiter's tray and in trying not to drop it, he tripped. Crockery and silverware flew in the air, then scattered all over the floor.

Giulia leapt to her feet to try and help, and as she reached out to steady him, she knocked into him instead, and the cold remains of his breakfast landed in Gil's lap. He, in turn, leapt to his feet and attempted to brush off the mess with a napkin. The poor waiter started to apologize profusely, but Gil cut him off.

"Shit - are you alright?" he asked, helping the waiter to his feet. "You haven't hurt yourself, have you? Are you okay, Giulia?"

Giulia nodded, her face crimson with embarrassment.

The waiter's mouth dropped open with surprise and trepidation:

"But sir, it was all my fault. Look at you! Gil started to laugh.

"Oh, c'mon. It was just an accident, but I will go and change. You're sure you're okay?"

The waiter knelt to clear up the mess on the floor.

Gil left Giulia to explain the situation to the manager and went and changed out of his soiled clothes.

Giulia watched his retreating figure and shuddered. She always seemed to make an idiot of herself in front of Gil.

She tried so hard to play the sophisticated lady. and somehow always ended up looking like the child he took her for.

She was about to stamp her foot in fury at her stupidity, when she realized the waiter was standing by with a broom and asking her if she would mind moving to another table next to the windows, from where she had a clear view of the aircraft taking off and landing.

Gil was longer than he expected getting back. He'd been accosted by a dozen autograph hunters, sweet giggly girls with pink faces, in the hotel lobby. By the time he did get back, Giulia was nowhere to be seen. He tried to locate her but couldn't see her anywhere. Then he recognized the waiter who had had such an awful morning and called him over.

"Do you remember the lady I was with before the…," he grinned broadly – "disaster? Is that the right word?"

"I reseated her over there by the window sir, so I could finish clearing away, and where she could be more comfortable."

He turned, indicating the seat, but Giulia wasn't there.

Gil was worried she was missing. This was a busy airport and people were coming and going all the time. Giulia was very fond of jewelry and had been wearing quite a quantity of gold. It would have been easy to believe she could have been abducted and robbed. There was no chance she could fight off an assailant.

He sent the waiter for the manager who, once the problem had been explained, directed his staff to the exits to try and locate someone who might have seen her.

Meanwhile, Giulia finished washing her hands in the ladies' room and sponging off some egg from the knee of her jeans. Then, singing one of her father's favorite songs, perhaps a little more loudly than was ladylike, she returned to the restaurant. She was amazed to find the whole place, peaceful and orderly when she had left, completely upside-down with waiters and serving staff running in every direction.

She looked around for Gil. He was standing in the middle of the mayhem looking bemused.

"What's happened?" she asked looking about her fearfully. "Has someone been hurt? Can I do anything to help?"

It was at that very moment that Larry and Diana made an appearance.

"Wow, Gil. You sure know how to make an impression. What did you do to these poor guys? You clearly scared the crap out of them to get them to react like that," said Larry.

Gil considered, trying to make sense of the panic before him, then he began to grin. For the first time in an age, he actually felt like laughing.

"Ask your sister," Gil chortled. Giulia looked blank.

"All I did was bang into a waiter." she said in confusion. "Why?"

By this time Gil and Larry were convulsed with laughter. Diana frowned at Gil and her husband and went to call off the hue and cry.

Giulia stood all alone, tears brimming.

"What did I do? Did I cause all this?"

Her gesture encompassed the whole restaurant.

"You did, Gee. You sure did. You coming with us, Gil?"

"Nope, on my way to Anasazi before I bumped into Calamity Jane here," He looked at his watch and said:

"Sorry, got to shoot. I have a hire car to collect, and I need to get on the road. See you soon!"

He hugged Giulia to him and smiled at her indulgently. As he walked away, Giulia scowled - she'd actually excelled herself this time.

"He seems like a good guy," said Diana, watching him

go.

"One of the best," agreed Larry, taking her arm. "C'mon, my sweet, time for my sister to cook us breakfast."

He pulled her towards the exit and Giulia followed, wishing she was dead.

Chapter Thirty

Gil usually enjoyed the drive to Anasazi. Beautiful mountains loomed above, and icy snow-melt rills ran alongside the paved roads. Mountain flowers were scattered along the roadsides, and the sun was dazzling, striking sparks from the water. Today was no exception although Gil's good mood faded as the journey progressed.

He pulled into the compound and drove the car to a standstill.

"Hey, man," He was greeted by Dave Blane, a sideman from way back. "How've you been - you're looking good."

Gil snorted.

"I never looked worse in my life!"

"Well, I didn't want to draw attention to the fact you look like shit. But now you come to mention it......"

They walked, laughing, into the studio complex and were greeted by Jeff.

"Good to see you, man. Will you be staying a while? The Snowline cabin is available if you want to use it. I'll get one of the girls to make up the bed and light a fire. Gil smiled his thanks.

They had a short jam session with Jeff on bass and Dave on drums – which wasn't very successful, as Dave's instrument of choice was keyboards, but Gil got to play the improvised music he loved, and never got the chance to do with the band. It distracted him for a while.

Later, he walked to the cabin and dropped his bag on the bed. Now he was alone, his thoughts crowded in on him, and what had been a bright and beautiful day, began to turn sour. He pulled a rattan cushioned chair up to the fireside and stared morosely into the flames.

The end. It was the end. No new beginnings for himself and Connie. Over. The logs shifted and spat a cinder onto the hearth rug. Gil tossed it back into the flames.

He threw his bag on the floor and lay on his back on the bed, staring at the stripped-pine ceiling. There was nothing for him to do but agree to the meeting. It was time to end all this gloom. Shit, it was going to be awful.

He hadn't met Rachel. He just hoped he could rely on her to bring some sanity to the discussion, but since she had lost her temper when the idea was first mooted, he somehow doubted it. If it was left to himself, Connie and Oliver it was going to be disastrous. They would be a solid wall of opposition, and he wasn't sure what to do about that.

He put a guard round the fire, pulled on a parka and walked out into the cold night air. He was desperately miserable.

Stars studded the midnight blue and the pale contours of nearby mountain peaks rose to the sky. Gil took the path he'd followed with Jamie and crunched through brittle snow until it was to his knees. Then he turned, and sitting on a nearby rock, watched the lights below twinkling through the crystal night. He remembered a story Jeff had once told him about the studio's name, Anasazi. It was the name of a tribe of Indians who, according to tradition, just vanished into thin air. Perhaps they had frozen to death and disappeared beneath the snow.

Gil tucked his gloved hands under his arms for warmth. But the cold was beginning to penetrate through his parka and his cheeks and nose were numb. He shivered and began to feel as he had beneath the waters of the swimming pool.

They would look for him in the morning, and find him frozen to this rock, all his problems solved, all his pain gone.

Then he thought of Jeff and Dave and the people he called friends who would have to carry his body down the mountain side, and reluctantly rose and walked back to the cabin.

This was not the way out. He would have to face this. He'd call Connie in the morning and agree to the meeting and suggest Rick's as a venue. Then they could all get hammered if it got too much. The thought of Connie and Oliver propping each other up the worse for drink made him smile grimly. Yes, he'd call Connie in the morning.

The girl from Kentucky brought Gil his morning meal.

After she'd gone, he ate his cooked breakfast with relish and drank three cups of coffee. All the time, his attention kept returning to the telephone on the table by the door. Sooner or later, he was going to have to pick up the receiver.

Gil paced backwards and forwards. Then stopped in front of the telephone. He put his hand out and touched it, then drew back. Finally, steeling himself he lifted the receiver and stood listening to the tone for a few moments, before dialing his home number.

Jacob answered which took him aback. He had been so focused on Connie he hadn't considered the boys. Par for the course he supposed Connie would say.

"Hi, Jake. Is Mommy there please? Tell her Daddy would like a word with her."

"Sure. Ma! There's Pa on the phone for you!" Jacob bellowed.

"Don't call me that!" said an equally strident voice. "Hello, Gil."

She'd become so cold. He took a painful breath. He'd try once more, then he'd know he'd done all he could.

"Are you set on this, Connie? Have you thought of the implications with the kids and our families? About all the legal problems and bitterness?"

He couldn't see Connie's face, but he could picture her expression.

"Those are things we have to talk about'" she replied, tersely. "And not over the phone."

"In that case…," he had to take a couple of deep breaths to keep his composure. "I suggest all four of us meet at Ricks on Monday afternoon. They have a back room they hire out – we had one of our first gigs there as kids. I'll call them."

"I'm not going there, Gil, if you're going to get drunk. I'm just not."

"You have my word."

"Okay. I'll get Oliver to contact Rachel and see you two o'clock. If there's any change, I'll call you. Where will you be?"

"I'm at Anasazi at the moment but I can't stay after tomorrow. We'll be leaving next week, and we have rehearsals until this Friday, then studio work after. I'll stay at Mom's. You'll be able to get me there in the evening until I've to leave – probably Wednesday."

"You don't say! I'm amazed. Let's hope you can fit a couple of hours in your busy schedule to figure out four people's future. Oh, and the kids – that makes eight!

Then again there's our parents – that's twelve. You really are a first-rate son-of-a-bitch Gil. You care about no-one but yourself and your goddam career."

Gil returned the receiver to its cradle. He was distressed and confused by how much he'd hurt her over the years to make her say these things to him. He'd never meant to – never. He had loved her from the day they'd met.

After, the grief came in wave after wave until he was completely spent.

He slept until early evening, then washed his face in cold water. Although his eyes were still red, the puffiness was mostly gone from his face.

He thought about walking up the mountain again, but decided given his present state of mind, it might be safer to be with people for a while.

He stuck his hands in his pockets and wandered down to the complex below.

The first person he saw was David Elliot.

"Hey Gil - bad cold? Gee, too bad."

This was the second time he'd had this conversation Gil realized with annoyance.

"Touch of 'flu I think – started a few days back. I must have picked it up from one of the kids..."

"Coming for something to eat?" asked Davy. "There's the usual gang who never seem to leave," he chuckled. "Jeff must pay them to make the place look busy. Oh, and Harry's here....and Mickey Dalton's come with a couple of the other guys from Savannah. So, you'll appreciate it's party time!"

Gil shuddered. All he wanted to do was gulp down a burger, flee and hibernate for a year. But perhaps he might feel better for a few beers with the guys. He

209

guessed there'd be a bit more than beer on the go, but he could always leave before they got round to the heavy stuff.

He got an enthusiastic welcome. They played and sang with the same passion and liked to talk guitar just like he did. After they'd eaten, they all assembled outside at the wooden benches, talking about mutual acquaintances and telling stories that made them howl with laughter.

By ten o'clock there really was a party going on. Harry fell off the table and cracked his head which quietened things down for a few minutes. But after that, with glasses kept full by Jeff's waitresses, things livened up. Mickey Dalton got so drunk they'd to carry him back to his cabin. He could be heard singing all the way up the road.

Gil's good sense prevailed, and he headed back to his cabin before any one broke out the coke.

Gil was drunk. He'd been drunker. But he was definitely swaying, because he had to keep touching the furniture to keep his balance. He showered unsteadily and clambered naked into bed. The pillows felt so soft that he cuddled down into them and closed his eyes. Just let the world let me be, he thought as he dragged the bedclothes up over his head.

He was unprepared, therefore, for a crash as the door flew open, nearly taking it off its hinges. A blast of freezing mountain air blew sparks from the dying fire. Gil sat bolt upright in bed. What the fuck….

Grinning inanely were Mickey Dalton and Geordie Stanton, propping up either door jamb.

"Go out or come in, but shut the god-damn door," Gil said. "You're letting all the heat out. And shut up –

you'll have the whole village in here."

Mickey swigged the dregs from a beer bottle and tossed it into the log basket next to the fire.

"Hey Gil, got some blow?" said Geordie, swaying unsteadily beside him..

"No, I don't. Fuck off."

Geordie poked around in his jacket breast pocket and pulled out a little bag of white pills.

He grinned as if he'd just pulled a rabbit from a hat.

Swinging it in Gil's face he chortled:

"Wow, Gil baby. Look what I found. Wanna share?"

Gil went to grab the door handle to throw them out, but Mickey was already in the dinette looking for glasses.

"Ah! This'll do just fine," and he grabbed the bag from Geordie's hand and began crushing the pills on the worktop with the bottom of the glass, singing to himself.

"Your cabin, you first."

"No, no, no NO! Get out of here. Go on – git!"

Mickey quickly snorted the coke and disappeared grunting, out of the cabin dragging Geordie with him. Gil, still naked, banged the door shut behind them.

He ran his cupped hands down his face and shook his head. Fuck, that had been close. All those weeks getting clean…. he couldn't bear the thought. But he couldn't resist sucking his finger, soaking up the few grains left on the bottom of the glass and putting it on his tongue where it tingled pleasantly. Damn – it would have been such a relief. But Connie had warned him off getting drunk. If he turned up stoned at Rick's he'd never see his kids again.

There would be no more sleep that night. Wrapped in the bed-quilt, he spent it drinking coffee, smoking cigarettes and fighting demons until at four a.m. he could take no more. He dressed and threw his belongings in his bag, put a $20 bill under an overflowing ashtray on the coffee table and left.

Chapter Thirty-one

The first flight home was nine a.m., so he had an hour to kill until he needed to check in. He passed his time in the bar. Once back in LA he went straight to his mother's house.

Nancy fed him and put him to bed. Your child was still your child, even when a troubled man. He slept the clock round, then awoke to another ample meal. She asked him for no explanation, but she had been so good over the past few weeks, he felt he owed her something.

"Mom, things are bad at the moment and likely to get worse. Please let me explain when it's all over. I don't want to go through it twice."

Nancy said nothing, just held him. How could she not know what was going on? But then Gil hadn't been there when Connie had left the kids.

"I have to see Mr. Downey tomorrow about tax and the IRS. I'm long overdue at rehearsals, too. They're going to rake me over the coals for that, which is something I could do without. Then Monday, I have an afternoon meeting."

It was pointless to elaborate.

He buried his head in her shoulder so grateful for her love in that moment that he couldn't speak.

The door banged open and Monty strode in.

"Nancy – I need you to come and cook me a ...." He stopped in mid-sentence and his face took on that mean look. Nancy's own was frozen in a mask of trepidation. Oh, the shit was going to hit the fan here!

"Get out, Gil. Your mom and I have things to discuss."

"Sorry Pops. Nope. I'm staying for a few days."

"You'll do as you're goddam told. Fuck off! You can always be relied on to mollycoddle the little bastards, Nancy? Go to hell, Gil!"

Gil strode across the room and picked his father up by the lapels. They were much of a height, but his fury meant that Monty's feet left the ground.

"Don't you talk to my mother like that! I've listened to your bullshit for over thirty years. No more...no more!"

Monty's spectacles slid sideways off his nose and landed on the floor. It was all Gil could do not the stamp on them.

"Now, you fuck off! Git before I really lose it!" he yelled.

Monty picked up his glasses and made for the door in a hurry. This time he closed it quietly.

"I'm sorry, Mom. I shouldn't have done that," Gil said. But Nancy was grinning all over her face.

"Oh, thank you – thank you. That's the most fun I've had with your father in years."

Gil smiled, shame faced.

"Now I owe him an apology. And I hate owing him anything."

"You certainly do not. Let him stew," said Nancy, wagging her finger in Gil's face.

He rubbed his forehead and frowned.

"I have the mother and father of all headaches Mom. I'll go sit in the garden for a while."

"Yes, you go dear. I'll bring you out some coffee. You look as if you need some quiet time."

Nancy watched him from the window, sitting in a garden chair with his head in his hands. There was nothing she could do.

The meeting with the accountant should have been routine but went on an hour longer than planned, just silly niggling things, but it made Gil late for the rehearsal session.

Nobody was pleased. John, patient as a rule, was upset as he had arranged to take his kids to a ball game which would now be at half-time. Ed was his usual unpleasant self.

"You Robsons are not worth my time. You clearly have no fricking clue what you're doing. You're always late, usually because you're either wasted or stoned. Look at the state of you!"

Gil looked down. He was very overweight. He'd fastened his shirt wrong, and his belly was poking out between the buttons. His beard hadn't been properly trimmed in weeks. He did look a train-wreck. He couldn't bring himself to care. He still had the remains of his headache.

"I've no time or inclination for your bullshit today, Ed. If you can't be helpful, fuck off.."

"Just so's you understand when it comes to carving up the profits, you all owe me big time. I do as much as the rest of you put together."

Gil couldn't believe what he was hearing. This was from Ed. The laziest, most self-indulgent, selfish person he had ever come across in his life. He could never even get him to rehearsals for major gigs, where they earned thousands of dollars. For the second time that day he came close to violence.

215

And then there was the looming meeting, the thought of which was weighing on his shoulders, heavier and heavier until he felt his spine would snap under the weight.

He couldn't begin to imagine what was going to happen at Rick's, only that it wouldn't be good. Whichever way it went, Connie was lost to him forever, and probably his boys with her. Oliver, under other circumstances might have been an okay guy, but try as he might, Gil couldn't view him as anything but the enemy. His head told him this was wrong, but that he was sharing a bed with his wife…. well, he just wouldn't think of that. The meeting might end quicker than anyone imagined if he did.

Chapter Thirty-two

Monday morning arrived, and with it a sense of impending doom. The day before, he'd thought about accompanying Nancy to church, but he couldn't abide the idea of the polite chatter on the steps afterwards.

Gil sat in the garden again, drank half a bottle of bourbon and smoked a pack of Marlboro. He couldn't turn up stinking of whisky, so he took a cold shower to sober up and then did his best to trim his beard. His hands shook so much he kept dropping the scissors in the sink.

He only had the clothes he'd brought from Colorado, so he sorted out a pair of jeans and his cleanest shirt, creased from packing. He put it on anyway.

It was still only eleven thirty. He'd another two and a half hours to go and the drive to downtown LA was no more than forty-five minutes in bad traffic.

By twelve-thirty Gil could stand the inactivity no longer. He jumped in his car and drove to Rick's. But it was still only one-thirty, so he went around the block a couple of times until the dash clock read one-forty-seven. That would do.

There was only one other car in the lot and that was a Porsche. He and Connie had matching Aston Martins he'd bought on a recent England tour, and he'd had shipped over, his forest green and hers white. Unless she'd bought it since, it wasn't hers.

Gil pressed the button to close his car's hood, locked the door and stood for a moment or two wishing the next couple of hours were over. Then there was nothing for it but to walk into the bar.

"Hello, Pete. Anyone asked for me?" he said with forced

217

cheerfulness to the barman.

"Hey Gil. Yep, there's a pretty lady with dark hair and a guy with her. They're in the back like you said. Do you want me to get them drinks?"

"No thanks. They might want something later, though."

"What can I get you?" It was a foregone conclusion as far as Pete was concerned, that Gil would want a good stiff drink. He looked as if he was about to drop.

"Nothing just yet. I may get back to you on that one as well."

A lady walked through the door. She was a little older than Gil perhaps, and rather frail-looking with blue eyes and light-brown hair. Gil walked over and asked if her name was Rachel Maxwell and introduced himself. She put a delicate hand on his arm.

"I think you and I are going to find this very difficult. But perhaps it's better to have everything out in the open." She didn't sound at all like the wilting flower Connie had described.

Gil didn't read this in quite the same way. There was going to be nothing 'better' about this as far as he could see. There was only worse, infinitely worse. He drew himself up and wished fervently he was either drunk out of his head or stoned to oblivion. He took Rachel by the arm and led her towards the back door, nodding at Pete as he passed.

The swing doors had blacked-out windows, so Connie and Oliver didn't see them coming. They were standing looking down at the street, his arm was casually draped around her, and her head was tipped back on his shoulder. They looked right together. It was devastating.

The expression on Rachel's face stiffened and she moved a few feet away from Gil.

There were some baize-covered tables piled up next to a small stage at the far side of the room. Beside them, half a dozen chairs were stacked.

Oliver lifted down one of the tables and a chair for each of them. Gil went to fetch an ashtray from the bar. Finally, they could delay the moment no longer.

"Who's going to start?" asked Gil as he lit his first cigarette of many. They all looked at each other.

Oliver took the lead.

"The prospect of divorce has to be faced sooner or later. This meeting is to see if there is anything at all to be salvaged from the situation. Clearly things need to alter but..."

"Oh, come on," said Gil. "Let's get to the nitty-gritty. We'll be here forever unless someone makes a useful commitment."

"I want a divorce," said Rachel simply. Gil quickly lost the impression there was anything frail about her at all. Everyone turned and looked at her in surprise.

"What? That's what we're here for, isn't it? We can talk round and round in circles, but it won't change the fact that we are two couples who don't want to be with each other anymore. From there we have to consider what to do about property and children and any other matters we have to work out between us."

It all sounded so cold when put like that.

Gil looked at Connie, trying to gage her reaction, but she half-turned away from him and looked up at Oliver.

Rachel started again. For such a delicate looking lady, she sure had guts, thought Gil.

"I don't mind using the word 'divorce' since that's what I came here for. Oliver and I have been living separate lives for the best part of a year. I really can't see that it's possible we pick up and start again. While I respect him, I don't love him and I'm sure he feels the same," she looked at him pointedly.

"A fair summing up, I guess. Yes, I can go with that. So that takes care of our intentions at least."

Connie was next in turn round the table. For the first time, she looked at Gil, and spoke directly to him, as if there were only the two of them alone in the room.

"We have to do this, Gil. I'll love you always, but I can't live with you. The isolation would kill me."

There was such caring in her voice. Oliver shifted in his seat.

Gil reached out towards her, then his hands faltered in mid-air as he tried to find a response. He didn't have one.

"Please say something, Gil. Anything. We have to move on from here. Will you at least agree to a separation? A place to start?"

He was completely numb, but he managed to nod, and the room came rushing back into focus so fast that he almost fell off his chair. Although he knew it was useless, he said:

"Connie.... Connie." He shook his head to clear it. "How will I ever…"

He stood abruptly and walked to the window, turning his back on the others in the room. They saw him square his shoulders and he turned, new steel in his voice.

"So," he said. "We've all agreed a separation is the right way forward for all…," he paused, "all four of us. Now what?"

"I guess we find attorneys," said the practical Rachel.

"Before we commit ourselves to that, there a few obvious matters we need to mention," said Oliver. "The first and most important is all four children. I'm not suggesting we come to any conclusions today - that is perhaps best handled by lawyers in any case - but we can arrange another meeting if everyone is in agreement, to compare notes."

Gil was scandalized.

"You are talking about my boys as if they were a commodity. You can't do that."

For the first time, Oliver looked at him with sympathy.

"In a sense they are. For the time being at least. And what happens to them is likely to be the worst bone of contention. All four of us are going to claim custody. Does anyone know if kids get a say in California? It could have a major bearing on how we proceed."

No-one did.

Oliver took a pen and notebook from his inside jacket pocket and began to make notes.

"I take it we all have access to legal advice?" He looked around the table at each person in turn. Connie said:

"I'll have to look for someone new. Gil and I have always used the same company."

"Mine's a very good guy. I'll call for an appointment tomorrow," said Oliver.

Everything was happening too fast for Giltears r to take in. He actually was saying goodbye, perhaps for the last time, to the wife he had known for ten years. For ten years she had been his rock. Without her to come home to, what would he do? Why bother coming home at all?

Why the hell had he been so stupid? Why hadn't he seen what he was doing to her? He knew he'd believed she'd left over and over before, but in his heart of hearts he'd always thought there might be another chance. He was always distracted, always trying to keep everything together against all the odds for everyone but Connie.

"Are we done here?" he snapped. "It hardly seemed worth the effort. All we've agreed is we want to go our separate ways, some of us will lose our kids and we need attorneys to help us do it. I could have told you that without any kind of meeting."

Connie reached out her hand. Then dropped it. She no longer had the right to comfort him. That was gone forever.

The day had turned sweltering. The heat had softened the tarmac in the parking lot and wilted the few blades of grass struggling through the sandy soil next to a split rail fence.

Gil jumped in his car and took off down the Boulevard, without looking back.

He drove and drove until the fuel gage on his dash began to blink red, then he pulled into a gas station. While the tank was being filled, he bought a bottle of bourbon from the garage store and stashed it under the passenger seat. He paid the man, who looked at him with amazement as he swerved out of the forecourt. He'd left him a $100 tip.

Chapter Thirty-three

Although Gil had driven off some of his despondency, he still felt haunted by the day's happenings.

He pulled into a look-out point on the side of the road. Palm-studded coastline spread on both sides as far as the eye could see. Peacock-colored sea below with a gentle lace of surf, surged back and forth along a deserted beach. It should have been peaceful, a balm to his aching soul, but it wasn't. The scene was as sterile as an endless desert.

He lifted the bottle of bourbon and took a long, long drink. Then he wiped the neck of the bottle and drank again. If ever he needed cocaine, it was now. He drank again.

The sun was scorching, and he could feel it burning the skin on his forehead and cheeks. He drank more whisky then got out of the car and leaned against the rail, gazing listlessly at the bottle swinging from his right hand. He ought to throw it into the sea below. He didn't. He took another swig.

Gradually the alcohol began to take effect, but instead of allaying the pain, it added to his depression.

He tipped the last of the whisky down his throat and dropping the bottle over the rail, he watched it bounce and jerk down the cliff face to shatter on the stones below. He held tightly to a post and put his foot on the rail fully intending to follow the bottle down, but the impetus threw him off balance and he fell backwards onto the paving stones, cracking his head. He felt the pain from far away, then black and blessed oblivion.

Gil came to ten minutes later to the sound of his car engine revving loudly. He turned his head slowly, then

223

shut his eyes again against the searing pain in his head, and the merciless sun. His car was being backed out of the parking spot. He tried to sit up and shout but, still drunk and groggy from the blow, he couldn't do more than raise his head a few inches. His body refused to obey him. He lifted a shaky hand and felt the back of his head. It came away wet with blood, and he passed out again.

It must have been quite some time later when he came to. This time he was looking into the face of a middle-aged man who was shaking his shoulder and asking if he was all right. Dumb question but he appreciated the thought. He did his best to sit up, but his head was spinning and his speech, when he finally managed to talk, was incoherent. The unknown man took off his t-shirt, rolled it up and carefully slipped it under Gil's neck.

"Lay still. I've called an ambulance. Do you have a car? How did you get here?"

Again Gil tried to speak, again more babble.

"Shh, keep calm. Help will be along soon."

As he spoke an ambulance pulled up and a paramedic ran over carrying his medical bag. He shone a light in Gil's eyes, which did nothing at all for his headache, took his pulse and felt all over for broken bones.

"He's taken a blow to the back of his head," said the stranger. "He's been groggy like this since I came."

The stranger handed the paramedic a business card and excused himself.

The drive to the hospital, after the alcohol and the fall, was disorientating and Gil gagged more than once.

Apart from the bang on the head which had given him a severe concussion and consequent bruising to his face, he appeared to have sustained no further injuries. The hospital staff had searched him for clues as to his identity, but all they found was a business card with a Colorado number tucked into his shirt pocket.

As he had been put into deep sedation because of his head wound, they had no other clue as to the identity of their 'John Doe.' He didn't appear to have transport and as he was brought in just in a shirt and jeans, he had no pocketbook or driver's license to prove who he was.

The first time the hospital secretary called the number on the card there was no reply. The second time, a little under an hour later, the phone was answered by a man. The receptionist said:

"Hello, this is the City Hospital in San Diego. An individual has been admitted who has no means of identification other than a card bearing the name of a Giulia Giordano, a Denver address and this number. We need to verify his identity so we can pass on details to the police to inform his family. He was found in the middle of nowhere on the Pacific Coast Highway."

"Sure, go ahead – Giulia's my sister," said Larry Giordano, growing more concerned by the minute. Who the hell could it be? Giulia didn't know anyone from San Diego.... did she?

The impersonal voice on the other end of the line continued.

"The man is twenty-five to thirty-five, five feet ten inches tall, shoulder length brown hair and a heavy beard. He has grey eyes. He is of fair complexion and stocky build."

"That sounds like Gil Robson," said Larry. "He usually drives a dark green, right-hand drive Aston Martin."

"I'm sorry sir. He had no vehicle when found."

Giulia tugged Larry by the arm.

"What's that about Gil?"

Larry asked the lady from the hospital to hold the line and placed a hand over the receiver to explain.

"The hospital in San Diego is trying to identify a man brought to them after an accident. He appears to have had your business card. That's his only ID."

"Is he badly injured?" demanded Giulia, swinging on Larry's telephone arm. He shook her off.

"Is he badly hurt? We need to get there. How do we get there from here? How long will it take? Put the phone down, Larry. I'll call the airport. No, I'll call Poppa. Shall I call Poppa? Would that be best?" She was unable to stop the endless stream of chatter.

Larry put the phone back to his ear, trying to hear the hospital secretary as she said:

"He has a nasty head wound so it would be wise to leave him where he is for a couple of days at least."

Giulia began to panic again.

"Giulia – go grab a soda.... or something, preferably with alcohol in it. I'll sort this."

"But it's Gil, Larry."

"We don't know that for certain yet, Now calm down. We can't fix anything with you flapping around like a headless chicken."

"But it is. I put my new business card in his shirt pocket at the airport. It has to be him."

"We think it might possibly be Gil Robson," said Larry to the hospital administrator. "If you've any California Crystal Band fans amongst the nurses, you'll know for certain. If it is, tell him Paul Giordano is on his way down. I'll call my father now. He'll be there in a couple of hours."

"He's heavily sedated at the moment, but I'll be sure to pass on your message as soon as he wakes. Just tell Mr. Giordano to ask at reception and he'll be directed. Thank you and goodbye."

Sometimes celebrity was priceless.

"I'll call Pops," said Larry. "We can't do anything from here. Even if we could get a flight straight away its going to be at least three hours. Dad can get there in two from LA"

Giulia snatched the phone from his hand saying:

"Go fix me that drink. I'll call Poppa." Larry shrugged and went to the kitchen.

When Paul arrived at the hospital his first task was to have Gil moved to his own room. Then he arranged with the hospital for a private consultant and nursing staff.

By the time it was all as Paul wanted it, Gil was fully conscious but still had a drip in his arm to control the pain.

"If you weren't in bed and tied to that machine, I'd bounce you all round this room, you stupid son-of-a-bitch."

You had to know someone well to start a conversation like that. He spoke to Gil the way he would have spoken to Tony. Gil couldn't look him in the eye.

"I don't know exactly what you did, but I do know you weren't sober when you did it. And where's your car? You didn't flap your wings and fly. So where is it? You've scared the shit out of my daughter. I don't allow that – not from anyone."

He waited for Gil to reply. He didn't, so he went on.

"I'll have to call your Mom and Connie and let them know where you are. Great!"

Gil grabbed Paul's sleeve with such force that he pulled the IV out of his arm.

"No, no. You mustn't do that! Not Connie!"

"Why the hell not? I'd want Carrie to be the first to know if I was in your position."

So quietly Paul could hardly hear, and with his head bent, Gil replied:

"Connie has a boyfriend. We had a meeting today. Connie, me, her boyfriend and his wife. We agreed to divorces. Paul…. what…."

There was no kinder man than Paul. His face creased in sympathy, and he put his hand on Gil's cheek.

"I've been there, my boy. You'll come through it. It may not seem that way but there will be an end to it all. Just hold on and you'll come through. It'll be quicker than you think."

"I'm so tired, Paul. I need to sleep." He did indeed look at the end of his tether.

"No problem. I'll go get something to eat. Larry and Giulia are flying in - they'll be a while yet though. Sweet dreams."

'No…. please, no. No more explanations.' Gil thought. One had felt like the world's end. He couldn't do it again.

Chapter Thirty-four

Over the years since her marriage, young as she had been, Connie had become very adept at hiding her feelings. Recent years with Gil had been difficult because they didn't, it became more and more apparent, understand one another's needs.

The mood in the car back to Bel Air was quiet but not awkward. Both Connie and Oliver were concerned with their own thoughts. Oliver's feelings were very positive. Now he had Connie to himself with no outside distractions, they could begin to build a life together. Perhaps one day they would marry, but that would be for the future.

Connie on the other hand, had been reminded in no uncertain terms that her husband of eight years and the father of her children, was out of her life for good, and she had no other option than to treat him as a stranger.

That would be so difficult. And it wasn't only Gil. It was Nancy, who was her friend as well as her mother-in-law - and Lizbeth. Jamie who had been the bane of her life, was nonetheless always there should she need him. And John and Suzy, who were the essence of kindness. Even Steve who she hardly knew at all she was confident would have been there for her. All would become passing strangers.

And what of the future? Would her relationship with Oliver last? Would her children and his get on? What was Oliver's family like? She didn't know them other than by name so she would face the future blind and with no support. Oliver himself wasn't a picture clear in her mind - she'd seen evidence of his temper. It was as if he was two people – one kind and considerate and one cold and aggressive. Which was the real Oliver? She really couldn't say at the moment.

Connie's own parents still lived in Los Angeles, but the Robsons had pretty much taken over her life. She didn't see much of them anymore. Her brother Bobby played in Gil's band so she would see him hardly at all. She wondered vaguely whether Bobby would choose to be her brother or Gil's friend and was dismayed to realize she didn't know the answer. She sighed, then turned and smiled at Oliver. They could do it if they worked together. He smiled back and covered her hand with his.

"We'll make it. Don't worry. First job is a break, I think. How about Hawaii? Or Mexico? We could do with some 'us' time, don't you think?"

"What about the kids? Do we take them with us?"

"I said 'us' time and that's what I meant. My mother would be happy to have all four kids for a few days. She still lives in Illinois but has a holiday home in San Clemente. They'd enjoy the beach."

Connie was unsure. Jacob and Mylo had been through a lot of upset recently, just about living entirely with Nancy for the past weeks. It couldn't go on like this and they were about to have their world turned upside-down again. Would it be right of her to leave them with a stranger? She didn't think so, but Oliver seemed confident in his mother's ability to cope, so she'd go with it for now.

"Well...I've always wanted to go to Rome, Italy. Could we do that?"

"Excellent suggestion! I've never been there either."

The gloom and despondency of the afternoon lifted somewhat, and they walked into the house arm-in-arm.

Simm and Deborah were in the foyer. She had hold of him by the hair and was hanging on so tight he couldn't get free.

"I told you I'd get you, you little bastard!" the seven-year-old yelled.

Simm had tears streaming down his face and was trying to dislodge her without hurting her.

"Hey! Deborah! Let him go - you can't do that. You're not allowed to hurt your brother, you know that. Let him go - NOW!" ordered Oliver. It wasn't often he raised his voice to his daughter so Connie looked at him in surprise.

Deborah looked back at them both with a defiant expression.

"Well, she," she pointed rudely at Connie, "hurt me. She slapped me. You saw her."

"The difference is that Connie did it once and she's very sorry." He looked at Connie for confirmation and Connie silently wished she'd slapped her harder. "You're not. You'll be just as mean to him tomorrow."

Admonition from her father was a rare concept for Deborah, so she concentrated on keeping her one and only ally onboard.

"I'm sorry Daddy. I promise I won't do it again." said Deborah, launching herself into her father's arms and hugging him tightly. Oliver didn't see her poking her tongue out at Simm over his shoulder, but Connie did. Deborah grinned at her.

Oliver put her down and told them both to go play.

"Glass of wine?"

Connie was in desperate need of alcohol. She'd have preferred a joint, but a drink would do.

As he poured the wine Connie asked him with a worried

frown:

"Do you think Deborah will be okay sharing her grandmother with my two?"

"Sure she will. I'll have a talk to her later. She'll come round." Connie wasn't convinced.

"Anyway, three older boys against a little girl? No contest!" laughed Oliver.

"No," thought Connie wryly to herself, "Certainly. No contest."

Still there was safety in numbers and the children might come to terms with the situation easier if they were together. Perhaps it was a good idea they should go to San Clemente – she was curious to meet Oliver's mother herself.

Connie kicked off her shoes with a sigh of relief and put her feet up on a chair. It had been one hell of a day. She tried her level best not to remember the look on Gil's face when he had asked her to reconsider. She would carry that mental snapshot with her to the grave. She took a long swallow of wine and refilled the glass.

"Come and sit out here," shouted Oliver from the poolside.

"How do you think Rachel took it? She seemed pretty composed."

Oliver shrugged.

"Rachel's great with everything except children. I'd never have got any business enterprises off the ground without her. She's a superb accountant. Can add columns up in her head as fast as some people can use a calculator. She's a serious person which is why she probably isn't good with kids."

"Is that why you married her? I mean for her business

skills?"

Connie waited for the hammer to fall at the impertinence of the question, but he merely said:

"Partly."

She didn't dare push it further. The difference in approach between herself and Gil, and Oliver and Rachel was off the scale.

Later that evening, when the kids were tucked up in bed and Deborah finally fell asleep, Connie took some time alone to wander around the garden and consider her family's future. She picked a few bugs from the roses and broke off some dead flowers from a pot of geraniums by the front door. Deep in thought, she didn't at first hear the car come up the drive.

As it pulled up, she turned and was amazed to see Nancy behind the wheel, with Jacob and Mylo sitting looking hopeful on the back seat.

Nancy knew she wouldn't be welcome. She also doubted her grandchildren would like staying with their mother in this overextravagant luxury home. She didn't get out of the car and left the engine running. Connie began to run towards the car to kiss the children when Nancy stopped her.

"I thought you should know that Gil's had an accident and is in hospital in San Diego. They're not certain what's wrong yet but he's had a bad head injury."

As Connie was about to speak, she finished with, "That's all I know. I thought I should tell you."

And with that she reversed, swung the car round and disappeared as rapidly as she had arrived. Connie could see the shell-shocked little faces of her children pressed against the back window.

Oliver, who had heard the whole conversation from the shadow of the hall, watched Nancy's taillights as they disappeared onto the main road.

"Did you hear that? It sounds serious. I have to go," fretted Connie.

Oliver stayed silent for a few seconds then said quietly but with unmistakable emphasis:

"You will not go. Not again. If you take one step towards that car you will not be coming back. Ever. I won't take this again. He's no longer your responsibility and if you don't know that, you shouldn't be here – you should be with him."

Then he returned to the dim of the house interior, calling over his shoulder:

"And, if you decide to stay, you should get your children from your mother-in-law at the first opportunity. They've been there too long as it is, and if you're not careful, they could be there permanently."

Connie sat on the doorsteps, head propped in her hands, and remembered when she had first met Gil all those years ago on similar steps.

She had looked up to see this boy, not much older than her, with the sweetest smile she had ever seen, looking down on her and offering her his hand as if she were a princess. She had been too shy to take it but how she had longed to! How much had happened since then. How much they had been to each other. And now she prayed she and Oliver would have something equally special together and that was her future. He was absolutely right; she should not look back. Oliver, Simeon and Deborah were her future - and Jacob and Mylo, of course. The other Robsons were her past.

234

As she walked through the door, Oliver picked her up in his arms. She snuggled her head into his neck, and he whispered into her hair:

"I'm so glad you decided to come home. I love you, Connie. Please don't leave – ever." She kissed his cheek and lightly bit his ear lobe. Her voice became husky.

"Take me to bed, Oliver." Her voice softened and she whispered the last word in his ear.

He strode up the curved staircase and she waited for the princess feeling, which never came.

Chapter Thirty-five

When Gil woke again a couple of hours later, groggy from the effects of a light sedative, Larry was sitting on a couch near the wall. Giulia was in an armchair next to the bed, holding his hand and gazing out of the window. He managed a watery smile and whispered:

"Hey!" His throat was scratchy and dry. Giulia jumped to her feet.

"Larry, he's awake. Larry..." Her brother had dozed off and woke with a start.

"He's awake, Larry. Look!"

Gill had the feeling he had become part of the machine he was hooked up to. She didn't seem aware he was there.

"Hi, Larry.," said Gil, quietly because his head still ached like the devil and Giulia's exuberance was causing him pain.

"Can it, Giulia - have some consideration."

"Sorry Gil. Does your head hurt so much?"

She tiptoed over to the washstand and dipped a paper towel in cold water which she placed gently across his brow. Shit, that felt good. He closed his eyes in relief.

"Thank you. How did you know that was exactly what I needed?" he croaked with a wan smile. Giulia positively glowed with delight and ran over to fetch a glass of water for his throat.

Larry came and sat on the foot of his bed.

"In God's name what happened to you? Do you know you've got a doozy of a black eye?" Gil didn't. Larry changed the subject to something more practical.

"I take it you arrived by car. Give me a clue. It wasn't there when the paramedics picked you up."

"I think it was stolen. I have a vague recollection of seeing it being driven away. But that's all it was – a brief glance."

"No impression of who took it then? – how many, how old, what color? That sort of thing." Gil shook his head.

"I'd fallen backwards on the ground and banged my head, but I couldn't have seen anyway from that angle."

He didn't mention he'd been so drunk he wouldn't have remembered in any case.

"Well, we'll leave you to rest - you look as if you need it. C'mon Giulia. Be back in the morning," and he strode to the door dragging a reluctant Giulia by the arm.

She shook off his hand, straightened her skirt and said, with a pretty good attempt at composure:

"Good night, Gil. I'm relieved you're feeling better. We'll be back in the morning when you've had a chance to rest," then as an after-thought, "And do try to eat something."

Then the two of them were gone.

Nancy arrived at the hospital a little after 10pm. She drove at top speed after she'd dropped the kids off, protesting, with Lizbeth. Those poor boys were being tossed from pillar to post.

She dashed into the hospital foyer and asked the receptionist where she could find Gil Robson. The receptionist asked her for identification. She couldn't let just anyone in to see a member of 'the California Crystal Band' she explained.

"Goddam, I'm his mother!" Nancy fumed, poking through her purse for her drivers' license.

The receptionist straightened her starched cap, glanced at the paperwork and returned it.

"One moment please." She picked up the phone and within minutes one of Gil's nurses appeared and led her to his room.

He was dozing when she entered. She gasped at the damage to his face.

"Oh, Gil," she lay her cheek next to his and kissed him. He couldn't take sympathy at the moment, so he disentangled himself and pushed her gently away.

"Please don't cry, Mom - it's just a temporary set-back," and he made a weak attempt at a smile, But the one person he could never fool was his mother.

"Gil, I don't think Connie's coming this time. I went to tell her you were in hospital, but she didn't speak. I don't know what she thinks she's doing."

Gil changed the subject.

"How did you know where I was?"

"Giulia Giordano called. She was in a bit of a state, so I have been worried sick."

"Just for future reference, Giulia tends to be a bit of a drama queen."

Gil rubbed his forehead, trying to control the pain.

"Mom, you remember me telling you I'd a meeting yesterday afternoon? You probably assumed it was business, but it wasn't. Connie and I, and Oliver Maxwell and his wife, met to hammer out some details for divorce proceedings," his voice broke. "I kept my mouth shut because Connie seemed so set on it."

Nancy's hands flew to her mouth, and she looked at him in disbelief, so he added gently:

"Whatever happens, Mom, getting back together won't work if one of us is unhappy with the idea."

As Nancy looked down at the tissue she was twisting between her fingers, the door banged against the wall as Jamie barged in and took the distance to the bed in a single stride.

"Oh, fuck, Gil. What have you done? What's going on with you recently? You've looked worse in the past six weeks than you did in the whole of your life before!"

"Thanks brother. That's made me feel really great."

Nancy dragged Jamie backwards and pushed him into a chair.

"Quiet! Your input isn't needed."

Gil resumed his conversation with Nancy.

"I'm here for another couple of days then I don't know where I'll go. I could rent somewhere temporarily I suppose. I don't want to go back to Linden Reach."

"You'll do no such thing. You'll come home with me. You need looking after."

"You know I can't do that. I couldn't face Dad with all this going on - just not going there at the moment."

"You could always stay at mine," chimed in Jamie.

"Sure thing," said Gil sarcastically. "Sorry Jamie but look what happened last time."

"Regrettably I do see your point," shrugged Jamie.

Nancy looked thoughtful.

"You mentioned Giulia. Perhaps the Giordanos would put you up for a few days – they've always treated you

239

like family."

Carrie Giordano liked few people, and those she did like understood it may be on a very temporary basis. But remarkably she'd always had a soft spot for Gil. Even so, he was doubtful as he said:

"Might be worth considering, and I'd rather Connie didn't know where I was for a day or two at least. I'll be okay – don't worry." Nancy was starting to look panicky again.

"Mom, I'm not a fool. I promise you faithfully I won't do anything stupid."

"Well, not on purpose anyway." said Jamie. Nancy cuffed him and continued.

"I've brought you some clean clothes and there's some deodorant and shampoo in a bag. You might feel better for a clean-up."

She chattered on with mom-talk for a few minutes until she noted Gil was beginning to fade again.

"Come on Jamie. Time to go."

"Oh Ma! We only just got here. Now I have to drive all the way back to LA only to come back tomorrow. You don't suppose I could find some where to stay in San Diego?" pouted Jamie at the same time winking at Gil.

"No I don't. Move. Get goin'," ordered Nancy as she pushed him out of the door. She bent to kiss Gil who whispered in her ear.

"Please don't let him come back again. At least not yet. I couldn't stand up to him." Nancy nodded seriously.

"I'll take him home with me where I can at least try to keep an eye on him. He'll have to suffer your Dad for a day or two. Serves him right – serves them both right."

"Thanks Mom. If you see Connie…. Oh, never mind, it doesn't matter."

But of course it did matter – it mattered more than anything in the whole world to Gil.

The following morning, Giulia and Larry turned up bright and early, so Gil knew they must have found somewhere local to stay.

Gil had just been given a breakfast he couldn't eat, and helped by the nurse to shower and dress, which he'd insisted upon, although he was still very dizzy.

Larry was attempting to quell Giulia's exuberance. Gil thought she was a pretty, cute little thing but she could talk for America. She never stopped. But then, she'd been the same from childhood. He still wasn't aware of how nervous she became in his presence. Larry could have told him she was only like that around him, but in a brother's way he hadn't really noticed.

"Hello, Gil. You're looking better today. I brought you some grapes and bananas," said Giulia. "I can get you something else if you'd rather. Would you?"

Gil hated bananas, didn't go big on grapes either – more fries than fruit kind of man.

"No that's fine. Thank you, very kind of you."

Larry tossed a couple of magazines on the bed – one on military aircraft which was clearly his, and one on Fender guitars which he'd bought in town.

"Should keep you entertained for a couple of hours. I've to go back to Los Angeles. I'm looking at joining the Airforce. No idea if I'm the right sort. Probably not, but worth a try. I can't live the rest of my life as 'son of Paul Giordano', and it's been a couple of years since I

241

realized I was a crap guitarist. You could have given me some clue there, Gil. Come on Giulia. Time to hit the road."

Gil took Giulia's hand and kissed it, momentarily silencing her. She could feel herself melt inside. He smiled up at her.

"If I had a daughter, I'd want her to be just like you."

Chapter Thirty-six

Connie hadn't slept very well. They had made passionate, volatile love – not the gentle and tender sex she enjoyed with Gil - then Oliver had drifted off to sleep.

Connie lay staring at the ceiling and wondered about him. He was completely changing his life, but he seemed to be so confident and at ease with it all. She was terrified. And still felt as if there was a stone in the pit of her stomach which had persisted since the discussion at Ricks. Horrible place, she couldn't understand why Gil liked it so much.

The following morning, she pushed the scrambled egg round her plate but didn't eat it. Oliver noticed but said nothing. He figured she just needed more time. A visit to the lawyer's office the following week would help to concentrate her mind.

"If you're finished, we could take a swim. Then I have to go down to the salesroom. Do you want to come with me? We could have lunch and I could show you the track. There's a big international race next week."

"No, I should go pick up the boys from Nancy. You're right – they should be with me. Believe me, I'd rather be at the track with you. Gil is the center of Nancy's universe. It isn't going to be pretty."

"Please don't let Nancy suck you into this situation with Gil, Connie. You can't have both of us. It doesn't work like that. And the road we chose means you just have to let go. And the sooner the better for the kids' sake."

Oliver smiled, then bent his head and she kissed him quickly on the mouth.

"Have a good day. See you five-ish?" she said.

"Better make it six, just in case. 'Bye."

When she'd finished her coffee, she left Maria clearing the breakfast table and went to call Nancy. Maria, who wasn't above listening in, stood behind the kitchen door.

"Hi Nancy. I know you won't want to talk to me, but I really do need to pick up the boys. They've had enough upset. I really need them here with me. So, I'll be over in an hour if that's not a problem."

Maria couldn't hear Nancy's reply of course but was amazed at Connie's next words.

"You know he can't be there with them alone. I will have to be there too. Can you wait until I get there? It'll be okay. You can leave then. I know you'll be keen to get away."

Again, words from Nancy, and Connie said:

"Give him my love and kiss him for me. Tell him I'm sorry he was hurt. Goodbye."

Maria was delighted. She'd never liked that upstart woman. Rachel was far more to her taste – quiet, predictable and not very interested in what Maria was doing. Connie, on the other hand, missed nothing.

Once Connie arrived at Monty's house to pick up the boys, Nancy left for the drive back to San Diego.

She'd suggested to Jamie he might take the boat out. There was good fishing at the moment she'd heard in the Monterey Bay area, and he could take that nice new French girlfriend with him. That would keep him out of the way for a few days at least. The delight of Jamie's life was his yacht, with women a close second.

"What's going on?" asked Monty, suspiciously. Clearly Nancy had told him absolutely nothing about anything.

Connie proposed to keep it that way.

"Well, thanks a lot Monty. It was kind of you to look after the boys for me."

"In the past twenty-four hours they've been with Nancy, Lizbeth and now me," Monty glowered. "What the hell is going on?" and he stood practically nose to nose with Connie, intent on intimidating out of her whatever she wasn't telling him. But the days when Connie was scared of Monty were long gone.

"I just had to be out of town for a day or two."

"And look at the boy's legs," said Monty, talking over the top of her, "They're completely skinned. He's too little to be out on an ice-rink on his own. You should have been with him."

And this from a man who'd made mental and physical punchbags out of the little boys he claimed to love.

Connie picked up the boys' bag. They ran for the door and waited for her to catch up on the drive.

"Well, goodbye Monty," and under her breath as she walked away. "And go to hell."

"What did you say, Mommy?" asked Mylo.

"Oh, nothing honey. Just wishing grandad a good day."

Connie sat at the pool-side as the kids played together in the water. She relaxed watching them. Perhaps it was going to turn out alright after all. They seemed to be getting along fine. Deborah and Mylo were sitting on the opposite side of the pool, laughing and swishing their feet in the water. Simm and Jacob were diving for dimes.

She went behind the pool-bar and poured herself a glass of red wine. Yes, this was going to be okay.

Connie decided not to take advantage of Oliver's suggestion she work with his own legal team. Something about the idea seemed unethical when they were involved in two separate but linked divorce cases. So she sought out a firm her father had dealt with. They mostly were concerned with litigation, but they did have a department dedicated to marital disputes.

It turned out to be a smart move. They regarded Connie's father with a deal of respect. He had been a very good businessman and had made a sizeable fortune processing sugar cane in Hawaii before coming to Los Angeles.

They explained the process of legal separation and its purpose. It had never occurred to her she'd be given a breathing space to sort out parental obligations and financial settlements before the finality of divorce. Of course, it also allowed for a chance to resolve the relationship and avoid the divorce altogether. This just wasn't a possibility in their cases she thought glumly. Still, she could relax a little in the meantime. So, she left the signed document with the lawyer and went back to Oliver's.

Chapter Thirty-seven

Larry came back on his own the following morning to find Gil sitting ready dressed in the bedside chair. When asked, he didn't know why Giulia hadn't come with him. She seemed a bit nettled about something. He shrugged. She'd get over it.

"Something I said?" asked Gil, puzzled.

"Who knows?" Larry replied. "She's always been a bit hysterical."

"I'm glad she didn't come. It'll give me a chance to explain things. Man to man."

Larry doubled over laughing.

"What? You sound like Humphrey Bogart in Casa Blanca. Man to man?"

Gil brushed him off impatiently.

"This is serious, Larry." Gil took a deep breath. Connie and I are getting a separation – and its looking like it'll end in divorce."

"Do I know him? I assume it's a 'him'," Larry asked.

"You might – although he is only a symptom of the problems. He owns that big car dealership on Beverly Boulevard. His name's Oliver Maxwell. Under other circumstances he might not be a bad guy, but he's stolen my wife so not my number one."

He wiped his face with the back of his hand - he hadn't mentioned that the problem had been a long time in the making.

"Oh, Larry. He's everything I'm not and should be for Connie. He's monied – well, yes, I'm not short in the dollar stakes. But he's also educated and well read. And

247

confident. He knows how to dress and speak. I'm hopeless with the rich and famous – even though I'm rich and famous."

"Well, I'm bound to disagree with you. You're famous and loved by everyone who knows you. Dang it, even me!" he laughed ruefully.

Gil thought but couldn't find one positive idea to cling to. The band – with the possible exception of John – took advantage of him and undermined whatever he did. Ed was poisonous. He sneered and derided whatever Gil wanted to do to progress, and just wanted to play the same old crap over and over, because it brought in a fast buck.

He'd tried and tried for them all – including his wayward brother - and in the process he'd lost Connie, who had only got more beautiful and confident with time, and who had given him everything. He had just taken it all for granted.

He had to leave this hospital tomorrow and despite his fame and fortune, he had nowhere to go and no-one to call. He was floundering.

"This is such a big ask," he said to Larry then paused.

"If you don't ask the question, I can't give you an answer."

"Do you think your mom and dad would mind if I came to stay for a day or two? That's all. I really don't want to go back to Linden Reach, and I can't face my Dad at the moment. Jamie – well, you know my brother…. and Ed is……."

"Yes, no need to labor the point. I'll call them but I'll tell you now, there'll be no problem. My Mom likes you better than me anyway."

"I'm supposed to be here another couple of days, but we

have some TV dates in New York next week, and I need to be there for rehearsals. I don't have time to be an invalid. I need to be out tomorrow to at least try to get some action out of the band. It sure as hell's an uphill battle."

Gil still had a black eye, rapidly turning yellow, a sticking plaster on the back of his head where some of his hair had been shaved away and looked so distressed Larry rang his mother immediately and arranged for him to be taken to their house that afternoon.

"You realize you're a complete idiot? From being ignored you're about to have more attention than you can possibly stomach. Giulia will insist on waiting on you hand and foot."

"I'd like that," said Gil.

Paul met them at the door and took Gil's bag to a room overlooking a tiled terrace with no other access than from his bedroom. It would be so good to be alone and get his thoughts in order. If only he could think of something other than his wife.

As might be expected of Paul Giordano, every room in the house had a well-stocked bar. Gil's was no exception. A couple of glass shelves contained a few bottles of bourbon with mixers and a selection of beers. Perhaps less predictable was the large container of peanuts.

Larry took a handful, stuffed them in his mouth and said:

"See you later, pal. I'll try and fend off the Beverly Hills Hurricane for as long as possible."

Gil sat down with nothing to do. It was such an unusual feeling. He stood and walked round the room a bit, checked out the terrace, looked at the tubs of flowers then walked around the room some more. He took a shower then against all common sense poured himself a large glass of bourbon. He felt better. More relaxed.

Paul came in to see how he was doing and the smell of cannabis which accompanied him into the room was unmistakable. The feeling of relaxation disappeared in an instant. His first day on his own, and he couldn't afford to fall off the wagon. But he couldn't tell the man how to behave in his own house, so he tried to ignore it. Connie... think of Connie... but the more he tried, the more overwhelmed he became. Finally, when Paul offered the joint, he took it. He looked at it for a while, still trying to stay in control, but finally took a deep, deep toke, and held it inside until his lungs felt on fire. He so loved the flavor. Sure, it was an acquired taste, but one he'd picked up years ago. Gil took another drag and began to breathe easier. He leaned back on the sofa and smiled at Paul who laughed back at him.

"Better?"

"You have no idea..." said Gil and let his head flop back.

So gradually, Paul and Gil got drunker and drunker and higher and higher until neither knew what day of the week it was, and neither cared.

Gil hadn't seen Giulia around, but he knew she was in the house. He could smell her distinctive perfume. The higher he got the more pervasive the scent. It was glorious.

The next time Gil looked around Paul was gone. There didn't seem any point in doing anything other than wait, so he poured himself another whisky. He thought of Connie and the sadness returned, worse than ever.

By the time Paul came back, Gil was beginning to feel

the effects of the drug wearing off, the sadness intensified again, and tears began to roll down his face. Paul hugged him as he might his own sons, but it just made matters worse.

"This calls for something stronger." said Paul. He walked over to his grand piano and opened the lid. Within was his stash of coke.

"Jeez, Paul. You have to be kiddin.' You more than anyone know that it's a long downward slide. Throw it in the toilet."

Gil stood and walked to the door.

"I'm so sorry, Paul. I can't afford to go down that road again. I can't lose Connie and my mind. She got me out of it last time - I couldn't have done it without her. I'm sorry." He left and closed the door behind him.

The cannabis buzz had faded but the alcohol was still in his system. He swayed back against the closed door. Larry was in the room with Tony and Giulia. He was in deep conversation with Tony but turned and the smile faded from his face.

"Oh, damn, Gil. He didn't. Please tell me he didn't." said Larry.

Gil turned and banged his head gently against the door.

"I can't do this, I just can't. I have to go find Connie and tell her I can't do this - she has to help me. I'll persuade her - there has to be a way. I can't weaken every time someone waves a bag of blow under my nose. Sooner or later, I'm going to give in. The pressure is unbelievable."

Giulia burst into tears.

When Connie got back to the big house in Bel Air there was an ambulance parked outside.

251

The paramedics were carrying a gurney and on it, with blood running from a wound on his forehead, was Mylo.

"What's happened – what the hell has happened?" she shouted.

The paramedic adopted a placatory tone and sat her down in the ambulance.

"It seems there has been an accident in the swimming pool. Mylo was playing with the little girl. She slipped on the poolside and accidentally knocked him into the water. He banged his head in the process. Don't worry. He was shocked rather than injured. One of the other boys managed to pull him out. He'll be as right as rain in no time but its policy to bring all head wounds into hospital to keep an eye on them overnight, especially children."

Connie went with Mylo to the hospital and sat with him until he was calm. When she knew he was okay, she called Nancy and gave her an explanation of what little she knew.

Nancy dropped everything and came straight over. Mylo was sitting up in bed by this time, playing with some toy soldiers one of the nurses had brought for him. He smiled at his Nana who gave him a comforting cuddle. But he pushed her away, intent on his game.

"Seems he's alright," Nancy's attitude was still reserved.

"I was at the lawyers's office. The ambulance was in the drive when I got home."

Nancy bridled at the words 'home' and 'lawyer' but said nothing.

"Then you'd better get home again and find out exactly what caused the accident."

Connie picked up her bag and headed for the door before

remembering Mylo and returned to kiss him.

"See you later, sugar. Nana will stop with you until I come back. I won't be long."

Oliver was there when she got back and there was an unholy row going on.

"It doesn't help your cause to tell lies, Jacob. Deborah is too small to have pushed Mylo into the pool and even if she was big enough, she would never dream of doing such a thing."

When Connie tried to get to the bottom of the problem, a tearful Jacob told her Deborah had pushed Mylo into the pool. Oliver was adamant that wasn't so.

Connie glanced across at Simeon who looked as if he would like to sink into the floor.

"What happened Simm?"

Simm looked at Connie, then at his father then down at Deborah. Whether it was the little secret smile she gave him, or fear for Mylo was unclear, but Simm confirmed Jacob's story. Deborah had pushed Mylo into the pool. But he was very quick to point out that he thought it had been an accident. Connie was skeptical and it must have shown in her face because Oliver said:

"I can't believe you would consider her capable of such an act, Connie. She has repeatedly begged for you to come live with us."

Simm's mouth fell open in shock.

"Why the conniving little...." Connie couldn't finish the sentence. Oliver was taken aback by the collusion between her and his son, but he assumed there must be more to this than was immediately apparent and put off any further discussion.

"Time for bed, kids. I'll be in to read you a story in a

while."

Once Maria had taken them away, he turned to Connie.

"Is Mylo okay?"

"Yes. They'll discharge him in the morning all being well. Nancy's with him now."

"Her name comes up a lot when it comes to those boys. I seem to say that often and you have to start taking notice. We should try and find another way to take care of them. It must be quite a burden for an old lady."

The thought of Nancy being referred to as an old lady made Connie smile. She knew older teenagers.

"You can't separate my two boys from their Nana. It's not possible. I think in this case, we should let them stay somewhere familiar for a few days – with Nancy – and Simm and Deborah could stay with your mom."

Oliver was not happy with this.

Connie said, "There is a difference between Gil and Nancy's places in my life. Gil very soon will be my ex-husband. At the moment I can't be around him. Nancy is his mother, but she is also my friend. It may surprise you to know she has a problem with Gil and me too. She wants Gil out of my life as much as you do.

Chapter Thirty-eight

That evening a couple of officers from the LAPD turned up at the Giordano residence asking to speak to Gil.

Giulia ran off to find him. He was reading a magazine in the library and smiled when she came in. Her eyes wide with concern she said:

"There are two policemen. They want to speak to you."

"Oh, good," said Gil. "They've probably found my car, although it's sure to have been totaled by now."

In the hall, Gil greeted the two officers, and led them into the sitting room.

"Can I help you?" Gil said smiling pleasantly, although he did think the policemen looked rather strained.

"You are Mr. Gil Robson, son of Montagu and Nancy Robson, brother of James. You currently reside in Linden Reach?" Gil nodded, his smile fading. "You may want to sit down, sir."

By now thoroughly alarmed, Gil sat.

"We are sorry to tell you that the body of your brother James Robson was pulled from the sea near Santa Barbara at five-thirty this morning. A young lady was also found in the wreckage of his boat, also deceased."

Gil didn't react. He couldn't. He froze. But the policemen clearly had dealt with all kinds of responses, so they merely told him they'd inform his parents, asked him to contact his remaining family and said they'd be in touch when their enquiries were complete.

"In the meantime, we would advise you against watching the media. Your brother was a celebrity. The TV in particular won't take anyone's feelings into account." And with that they took their leave.

Gil stood up. His knees gave way and he flopped back into the chair. The blood had gone from his face and his eyes had glazed with shock. Giulia, who had been in the room throughout, sat at his feet and rubbed her cheek against his hand. He pushed her away and walked into Paul's den, sat down and accepted a joint from the box offered.

"Everything good?" asked Paul.

"Fine." said Gil and smiled. "Just dandy." He took another toke and wandered out onto the terrace. Paul went back to reading his magazine, then Giulia came tearing in.

"Where's Gil? Where did he go."

"He's out on the terrace," said Paul, confused. "Why?"

Giulia didn't bother answering but ran onto the terrace. She found Gil hunched over on his knees. When she tried to speak to him, he just looked at her blankly as if he'd never seen her before. The joint was burning his fingers, but he hadn't dropped it.

"Poppa…Poppa come and help me!" Giulia screamed.

"What's happened? What's going on? Gil?"

Between them they managed to get Gil inside and sat him in a chair. Giulia dragged Paul outside by his shirt sleeve and whispered.

"It's Jamie. He drowned off Santa Barbara. The police just came and told him. What do we do? What shall I do?"

"He's dead?" said Paul incredulously. "Are you sure?"

Giulia stamped her foot.

"You think I'd make that up? You think I could make

256

that up. What do we do?"

"Get Larry. We need to get him into bed – he's suffering from shock – then go call the doctor. Tell him it's an emergency."

She was out of the door before he finished speaking and Paul heard her on the hall phone.

Larry arrived and together they managed to get Gil to bed.

The doctor arrived, checked him over and gave him a sedative.

"He's going to be so full of fucking tranquilizer he'll never wake up," said Larry to his father when the doctor left. "How is it possible one person can have so much grief and still manage to operate like Gil does?" Paul shrugged and said:

"Guess we'll have to help him get through this. His father won't give him a thought, and his mother will have enough on her plate. We can deal with the press and help him arrange the funeral. We'd better go see Nancy."

"We'll have to get him in a fit state to cope with press conferences. He'll feel torn in two for the rest of his life," Larry said.

When Gil woke, Giulia was by his side. That she'd been there for some time was obvious from the cold coffee and empty plate on the nightstand. When she saw his eyes were open, she said:

"I once told you I'm not a lot of practical help, but I can listen."

Gil shook his head and turned away from her. No sympathy. Not now.

Larry arrived and took charge.

"Good, you're awake - we need to talk. First thing I need to know is if you have anyone you'd like to help with this little lot?"

He waved a piece of paper covered in writing in Gil's face.

"Things to do, my friend." Larry's tone was unnaturally bracing.

"Then call Steve, my manager. His number's in my pocketbook."

"Where's your pocketbook? Never mind – I'll find it. Giulia, go make Gil some coffee. And a sandwich." And after she'd left - "Not for you - for her. It'll keep her occupied for longer."

"First, identification. Dad can do that unless you'd rather go."

"I have to do that. If I don't I'll never believe it. Besides, I doubt anyone else could face it."

'And you can?' thought Larry.

"Next. Dealing with your family. The police will have informed your parents, but they'll want to speak to you again, I would think."

Gil rubbed a hand over his ashen face.

"Next. The funeral......."

The list went on and on. It made him dizzy, but at least Gil was functioning by the end.

"But please Larry, please - the police have advised me against watching TV reports and I don't want to see him all messed up."

Larry nodded. Gil's face creased and tears seeped from

the corners of his eyes onto the pillow.

"You've got it, my man."

Larry brought him a phone and Gil called Lizbeth. She was home, thank God.

"Oh, hi Gil. You good? Rosie wants to come see you - where are you by the way? Don't seem to have seen you in ages."

Clearly Nancy had yet to pass on the news.

Lizbeth would have rattled on, but Gil finally found his tongue and said:

"Liz, there's no easy way to say this," he took a deep breath and his hands tightened on the bedclothes.

"Jamie was washed overboard near Santa Barbara and he's...," but he couldn't bring himself to say the word.

"He's not.... Are you telling me he didn't survive?" He wasn't the only one who couldn't say the 'd' word.

"Please Lizzie, please help me. We were the ones who loved him most in the whole world. We need each other's support."

He collapsed under his grief for a few moments then pulled himself together

Through her shock, Lizbeth's heart was full of pity for him, as well as grief for her husband. She knew how much of this he'd have to shoulder for her sake.

"Do you want me to come and identify him with you?"

The first Connie heard of Jamie's death was on the eight o'clock news. It was being brought home to her she was no longer considered a member of the Robson family. No one had called her. Of course, she knew this in her head, but it had come as a shock how excluded she actually was. Technically, Jamie wasn't her brother-in-law anymore.

She listened to the news report with growing horror. They didn't know why, but his yacht had been blown off course and had ended up on the rocks off Santa Cruz, part of the Channel Islands up the coast from Santa Monica. Initially, there was no sign of Jamie, but his body was washed ashore and discovered a couple of hours later. The local police, said the announcer, had been informed and were carrying out enquiries. Foul play was not suspected.

Oliver had been to a meeting at the track and didn't return home until ten-thirty. He found Connie sitting in a chair in front of a television, watching intently a news program where paramedics were carrying a body on a stretcher to a waiting ambulance. The body was covered with a blanket but not yet enclosed in a body bag. One leg and one arm hung over the side and hair and the side of a face were briefly visible.

"What's the matter Connie? Was it someone you knew?"

He went to pull her to him, but she pushed away, her eyes still glued to the screen.

"I just don't believe it, Oliver. He'll jump up any minute and shout 'Gottcha!' Please tell me he will."

"Shit, it's not Gil, is it?"

"No, Jamie. They say its Jamie. I keep watching it over and over just to make sure, but they keep saying its Jamie Robson, founder member of the California Crystal Band. It's Jamie," she sobbed. "I have to go see Nancy. Now - I have to go now." She lurched from the chair.

Oliver took her gently by the arm and sat her back down.

He knelt at her feet, stroking her cheek.

"Sweetheart, you can't. You would not be welcome. Surely you can see that?"

"But I know.... knew Jamie. He was always good to me. I have to go."

Oliver shook his head.

"You can't and that's that. You have to know there is no place there for you."

Chapter Thirty-nine

After the funeral was over, Gil wondered how he'd survived.

All Jamie's friends and acquaintances were there, and Liz who, despite their difficulties had truly loved him. Despite his sometimes violent and erratic behavior, he had been a generous friend to more people than anyone had realized.

After the private family service, they arrived at the burial in a steady stream.

Gil also realized what a wealth of good friends he had himself. Many hadn't known Jamie well, but they turned up, one after the other. All the guys from Anasazi, including Todd and Jeff. The guys from his own band with their wives - including Ed, who inappropriately turned up with a crate of expensive French champagne.

"Jamie would have liked it like that" he said, but no-one was fooled.

Some of the mourners, he and Jamie had known from their teens in this band or that, including Harry Forster and David Elliot and even people from England and Europe. Gil felt himself cocooned in their sympathy.

Liz stood composed to an impossible degree, and grey-white beside the grave, brushing off any attempts at comfort. Nancy stood several yards away, trying but failing to put on a brave face for her sake.

His father's grief made him look mutinous, as if Jamie had done this on purpose to gall him.

Gloria volunteered to look after the family's children until Gil and Liz could take over. From the look of both, it probably wouldn't be any time soon. He stood,

262

withdrawn and silent on the gravel path outside the gathering of mourners, unable to believe what was happening.

It was a really beautiful funeral, full of love for Jamie and followed by a small reception, lightened by affectionate laughter at Jamie's exploits. Wine was drunk but no-one touched Ed's champagne.

Connie hadn't been contacted at all.

She spent the whole night in such agitation, that the following morning Oliver offered to take her to buy some flowers and drop her off at the cemetery on his way to work. It was the day after the funeral so it was doubtful anyone would be there.

Connie shook her head:

"I'd like to go alone. Otherwise, you'll have to wait for me, and it would make you late. But thank you – it was good of you to offer."

The truth of the matter was she wanted to grieve alone – it would be her only opportunity.

She rested her head wearily against his shoulder, then stood back and gave him a watery smile.

"Thank you for understanding. It's important to me. Jamie was a true friend but not many people would have appreciated that about him."

"Call me when you get home," said Oliver and kissed her on the forehead.

The boys were with Liz. Connie would have to tell them eventually but now was not the time. When she felt sure of being calm herself, she could offer comfort. But not now.

She stopped at a local florist and bought a big bouquet of white orchids and roses. Oliver would have thought them beyond ostentatious, but to her they were perfect. On the card she wrote:

"Oh, Jamie. I will miss you. I will miss the very fact you annoyed the hell out of me.

Yes, even that.

Love always, Connie."

She drew a smiley face next to the words.

Pulling into the small parking lot near the gates, she spent a few moments collecting herself, then put on her sunglasses and picked up her purse and the flowers.

Jamie's grave was piled high with bouquets and wreaths of every imaginable color and shape. Fans had left letters and little gifts, and here and there were candles in storm-lanterns, some still burning. Connie was choked at the beauty of it all and the expression of love it represented.

She knelt and placed her flowers amongst the rest, then stopped to read some of the cards.

As she rose, wiping the soil from her fingers, she caught sight of a shadow disappearing amongst the trees. Its owner was gone before she could tell who it was.

Connie sat for a while on a nearby bench by a gravel path, and just felt sad for the wasted life that had been Jamie Robson's.

She rose to leave, and when she was just a few yards from the gate she was knocked down from behind, and a hooded figure grabbed her purse. She hung on as hard as she could, but he wrested the bag from her hands by punching her in the face. She fell to the ground, stunned.

As her heart stopped pounding and she came to, the first thing she saw were white lilies scattered on the ground all about her. She felt an arm gently lifting her and a familiar voice said:

"Are you okay? You're going to have a real bruise on your cheek."

She looked up into the gentle, cloud-blue eyes of the man who was still her husband.

"I'm... I'm okay," she stuttered, embarrassed and apologetic. "I brought some flowers for Jamie. I thought no-one would be here the day after the funeral."

"It was such a circus yesterday – I thought I'd come back today so I could talk to him quietly. Why don't you help me pick up my flowers then if you like, we can talk to him together?"

She knew he desperately wanted her to stay although he would never say so. She began to pick up the flowers and put them into a neat bunch. Gil joined her and, side by side, they reassembled the beautiful bouquet.

Connie put a comforting hand in his. His eyes lingered on their intertwined fingers before he turned his head away.

Gil lay his flowers next to hers on the grave, kissed the tips of his fingers and ran them over the top of the headstone. Connie knew that in his silence, he was talking to his brother. And what's more, in his mind, his brother was answering him.

She put her arm around his back and, against his will he was sobbing uncontrollably into her shoulder. After a minute or two, he sat upright and said in a tired and worried voice:

"What will I do now, Connie? I've lost you, and now I've lost the only other person on the planet who fights – fought – my corner. What do I do?"

"You have more support than you can possibly imagine. Who showed up yesterday for you? It wasn't only Jamie's friends but your own too – I recognized them on TV."

"You always told me," said Gil, "what matters is who you go home to at night. I love them all, but I have no-one to go home to anymore."

He looked so bereft she put her arms around him and hugged him close. He turned his head and without conscious effort by either his lips were on hers, and the kiss which began as a gentle comfort, became searing.

Gil pulled away, jumped to his feet, and began striding back to the gate. No matter the cost, he would not compromise her like this.

So surprisingly, it was Connie who dragged him into the trees she had been mugged beneath not a half hour before, pulled his head down to hers and kissed him viciously.

His resistance snapped. He backed her against a tree and his hands were all over her, tugging at her dress pulling her body to his. They made love desperately, blindly oblivious to all but themselves.

After, Connie slid down the tree to sit breathing heavily on the soft leaves at its base. Gil sank down beside her, and they sat like babes in the wood, leaning head-to-head. Neither spoke for a minute or two.

"What are we going to do? This is insane," said Connie looking seriously into his eyes.

"Perhaps in time, we may look back on this as the swan song to a beautiful, but tragic love affair," whispered Gil.

It was hopeless…. hopeless. For him it could never be, but he couldn't help adding:

"You can bet your life on one thing. Jamie is sitting up there laughing fit to bust. Especially if someone else was in the cemetery. We weren't exactly quiet."

"Damn!" exclaimed Connie, "That bastard stole my car keys!"

Connie walked back to Jamie's burial plot, and like Gil had done, kissed the tips of her fingers and ran them along the headstone. She was so preoccupied she didn't hear Gil start his car and leave.

She whispered:

"Oh Jamie, if only you were here to tell me what to do. But of course you would always choose Gil. You always did. But this time you broke his heart far worse than I ever could."

She turned sadly away and walked back towards the gate. In passing she couldn't resist looking at the scene of their 'afternoon delight', well, "morning delight" to be exact. There was a hole at the base of the tree where she'd dug her heel into the soil for purchase. But Gil was gone and she was alone.

Chapter Forty

It was a very confusing situation. On the one hand, Gil's heart and soul were soaring, on the other, he knew it could never happen again. But the one thing the occurrence had confirmed to him was that Connie felt as he did.

He couldn't see what he could do about it. He would gladly take her with him everywhere he went, but the children needed her. It was the wickedest thought in the world, and he would rather have died than admit it out loud, but if there were no children, there would be no problem.

There was no way out because the band had to come first. His own family wasn't the only consideration. He was responsible for dozens of other families too. And his brother, out of control on drink and drugs, had needed him to keep him together. Now he was gone forever – gone from his life for always.

He sometimes felt squashed flat by the weight of responsibility. Before the boys, Connie helped him, supported him. Now Connie was gone. And Jamie was gone too – his shield against Ed's bullying and malice; his supporter in his ambition to create inspirational music rather than Ed's laisse faire attitude to bring in the big bucks.

He could see no future, yet Connie had made love to him, and he was flying with the angels.

Gil went back to the Giordano house to pack his things. He had trespassed on their hospitality far too long. It was time to face Linden Reach again.

Giulia greeted him at the door in her usual enthusiastic

manner.

"Come and see, Gil. I made something for you."

Her smile lit the room. She had flour on the end of her nose.

She led him into the kitchen and made him close his eyes. There was the sound of a cupboard opening and crockery rattling, then at her say-so he opened his eyes to a plate of home-baked chocolate chip muffins.

"Did you make these yourself? Wow! I never took you for a chef. You've really surprised me."

Giulia was delighted.

"I did – but Betty Crocker helped a bit," she giggled.

He couldn't suppress a grin. She was such a cutie. He had been right: if ever he had a daughter, he would want her to be just like Giulia.

"Come and eat with me," he smiled.

As she sat, he eyed her thoughtfully. Could he share with her what had happened with Connie? She gazed back adoringly, which he totally missed.

"Giulia…." he paused. She nudged him to continue. "Can you keep a secret?"

Giulia nodded and put a hand on his arm. He looked down and remembered Connie's fingers intertwined with his. It made him sad.

"You know I went to take some flowers for Jamie today? Well, I bumped into Connie. She had gone to lay flowers too."

His face lit up like the sun. Giulia's heart plummeted.

"We… well, for a little while it was as it had always been. We were so close, Giulia. Nothing can come of it I don't think. Nothing else has changed so I don't see how it could."

He was clearly still thinking hard how he could fix things.

"Can you think what I can do to put things right with her? You're a girl – how can I make it work?"

Giulia wiped the chocolate from her mouth with a napkin, stood stiffly and walked from the room, banging into Tony in the doorway.

"What's her problem?" asked Tony. "She's always in such a rush to be somewhere else. You okay? You're grinning like a Cheshire cat and your brother was buried yesterday. There's something not quite right about that."

Tactless and direct, but entirely accurate.

Gil was immediately contrite. His behavior was inappropriate. Jamie was hardly cold in the ground and the thought of Connie was making him act like a schoolboy. How Jamie would have loved it!

"Is your Mom here? I've come to pick up my things to go home. I wanted to thank her before I went."

"She's at some committee meeting somewhere," said Tony who was always vague about these things. "Pops is here, I think. Oh no, he isn't - Uncle Peter called and they've gone to play golf. Oh, well, never mind. I'll tell them you left."

"Just how many uncles do you have? Never mind…can you remember to tell your mom and dad I said thanks and I'll call them later?"

"Sure," he shrugged and left. Gil raised his eyes to the ceiling.

"Just where had Giulia gone?" he mused.

Going to Linden Reach was harder than he'd imagined. The cupboards still contained Connie's belongings – a silk kimono he'd bought her in Japan, a belt with a jeweled buckle from Paris - she'd worn it every day for a month when he first gave it to her - in a drawer with her silk and lace underwear. On a shelf on her dressing table, sat a large glass bottle with a cut-crystal stopper containing her favorite perfume. So much of her was still there.

He shut the door firmly. He'd pack some of his things and move them to one of the guest rooms.

Mid-afternoon, his mother arrived with the two boys. She'd got into the habit of picking them up from school recently. They leapt at Gil, and Mylo hung round his neck and refused to let go.

"Daddy, Daddy, Daddy, Daddy...," chanted Jacob, clinging to Gil's sleeve. Then quietly:

"Please don't go away again, Dad."

Gil dropped into a chair and pulled a child onto each knee.

"I know you are big boys now. I know you will listen to me and try your best to understand what I say. Then you can ask me whatever you like, and I'll do my best to answer.

"You know that Mom and I have had an argument and that we have fallen out. You must ask your mother to explain her side of things too. That's only fair, wouldn't you say?"

His big boys nodded seriously.

"Well, this is my side of things. I have to go away all the time because I have to work to get us money to live. I

271

work with Uncle John, Uncle Phil and Uncle Ed and we travel all over the world. People like to come and hear us sing and we are pretty good at it," He hugged them both to his chest.

"Uncle Jamie is a bit complicated. If you like, we'll talk about him later."

They knew something was going on with Uncle Jamie, but every time they heard the grownups mention him, they stopped as the children came in the room.

This was seriously big-boy stuff. Jacob decided to look as if he understood.

"Do you know what 'famous' means?" continued his Dad.

"It means lots of people know who you are."

"That's right. You've seen people sitting on the wall outside the house making lots of noise, and shouting my name until the policeman has to come and move them away? That often happens to well-known people. Sometimes it means I don't get to spend all the time with you I'd like. I have to spend time with those people as well.

"That's my job. As well as bad things, there are also good. It means we can go tobogganing in Colorado whenever we like. It means we can go anywhere we want in a plane, and you can have new skates and baseball gear whenever you feel like it. It isn't the same for most kids. Most kids' dads don't get as much money as I do."

He'd to hold back his emotions as his mind was filled with recollections of his own childhood.

"Can I ask questions now?" said Jacob, patience wearing thin. Gil nodded.

"Why don't you and Mommy talk anymore?"

Damn, he'd been waiting for that one. There was no answer that would satisfy a small child. They couldn't even begin to understand the implications of the unbridled passion in the cemetery.

"She thinks my being away so much is bad for you, and she gets lonely."

"We get lonely too," said Mylo. "Don't you want to stay with us?"

"More than anything in the world. But we can't always have whatever we want. Sometimes we have to choose, and that's why Mom and I have fallen out. Mommy thinks I should be more with you and her."

"I'd like that too," said Jacob.

"But then I have to make the dollars to give us a home, send you to good schools, buy you the things you need. I also need – *'needed, that's gone now too'* - to write songs with Uncle Jamie, and the band has to travel all over the world to sing them for other people, some of them boys like you.

"But don't the boys have daddies of their own?" asked Mylo, puzzled.

"But their dads aren't clever like ours. Our Dad is special."

"No, but God has given me a special gift – a very special gift. He has given me a voice people want to listen to. Don't you think it would be wrong of me not to use it?"

"Yes, I understand Daddy," said Jacob sagely. "But why doesn't Mommy understand that?"

"I think she does deep down, but as I told you, she does get very lonely when I'm away so much."

Gil didn't want to think about this, but he had promised he would answer whatever they wanted to know.

He was fortunate in his compassionate mother who came to his rescue.

"Pizza's ready, boys. Who wants Cola?" There was a mass exodus

Gil rubbed his hands over his face. He suddenly felt tired to the bone.

It had been a day of sky highs and deep doldrums. He needed some alone time to sort out his thoughts. At the moment he was completely overwhelmed. It was so difficult explaining to two innocents, things he didn't fully grasp himself.

But he'd to be in Seattle Tuesday afternoon, and the weekend would be taken up with rehearsals and packing. They'd be back Friday, but then there was more work to be done on the new album, and the slog of getting everyone to turn up on stage.

Perhaps he could get some time to himself on the plane.

Chapter Forty-one

Maria was fixing milk and cookies for Simm and Deborah when Connie got back. She could hear them outdoors playing catch around the trees.

"Hello Maria. Good day? Anything I can help with?"

"Oh no, Mrs. Connie," there was the slightest emphasis on the word Mrs. not lost on Connie.

"Then I'll go and take a bath. Hot day!"

Her smile was deliberately bright. She imagined Maria's reaction if she could have seen her a few hours earlier. Sometimes being smug was just the best thing.

The skin on her thighs was still tender from the force of their lovemaking. She soaped them gently, lost in the memory. Then she thought of Oliver, and how she might face him, and it pulled her up short. She had no other recourse than to lie, although she hated the very thought.

Simm and Deborah bowled in from the garden, sticky with sweat and streaked with soil, for once happy together. Their laughter had given Deborah hiccoughs. Maria made her stop, hold her breath to ten, drink a glass of water then ordered them both upstairs to shower and change before daddy came home.

"You look like a couple of *erizos*. Your papa will not recognize you. Mrs. Connie is upstairs. Be sure not to disturb her."

Connie decided fixing dinner herself that evening would be a distraction. Something special, linguine with clams in white wine sauce – easy and effective. She gave Maria the rest of the day off.

She was just tossing the salad when Oliver walked in.

"Hello, gorgeous," he grinned, and whipped a bunch of cream roses and gypsophilia from behind his back. "A beautiful bouquet for a beautiful lady."

"Thank you – how kind." It was a bit lame given the guilt she felt.

He trawled his finger through the creamy sauce in the pan and licked it suggestively, grinning at her expression.

"Mmm, good!"

"Out – out...." And she shooed him from the kitchen like a mother hen.

She was very quiet through dinner which Oliver put down to depression caused by Jamie's death. A couple of days should do the trick.

Personally, he thought Jamie was a low-life, but it was true he had been Connie's brother-in-law.

The atmosphere at the table changed abruptly. Deborah sniffed at the pasta with a look of distain on her face.

"Ugh, what's that?" she said loudly, indicating the delicious meal. "It looks disgusting. I want tacos."

"Well, you can't have them," said Connie. "Today's dinner is pasta."

"I can too have them. Daddy, can I have tacos?"

"Of course you can sweetie," said her father, absently. Connie felt less guilty about her own transgressions.

She took off her apron and tied it round Deborah's waist.

"I'd like extra cheese on mine," she said. Then, when three-quarters of the diner's tucked into their meal, even Oliver was laughing.

So, Deborah went to bed hungry and humiliated.

Connie collected the boys from Lizbeth who looked torn in two by the impending separation. Gil was her husband's brother, but Connie had been her friend for ten years, since before they were married. Choosing between them was heart-breaking. The boys hugged their Auntie Liz tightly. Lizbeth realized she would pretty much be saying goodbye to them too. Their closeness would be gone forever.

"Gil isn't going to be pleased I've collected them Liz, but Oliver thinks they've been with Nancy long enough, and they should spend time with us."

Gil would be distraught that because the whole family was grieving, Connie had managed to sneak in and snatch both boys from under the Robsons' noses. He would be hurt she would do such a thing when he could do nothing to stop her.

Lizbeth hugged her tight and when they parted, she was crying.

Tug-of-love children. Nothing good could come of it.

"You will call Gil, won't you Connie? You will tell him yourself where they are?"

"Of course I will!"

Oliver arrived home at five-thirty. Connie had yet to come back from collecting the boys.

Simm and Deborah bowled down the stairs to greet him and Mary Jane stood by, smiling as they jumped into his arms.

"Hello, monsters! Where's Connie?"

"She's gone to pick up Jacob and Mylo from their

auntie's so they can live with us," said Simm. Deborah screwed up her face but Oliver smiled.

"That's really good news! Won't it be great to have more brothers, Deborah? You'll love it. Wait and see." Deborah didn't look so sure.

"As soon as Connie comes back, I have a little surprise for you all."

Shortly after, Connie and her two boys came bowling through the door singing an enthusiastic chorus of 'Coming Round the Mountain'. Simm burst out laughing. It was going to be fun being part of another family.

Connie whispered in Oliver's ear as she walked past: "Don't mention Jamie. Lizbeth says Gil hasn't told them." Oliver nodded.

"Right, gang," said Oliver. "I've been on the phone to Grannie, and we are all going to San Clemente for the weekend."

So they weren't going to Nancy's as she'd intended.

Jacob and Mylo looked at each other. They'd heard of it, of course, but never been there. Simm and Deborah let out a loud cheer.

"Jake, you'll love it. It has a long pier and you can watch the surfers and further down on the other side you can swim and you can go fishing from the pier and there a loads of great restaurants with clams and shrimp and lobster and everything. It's really really great."

"Better stop talking, Simm – you'll run out of breath," said Oliver. Simeon was now panting and red in his beaming face.

"And Grannie's lovely," said Deborah, not to be outdone. "She has a big broomstick in the kitchen which she uses to kill rats."

"She does not!" said Simm, outraged.

Chapter Forty-two

In a beautiful county, San Clemente stood out. Golden beaches, tasteful restaurants and, as Simm had said, a long, long pier with a wonderful view at the end.

Grace Maxwell's villa was built into a cliff-side and had an extensive tiled patio with shaded sofas and upholstered armchairs. Set under an awning, were three large coolers for white wine, beer, juice and soda. There were also barbeque and pizza ovens.

Grace herself, was a silver-haired, sylph-like lady in her sixties. Her facial resemblance to Oliver was remarkable, and she had the same smooth skin and slender build, but where Oliver was tanned from outdoor living, Grace was pale-skinned from wearing wide-brimmed hats outdoors.

She didn't smile much which Connie found disconcerting. Mylo and Jacob were nervous around her, but her own grandchildren hugged her enthusiastically, kissing her cheeks over and over. She brushed them away.

"So, this is Connie. And Jacob and Mylo I assume." Still no smile. She leaned over and taking both boys by the chin, turned their faces this way and that and looked deep into their eyes.

"Hmm...," she said. That could have meant anything.

"Jeez," thought Connie.

It was then she caught the glimmer of a smile and realized this was a lady, for such she was, of great character and intelligence.

"Come on in children, there's cake and orange juice - she didn't approve of soda pop - in the kitchen."

Jacob went indoors, bypassed the cake and began poking

around in corners and opening cupboard doors. Connie cringed.

"There isn't, Deborah. There's no brooms in here and it's too clean for rats."

"Idiot!" exclaimed Deborah and got a tap on her bottom for cheek from her Grannie.

"That's no way to treat your guests, Deborah. You're a Maxwell – you should know better."

"Now, Connie. Would you prefer coffee, or perhaps a glass of wine?"

"I'll have a glass of Merlot, please, Grace," said Oliver.

Grace didn't like being called Mom – she said it made her feel old - but she was always 'grannie' to her grandchildren. It made her feel like a matriarch.

"I didn't ask you, Oliver. What will it be, Connie?" It was a lifetime ago in her childhood that Connie had been treated with such courtesy. It suddenly felt so familiar, almost homely.

"Coffee would be nice, thank you."

Grace waved her hand and a maid curtsied and returned to the house interior, emerging a few minutes later with a tray of drinks and a dish of green and black olives.

"How was your journey from Windham?" asked Oliver. Grace turned to Connie.

"Oh, the usual. I have a place just outside Windham in Illinois. My husband – he's dead now - was a psychiatrist. There are plenty of crazy people in Illinois, so he did quite well."

"Connie'll think you were one of dad's patients," persisted Oliver

"And so I was, for a while."

She was so enigmatic Connie wasn't quite sure if it was a family joke, so she changed the subject.

"What a lovely home you have Grace. It must have one of the best views of the beach in San Clemente."

"I suppose it does. The tourists do look a bit like ants from here."

There was a sudden shout from indoors, and Mylo appeared, orange juice dripping from his t-shirt. Connie was about to go to him when Grace commanded:

"Deborah – come here. Now, Deborah…. not next week."

The little girl appeared her expression neutral. She didn't dare sass her grandmother, but Grace knew what was going on. She seemed to have a sixth sense.

"You will apologize to Mylo immediately. Simeon, help him clean up. There's an old t-shirt of yours in your dressing room which should fit him."

"Well? What are you waiting for?" Grace snapped at her granddaughter and rapped her knuckles smartly on the chair arm.

"Sorry," muttered Deborah in a voice which was anything but. Grace waved a hand.

"I suppose that will have to do. Now go away and play."

After the children had gone, Grace gave her son her full attention for the first time.

"You have to do something about that child. She needs a good spanking. Her manners are appalling."

"She's good-hearted. She'll grow out of it in time."

"She isn't and she won't."

Oliver changed the subject.

282

"We've brought the kids here for a holiday, of course," said Oliver almost defensively. "But I'm afraid we have an ulterior motive."

Grace raised an eyebrow.

"We wanted to tell you face to face what is going on. Rachel and I are going through a legal separation…….."

"Thank the Lord for that!" Grace exclaimed, and she turned to Connie.

"A faux aristocrat. Very tedious woman. Do you like books, Connie? Come. I'll show you my library." She pushed her chair back. "Come along."

Connie dumbfounded, dutifully followed her to a large cool room at the rear of the house, one wall of which appeared to be composed of the natural stone of the cliff into which the house was built. The other three walls comprised floor to ceiling shelves, each full of books. In one corner was a wrought-iron spiral staircase presumably leading to the roof.

Connie walked along the shelves examining the titles. There were the obvious ones – American authors like Steinbeck and Walt Whitman, and the English classics, Charlotte Bronte, Jane Austen and an extremely old folio edition of Shakespeare's "Merchant of Venice."

"May I look at this, please?" Connie was fascinated.

Grace pulled it off the shelf and dropped it unceremoniously on a table in the center of the room. Connie was aghast. The book must be priceless. When she saw the look on her face Grace said:

"It's alright, dear. I've had all the spines reinforced. I'm notoriously clumsy."

They spent an hour in the library until Grace looked at her little Cartier watch and said:

"We'll have some tea then take the children down to the beach. Do you like beaches? I must confess to not caring for them myself, but one does have to indulge the brats from time to time I suppose."

They returned to find an English cream tea of dainty cucumber sandwiches and cream cakes with a large pot of hot Darjeeling tea.

"Just a snack, dear. There's a remarkably good fish restaurant on the pier. You do like fish, I take it? We'll go there when the children have had enough of the beach."

Only once had Oliver been unable to get a word in. Every time he tried, his mother would turn to Connie with another query.

The beach was typically Californian. Fine golden sand and although the waves curled to one side of the pier, on the other was gentler water for small children to play.

Grace kicked off her sandals and pulled her sundress over her neatly coiffed hair. Underneath she wore a tankini in bright blues and greens.

"Right, infants, last one in's a sissy!" and with that she raced down the beach and into the sea, the children whooping and hollering behind.

"That's my mother," said Oliver awkwardly.

Connie had only known Grace for a few hours and already she'd made an indelible impression. She supposed there was no middle road with Grace Maxwell. You either loved her or hated her.

They stayed for three whole days, each of which was an adventure, led by that amazing and original old lady. On the last day, Grace's lady's maid was packing her belongings for her return to Illinois.

Suddenly there was an ear-splitting scream. All the adults, including Grace, rushed to the doors and there was Mylo, laying at the bottom of a flight of marble stairs, his ankle twisted at a peculiar angle.

Connie went to pick him up, but he screamed in agony.

Grace took over.

"Tina!" she shouted and a small, plump Mexican woman in a black dress dashed out of the kitchen. "Call Mr. Craven. His number is in the pocket of my purse. Tell him I say to come immediately. Immediately!" Tina dropped a curtsy. "Then call 911" Grace ordered, as an afterthought.

Under her auspices, Mylo was having pain medication and his ankle set within the hour. Connie accompanied him to hospital with the surgeon, Mr. Craven.

Grace's hair had escaped its clips. She wound it round her finger and shoved it back in place.

She looked around. Simm was sitting on the stairs, clearly horrified by what had happened and Jacob, his friend, sat next to him. Deborah was on Oliver's knee, cuddled up to his chest. Her expression was not visible.

But grannie Grace was nobody's fool.

"Right!" she exclaimed. "I've had enough. Tomorrow I'm going back to Windham and that little minx is coming with me. If you won't discipline her then I suppose I'll have to."

Oliver's mouth opened and closed like a goldfish.

Chapter Forty-three

Gil's grief for Jamie came in waves. Sometimes he would feel fine and function normally, and at others all he could think of was how much he loved his brother, and how unbearable life was going to be without him. The time spent in the studio was the worst.

"Huh! Little baby Gil. The Robson with no brains and no looks. The expendable one! Why don't you piss off back to Briarside where you belong, and leave the professionals to it? You'll still get your cut."

Ed was having a field day, now free to attack Gil anyway he wished with no interference from Jamie.

While Gil was no push-over – he was a kid from the wrong side of the tracks in Los Angeles – it would have broken his heart to resort to the same kind of invective. So, he kept his temper.

But the sheer cruelty wore him down and added to the burden he already carried. Until he was no longer there, Gil hadn't realized how much of Jamie's high spirits had been aimed at protecting him. Everyone thought of his brother merely as a drunk and drug addict – a low-life who had no serious thoughts in his head.

Gil knew different. He was a serious song writer and starting as he did, derided at every turn by his sarcastic and abusive father, he had managed to pick himself up and teach himself to master of keyboards of all kinds. He had been involved in the writing, singing and production of his own solo work at Anasazi when he died.

Of course, that had been very carefully hidden from a jealous and vindictive Ed. Secretly helped by Gil, together they constructed a masterpiece of originality and great beauty. It had been in its final stages when

Jamie died, and Gil was determined that he would see to its completion. It would be his own personal eulogy to his beloved brother.

Meantime, he had to find a way to cope. But he was buckling under the strain. He fulfilled all his studio work but now dutifully. It had ceased to be the joyful experience of his youth. The stage work was beautifully prepared and crafted, the support musicians treated with the same consideration and respect, but increasingly they began to notice that Gil's heart wasn't in it.

Almost imperceptibly at first, his drinking increased reinforced by the occasional snort of cocaine, which he was careful to keep well-hidden but which was beginning to take control again as the weeks went by.

And his recovery had started so well.

Chapter Forty-four

Connie woke one hot Sunday morning in May feeling very unwell. It had been coming on for the past couple of days but on this particular morning, she felt dreadful. Jacob was just recovering from a bug he'd picked up at school. It may have been that.

She lay on her back, Oliver snoring gently beside her, feeling her stomach churn and the sweat break out on her brow. When it became unbearable, she ran to the bathroom and was violently sick.

Oliver had slept through, so she took a glass of water and sat in the cooler air next to the pool.

Maria the housekeeper, arrived on time at seven-thirty, and set about her chores in the kitchen. The banging and clattering of pans and utensils was more than Connie could bear, so she went back to her dressing room to change.

She put her head round the bedroom door, but Oliver was still sleeping.

This same routine continued for nearly a week until Connie began to suspect another cause for her illness. She'd been unwell through a couple of months of her pregnancy when Jacob came but had sailed through Mylo's birth. She had been so young herself when her boys were born, and anyway her life then had been a rollercoaster.

Perhaps she might have more leisure to enjoy her pregnancy this time round. She was going to the Track with Oliver this evening. She'd talk to him when they got back. She was beginning to like the idea of a new baby.

The visit to the track, with the heat and dust, had begun

to make her feel queasy again, so they came back earlier than planned. She showered, changed and twisted her damp hair into a bun on top of her head.

Oliver always thought she looked at her best like this. You couldn't embellish a lily and with her skin glowing from the shower, and the perfume of her shampoo drifting around her, she was his idea of perfection.

Connie smiled, sat on his knee and kissed him quickly on the lips.

"I have something to speak to you about. I promise you a night of bliss afterwards!" she laughed.

"Oliver...," she was suddenly unsure of herself. "I think there's every chance we might be expecting a baby."

"No. It has to be something else. Now come back here. You made a promise!"

"I think you're wrong. I have all the signs," Connie persisted.

"Can't be. Because Rachel had been ill, I had a vasectomy directly after Deborah's birth, so it must be something else."

"Oh, okay. I'll make an appointment with the doctor in the morning. So.... where were we?" She kissed him sweetly and parted his lips with her tongue.

The following day the doctor confirmed her suspicions. The baby was due in January. She fainted, collapsing into the doctor's arms. There was only one other possible explanation.

Connie was still shattered as she went down the steps from the obstetrician's office. He had tried to persuade her to stay until she felt well again, but all she wanted was to get out into the air and be alone to think.

She had to put aside her feelings and consider the

practicalities first.

She didn't have the support system she'd had when she was with Gil. Jamie, who might have defied convention, was gone. There was her mother. But how could she explain this to her own mother?

And how was she to tell Oliver? He was no Gil who would have put her first in all things – even this – no matter the cost to himself.

But the only viable way forward was Gil or her mother. Gil was definitely out of the question so it looked like she would have to go to Kelani.

Whatever Oliver's response it wouldn't be possible for her to stay at his home. They could never explain it to the children. She had no doubt Nancy would take her boys. Oh Lord, she hated this. How could she have been so irresponsible?

If she left the boys with Nancy, she would have to tell Gil. She would know he wouldn't want to be excluded. But Connie's major problem was there was no way on earth Gil would dream of giving the baby up. He would see it as his responsibility – and hers too – which was a huge chunk of hypocrisy given their situation.

She had a little time yet. She wasn't showing. She would see her mother.

Kelani wanted to be helpful, but she was an old-fashioned lady who set great store by the opinions of her neighbors. How could she explain an obviously pregnant daughter with no husband? But Connie was her daughter nonetheless, and she had a duty to help her if she could. She could appreciate Connie would only come to her as a last resort. Such was her quandary that she burst into tears in Connie's arms, and her daughter knew there could be no help from that quarter.

This was just awful. Oliver would have to be the next to know. That couldn't be put off.

Oliver stood stiff as a board and regarded her through cold, expressionless eyes.

"Again. You've done it again. You've treated my family like shit."

That was all. He walked out of the house and didn't come back for the rest of the day – or the next. She was left to cope with the children without a clue what to tell them and no idea when, or if, he'd be back.

Her pregnancy continued to be difficult.

On the third day after his departure, Oliver came back with a partial solution. She should go and stay with his mother in Illinois. Connie feared Grace would not only turn her away but eviscerate her.

"I don't really see you have any other option. Running the gauntlet with my mother or going to Gil. If you do the second, I swear to God, I will kill you with my bare hands. So, my mother it has to be."

This time, Connie's tears were useless and she prepared for her journey to Illinois.

Grace looked her up and down.

"Make yourself scarce, Oliver. I need to speak to Connie alone."

Oliver looked pleased but he needn't have.

Once he'd left, Grace led Connie through to an exquisite sitting room overlooking Lake Michigan. It had cream chintz upholstery and light oak furniture and positively glowed in the sunshine.

"Sit down, sit down," she said impatiently. "I suppose

that stupid son of mine has been a complete bastard. Who knows? He may have been born on the wrong side of the blanket himself,"

Grace came as close to a grin as Connie had ever seen.

"Now.... I want the full story. And I mean the full story. Nothing missing because you think its distasteful. Nothing missing because you think it's none of my business. Everything."

Connie began. It was a story which lasted until the bright sunlight moved to an evening glow.

She told about her breakup with Gil and her relationship with Oliver. About her problems with Deborah. Grace sniffed. About her leaving Oliver to take care of Gil when he was so ill with drink and drugs; about her return; about the agreement thrashed out at Rick's Bar; about Jamie and his death and his closeness to Gil; about meeting Gil at Jamie's grave, and what happened then that put her in this situation.

Grace sat, expressionless and thoughtful throughout.

"Bit of a pickle then? Sounds like your feelings for this Gil are the problem for Oliver."

"It's the truth. I do still love Gil and always will," she said and looked Grace bravely in the eye, "but living with him is impossible. He's rarely there, and when he is, his mind isn't. Oliver loves me and I'm sure given time things will work out," said a troubled Connie.

"In that case, I can only see one way forward. We'll send the brat back to Los Angeles with her father, and you stay here through your pregnancy. I could use some intelligent conversation. But I have one stipulation. I want you to have the baby in Los Angeles."

Connie supposed she had her reasons, but she was wary of asking someone she knew so superficially what they were. She was just so unbelievably grateful that Grace had been more of a mother to her than her own.

"Now, come on. You can have your last glass of wine for quite some time, and first thing in the morning I'll pack Oliver off home with his delightful daughter."

Chapter Forty-five

That autumn the band began a tour of Europe finishing with a gig in England on the way home. It was going to be grueling with most venues having two performances.

It didn't help that Gil's health was at a low point before they even began. The drinking had led to big weight gain and hiding his use of cocaine was making him paranoid. But he just wouldn't have been functioning at all without it.

Increasingly, the band members were beginning to panic. Gil was musical director. Without him, the music cues to everyone on stage didn't happen. There was no-one to make sure the sound checks were carried out and instruments up to par. And, worst of all, he had begun to sing off-key. As all the harmonies were keyed to his voice this was more than disastrous.

Even Ed had stopped making snide remarks, if he wasn't entirely helpful.

The hammer finally fell when it occurred to Nancy that she didn't actually know where Connie was.

It was something as small as needing her to sign a form so that Jacob could go on a school trip to the zoo. She called everyone she knew trying to locate her. Jacob was going to miss out. Connie was nowhere to be found.

Assuming, therefore, that Gil had forgotten to tell her Connie's plans in the rush of getting ready to leave LA, Nancy picked up the phone and called his hotel.

"Can you give me a number for Connie, Gil? She's not home and neither Lizbeth nor her mother have seen her. I need her to sign a form for Jacob. Who else can I ask?"

The last time Gil had seen Connie, they had both gone to

lay flowers on Jamie's grave and all hell had broken loose. That had been a while ago now – just how long he couldn't quite remember – but he'd done his best to stay away. He'd only seen her the once and that was getting into her car outside Oliver's house. What had he been doing outside Oliver's house? His memory was vague on that point.

"Nope, sorry Mom. No idea where she is. Did you ask Lizbeth…oh, yes. You said you did. Don't know, sorry, don't know."

"You're alright, Son?"

"I'm fine, Mom. I'll make a few calls and get back to you."

He turned on the TV and fell asleep.

The following morning Gil awoke with an appalling hangover. He could barely see from the headache and his mouth felt like shit. He tried to bring himself round by taking a cold shower and felt marginally better, but he recoiled when he saw his reflection in the bathroom mirror.

There was no way he could face eating, so he picked up his overnight bag and headed for the door. Then he half-remembered something about his mother….and Connie. He'd better call. He looked at his watch. His Mom would still be in bed. He'd call later from the theatre.

But of course, with all that was going on he forgot, even if Connie's name kept pounding in the back of his mind through the bourbon he'd consumed.

When he finally got round to calling, it was after the afternoon gig. Nancy was frantic. She couldn't find Connie anywhere. She'd even been to Kelani's in Santa Monica, and she hadn't seen her either. She'd been oddly hesitant, Nancy thought.

"Calm down, Calm down, Mom. I'll give it some thought and get back to you."

"That's what you said yesterday. What the hell is wrong with you, Gil? You and Connie might be breaking up, but I'd have thought you'd be a little curious as to where she is."

Gil held his head between his hands and screamed inwardly. Again, the whole world was revolving round his decisions, and he couldn't do this anymore. He slammed the phone down.

"Gil, Jeff needs you backstage. Don't know why."

"Fuck off!" Gil yelled at the top of his lungs and marched out of the room.

He'd found a little curtained-off area backstage and crawled in there for some peace. Now no-one knew where he was. But he was kind of worried about Connie, now he had time to think about it.

He emerged from his hidey-hole and picked up the nearest phone. Who to call? Nancy'd been round everyone he could think of. Except one. Oh, crap no. NO!

The last time he'd felt so bad about making a phone call was when he'd to tell Connie about the meeting at Rick's. But he had a premonition this was going to be much, much worse. He leafed through his pocketbook until he found a dog-eared card he'd kept from when he'd had his addiction problems....... last addiction problems. He felt for the little bag in his jacket pocket.

"Hey – whose calling?" Simm asked.

"Is your dad there, Simm? Its Gil Robson. I need to

speak to him urgently."

He took a slug of whisky.

"Hello, Oliver? My mother is trying to get in touch with Connie and no-one can find her. Do you know her number?" There was a protracted silence.

"Indeed I do."

He reeled off a number in Illinois and put the phone down.

Gil was perplexed. He coped with it in the way he coped with most stress these days. He took out the little bag from his pocket.

Gil called Illinois. The phone was answered by a servant. He asked for Connie. Connie, thinking it was Oliver and a chance to apologize, picked up the phone.

"Hello. Oliver?"

"Connie its Gil. Where are you? The whole of LA is upside down looking for you. Mostly because my Mom needs a paper signed for Jacob's school. What the hell are you doing in Illinois?"

Connie sat down with a thump on a hall chair. How was she to do this. On the phone? Well, she could hardly go and see him. On the phone, then.

"You'd better sit down Gil. This is going to come as a shock."

Silence.

"I'm pregnant." She heard him draw a deep breath.

"Oliver must be delighted," he said grimly.

"Oliver had a vasectomy after Deborah was born. Not his. Yours."

For a moment he just refused to believe it, then he sank to his knees and wept silently into the floor. He could hear Connie calling down the phone.

"What do I do Connie? Tell me what to do. Do you need anything? Money? Somewhere to stay? Is your Mom there with you? Why the hell are you in Illinois?"

"I'm staying with Oliver's mother. She's been very good to me. I don't need anything. I'm fine. I'll call you when you get back."

"You can't drop a bombshell like that and just hang up!" he screamed down the phone, but she had already gone.

It was only one hour before show-time and Gil would usually be doing last minute checks. He was nowhere to be found.

Eventually Bill, the percussionist, found his little hide-away behind the curtain. Gil was lying on his back, a spent bottle of bourbon on his chest and another, half-full in his left hand. He was completely unconscious. John shook him but the only response was an incoherent mutter which quickly faded. He called Ed over. Gil was so intoxicated they couldn't wake him. They tried to lift him, but he was a dead weight in their arms.

Between them, they managed to carry him, feet dragging, to the dressing rooms.

Thirty minutes to curtain up.

No time for consideration - Gil was shoved unceremoniously under a cold shower.

Gradually, some sense returned, and he struggled to stand. Time was short. He was toweled down by three pairs of hands and dragged into the first of his clothes they could lay their hands on.

Curtain up.

Curt, one of the sidemen, shoved a guitar in his hands and they pushed him on-stage.

He tripped but regained his footing.

Ed opened the performance with his usual prance across the stage, this time dressed in purple sequined trousers. Gil knocked into one of the amps and sent a capo skidding across the floor.

The music started up. The opener was one of Gil's best compositions. He sang it seated at a small Wurlitzer. His excess weight caused him to lean slightly to one side. John had the awful impression he was going to slide off his seat. But he got shakily to his feet and tinkered with the mic on top of the piano, trying ineptly to adjust it to the right height.

He tripped on a piece of loose wiring.

Jamie, who might have saved the day, had died. Phil was a good keyboard player but couldn't play guitar though his singing was good. John could play guitar but not lead. And Ed? Well Ed could entertain but had no musical skills at all – just attitude and a big mouth.

It was Gil who played keyboards and guitar; Gil who had perfect pitch to anchor the harmonies; Gil who, now Jamie was no longer there, had to attempt to duplicate his talent for weaving everything together into a seamless whole.

The audience began to look at each other and mutter, then first one and then another stood quietly and filed out of the auditorium.

Then Gil collapsed altogether and lay amongst the guitar pedals and set lists on the wooden planks of the stage.

John went out front and sang one of Gil's beautiful solos to the best of his ability, simply to give them time. But the audience had filed out and the auditorium was by now empty.

Chapter Forty-six

It was four in the morning. The alcohol had largely disappeared from Gil's brain, and he had learned to wait out the downer from the coke long ago. It made him shudder for a while, but it passed.

He felt as if the heart had been torn out of him. He could outlive the rest of his problems, but he couldn't do without the friends in his audiences and the music they shared with him.

He was looking at the scene of his disgrace from the night before. They had the following day off, so the stage was still littered with equipment to be packed in the morning.

He put both hands on the seat in front and rested his head on them. He couldn't think of a way to extricate himself from this. If his fans left him, he could see no way forward. His life would be finished.

Afterwards, he came to believe the thought had been put in his head by some entity greater than himself. Some spirit above the banalities of this world.

"Call Giulia," it whispered in his ear.

She at least would listen. He hoped she wouldn't judge him too harshly although he couldn't see why she shouldn't. It would be around two in the morning in Denver – he hoped she'd be there and not at the family home in Los Angeles.

He ran for the back-stage phone and dialed her number. It called for what seemed hours and at last, a sleepy voice on the other end of the line said:

"Yes? Who the hell is it at this time in the morning?" Then as consciousness returned: "Is that you Tony? If this is a joke, it's not funny. Go to hell!" She almost slammed the phone down.

"Giulia – please don't hang up. Its Gil."

"Gil – where are you, for God's sake. Do you realize it's …," there was a significant pause, "two-fifteen?

"Yes… yes..." There was no time for explanations. "Do you remember, twice you told me that you would listen if I was in trouble? Well, I'm in trouble – of the worst kind."

"Of course. Go on." She had sat up in bed and pulled the sleep mask from her eyes.

He didn't want to tell her what Connie had said to him to completely throw him off-beam. It wasn't important. His substance abuse would probably have led him down the same road.

"I'm right back to square one. I've broken every one of my promises and I'm off the wagon big time. I can't believe I could be so stupid. You don't need to say anything." He paused. Could he get through this conversation without his usual prop? He'd have to, although he'd be in one hell of a state afterwards.

"Go on.": her voice was neutral, so he continued:

"Last night I completely lost my mind on stage……"

He let her have all the gruesome details, leaving nothing out and making no excuses. He talked for an hour uninterrupted and because she hadn't spoken throughout, he thought she might have dropped off to sleep again in the middle. She hadn't.

After a brief pause during which his foot began to tap, uncontrolled against the seat in front and his knuckles to rap on his chair arm, she answered:

"So, what's the problem? If you've upset someone,

apologize."

Shit, if he'd realized she was that good, he'd have called sooner. Without anything from him, she'd got right to the crux of the matter – his music and his fans.

"Thanks Giulia… Thank you. You can go back to sleep now. I'll let you know what happens."

He slapped the phone down, took out his notebook and dialed the number of the promoter who had walked out in a fury the night before – that much he did remember. It didn't even register it was only six a.m.. Poor guy had probably had as much sleep as Gil had. A phone conversation later, more powder up his nose and he had taken a cab to the promoter's hotel, where he was met in the coffee shop by a furious, but thankfully silent, businessman.

"You don't need to say a word," said Gil holding up his hand, "but I'd like you to help me put things right – well, at least to try."

The promoter tapped his fingers on the tabletop and invited him to continue.

"I will probably have to lie through my teeth, but I would like to speak to the press. I want to take out a full page in the local newspapers."

The promoter looked at him, trying to figure out if he was serious. He'd met some weird people in the music business. Gil's eyes looked steadily back into his.

"It may be difficult at such short notice, but I'll try," said the promoter. "Did you speak to the rest of the band?"

"Shit, no. They'd be furious but I need to apologize to them publicly too. The whole world needs to hear how sorry I am."

The promoter made the local paper deadline with minutes to spare. Gil's pictures were splashed across the page with the headline

TOP POP STAR BREAKS SILENCE ON DRUNKEN SHAMBLES

Gil Robson of The California Crystal Band offers public apology to fans.

Gil wasn't aware of being silent, but the rest was true enough. His behavior had been shameful.

Chapter Forty-seven

At the press interview Gil had stumbled through the questions more or less successfully, praying that no-one would pay too much attention to his answers. He had had no sleep, so he certainly looked rough.

He still hadn't spoken to the guys, so he had that to do. Depending on their reaction the pressure might ease a bit. It felt like a cataclysm waiting to happen, but it didn't turn out that way.

John, who had taken on most of the vocals, hugged him, aware of how distraught with embarrassment he was. Ed and Phil hung back, reserving judgment, although they were impressed by his public apology. The most precious reaction to Gil came from the guys in the backing band. To a man they supported him, although it was possible his actions might affect their futures.

Gil made two resolutions as a result of this trauma. He would never again drink or take drugs before a performance, and he would never take for granted the devotion of the fans he thought of as friends. He just hoped they would forgive him – and of course they did.

He was so exhausted by all the trauma, he slept the whole of the long journey back, and once in Los Angeles he lost no time in calling Denver to thank Giulia.

Diana was there but Larry and Giulia had gone back to LA for a few days.

When he arrived unannounced at the Giordano home, Giulia was red in the face, sweaty and smarting from a thrashing at tennis by her mother.

She smiled, but clearly upset by her appearance, rushed

into the house to shower and change. Carrie kissed him on both cheeks and pulled him inside by the hand.

"That girl goes to pieces when you're around. I can't think what's wrong with her," she said with a wink.

Gil, who habitually missed all the clues, winked back. Carrie lifted her hands in despair. Gil was confused but accepted the glass of iced lemonade she handed him.

Giulia soon reappeared, glowing from the exercise and her shower. Gil held her face between his hands and kissed her on the forehead.

"Why don't you two spend some time in the den? I've to go visit some friends. Back in a couple of hours. Paul's out until tonight and Larry's watching Tony play football."

Carry looked pointedly at her daughter whose blush was apparent even through her tan.

They sat on the sofa, and Gil pulled Giulia close in a grateful hug.

"I can't thank you enough for your advice."

He gave her a long explanation of what had happened, his face becoming increasingly haggard. Giulia felt so sorry for him, she leant over and gave him a sympathetic kiss on the lips. Gardenias.

"That's enough of my problems. How've you been? I'm sick of thinking about me."

"Oh, good, I guess. The apartments are pretty much finished now. Diana's sorting out the last details. I honestly don't know what I'd have done without her. And Larry of course, although now he's in pilot training, we don't see him so much. Gil, why didn't you tell me things were so bad before it went this far?"

"I don't know. Didn't want to worry you, I guess."

She leaned in and the kiss she gave him this time was anything but sisterly. He looked shocked, as if he'd been kissed sensually by an eight-year-old. But she wasn't eight, was she? She was ten years younger than him so that would make her.... twenty-three in December. Twenty-three! Connie was rearing two babies by that age. Twenty-three! He looked at her with new eyes.

She was very pretty, petite and delicate. He took in her appearance for the first time with admiration.

She told him of a pet charity she was sponsoring and about Larry joining the air force. He was completely distracted. This was not good. The Giordanos were his friends — all of them. They were where he went to be safe, to be happy. He couldn't endanger that for a fling with Giulia. So, he left.

But he had noticed Giulia was no longer a child.

That evening when Giulia arrived at the house in Linden Reach she was carrying one of Larry's guitars as an excuse to ask Gil to fix a new string. Guitars were becoming a regular pretext - she just hoped he hadn't noticed.

He was as usual down at the pool-house. He had yet to see her, so she observed him for a few seconds. The multitude of candles he'd lit softened his features and struck highlights from his guitar and his hair. The scent of rosewater filled the air - it was always there when he was deep in thought. She wondered why it relaxed him so.

He was such a beautiful man, with the gentlest blue eyes imaginable. He had always been the center of her existence, even though he was besotted by Connie.

He looked up and smiled that smile which since she was

eight years old could turn her insides to jelly. She offered him Larry's guitar.

"Can you fix the A string on this? My fingers aren't strong enough to stretch it."

He took the instrument from her and reached for his guitar case with its spare strings. She sat cross-legged on the lawn in front of him. The grass was slightly damp, so she ran her hands along her jeans to dry them off.

Giulia took the repaired guitar from his hands and laid it carefully next to her on the grass. She kissed him and removed any lingering doubts he may have had she was still a baby.

"Giulia – please, please don't do this. Please – I don't want to hurt you."

The stress started him trembling again. This time it was severe enough to cause a small seizure. With no-one else to help, Giulia sat next to him until he'd recovered sufficiently to speak. He reached into his pocket for another small white packet.

"You really don't want to get involved with me, Giulia. I just make the same mistakes over and over – I don't seem able to help myself. Find someone who will treat you the way you deserve."

"You're getting too good at not facing facts," said Giulia, ignoring the facts he'd clearly laid before her. "You will get a hold on this. And you will accept help. Here."

She opened the packet and handed him the coke.

"Take it. I know my Dad well enough to know you can't just stop without medical help. I'll help you the best I know how."

He took the cocaine and his worries receded. He kissed

her passionately, overcome by the 'high.'

Chapter Forty-eight

Connie had never been so relieved to see the back of anyone as she was Deborah. She was relieved to have her problems with Oliver put on a back-burner as well.

Telling Gil about the baby had just about wiped her out, and the fall-out from that conversation was not yet apparent.

Grace was her usual acerbic self and maintained her coldness to her son, at the same time treating Connie like a beloved daughter. Best of all, she was clearly looking forward to the birth of another grandchild 'to make up for that idiotic brat'.

Grace never asked about Gil, for which Connie was profoundly grateful. She didn't like to think about him either, but she did find it a bit puzzling he hadn't tried to get in touch.

Her time neared. She was worn out and aching. This baby pushed and kicked harder than either of her boys. It was as if it was desperate to be born.

Grace had Connie's bags packed and sent freight to Kelani's home in Santa Monica. Connie had rung her mother and arranged to have the baby there. Even Kelani couldn't deny her that as Christmas approached.

Once she'd settled Connie with her mother, Grace returned to Illinois.

The baby was due at the beginning of January but caused havoc by coming three weeks early. Nobody but Grace and Kelani, and the gynecologist and his nurse who Grace bribed to silence, knew of the birth.

It was a girl – five pounds twelve ounces but vigorous

and healthy. She needed no help starting to breathe and her first cry was ear-splitting.

Grace had allayed her nervous excitement by endless shopping trips. She bought tiny little dresses – 'no lace, horribly unhygienic' – thumb-sized socks and mittens and delicate, hand-crocheted blankets. And nowhere was there a single hint of pink. The baby couldn't possibly use it all but that was beside the point.

Grace couldn't bring herself to buy diapers which Connie in frequent phone calls, found hilarious.

Connie and the baby were to return to Windham with Oliver. Clearly Grace wanted to keep an eye on him.

Kelani registered the baby's birth and Connie decided to name the baby Anna Robson Maxwell, hopefully to keep everyone happy, especially Grace.

Once back in Windham, there was a long discussion - a very long discussion - before a consensus of opinion on what to do next was reached.

Connie had formed a bond with the baby, stronger than with either Jacob or Mylo. It would be bad enough not being involved in her life, but it would break her heart never to know where she was. And to Grace, the first time she held her in her arms, she was her darling granddaughter.

If Gil found little Anna, the complications he would certainly cause would be off the scale. He hadn't been in touch again since that dreadful telephone conversation when she had hung up on him, but he knew of the pregnancy, so he would guess at the birth date. He might even make an intelligent guess at her name. Connie just prayed his head would rule his heart and he would leave the little mite time and space to be carefree and happy.

It was then that the reason for Grace's insistence baby Anna was born and registered in Los Angeles became apparent. It would throw Gil off the scent long enough for them to hide her.

And Grace had another surprise for them.

"I do hope you don't think I'm jumping the gun, dear," said Grace "but I have made one or two enquiries."

She had been looking round for a family to adopt the little one privately to avoid official records. It was highly illegal and the new parents would have to be on board at the risk of losing their child, who could never therefore be told until she reached the age of discretion. Connie gave Grace permission to continue her enquiries.

Oliver was very unsure about the arrangements, but above all he didn't want Connie involved with Gil in any way whatever. So in the end he agreed to keep his mouth shut.

His mother was disdainful and entirely distrustful. He had already pointed Gil in the direction of Illinois by giving him the number for the Windham house. She believed him to be the weak link in her plans.

Eventually baby Anna was adopted privately by a family in Champaign in Illinois, less than three hours' drive from Windham. At Connie's request, her name was changed at her baptism.

Chapter Forty-nine

Connie and Oliver were back in Los Angeles as soon as the business with the baby was concluded. They had left the finer details to Grace who called to say the new parents had named her Christina. There was another name but that and the surname stayed Grace's secret until she saw Connie face to face. She didn't want Oliver overhearing.

Nancy, who all this time had been caring for Jacob and Mylo, was unaware of all this. The boys had now been with her for almost a year. Connie had been totally cut off from happenings in Los Angeles so she had no idea what was going on.

When Connie turned up at her front door to collect her sons, Nancy very firmly said no. She could not have them again. It had taken them ages to settle into a routine and they were now content and doing well. She would not see that ruined.

Connie turned to the boys who glanced at each other anxiously.

"Wouldn't you like to come home with me and see Oliver and Simm?" She left Deborah out of it. "We are going to have a barbeque this afternoon. Wouldn't you like that?"

The boys both looked at Nancy for reassurance.

"Do we have to, Nana? I'd rather stay here," begged Jacob.

A single stray tear ran down Mylo's cheek.

"That a clear enough answer for you, Connie? I've only seen Gil twice since you disappeared, and the boys felt the same about him. You can imagine no doubt how that made me feel - or perhaps not. I thought I knew you, but it seems I was wrong."

Nancy pulled the boys back inside the house and closed the door.

"She can't do that with my kids," muttered a furious Connie. She banged on the door with her fist, but it didn't open again.

The boys, who were clinging to each other, suddenly reminded Nancy of Gil and Jamie with their father at the same age.

In retrospect, Connie thought perhaps she should have made more effort to keep on the right side of Nancy. If Gil had told anyone about the baby, it would be her. As far as Connie knew, this close little group, which may or may not include Nancy, were the only ones who knew. Even Lizbeth didn't – or Monty, thank goodness.

Whatever Oliver might think, she had to see Gil and thrash out an agreement. She needed to explain what had happened and why she'd done what she'd done without his consent, about their daughter. Their daughter! He was going to be devastated.

She drove to Linden Reach, but the house was in darkness, so she tore a page from her pocket diary and scribbled a message that she'd be over in the morning. She had important matters to discuss. She put the note in the middle of the front steps, weighed down with a stone from the garden, so he couldn't miss it.

The following morning, she arrived at ten-thirty, and when Gil opened the door to her knock, she was shocked to see Giulia standing behind him in the kimono Gil had bought for her in Japan. It was too big for her and trailed on the floor.

"Can we sit down. I'd like to speak to you privately."

She looked meaningfully at Giulia. Giulia was pleased to leave.

Gil didn't offer her coffee so she launched straight into the disaster she knew was about to unfold.

"The baby came early."

Gil automatically looked down at her belly. She had pretty much got her figure back.

"How early? She? We had a daughter! Is she well? Have you left her in the car? Can I fetch her? What can I do? Just ask!"

Prepared as she thought she was, she was still surprised at his enthusiasm.

"She's not here."

"At Oliver's?" he frowned then beamed. "At your mother's? Or mine?"

"No Gil. She's safe where you'll never find her. Your life will not ruin hers the way it did mine and the boys. I won't allow it. She will grow up happy and carefree….and not knowing who her father is until she's older - perhaps."

His mouth dropped open. Was he hearing her right?

"You can't do this, Connie. Have you come to hate me so much?"

"I don't hate you, Gil," she said with resignation. "I have come to tell you she was born safely, there were no complications, and she is well. That's all."

"But she's my daughter. She will not be brought up as Oliver's - I will never accept that. Never. I will steal her first."

His eyes had filled with unshed tears.

"There are two things wrong with that statement. Firstly, she will not be brought up as Oliver's. I'm not so lacking in feeling," she scowled at him. "Secondly, you won't steal her because you'll never find her."

"Lacking in feeling? *Lacking in feeling?* You heartless bitch! Get out of my house!"

"But it's not your house, Gil, its mine. If you don't believe me, check the deeds. But I have no need of it now. I'll have it made over to you."

"Leave...leave now. You can have the fucking house but I promise you this, I will find that child if it takes me the rest of my life."

His determination unnerved her.

"Goodbye Gil. Goodbye," and she walked out of the house and quietly closed the door on her past. The matter of the boys and the divorce hadn't even been broached.

Chapter Fifty

He remained bereft, staring at the door. Giulia – where was Giulia? He needed more coke. And he wanted this time to take it in the pool-house.

That day he needed four hits. By the end he was almost comatose. He so needed to be comatose.

Giulia looked on in pity. She couldn't touch his heart this time - it was truly broken. The last time he asked, she said she had no more and couldn't get it. To cope with a massive downer, he broke out the Jack Daniels. Then he lurched out of the door, got in his car and swerved off down the drive.

Giulia had to find him and fast. She had no idea where he'd gone, and when she couldn't find him she started to panic. She couldn't call the cops, so she jumped in her car and started trawling the streets of Los Angeles, visiting his known haunts. She started with Rick's. It was Gil's go-to bar as it was Larry's. But Pete hadn't seen him. She checked out the band's management office on Sunset Boulevard but didn't go in. She could see he wasn't there.

She parked up in Venice and fearfully checked out the bars along the boardwalk. No joy.

So Giulia resorted to driving slowly along the sea front towards Santa Monica, checking face after face. It was now five in the morning, and she hadn't found him.

Then she had a sudden inspiration. Who always had his back in times of crisis? Jamie. He wouldn't be at his grave. He would want happy memories. Suddenly, she knew where he was.

Giulia drove as fast as she dare to Santa Monica pier – she couldn't afford to be pulled over. Gil had once told her he and Jamie used to fish there as children. Usually when they needed to escape Monty.

She jumped from the car too distracted to shut the door and ran for the pier gates.

Gil was standing half-way along, where the water below started to deepen. He was staring, unblinking, into a glorious pink and gold sunrise which reflected on the sea. Giulia could tell from his expression he was blind to it. His chestnut hair was blown back from his face by a gentle breeze. An empty bottle swung from his hand then dropped with a muted splash to the waves below.

Gil turned unsteadily and slid down a rail post to sit on the planks of the pier, his head on his raised knees. His shoulders began to shake and even from where she was standing, she could hear him. He threw back his head and screamed at a world which was slowly but surely crushing him to death.

Giulia ran. Then slid the last yards and dropped to her knees. He raised his head and for a moment or two didn't recognize her through the haze of substance and alcohol. She put her hand to her mouth and her eyes filled with tears.

Giulia held him to her. He slipped sideways into her arms and really let go. He cried as he hadn't since Jamie held him when Monty threatened to kill him when he was six.

After a few minutes, he pulled away and dried his eyes on his sleeve.

"I'll be okay in a minute. I just need a minute."

His speech was slurred and she had to steady him when he swayed sideways. Giulia sat back against the rail beside him and he rested his head wearily on her shoulder. He took several deep, steadying breaths.

"I need to tell you what's happened. But not here…. not like this."

Giulia nodded and helped him to his feet.

"Let's go. My car's parked right outside."

They went to the Giordano house – Gil didn't want to go to Linden Reach. She had her own suite of rooms and took him there, walking straight through the house before anyone could ask questions.

Giulia sat him on the sofa and fetched a bottle of water from the cooler, tipping some of it into a face cloth and wiping the sweat and tears from his face with loving care. There was no other way to express what he felt than to brush a kiss as soft as a butterfly's wing against her lips.

She waited.

"You do know you have to stop this Gil," she said quietly when the silence went on and on. "If you don't, you'll end up at the bottom of the Pacific with Jamie."

His hold on her tightened but he nodded.

"I am just finding it difficult to come to terms with what she's done. I must have cut her so deeply and for that I am desperately sorry."

Again, she waited…and then it all came tumbling out.

Once or twice through the story of the baby, Giulia had to consciously suppress a gasp. She would do what she could to help him find her, but what then? What if they did find her? Gil, kind as he was, would not let this go. The poor little one would be torn apart by warring parents. Giulia was beginning to see Connie's point of view – she wouldn't be involved in the child's upbringing either. Gil was not being targeted.

This was not the right time to mention it though. There

were more pressing matters to address.

"I know this is difficult Gil, but if you want to do your best for your little daughter, you are going to have to straighten yourself out first. If it came to a court case the lawyers would destroy you."

"I'd thought of that. Of course I had. The first thing to do would be to get out of LA - away to where drugs are less acceptable. They're a way of life here."

Giulia brightened. This was something practical she could help with.

"We'll go to Denver! To my apartment. Would you be okay with that?"

"Of course I would, but you should be very sure you're up for this. I'm likely to be out of control for some time…maybe a lot of it. That's if I can kick the habit at all this time round - it takes will-power I don't know I have without Connie."

She snuggled under his arm, then tipped her head back to smile up into his eyes.

"We can do this, Gil. And life will be good again. I promise."

They only stopped a couple of nights in Denver. Gil decided there was too much of the city life there.

Meantime, he called Jeff at Anasazi and arranged the long-term rental of the Snowline cabin. He thought of the glorious peace of the ageless mountains, and access to music might go a long way to healing his spirit.

Perhaps Giulia could help with the rest. He had started to realize she was becoming more important to him, but in what way he couldn't figure out.

Giulia had never been to Anasazi before. It was very different from the luxurious residences owned by Paul Giordano.

The Snowline cabin was not the largest but when its wood burner was lit, it was warm and cozy. Perfect for two people embarking on a love affair. Except there was a long way to go before Gil and Giulia got to that point.

First there was his addiction to conquer. Giulia was in charge of his drug supply, which she carefully secreted away, and day by day she reduced the quantity, afraid she couldn't cope with the effects of total withdrawal.

Some days were better than others. Some days he was a screaming wreck and Giulia had to wait out his paranoia elsewhere. Some days he was calm and rational and it gave them both hope for the future.

But Gil was so tired, so weary with all the drama and unpredictability. Yet the cocaine kept him edgy and he was unable to sleep. It was a vicious circle.

Giulia had taken to going down to the kitchens and carrying their meals back to the cabin. It was a long walk but soon she had more offers of help from Jeff's staff and Gil's friends than she needed. She was very careful where she placed her trust.

In the end, there were two people apart from Jeff she came to regard as 'safe' – both friends of Gil's from his teens – Harry Forster and David Elliot. Harry was a slender, gentle soul with long flaxen hair and a penchant for romantic poets, and David, who loved the wildness of the Colorado landscape, took frequent lone hiking trips in the mountains.

Sometimes Harry and he would go riding through the narrow passes which ran between the peaks. Both loved horses, and they'd dragged Gil with them on the rare occasions all three were at Anasazi together.

Catch a Falling Star

Unbeknownst to Gil – although he must have realized something was going on – Giulia and the two friends organized a rota whereby one of them was always nearby. It wasn't so much to keep Gil in as to keep the wilder elements amongst Jeff's associates out. And they managed very well.

Gil had good reason to get clean - the baby daughter he had never seen. But he also wanted to do it for Giulia. He was ashamed that she should see him at his lowest.

The only time they let him out of their sight was when he wanted to wander above the snowline as he had with Jamie.

He became lost in the beauty of the sparkling snow. Gil would sit for hours watching a hawk fly circles in the ineffable blue of a cloudless sky. To him, this was paradise.

But the darn addiction nagged at him night and day, pulling him in directions he didn't want to go, and leaving him worn out and despondent.

On only two occasions did it get the better of him. Only twice did he lose his fight.

The first time he was sitting on the same rock he sat on when he came through the last period of withdrawal. That's what he was thinking of when he keeled over in a seizure. That time he had to lift himself out of it because no-one else was around. It scared the shit out of him.

And the second time he was in the studio alone when an acquaintance came in carrying cocaine. Gil had it in his fingers and was at a low enough point to use it. Fortunately, Harry walked in. He leaned against the wall, arms folded, and glared for Gil to give it back. As the rejected dealer walked by in fury, Harry said in a quiet, even voice:

"If you so much as show your face within a hundred yards of Gil again I'll see you're dealt with. Permanently."

The dealer took an aggressive step forward, but Harry didn't flinch, and Gil stepped forward and punched the guy in the face.

"Now, git! And don't come back." said Harry.

"Nearly had you!" said the dealer with a smirk. "I'll get you next time round. You need it – you really need it. Don't you?" he smirked

Once he had disappeared out of the door, Gil turned desperate eyes on Harry:

"He's right, I really do. It would get me through the bad times when Giulia isn't around. Call him back I have the bucks."

Harry pushed himself off the wall and pulled Gil to the door.

"No you don't my friend. You may think you do now, but tomorrow you'd hate yourself. Next time you're in LA, you're coming with me to see Daniel – you need help."

It was so long since Gil had seen Daniel Jones, he'd almost forgotten the Teacher and his sect of the Soul.

"When you're ready to listen, Davy and I have a proposition for you. No pressure – time's not an issue." He smiled and put his arm round Gil's shoulder. "Come on – let's get some air."

Harry and Gil sat at one of the outdoor tables in the crisp air, and Giulia joined them. Gil put his head down on the table on folded arms, tense and shaken by his encounter with the dealer. Harry put his hand on his shoulder and gave Giulia a meaningful look over Gil's head.

"Nearly," he mouthed.

"Come on, Gil… lets go back," Giulia whispered gently. "You look as if you could use a rest."

Gil jerked upright.

"NO!" He stood and squared his shoulders. "I will NOT be beaten by this – there are other considerations now. What's the proposition, Harry? Sounds interesting."

He reached a shaking hand for Giulia's.

"C'mon, we'll go to our cabin. David's there now. Coming, Giulia?" asked Harry.

The interior of the cabin was smaller than Gil's, but with the same stripped pine interior. A glass porch facing the mountains almost doubled its size.

David had dragged some chairs into the porch, and the indoor fire and bright sunlight made it warm and comfortable. A glass table held a huge ash tray and a marquetry box of cigarettes.

David took their coats as they walked through the door. The smell of coffee was all-pervasive. It seemed almost like a home.

Once settled, cigarettes lit and scalding coffee accepted, Harry launched into their plan. Giulia sat a little back from the men, quiet but all attention.

"Dave and I were talking about a collaboration album and we'd like you in."

David took up the conversation:

"We were in the studio the other day and the topic of our bands came up. My guys are all pulling in different directions now. We've been together so long that our new songs are beginning to sound like the old ones," he grinned ruefully. "Harry feels the same."

Gil could see that Harry was nervous about approaching him, so he smiled in encouragement.

"We were in the studio, and no-one was around so we had an exploratory jam session, but it sounded flat," explained Harry. "We need a third voice, a higher voice. We both said your name at the same time."

"We know you have commitments to your own guys – we wouldn't want to interfere with that - but if you could at least help us out from time to time on passages out of our range, it would be so good - or more if you think you could," David finished hopefully.

They both looked at him expectantly.

Gil lit another cigarette and sat back in his chair. He had no idea how he felt about this. It would take some consideration. He looked out of the window at the row upon row of jagged mountain peaks stretching from horizon to horizon.

"Could you leave it with me for a while? How long are you here?"

"I've to leave tomorrow night. Gig's Saturday," said David.

"I'm okay for a day or two," said Harry. "What do you think of the idea. Generally."

"It's interesting."

No more was said but they chatted on for an hour or so, old friends with catching up to do.

Gil and Giulia strolled together, arm in arm, to their own place.

"I think it's a great idea," she said into the silence.

Gil thought for a moment.

"I need to think. I'll walk up the mountain before it gets dark. Will you be okay on your own?"

She squeezed his waist by way of reply.

It was Jamie who came to him on the mountain side. Gil clearly felt his presence and heard his voice.

"Do it. All." Then he was gone.

Gil ran down the mountain and burst, panting through the door.

"Oh my goodness, are you alright? What's happened?" Giulia was thoroughly alarmed.

He told her about Jamie and what he'd said. Perhaps the stress was getting to him worse than she had ever imagined, if he was hearing his dead brother on a mountain side in Colorado. She was silent, waiting expectantly for him to continue.

"But there's so much to consider. What about the baby? What about Connie - and the boys?"

'Connie again' thought Giulia gloomily, but she put that persistent thought to the back of her mind and replied, getting to the crux of the matter with her usual insight:

"Well...," she said, "I don't see that there's anything there that won't wait – for a few weeks at least. This is only my opinion you understand, but I'd like you to take Jamie's advice."

Gil was amazed at her trust. He'd thought she might doubt his sanity when he started talking about voices of dead people on the mountainside.

"Get out of Los Angeles," she advised. "Get away from the people who have used you for almost all of your life, and the people who will harm you for money. Learn to live again. Learn to think what's best for you."

He considered for a moment, his head on one side.

"I like the idea of ditching my connections to LA It's so peaceful here I can feel the place repairing all the broken parts of me."

"I'm sure Jeff would let us stick around for a few months at least. Then you can get properly free of this poison and work with the guys. Are you going to agree? And if so, how much will you commit to it?"

"I don't know. I know what I'd want to do but it would mean destroying the life I have. Can I do that?"

"Don't you think it's pretty much in pieces now? Your marriage is a thing of the past and your kids are all strangers. It must be like dragging a ball and chain. No wonder you're losing it – you must be exhausted."

He rested his head in her lap. The room was chiaroscuro from the banked-up fire. He was warm, rested and free for the moment from cravings. He closed his eyes and breathed in the scent of gardenias, the restfulness.

Gil jerked upright, grinned and looked her in the eye.

"I'll do it! But the only way to do it is like Jamie said. I have to do it all. I'll hand the band over to Ed and watch him screw it into the ground. I'll start the separation rolling with Connie and fight out the problem about all three kids as we go along. If it turns into a legal matter… well it does. I'm sure she will want damage limitation for them."

Giulia clapped her hands.

"I am so pleased for you! Will you take the guys up on

their offer? Together the three of you could create something completely new. It'll be like going back to the beginning and starting over, but this time you'll be doing it for you."

"But there's Mom. What do I do about Mom? She has Jake and Mylo to care for as well as coping with my Dad"

"I'm sure your mom will manage with Lizbeth to help her. I think you're worrying unnecessarily."

Gil called Liz and his Mom and they both wondered what he was worried about.

Chapter Fifty-one

Connie went back to Oliver's in Bel Air. Oliver had had a choice to make which Connie awaited nervously. But if he wanted her, life would have to go on. By mutual consent, ostensibly for the sake of the children, things gradually returned to normal. No mention of Gil was made in Oliver's hearing again.

Simm was a sweetheart, Deborah needed putting down. Connie was concerned about Jacob and Mylo but Nancy had been right. Their Nana could provide them with a stability which had been missing all their young lives.

She and Nancy had agreed to a truce. Connie visited the boys a couple of times a week and took them out to the beach or to a movie. Everything had settled down very nicely.

Connie had even been a couple of times to visit her daughter at Windham. Oliver didn't go with her on either occasion. Grace stayed silent on the subject of her son's reaction.

Christina was going to be a real beauty. But then Connie was her mother so she was bound to think so.

To the best of her knowledge Gil had yet to make a move to find the baby. Connie prayed he would see sense and leave her alone. She had had no contact with him. He just seemed to have disappeared from LA Even Nancy didn't know where he was.

Connie took fresh flowers to Jamie's grave occasionally. She knew if Gil was in Los Angeles, he would do the same. But so far there was no sign of him.

One morning, which thankfully had gone without a hitch, she walked down the drive to pick up the mail. Mary Jane usually did it but it was a pleasant stroll through the gardens when the pristine lawns were covered in early morning dew.

On her return, she handed the envelopes to Oliver as he went out the door to work. His secretary would see to any bills and file away the business paperwork.

Connie was dressing after her morning shower when there was a gentle tap at the door and her maid said

"There is a gentleman to see you, Ma'am."

"Thank you. Ask him to wait in my sitting room. I'll be there directly."

Connie greeted her visitor strapping on her watch.

"I hope I haven't kept you too long. May I help you?"

"I have a letter for you Mrs. Robson. Legally, I am obliged to place it directly in your hands."

He handed over the envelope.

"Good day to you madame." And he saw himself out.

Enclosed was the legal separation document from Gil's attorneys.

The same document was with her own attorney. She'd forgotten completely to instruct its exchange.

Connie read the standard letter briefly, then again in more detail. Gil was slipping further and further away. Soon he would be gone completely. She was overcome with sadness.

She was surprised Gil had been the one to be so decisive when he'd fought against it for so long. Perhaps his fury over the baby had tipped him over the edge. At least this meant the inertia had ended. She'd have a word with Oliver. She need do nothing, but she'd see her attorney to check everything was in order and the documents sent.

Oliver's response was predictable. He offered to drive her over.

She called Grace who for once agreed with her son.

"Better to get it over with and get on with the rest of your life."

Meantime, Gil waited at Harry's apartment until it was time for the meeting at the band's office on Sunset Boulevard.

He'd called a full meeting of the guys and their legal people, record company and their representatives and his own lawyer. His father would be tackled separately later to avoid muddying the waters.

"I'm quitting," he stated baldly.

There was a moments silence then all hell broke loose.

The loudest voice, he wasn't amazed to hear, was Ed's. He was in tears and threw his representative's clipboard at Gil in fury. It missed by a mile.

"You can't do that you bastard. I've put up with you all these years. I'll sue you to hell and back."

Gil refused to be drawn and smiled at him. Ed became speechless with fury. His representative put a calming hand on his arm and drew him back into his seat.

"That's why I'm here Mr. Morris. Let me do my job."

And the meeting went downhill from there. Gil let them shout it out. Strange how calm he felt. He'd thought he'd be terrified, but his troubles just seemed to be melting away. He felt almost euphoric and suddenly realized he hadn't needed a hit once.

The essential points were covered pretty quickly. The company as it stood would have to be wound up, and a business with a different name formed to exclude his cut from performances, and any future record deals. Gil would simply retain the rights to existing recordings, to his own compositions and any past contracts. An appointment was made for the following week for him to sign any necessary paperwork.

He was sorry for John and Phil. And desperately sorry for his backing band, some of whom had been with them for years. He hoped they would understand, but it was a foregone conclusion that some of them wouldn't. He could be fending off legal challenges for years. Well, so be it. He paid a lawyer for that.

The meeting broke up acrimoniously. All the band members stalked out to their cars and drove off without saying one word to each other. Ed would come in for most of the flack for his behavior to Gil over decades.

He grinned and rubbed his hands together – as far as Ed was concerned, retribution was sweet!

There was much work to be done to extricate himself from his life since he was sixteen, but the shillyshallying was over and done with.

Now to tackle his father and for that he did need a little substance support.

Gil could have written the script for his meeting with his dad.

"You stupid bastard. What the fuck have you done, you selfish son of a bitch?"

Gil had a quiet smile at that – pot calling the kettle black. Monty's income was being threatened. Gil was surprised to find he was enjoying himself hugely.

Monty took a swing at him. Gil ducked. This was being made so easy.

"Deal with it Dad. I'll get Downey to send you the legal releases to sign."

"The fuck I will!"

"I think you'll find you have little choice."

"You can't have the publishing company. I'll see to that."

"Nothing to do with me anyway. My attorney will sort out the rights to my own compositions but apart from that there's no problem."

Monty looked as if he'd explode. He was speechless with rage. Gil turned on his heel and left.

Now for his mom. She kissed him lovingly and said he should have done it years ago.

Oh, this was turning out well.

Lastly, Lizbeth.

She answered the door to his knock and pulled him into a fierce hug. Strangely, she seemed to have taken on a whole new lease of life without Jamie.

"Where've you been? Come on in."

She tugged him into the house and hugged him again.

"Connie came to see me after Jamie's funeral when she picked up the boys," said Lizbeth. "We had a sad goodbye."

Her eyes filled with tears.

"It's so difficult, Gil. I have to choose between you – my brother-in-law – and my friend for years. What do I do?"

Gil took her hand.

"You must do as you see fit Liz. If you want to keep Connie as your friend its fine with me. All I ask is for your own peace of mind, you don't take sides."

When he finally got round to broaching the subject of his leaving the band, he found that interested her far less and she shrugged her shoulders.

"Whatever makes you happy. Makes no difference to me."

Everything had now been set in motion, so for the moment there was nothing to do.

He flew back to Denver with Harry, and Giulia picked them up at the airport. They stopped at her apartment overnight, then she drove them both to Anasazi.

Gil still wasn't completely off the coke, but the action had made him less depressed, so he felt better able to cope. In fact, he was doing pretty well without help.

By the time David had made it back too, Gil had already worked out some ideas on paper. They were mostly only snatches but they were a start and he kind of liked most of them.

Starting work at sixteen had meant his teenage education was sketchy – it really wound him up that he needed to call in favors for help with lyrics, but once there was music to work with, that was what he'd need to do.

Harry, David and Gil mostly worked seriously together, but every so often the joy of what they were doing would break loose, and they would revert to childhood. Gil was the worst for this.

Occasionally, when work allowed, they took frequent rides in the mountains, explored caves and forded rivers. Giulia stayed home. Amongst all her family and friends, she alone was terrified of horses.

On one ride they came across a small village, miles from anywhere. It comprised dwellings of all sizes and shapes. It was clearly some kind of religious settlement. There were monks with shaven heads and linen robes, some of whom sat cross-legged on beaten earth. A group of women in brightly beaded clothing sat before a teepee, and a class of children chanted their catechism in a hut with a large cross on its apex. People of all races wandered chatting and laughing together. There was even a group of hippies, arms round each other's shoulders. The atmosphere was one of peace and contentment. Gil had never seen its like. Not only a religious settlement but a place for all creeds.

Gil felt it first. An almost imperceptible vibration, a buzzing, which started in the soles of his feet and gradually increased as it travelled up his body. With it came a feeling of well-being so profound it took his breath away.

The other two felt it also, but it didn't seem to hit them in quite the same way.

A tall spare figure in the linen robe of a monk, walked over and smiling, took Gil's hand.

"Welcome, brother."

The other two looked at each other and David shrugged. It was as if they weren't there.

The stranger led Gil to a cabin with a porch, where from gilded hooks wind-chimes tinkled softly in the crisp breeze. Harry and David followed, leading Gil's horse.

Inside, the room gleamed with bank upon bank of white candles of every size and shape. A small boy was wandering around with a taper replacing and relighting ones which had burnt out. He put the stubs in a satchel over one of his shoulders.

Gil's eyes were wide with wonder. He had always loved and been drawn to candlelight. When he was troubled or unhappy its gentle glow calmed him.

The monk led him to a low stool. The others had remained in the doorway, transfixed by the look on Gil's face.

"You have been deeply honored," said the monk smiling kindly at Gil.

David and Harry had no clue what was happening.

"Our brotherhood is built upon the largest crystal deposit on earth to partake of its spiritual strength. I can see you feel it deeply. So few of us are granted that honor.

"I saw the shadow of your protector - the lady on the horse - as you rode out of the pass. Who is she?"

"There were just the three of us," Gil said, puzzled.

"No there were most definitely four. Perhaps bringing her here hasn't happened yet. The present and future often intertwine here."

This meant nothing at all to David and Harry and it was apparent Gil hadn't a clue either, but nevertheless he breathed a sigh of relief when the monk said:

"I feel your agony, brother. Be patient – help is on its way,"

He smiled gently and spoke in a formal, almost stilted fashion.

He reached into a cupboard set into the wall behind him.

From it he took a small but whole deep purple crystal, which he folded into Gil's hand where it pulsed gently.

"Don't carry it with you. Hide it in a secret place and only use its strength when all else fails."

It sounded to David like substitute cocaine.

"This is not the place for you yet. We may never meet here again, but our souls are intertwined – I feel it."

Gil struggled to put his thoughts in order.

"I would very much like to know who you are though," said Gil, respectfully.

"We don't use names here in that sense, but you may call me Anukulah. It simply means 'Brother' in Sanskrit for that is what I am to you.

"We will meet again in another time, but not soon. Goodbye," he smiled, squeezing Gils hand and bowing briefly.

Then he disappeared into the brilliant outdoors.

Harry and David were at a loss as to what they should do next, but they needn't have worried. Gil rose to his feet and beamed at them.

"C'mon you guys. Let's go home."

He mounted his horse and began the slow trot back the way they had come, wondering who the hell the shadow lady could be.

Chapter Fifty-two

Connie's attorney confirmed that Gil's separation papers were in order. There only remained the settling of property and what would happen with their children.

Connie knew Gil wouldn't contest any property questions. It was a different case with the children.

She wondered if she could possibly get away with not declaring Christina. Her birth had been registered in the usual way by Kelani, but once her whereabouts became difficult to trace, perhaps the authorities would give up. She could always say she was living abroad, couldn't she? There were so few who knew of her at all.

What about Gil? Was he going to make an issue of this? But she really didn't want to see him again – it was just too much for him.

Regarding Jacob and Mylo, she would put everything in the hands of her lawyers and hope Gil would do the same – but Connie would have to see him about their futures at some point.

But she was wrong on that count - Nancy had petitioned the court to have the boys stay with her. Neither wanted to be with Connie or Gil. They had been tossed from one to the other all their lives and nothing was about to change. Gil would still be away most of the time and Connie would be with Oliver.

Nana's house was the only place they had truly considered home. They wanted to stay. Equal visiting rights were arranged but neither parent wanted to fight over these.

Both just wanted to rebuild their lives. But it was a state of affairs both were thoroughly ashamed of. Without Gil's mother, two little lives would have been ruined by their own selfish concerns.

Work continued on the album at Anasazi. All three guys were so happy away from the slog of their own bands. This had been a long time coming and it didn't take much discussion to decide they wanted their collaboration to continue.

Both David and Harry had parted on amicable terms with their bandmates. It was only Gil who had problems. Ed was still threatening him with court action.

Gil was too relaxed to care.

His life with Giulia seemed stable. Both were satisfied with things the way they were for the time being. Both loved the Colorado mountains and the peace, although Giulia still occasionally longed for her mother in Los Angeles, and her favorite operas in San Francisco, but it was an occasional want not a need at least for the moment. Both loved Anasazi with its companionship and creativity. But Gil knew a long conversation was due.

He wrapped his crystal in one of the soft cloths he used to polish his guitars and hid it in a niche in the pine wall behind a picture. His cravings had totally disappeared.

Shortly after, he received a phone call from Connie.

Giulia saw his expression change and the old sadness return. Would he ever get over her? Never completely she guessed.

Connie wanted to know what Gil intended to do about the baby in the legal proceedings. She explained that she wanted to leave her out of it and why.

"I'll get back to you." Gil said abruptly and put down the

phone.

He really didn't want to dig up dirt from his old life, but this was his little girl, the daughter he had never met, and probably never would if Connie had her way.

"What should I do Giulia? This is my child – I can't abandon her. I'd considered hiring a P.I. What do you think? The boys have chosen to stay with my mom. She can give them the home I can't, and I know they will be happy as they are. But what of this poor little abandoned child?"

He was so sad, Giulia wondered if he didn't see himself as the abandoned child.

She considered for a moment.

"Well…. If you are bent on your responsibilities, it would probably be easy enough to find her – but you should consider carefully what you do or you may put her in the same position as Jacob and Mylo.

"The difference there is you know them and how they feel. The baby has never known you. If she's to leave her foster parents, it will have to be now before she understands. Can you make the home for her you couldn't make for the boys? Of course you could probably push things and force Connie's hand – you'd be able to trace the baby. But is that worth breaking so many hearts when all you have to do is wait?

"It depends on what you feel is right. Is it better to be with the birth father she doesn't know, or an adopted father she does? And besides, a baby who has two groups of people vying for her, can hardly be called 'abandoned'"

Gil paced the room. Every so often he stopped, frowned, looked about to speak then thought better of it. Giulia made some herbal tea and sat sipping it until he was ready to talk.

"What do you think of this? I give Connie what she wants for now and leave the matter of the baby. Then when she's old enough to understand, and if her adopted parents agree, we can rethink the situation?"

Giulia could see gaps in his logic, but if it was something that gave him a peaceful way out, she wouldn't contradict him.

"Sounds good. Why don't you call Connie back now and tell her?"

His unease lingered for days. Was he taking the easy way out? Should he have been more assertive?

As usual, the music healed him.

When Gil went down to the studio in the morning, the other two were already there tuning up.

"Hey, Gil. What kept you?" David looked as if he'd just tumbled out of bed.

"Oh, y'know. Just knocking off a couple of masterpieces."

"I'd laugh if I didn't know that's a possibility." smiled Harry. He pushed his wire rimmed glasses up on his nose and unwound a broken string from a guitar peg.

"Ready to go, guys?" Gil was impatient to begin.

"Sure," said Harry, "Just let me finish this."

Gil did his usual vocal exercises to loosen up his throat. The other two fell about laughing.

David was checking out the Neve console. He hadn't seen this particular model before, so he spent half an hour fiddling with the sliders and controls.

"Man, I like this!" he exclaimed, like a child on Christmas morning. "Let's get something on tape so I can play around with it a bit."

"Don't you think it'd be worth getting Todd in?" asked a worried Gil.

"Is the grass green?" said David as the man himself walked through the door.

"Hey Todd!" Todd strode into the booth and pushed David off his 'baby'

"Don't you dare touch that, Elliot. It's a delicate piece of equipment."

"Gil's the producer. Why don't you give him a quick lesson then you can have the afternoon off?" said David, and Todd glowered.

"You touch that fucking console – any of you – and I….and I won't be responsible for the consequences."

By this time, all three of them were laughing at Todd's expense.

As usual, it was given to Gil to smooth things over. He made a monumental effort to control his own features and turned a stern eye on the others, which did the opposite of what he'd intended. By this time even Todd had begun to smile.

Gil had been noting some minor corrections to one of yesterday's tapes. They gathered round the microphone, listening to the backing before joining their voices in harmony. Sounded good but Gil thought it could be better.

"Oh jeez, Gil. It can't be better – it's perfect." groaned David.

They had been working on this particular track for what seemed like forever.

Harry offered round his cigarettes and quietly picked up the headphones and sang a few bars against the backing track.

"Is that better? I pitched it slightly lower. Todd, can you mix that and adjust the volume on the top notes, so Gil's voice blends smoother."

That's it!" said Gil at the playback. "Can it, for God's sake before we all go crazy!"

His exasperation made the others grin. He'd been the one being so picky.

It was such a feeling of accomplishment when they knew they had it exactly right. Why the hell couldn't Ed understand that?

"Okay, another couple of hours on "Moonlighting" then we'll break for something to eat," said Gil, and the others groaned. He looked at his watch.

"Shit, its nearly two o'clock. I've been saying we'll stop for the past two hours. I'm going to slide through the slats on the cattle grid if I lose any more weight."

No-one said anything. Gil was notoriously sensitive about his weight. It was good at the moment, but a burger and fries and a couple of beers could soon put paid to that.

Despite his life-long dependency on his brother, Harry and David became more family than friends, and were decidedly less stressful than Jamie.

The autumn was gradually giving way to an early winter frost, which rimed the frozen leaves and crunched underfoot. As long as he needed him, Jamie still spoke on his lone walks through the snow. But the occasions became fewer and fewer.

The last time he said, 'Be a brother, Brother.' Nothing more.

Gil had known it was the end. It had been devastating to let him go, but his need for him was gone.

Work on the album continued to satisfy his creativity, and Gil threw himself into it with all the enthusiasm he had once felt for his brother's band. He was loving working again.

The music was flowing out of him as never before. Snatches of it would come in the middle of the night and he had taken to keeping a recorder by the bed. Even so, Giulia frequently woke to the sight of Gil, sitting naked on the sofa with his guitar in his hands, humming a tune. She always had to disappear beneath the covers to keep from giggling out loud.

Gil was occupied and happy and with people he loved, and who loved him. It had been a long time, if ever before since he had felt like that.

The one cloud on the horizon was Monty. He'd taken to calling often.

Monty had abused Giulia even worse than the others, calling her whore, and marriage-wrecker, destroyer of children's lives and so many other things. She'd learned to switch off. After she'd managed to deflect him a couple of times when Gil had been at the studio, she went to Jeff's office and asked his secretary not to redirect the calls to the cabin. Shortly afterwards they stopped.

They had gone to Denver for Giulia to do some shopping and visit the hairdresser. Gil had flown on to Los

Angeles to sign some documents concerning the winding up of the band. He'd be gone a couple of days.

He hated to swap the silent mountains for the traffic fumes and madness of the city. Never before had Gil noticed the distressing underbelly of the streets – the ragged homeless sleeping in cardboard boxes and dumpsters in back alleys, gaunt drug addicts leaning unsteadily against walls. The last scared the crap out of him.

The situation with the boys had stabilized now no-one's future was threatened.

On the first day, he visited his mother, kissed the boys and told them how much he missed them. God forgive him, but it was a lie. Nancy who could always read him, hugged him close:

"I'm sorry I'm such a failure, Mom. I'm sorry."

"You're not a failure, honey. Life just came at you in the wrong order. You never had time to be a child. Take time to be one now. Now, get going. Your dad's coming for dinner."

At one point, he thought he glanced Connie across the street, but he wasn't sure.

He took flowers to Jamie and thanked him for his help. As he laid the flowers down, one broke loose from the bunch and stayed in his hand. It was a white rose bud. He put it in his buttonhole. He would press it when he got back to Anasazi and keep it always in his pocketbook. But he wouldn't come back. Jamie had gone.

The next day he visited the office at Sunset Boulevard to sign the documents. He'd have to come back a time or two before his business there was completed.

He didn't need to see Connie. The separation had been taken care of by their lawyers. The divorce proper would be the next step.

He was so relieved to leave LA If he could fix it, he would never, ever come back.

Giulia met him at the airport, and they had a few days at her apartment in Denver before setting off back to the mountains.

It gradually became obvious that Gil had something on his mind. It didn't interfere with his work, or even with his life with Giulia. But there was something he wasn't saying - Giulia could feel it.

After a week she'd had enough of the suspense.

"Come on, spill. What's going on?"

He feigned surprise but she seemed to know him almost as well as his mom.

They were tucking into pizza in the cabin and Gil put down the huge slice he was biting into, wiped his hands and mouth and looked at her earnestly.

"Do you want us to continue with this relationship? I was a fool the last time round, and I intend learning from my mistakes."

"I'm listening," said Giulia.

"No children. I will never be in a position to provide a settled home for them. This is a terrible thing to ask of you – I am truly sorry but it can't be sidestepped."

Giulia melted into his arms. He was a little unnerved by her devotion, but he needed different things than he had from Connie. He had been so young then, and the future stretched intriguingly before him. Now he was weary, and from Giulia he needed kindness, stability and support, and that she gave in plenty. In return he could offer her safety and comfort when she needed it most.

At the moment she needed that desperately. Her beloved Poppa had been diagnosed with a tumor in his right lung, and things were not looking good. Gil would be there for her.

They should do very well together.

"Well, that's that then," he concluded. "We understand each other. If anything alters, we can talk about it again, but we must always be honest with each other."

Connie was only mentioned briefly in passing, although both were aware of her presence.

Thanks to Ed, The California Crystal Band was more like a circus act than a group of experienced musicians. Gil blessed the day Giulia had given him the courage to turn his back on them.

Gil, David and Harry were still in the process of fulfilling contracts and, where they could, wriggling out of them. They tried to arrange things so they could spend as much time as possible finishing their album. It was going much better than any of them had dreamed. Jamie was correct. It had been right to let him go.

Giulia got bored being alone all the time, so she arranged to meet her sister-in-law Diana in Denver. Larry was still away. He was ecstatic as his slim frame meant he was eligible for pilot training, but the course was intensive, so he rarely got home these days.

Giulia was alone too much, but she had unwavering family support which Connie hadn't. Her situation wasn't unbearable, but she would talk to Gil about it anyway. He had made her promise to be honest.

The last time Gil had been to Los Angeles, he had brought back an exquisite suite of antique jewelry. Giulia adored it. It was a white gold choker with matching bracelet and earrings. It was hand-crafted and delicately scattered with bright diamonds. The whole was enclosed in an abalone and gold case. For the first week she kept taking it out just to run her fingers over its beauty. Then she'd put it back, only to take it out to admire again.

Giulia loved it so much she vowed to give Gil something priceless in return. Not necessarily expensive – money was never in short supply with the Giordanos - but something to melt his heart.

When she got back to Anasazi, she discussed her loneliness with Gil, and he was instantly sympathetic. He had been through this before with disastrous consequences. He recognized the signs now.

He made sure she was in the studio with him as much as she wanted, and when they broke for coffee or to eat, she was always included. The other guys had both been through this problem. All three of them had a track on the album about the same thing. There was no conflict.

It left Giulia with freedom for family visits, especially to see her adored father who was not recovering as she had hoped. Gil was busy in the studio so he probably wouldn't even notice. His guitar was his true mistress, she thought regretfully. Always had been – always would be.

It was late summer, and she was in Los Angeles. She'd gone shopping with Diana and Lucy Romano and bumped into Lizbeth Robson. The greeting was cordial, but nothing more. With her fingers crossed behind her back, Giulia asked for news of Nancy, Jacob and Mylo, and said Gil spoke about them all the time, which at the moment wasn't true. The album took all his time. He talked of little else.

But the seed of another idea was sown in her mind later that day.

After they had had lunch, Diana called in at a jewelers to pick up a watch she'd had refurbished. While she was waiting, Giulia looked idly into the window of the realtor next door.

It had all the usual Beverly Hills mansions and extravagant estates on the California coast. All very expensive and exclusive.

Then Diana rejoined them and they walked back to the car.

Giulia was becoming increasingly worried about her dad. She'd had to face the fact he wasn't going to pull round from this. He was looking gaunt, and pallor had long since taken over from his usual healthy tan. Her mother was relying on her increasingly for help, and her dad wanted to be with her – she had always been his favorite, his baby.

She'd ask Gil if it was okay to come back and stay for a couple of weeks just to help out.

Then Paul took a sudden turn for the worse and died within a matter of days. She only found out when she was shown his death certificate by her mother, that the tumor had spread. He'd kept that to himself, even Carrie hadn't known.

Screamed.

The funeral was a typical Catholic affair, with the ritual

Italians found such a comfort. The ladies all wore black lace veils and gloves. The men had black suits and ties and wore arm bands.

Gil didn't think it would be appropriate to attend such a private affair, although Paul had been both friend and father to him for many years. Instead, he collected Giulia and took her straight back to Anasazi, where through the night she lay weeping in his arms.

The following morning, she told him to go to the studio. She needed some time alone. Unlike Gil, who loved the snow, she preferred walking along the banks of a small lake on the boundary of the village, where she could watch the shadowy fish slide through the still water and the grebe swimming amongst the reeds.

Her thoughts about her dad were sad and filled with longing. But she was glad his final suffering hadn't been long. She was also cross with Gil because he hadn't attended the funeral, but then she realized he had been exactly where he was most needed.

Giulia was morose for some time, but she had a naturally sunny nature, which in the end prevailed.

Gil took her to his mountains, on hikes along rarely trodden paths through pine glades which smelled fresh and earthy.

"Don't you think it's just beautiful? So quiet you can hear a stream rushing half a mile away."

He began to sing a stirring hymn from his childhood, the shimmering notes soaring through the branches overhead. Giulia was mesmerized. When he was in a place like this and sang, it was as if he became one with the forest and streams, the mountains, the very air they breathed.

"I would stay and never leave if I could."

He kissed her affectionately and they walked together, back the way they had come, each wrapped in private thought, and by the time the stars began to twinkle in a velvet sky, they were at Anasazi.

Chapter Fifty-three

Winter passed into spring and aspens awoke, softly green and silver.

The album was finished, but for the final mix and mastering which Gil was working on with Todd. It had been such an enjoyable experience.

They were so proud of the finished music. They'd written and sung everything themselves and backed one another's tracks. They'd even managed most of the instruments between them. Gil thought it was the best thing he'd ever done. Harry hugged him warmly as he left and in his quiet voice said:

"I am so glad to have shared this with you, brother," He stowed away his guitar in its case - his bags were already packed and in his coupe.

"I'll call you."

He loaded his guitar and was gone.

David was right behind him. Lacking Harry's methodical nature, he'd thrown a couple of bulging sports bags in the back of his Mustang, gave Gil the peace sign, winked and screeched off down the track.

Gil grinned as his taillights disappeared round the corner. He would miss them, but it wouldn't be long until they were together again. They'd finished the creative part of the project. Now came the tedious business end. He'd rather have just taken his guitar and played to the seagulls on a desert island.

Connie had reached a truce with Deborah. They agreed to disagree... on everything.

Catch a Falling Star

Simm loved Connie with an intensity he'd never displayed to his own mother, who had always been cold with him. Simm, encouraged by Grace who thought nothing at all of Rachel, had learned to love books.

Connie had converted a small attic room into a library for him. They'd splashed more paint on themselves than on the wall in the process of decorating it, and Connie had had a cabinet maker come in and make fitted shelves and cupboards to Simm's design. Together they visited bookstores, markets and second-hand charity shops to buy books from very old to very new.

Deborah would come occasionally and stand at the library door with an unfathomable expression on her face. Then she would turn round and walk off down the hall.

This gradually became an increasingly frequent occurrence. She would arrive silently and leave the same way.

One day Connie walked into the library and on a small, upholstered stool was a copy of 'Wind in the Willows'. It was dog-eared and not very clean. Deborah was standing at the door. She turned and walked away. Connie put the book on one of the lower shelves.

The following day, no Deborah but on the same stool were copies of 'Tom Sawyer' and another by Betsy Byers, also well used. Connie put them on the shelf with the other books.

This went on for over a week until there was quite a little row.

On the next day, Deborah sidled into the library and picked up one of her books. She looked at Connie uncertainly then sat on the stool and began leafing through it. Five minutes later she closed the book, put it in its place on the shelf and left without saying a word.

353

Catch a Falling Star

Connie didn't mention this to Oliver.

Another week passed and Connie found a chewed pencil stub on her dressing-table. Then, following the same routine as before, there appeared a small coin, a hair-ribbon and a doll's shoe. What would she do next?

Next time they had dinner, Connie gave Deborah an extra big piece of apple cake and passed her the cream. She smiled, only briefly, but a definite smile.

The days went past and a little gift would appear or another book would be added to Deborah's shelf.

One day, Connie's friend Jean came to visit. They sat in the pagoda in the garden gossiping and drinking wine. Spring had brought out the blossom on the cherry trees and their petals lay thick as snow on the grass and on the surface of the little pool.

Deborah appeared. She was grubby and not a little sweaty from play. In her hand was a wine glass with orange juice in it. Connie, afraid she might break it and cut herself, leaned over to take it from her, but Deborah twisted away. She put her glass next to the others on the table then hoisted herself onto the seat next to Connie. No words were exchanged.

Jean was fascinated. Connie pulled a face out of Deborah's sight, and they relaunched their conversation. Deborah crossed her legs neatly at the ankle and listened. When Connie picked up her glass and took a drink, Deborah jumped off her seat and took an untidy slurp too. Then she clambered back and sat quietly again.

After a while Connie felt a sticky little hand creep down her arm and rest trustingly in her own. She nearly fell off her seat.

Deborah had made every move herself with no

encouragement. It had been a long process for a little girl. Connie pulled her onto her knee and continued her conversation with Jean. Deborah put both arms round Connie's neck and went to sleep. She smelled.... sticky.

Then things began to get very weird.

Deborah started the same process with Simeon – giving him little gifts and putting her books on shelves next to his.

A week or so later, Connie saw them walking hand in hand up the school drive. She started to laugh. Three weeks ago, Deborah had been swinging from his hair and scratching his face.

She told a bemused Oliver. "Be grateful for small mercies," he said.

Unfortunately, the mercies turned out to be very small. A few days later, Deborah took two of Simm's precious books from the library shelves, ripped out pages, then blamed it on Simm. She had regained the spotlight.

Chapter Fifty-four

Giulia got a letter.

When Gil walked back into the cabin after breakfast – Giulia never ate first thing in the morning - he had brought it with him.

She jumped up and down, beaming:

"Oh Gil. Larry's finished his training and has a whole three week's leave. He's taking Diana to Hawaii for a few days, then he's going to spend two weeks in Los Angeles."

Gil hugged her and kissed her on the forehead. He knew how she missed him. All her family, in fact.

"Will you want me to come to LA with you?" he asked.

"No, it's not important. I'll ask Larry to come to Denver for a few days before he goes back. You can see him then."

She paused and looked into his eyes.

"I know you have to go to LA from time to time for business. But I worry every time you're away from here. There's so much temptation. I know you're over it all now, but I still worry."

"I can't blame you. I've been through the coke scene before, and I still did it again. But now is different. I could see no future then. Don't worry."

"If you'd rather I didn't go then I won't. I'm fine with that. It'll be good for you to spend time with you mom and all the little Giordanos."

Gil loved to tease Giulia about this. She was the baby of seven and most of the children of Paul's first wife were older than he was. Giulia scowled at him.

"You're very cute when you pull that face." She hit him with a cushion from the sofa. They fell to the hearth rug, and he tickled her until she screamed.

Once Giulia had gone, Gil went back to writing again.

That Spring was warm, and he sat down at a picnic table outside the canteen. It was mostly quiet at the moment.

If he'd been with the band, he'd have been in Europe now. He blew out his cheeks in relief. He never need go again if he didn't want. He'd never have to leave unless he chose to. If he'd left the band earlier, he might still have Connie, and not have been stupid enough to hit the coke again. How different life might have been.

No point in dwelling on the past. He and Giulia were doing okay together, and he was more content than he ever remembered being.

After he had been basking in the sunshine, scribbling down the occasional lyric for a while, Jeff sat beside him.

"How'd it go?"

"Better than we could have imagined. It helped that we pretty much had the studio to ourselves, and Todd managed to keep David off his new console."

He gave Jeff a sideways grin.

"We got the whole thing done in half the time it'd have taken with the band, and I think the other two felt the same."

His expression changed and he sighed.

"Now all we have to do is market it. We don't have our own label so we're going to have to go shop it around the independents for now. Won't be the first time I've hit rock bottom. The bigger studios will soon pick up the next project if this one does well."

"And will there be a next project?" asked Jeff. "I understood this was a one-off."

"Yes, that's what we thought, but this one came so easy and was such a blast I think the other guys will be up for at least one more."

"Love to see my favorite musicians getting it right. Be cool," and Jeff left.

Giulia spent time with her family, especially Larry. It was lovely to be the coddled baby again.

Her mom seemed to be coping quite well. She had thrown herself into charity work. Giulia was astounded to hear that her nail-painted, perfectly coifed mother was helping out at a local school.

"What's the name of that guy Connie took up with?" she asked Giulia in her usual blunt manner." Maxwell, wasn't it? There are a couple of kids of that name at the school. Little boys okay but the girls a brat. S'pose they're his? And hers as well by default."

Giulia wasn't interested in Connie. She changed the subject.

"Larry looks so handsome in his uniform."

As she spoke, Larry walked in and took a soda from the refrigerator. He sat next to them at the kitchen counter.

"How're you doin' lovely ladies?"

"Fine," said Giulia, accepting the compliment without a second thought. "Where's Diana."

"She's gone shopping with one of her friends. You'd think she'd be falling all over herself to be with her handsome husband, wouldn't you?"

He had heard the conversation then.

"Got your wings I understand?"

"Yep! First in my class – can you believe it? Either I'm smarter than I thought or the rest of them are dumb!" He managed to take a drink and laugh at the same time.

"Gil not with you?"

"No. He's been working with Harry Forster and David Elliot on a collaboration, and he's exhausted. He wanted a bit of down-time, so I left him to it."

Larry who understood her better than anyone else, easily saw through and understood the lie. He pulled a face at her.

"Pigs do a pretty good job of flying too, I'm told." Giulia sighed,

"He wanted to come see mom but I'd rather he didn't come to LA if we can avoid it. He'd rather be up in the mountains anyway. Can you come up to Denver for a couple of days before you go back? He does want to see you."

"Sure. Okay with you Momma?"

"'Course. Put your pots in the dishwasher before you go."

Carrie picked up her purse and left.

"Don't you dare say it, Larry! No, we don't have servants to fill the dishwasher! You're not suffering from paralysis. Put the glass in yourself." Larry chuckled.

"When are you going back?" she continued. "Will it be the full three weeks?"

"No, I have to report back the day before, so I'll have to leave Wednesday."

"Can you come to Denver Sunday or Monday then?"

"Yep. See you at your pad Monday morning, I'll catch the early plane. Diana may come. Depends on her mood."

Giulia arranged to meet Gil at the Denver penthouse on the Sunday afternoon. That'd give her another couple of days with her mom.

When she arrived at the apartment, Gil was laying on his back on the sofa watching football on TV. He had a big bowl of potato chips balanced on his chest and a bottle of beer in his hand.

"What are you doing Gil? You look like a beached whale. You have a photo-shoot in a couple of weeks - we're going to have to do something about you by then. As of today, you're on half-rations,"

Larry laughed out loud.

"And tomorrow I'll call my beauty parlor and get you fixed up with an appointment."

She looked at him critically.

"Haircut. I suppose a shave is out of the question?" Gil jumped to his feet scattering chips everywhere and backed away.

"No scissors-totin' hairdresser is coming within a mile of my beard." He stroked it lovingly. "It will be properly barbered or nothing."

Giulia rolled her eyes.

"I've also made you an appointment with 'Jones and Tyson' on Wednesday afternoon. We can see Larry off, then you can have your first fitting."

"Who the fuck are Jones and Tyson? They sound like a comedy act."

"Jones and Tyson…. the best tailors in Colorado. You're not going on that photoshoot looking like an unmade bed!"

"I don't!" said Gil, offended. "I used to get measured for my suits at Nudie's."

"Well, you're too old to wear cowboy suits now."

Larry was doing his best not to laugh and failing miserably.

"You're not married but you might as well be! Oh, are you in trouble!"

Larry or no, Gil spent the next two days with his barber, then Giulia's beauty parlor to have a manicure and his hair cut and styled. It looked pretty good, but he wasn't sure it was 'him'. Somehow it looked wrong with his jeans.

The whole time Larry kept up a running commentary. What amused him most and could reduce him to tears, was that Gil was a substantial man and Giulia was so very tiny. Every time Giulia laid into him, Gil looked beaten, and Larry would go off into hysterics.

Wednesday morning came, and Larry packed his bags ready to board his plane. Gil hugged him.

"Sorry to see you go, brother," said Gil.

"The hell you are!" said Larry. "I can't wait to come back. You'll look like Cary Grant by then."

"Yeah, yeah!" said Gil. "You just wait until they let you out of that monkey suit. I'm gonna have some fun then. At the moment you look like a freakin' super-hero. It won't last. Then I'll be waiting for you!"

Giulia gave her brother a nudge.

"Pick up your bags Larry. You're going to miss your plane. I'll drive you and..." she rounded on Gil, "you stay here. We have a tailor to visit when I come back."

Chapter Fifty-five

The tailor looked Gil up and down and said to Giulia:

"I think Sir requires a suit in black. A very light-weight wool perhaps, double-breasted. Standard lapels"

He walked round Gil, scratching his chin.

"No, no vents but slightly longer than usual. And trousers? Hmmm.... slightly tapered, I think, with a double pleat."

Gil may just as well have been one of the green plush chairs which were scattered around the edges of the room.

The tailor began taking measurements and noting them in a black leather book. When he got to the leg length the tailor asked:

"Left or right, sir?"

At last, a question he could answer.

"Left," said Gil tersely.

The tailor led them into a large storeroom filled floor to ceiling with racks containing bolts of cloth. He studied for a few moments before hefting one onto a long table in the center of the room.

"No. Too heavy."

Looked okay to Gil.

"This one should be better. What do you think?" he said to Giulia taking down another.

She rubbed it between her fingers

"Wouldn't a silk mix be better? Make it lighter weight?"

He pulled another bolt.

"Only if you want a slight sheen." Giulia shook her head slowly.

"No," said Giulia, rubbing the fabric from the second bolt between her thumb and forefinger. "You're right. This is the one."

Gil shrugged. So far, he had uttered one word and he suspected only because it concerned his dick. Otherwise, this was Giulia's show.

"If you don't mind, honey, I'll go now and get some things I need," said Giulia.

"How long?" she asked the tailor.

"Oh, an hour should do it for the initial measurements," he looked appraisingly at Gil. "No, perhaps an hour and a half."

Gil wondered idly what it was about him that needed an extra half hour.

The bell tinkled as the door closed behind Giulia. The tailor approached him with a look of determination. Were some customers awkward? Gil couldn't blame them.

Giulia went shopping for toiletries and a lipstick. She glanced casually into one or two windows as she walked past. One was a very large realtor's office with brightly colored photographs of homes from rentals to expensive country houses.

The office she'd seen in LA, had been from the same chain, so she stopped to check it out.

One particular property took her eye. It was surrounded by the mountains but had a spectacular view from a glass wall at one end of the living area, which was huge.

From the very first moment she saw the house, she so wanted it for Gil. He would adore it. It was at the end of a long trail through pine trees.

What was she thinking? It carried a price of $73,000. That was outrageous.

She walked on and picked up her shopping.

On the way back past the realtors she couldn't resist taking another look. The salesman had noticed her the first time so when she returned, he greeted her at the door and asked if she would like to take a look at more photos.

Giulia checked her watch. She had a little over a half hour left. Why not? It would satisfy her curiosity if nothing else.

The photographs showed a kitchen and dining room with French windows. The four bedrooms, each with its own bathroom, were on the first floor. There was a long curving open stairway and garaging for three cars under the house which was built into a slope.

The rest of the photos showed the front of the property. Near the gate was a small cottage. She could fit that out as a music room for Gil, like the pool-house at Linden Reach.

"$73,000 is on the pricey side," she said looking at the flyer the realtor handed her.

"Perhaps if you were to take a look, you might get a better idea," he said. "It's only a few miles from Riverside, on the mountain road."

But how to slip away from Gil for a day? He'd be going back to Anasazi soon. She'd think up an excuse to stay behind.

"I have a window in my schedule about eleven Monday.

I assume that will be satisfactory?" she said, taking out a small appointments diary.

Giulia managed to keep her cool until she was out of sight, then fairly skipped down the road to collect Gil from the tailor's.

Gil was not in a good mood – he looked defiant. She didn't know what the tailor had done, but it didn't matter just so long as he went along with her plans.

She clung to his arm and gave him the same winning smile that used to work wonders on her father.

By the Friday afternoon her impatience to see him off, made him suspicious and he asked her if she had a gigolo stashed somewhere. Giulia batted her eyelashes at him, told him she'd a viewing for a vacant apartment. She'd be back Monday, or maybe Tuesday morning depending on the traffic. That took the pressure off – great!

Time seemed to have stood still. Monday felt like it should have come one hell of a lot sooner. The house occupied her thoughts every waking hour and featured in some of her better dreams as well.

The day before the scheduled viewing, Giulia could stand it no longer. She drove to the address provided by the realtor, parked up under some trees and explored.

The house seemed to be empty, so she had a look round. The little stone cottage next to the gate was absolutely perfect for Gil's own private place. From what she could see peering through a window, it was a biggish room with what she took to be a bathroom and bedroom or kitchen through two doors at the back. It would need carpets and new drapes but it seemed to be pretty well decorated..

The house itself would belong to them both. It was a lot bigger than she had assumed from the photos. It was pristine, newly painted and stained, with the towering front window gleaming brightly in the sunshine.

No need to spoil tomorrow morning. What she'd seen so far of the exterior pleased her. It was the right thing to do. She could feel it. If she could knock down the asking price a little it wouldn't be much more expensive than the annual rent paid for her apartments.

Giulia needn't have worried about getting a little free time for her own concerns. Despite her misgivings Gil had to be in Los Angeles for meetings with the band and his attorney.

He also intended to spend some time with his mother and asked if she'd like to come and meet her and get to know her better?

Gil had to admit to himself it was more about Nancy accepting Giulia, but he didn't say so. The boys were at Oliver's mother's holiday home in San Clemente with Connie, so there were no complications.

Giulia agreed to meet him at the airport on Tuesday evening and they would stay until Thursday. Part of the time he'd be concluding business, so she'd be alone with Nancy briefly.

"Oh dear Lord," Giulia said to herself as she replaced the receiver. 'I knew this day had to come, but I never thought I'd be so terrified.'

When he visited the band for the last time, as expected, Ed was his usual self and pulled no punches.

"Typical Robson. His brother's at the bottom of the

Pacific now he's not floating around in the ether."

"I thought the universe was your domain," Gil muttered under his breath referring to Ed's obsession with meditation. Ed ploughed on:

"And one who thinks he's already God and dumps on us lesser beings."

"I thought all you ever wanted to do was take charge of the band. Since we were kids in Briarside you've been telling me everything I said or did was crap. Well, here's your chance to prove yourself right.

"I will give you whatever help I can, but you must understand I am here to wind things up for me and my part in the band. I will not be coming back."

Ed's bottom lip trembled, and his voice was taut with panic. His tone turned from aggressive to wheedling and it occurred to Gil, Ed's reliance on him had been total for his entire life.

"Please stay. Another six months and I'll get a handle on it. You can teach me."

Gil shook his head, saddened by Ed's inadequacy.

"I've been trying to help you out as long as I can remember. All you've done is to make my life not worth living. I can forgive that Ed, but I will never, never forget."

"You can't blame me for that sorry fuck-up you call brother," sneered Ed defensively.

"I sure do. If in all our lives there had been one word of kindness, one word of encouragement, I would go to the ends of the earth for you. But you hurt my brother beyond fixing Ed, really damaged him."

Gil had never understood how someone so intent on displaying his spirituality and loudly proclaiming his adherence to cosmic forces Indian-style, could miss the point so completely. Gil understood what 'Spirit' was – he had all his life. But Ed's spirit was paid for with donations.

Gil thought it was stupid to have people telling you what to feel when you could just…. feel. Spirit flowed everywhere. All you had to do was stand still to tap into it. No mantras at all, just quiet and stillness. It's why he loved the mountains so much.

Gil knew the musicians amongst his associates would survive, including John, who sang well and also played guitar, and Phil who played keyboards and had a good range to his voice.

His sidemen were the very best, so always sought after. They also knew he would re-employed them when he could. It never entered their heads he wouldn't stay in the business. He was just too good to fail.

Chapter Fifty-six

Giulia was a full half hour early at the house on Larch Road. She wanted a better idea of what she'd be signing her name to.

While the exterior of the house itself was pristine, the acre plot it stood on had been neglected, so she guessed it had been empty for a month or two. That didn't matter. She'd have to employ a gardener in any case.

Behind the house was a shed with a covered wood-store attached. There was an over-grown path running up through the trees to the top of a steep slope, which ran the full width of the garden plot.

Giulia climbed to the top. The view was beautiful – sweeping meadows to the mountain foothills. They were carpeted with wildflowers - poppies and columbines, buttercups and cornflowers. She'd coat the entire banking behind the house with early-blooming snowdrops. There were honeysuckle vines twined around the lower branches of nearby pines. They needed cutting back, then next summer they would make a sweetly scented cascade of pink and cream blossoms.

She heard the realtor's car pull up in front of the house and ran down to meet him.

He shook her hand and gave her a small bunch of keys.

"I thought you might like to take a look around the house on your own first. We can discuss everything else after."

The interior was not as she had imagined. The outside of the house had been renovated, no doubt to make it more saleable, but the interior was in places rather tired.

The door opened into a cloakroom, with hooks for coats

and racks for boots and shoes.

A pine door led into a good-sized hall, with an open wood staircase sweeping up to the second floor. Behind the stairway was another door leading into a shower-room. She'd replace the staircase. It was ugly.

The sitting room had faint marks on the walls where pictures had been hung, but she had expected the house would need a complete overhaul. Besides, primrose was not her color.

But she wasn't prepared for what she saw on opening the door to the left of the hall.

The room inside was vast, with a gabled roof like a cathedral. The wall on the far side was entirely of glass. It had an unimpeded view of layer upon layer of glittering mountain peaks with blue and dark violet shadows between.

Because it was summer there were horizontal shelves of emerald grass on the lower slopes. It was entrancing.

If Gil could have designed his ideal house, she was sure he couldn't have planned anything so perfect.

There was no point in bothering with the second floor once she'd seen this. Whatever it was like, she'd fix it.

Beneath the enormous window of the cathedral room, Giulia could see not only the drive but a large, secluded garden, again with a lawn, at present bleached by the summer sun. It had flowerbeds which she would fill with all the colors of the rainbow.

She schooled her face not to show her delight, and the fact she was going to have this house if it took every cent she had.

"Would you like to go back to the office to discuss the details?" asked the realtor.

Giulia passed the bunch of keys through his car window and nodded, her expression so blank he immediately knew his commission would take his family to Hawaii in the fall.

From joy to worry of the worst kind. She'd to face Gil's mother and she'd never been so nervous in her life.

Gil was surprised by Nancy's reaction to Giulia.

She seemed to take exception to her from the start. He'd never seen her do that before. He thought she'd at least give her a chance.

Nancy wasn't rude – she never was – but the kiss she gave Giulia was not the same warm hug she gave everyone else.

He could only suppose it was to do with her grandchildren and a lingering attachment to Connie. He had one of those himself so he could sympathize. But like him, she would have to move on. Perhaps she thought he'd moved on too fast.

He and Giulia would just have to be patient. Things surely would come right, and in the meantime he could only pray she could never learn to read his mother like he could.

Nancy made coffee for them and Gil followed her into the kitchen under the pretext of helping with the tray, but really to speak about his dad. A visit from him would be a total disaster.

Connie had learned to stand up to him, but despite the telephone calls to Anasazi, Giulia wouldn't have a chance face to face. She would take it extremely personally because in her own family she'd never come across his like. Her mother could be cantankerous but with her family it passed in moments.

"I don't think you'll see him. The MLB's on, so he'll be glued to the TV. He's even worse than Jamie for baseball."

The elephant in the room came next:

"What's wrong Mom?" She looked into his eyes for a long moment.

Nancy sighed, and with some effort continued:

"I can't believe what you and Connie have done to those children. I am so disappointed in you Gil.

There was the sound of Giulia putting down her coffee cup next door.

"Now isn't the time to discuss this. We'll talk in private later."

"I don't have secrets from Giulia, Mom."

"Oh yes you do. And if you don't recognize that, you're a bigger fool than I took you for Gil Robson."

He, Giulia and Nancy spent the afternoon in more or less convivial conversation, and the following morning, Gil left to conclude his business with the record company.

Once the papers were signed, he heaved a sigh of relief.

He would still be responsible for the completion of an album already in production – a depressing prospect – but he'd make sure his own parts were recorded separately to save animosity. The record company agree to this, providing he oversaw the mastering.

Gil shook hands with them, but their faces were grim, and he knew for a fact there would be no further association with that particular label. He just hoped the animosity wouldn't spread through the industry.

Then apart from any litigation from the rest of the band, he was free. It remained to be seen how he would cope without his friends in the audience. No doubt something would have to be done – perhaps Harry and David had shown him the way forward but there would have to be live performances.

The end was in sight.

Gil met Harry immediately afterwards and spent an hour or so in pleasant conversation with Daniel Jones, the Teacher, at the US Movement spiritualist church. Harry had had to dash off in the middle, and Gil and Daniel were left chatting together.

Their talk appeared light and inconsequential, but Gil was surprised when he left, that he felt a distinct lifting of his spirits.

Who cared

Gil arrived back at Nancy's to find Giulia alone.

He sank almost to the waist in one of Nancy's armchairs. Giulia was sitting on the edge of the sofa and leafing through a copy of Harper's Bazaar she'd found on the shelf under the coffee table.

"Where's Mom?" he asked.

"Your dad rang. She was out of the door like greased lightning. Is she alright?"

Gil grinned then laughed out loud.

"Oh, she's okay. She's just making sure you're the same. Did she say when she'd be back?"

"She didn't say anything much. We were only alone about half an hour. It was quite awkward. Did I do something wrong?"

Gil heaved himself out of his chair and sat beside her on

the sofa, pulling her onto his knee. They sank deeper into the upholstery.

"Promise me, Giulia," he said with a deal of irritation, "If ever we have to furnish a house, you'll choose wooden furniture. One day I'll sit on this freakin' suite and disappear completely."

"Well, did I? Do anything wrong, I mean?"

"No, of course you didn't. You've never met her before. How could that be possible?"

Nancy returned about an hour later. She shared an intimate glance with Gil.

"What did he do?"

"Oh nothing. But he had plenty to say. He has a temperature so I managed to convince him he might have pneumonia."

Giulia gasped and Nancy turned to look at her.

"Not really. But he doesn't know that."

"My dad's a character," said Gil voicing the understatement of the decade.

"He's a monster," said Nancy with no inflection. "He beat my boys when they were small."

"Hush, Mom. Its water under the bridge now." said Gil completely dismissing his own recent run-in with his father.

"For you, maybe," said Nancy bitterly.

"You do realize what'll happen if he finds out Giulia's here?"

A small voice from the background said:

"I guess we'll have to meet sometime. Wouldn't it be better sooner rather than later?"

Gil snorted.

"When you meet my dad, you'll know why not. He has a very twisted way of looking at things. Better to leave it as it is for the time being until we can choose our own battlefield – preferably as public as possible."

Nancy sighed and relaxed into her armchair. Strangely, it didn't seem to engulf her. How odd, thought Giulia.

The next day, Gil got up before breakfast to go and meet Mr. Downey, his attorney. He had a few more papers to sign for the record company and the other band members. He was hoping and praying that for once in his life Ed would be a gentleman.

The other guys had eventually agreed to the arrangement with little argument. They knew Gil would be more than generous. Ed's legal representative had forwarded a list of questions - some of them not exactly pertinent.

While he was there, he asked Mr. Downey about re-starting the divorce proceedings. He thought he would have become used to the idea by now but it still pulled hard at his heartstrings. Giulia wasn't the only one doubtful of his ability to pull free.

He was going home the following day, so he arranged to meet Harry and David later for the photo-shoot. He had a feeling that when he turned up in his new suit with clean fingernails and his blow-dried hair, he'd never live it down.

'Well, let them laugh!' he thought with absolutely no conviction at all.

By the time they were ready to leave, Nancy had thawed a bit as if accepting the inevitable, but she was annoyed that Gil should choose to visit when he knew the boys would be away.

She blamed it squarely on Giulia. Giulia would have to accept Jacob and Mylo if she wanted Gil. There was no way round that, otherwise Gil would have to say goodbye to them. Although Gil's children were now living with her, Nancy could never accept he might want to give them up entirely. Oliver put up with them grudgingly. This divorce was going to be very painful. Where the children were concerned, was she the only one who cared?

Back in Denver, they stopped overnight at the apartment so Gil could go and reacquaint himself with his new suit. The trousers fitted like a glove and the jacket was three-quarters complete. The lapels needed to be finished and the lining stitched. He looked at himself in the full-length mirror and had to admit that perhaps the tailor and Giulia did know a thing or two after all. The longer jacket took pounds off him and the light wool was very comfortable.

Gil told the tailor he would return on the Saturday for the final fitting and to collect the suit for the photo-shoot on Tuesday morning.

Gil met up with David and Harry at the Carlton Hotel.

The appointment with the photographer was at two-thirty next day, so they called in at Rick's for a quick beer. There was a girl behind the bar Gil didn't know. Perhaps as well - Pete knew far too much about the bad side of his life.

The shoot went like clockwork which they usually did. Gil could smile and pose with the best of them, but the photographer decided 'mean and moody' would be best. Gil and David were okay, but sylph-like Harry had a problem with that – he couldn't do 'mean and moody' to save his life, so they had to go with serious for him and angle the lighting slightly.

Then came the hard part.

Gil had brought acetates with him from Anasazi and doled them out to the others. They would have to hawk them over town until they found a label which would take them on. This was virgin ground for them – at least it was now. The last time they'd had to do this they'd been teenagers, and Gil had had his dad to do it for him even then. You couldn't just walk in and see an A&R man now. You had to make advance appointments. And the decision wasn't made on the spot, as it used to be when the artist had personal contact. It could take weeks if not months.

They made a list of the major labels and divided it up between them. They had a pedigree as the leaders of prominent bands for the past twenty years. They didn't think there'd be a problem.

Gil decided to pay an agent to do the legwork for him, then he could get away from Los Angeles, and back to the peace of his mountains. David had to leave anyway as he was about to tour.

Gil dropped in to see Mr. Downey again for further news on the separation before going home. The office was about to close, so the visit was necessarily brief. Mr. Downey had handed the case and its paperwork over to a colleague, who dealt with marital issues. As far as he knew, the papers had been served and it was progressing smoothly.

Chapter Fifty-seven

Giulia had not been idle. She used Gil's absence to get things rolling at the house.

First job, employing a gardener. She was just in time to get the autumn pruning and planting done. She found an excellent man who got to work immediately by cutting back all the undergrowth and treating the lawns. In the Spring with the flowering cherry and apple trees, the back of the garden would be a cornucopia of color.

Now for the cottage. Giulia managed to spend a full day there while Gil was away in Los Angeles seeing to the mix on his final album. She had a heavily scented climbing rose planted on a trellis around the door.

She planned to have all the work done by late October before the frosts set in. She was delighted with the gift she had planned for Gil, and all the unease with Nancy was forgotten.

The finding of a label to take the album which had given them so much pleasure, was not as straight-forward as they had anticipated.

Harry, David and Gil had been responsible for making a lot of money for a lot of people. All three had decided to separate from very lucrative situations for hardnosed businessmen – not only for record companies, promotors and associated professions, but for others such as lawyers and photographers, designers and radio stations. The effect spread like ripples on a pool.

Such was the animosity they failed to find a single interested party amongst the major labels, who were convinced they were washed up without their former bands.

Most of the record company representatives hadn't even bothered listening to the acetates, but those who had, heard no echo of their former successes in their new material. As far as the three of them were concerned, that was the whole point. They were freeing themselves from the shackles which had tied them so rigidly for so many years. With the labels there was absolutely no meeting of minds.

All three had called in personal favors and all three had drawn blanks.

They were all devastated in their own ways, but to Gil their lack of success was a calamity.

His life had been in pieces when he first went to Anasazi. Working on this album had allowed his creativity to take wing, to soar. After the disaster of his marriage, his beloved Jamie's death and his disgust with the band he had been tied to since childhood, it had been his liberator.

He felt soul-sick. The others tried to lift him out of the depression which so completely claimed him. Even Giulia couldn't break the black humor which took him this time. All her love, all her care and attention seemed to bounce off him.

His soul wilted under the rejection. The other two found it the same. This kind of rebuff you took personally.

But Harry and David had inner reserves Gil was too exhausted to tap. They'd check out some of the smaller independents of which there were hundreds.

First, they made sure Gil was ensconced at Anasazi with Giulia.

After Harry and David had seen him home, Gil had finally had to admit to himself they had been unsuccessful. Professionally, if not personally, he'd been used to being in command. He got what he wanted usually, even if it took time.

The house might break through his despondency Giulia thought. But she had been bent on giving it to him as a birthday gift in December. She'd try to cope for a few more weeks. It was nearing the end of November.

In his absence, while he had been in LA working so hard to no end, she had completed the house. The gardens were tidied ready for the Spring. The interior colors of the house, restful and harmonious, chosen and applied.

Giulia hadn't wanted to employ an interior designer. She wanted this gift for her darling Gil to be from her alone, to contain all her love. She looked about her with satisfaction, knowing she'd done a good job. It would be their home – no more city apartment or rented cabin at Anasazi.

Back at the cabin Gil tinkered with his guitar, but there was no enthusiasm to work since there was no longer anyone at all to share his music with.

Giulia contacted one of his lyricists. They'd worked together so often they'd become friends - she thought he might entice him to work again. Gil spoke to him briefly and was friendly enough but turned away at the first opportunity and went back to gazing through the window at the darkening sky. Even the mountains were failing to lift his spirits.

Chapter Fifty-eight

The first flakes of winter snow drifted down from a leaden sky. Giulia banked up the fire. The cabin was as cozy as she could make it, but it was a cabin. Not the home she had so carefully built for him in the mountains, but snow just seemed to make him sadder, as if nature was dying and he was dying with it.

Stuck for anything practical to do, she left him to brood in front of the fire and wandered down to the studio to see some smiling faces and have some cheerful conversation. His mood was dragging her down too.

Jeff was balanced precariously on top of a ladder in the players' lounge retrieving large cardboard boxes from the loft.

"What on earth are you doing?" asked Giulia. "There are plenty of guys around to give you a hand."

"I like doing this myself," said Jeff, and Todd smiled his agreement.

When all the boxes had been spread out on the floor, Giulia saw that they were Christmas decorations. Shiny baubles of red and green and the glitter of gold and silver tinsel and artificial snow. Stars, Santas, reindeers, glass apples and grapes emerged from boxes sealed with parcel tape. A treasure trove of colors of every hue glittered and sparkled in the firelight.

"Well," said Todd looking at the gems spread before him, "The one thing we've no dearth of here is Christmas trees."

Giulia brightened. Now how could she get Gil to help cut Christmas trees? He'd be out in the fresh air with people he liked.

"Todd, would you go ask Gil to help bring the trees in? Since they've been in LA he's been tired and it's making him depressed. I've begun to annoy him nagging all the time. Perhaps if you asked?"

Against his inclination, Gil helped cut down three good-sized trees and heft them into the lounge and studio. It was amazing how many guys made themselves available when it came to decorating a Christmas tree.

Giulia stood back and watched the laughter and good humor, and noticed Gil's lips give an occasional twitch, especially when Mickey Stone tripped over a box, and landed on his ass with his head buried in the prickly branches hanging from the bottom of a tree.

'Funny how guys never grow up,' Giulia thought, as they all gathered round to admire their handiwork. Jeff switched on the lights, and they actually gasped. Gil too, she noticed, although he didn't smile.

Later, as they walked towards the cabin the snow began to fall faster. She'd need to go back to Denver that evening to pick up the jeep and snow-chains or they may not be able to get to the house at all. She didn't have to think hard to come up with a story for that.

"I need to check up on the apartments and see they're okay before the bad weather really sets in. Can't wait until tomorrow – the weather might get worse."

"Will you be okay driving in this? Shall I come with you?" asked Gil, without conviction.

"No, I'll be fine, but I'll need to leave now - I'll go round by the freeway. My only concern is you. Will you be okay? Please don't sit and brood - spend some time with your friends. I'll be back tomorrow all being well. I'll call you."

He bent and kissed her, but it was a reflex action.

The snow continued for that evening, then the sky cleared and the temperature dropped.

She had had to call Gil. The snow wasn't deep yet, but the local news media had reported a truck stuck at an intersection. The police were working hard to clear a build-up of traffic near Riverside.

Gil didn't want her to fight her way through traffic in the snow, so he told her to stay where she was for the time being.

Fortuitous. She had things to do.

With some trepidation she tackled the first item on her list - a phone call to Nancy. She told her all about Gil's lack of success with the album, and how disappointed and miserable he was. Then she told her she had planned a holiday break for him in the mountains. Weather permitting, would Nancy come and bring the boys to a surprise birthday party she was organizing?

Nancy was delighted. Could she bring Rosie and Carly? Giulia paused. That would mean Connie's friend and sister-in-law Lizbeth too. But she and Gil had helped each other out when they most needed it, so she agreed.

It was still the beginning of December and the snowfall resumed. Large drifting flakes of frozen lace meant one day had turned into four before Gil would let her drive to Anasazi. Panic off – except for the weather. She'd another couple of weeks to get everything arranged. Another two weeks of bad weather, perhaps? She'd just have to cross her fingers and pray.

The snow had stopped again.

Once she'd tackled Nancy, there was phone call after phone call. All the friends special enough to be in his notebook with all the phone numbers in it, which she'd stolen.

Finally, Giulia called her mother and told her about the house and how she wanted to dress it up for her own and for Gil's birthdays. She 'forgot' to mention she'd actually bought the house and didn't correct Carrie when she'd assumed it was a holiday rental.

After she'd explained what she wanted to do, her mother set the wheels in motion. She was the most organized person Giulia knew.

The pines close to the house were not suitable for the cathedral room – either too big or too small – so Giulia ordered one from Riverside.

She trawled the local shops for Christmas decorations. Her eyes sparkled as she ran around the store which stocked everything she needed, gathering boxes of multicolored baubles here, lights there until the cart was full and a shop-assistant was straining under the weight of boxes he carried.

Giulia called the electrician who had handled her house renovation and had him buy and run fairy-lights from tree to tree the full length of the drive. Her gardener cut long strands of ivy and branches of holly from the forest for the windowsills and mantle-shelves.

The house was only a few miles from Riverside, and as school finished a small bunch of kids of various sizes had gathered at the end of the drive to watch what was going on.

That wouldn't do at all for Giulia. They were drafted to build a small family of snowmen to stand to one side of the door.

With the renewed snowfall, arrangements were put on hold and the house temporarily shut down, the power turned off, the door locked, and everyone left for home.

Carrie decided she may as well stay at the Denver apartment as the weather was so uncertain. Giulia took the Jeep and drove to Anasazi.

Gil was sitting in front of the fire. The bed was rumpled and there were empty plates and pizza boxes on the dinette counter. The fire had been kept going but the hearth was dirty with ash and the log basket almost empty.

"Oh, Gil. You have to snap out of this - no-one can do it for you. You have to try."

"I know," he said but he made no move to greet her, or even to stand up.

But she had to be grateful for small mercies – he wasn't high, nor was he drunk.

"Come on. Let's get some fresh air!"

She threw his parker at him. He was too disinterested to care.

The cold air pinched his nose and ran icy fingers through his hair. Giulia pulled up his fur-lined hood, pulled gloves from his pockets and made him put them on.

"Which way?" she asked. He pointed towards Giulia's favorite little pond. No people and no walks he'd shared with Jamie there.

The water was steel grey and semi-frozen with patches of wet snow around the banks. Bullrush and iris stood, ice-stiff but drooping.

Giulia had always thought of it as verdant and full of life, but this time it seemed to look like Gil felt. Her eyes filled with tears. She reached up and hugged him and he buried his head in her hair as a child would.

"Come on. Let's go. There's nothing for us here," she said.

Each day that passed seemed like a week to Giulia. She had put all her faith in the house and hopes of it breaking through the ice which seemed to hold his heart in its grip.

Then the day of her own birthday dawned and it was time to leave for Larch Road.

But he didn't want to get in the car. This time she lost her temper and yelled at him.

"Get your ass in that god-damn car, Robson. Or I'll.... I'll ...," she looked around. There was an axe propped next to the door for chopping firewood. She brandished it at him, "I'll put this cleaver through your stupid skull!"

He got in the car.

Chapter Fifty-nine

The town of Riverside was dressed in its Christmas best. There were trees and sleighs full of gifts in every store window, and artificial icicles hanging from all the house eves. A huge, decorated tree graced the center of the square with a large notice advertising the switching on of the lights the next evening.

Once out of town the road narrowed, and Giulia had to slow right down to tackle snow ruts and pitch dark. She had thought and thought how she could get away from him long enough to switch on the lights before they both arrived but couldn't figure it out. Oh, well it couldn't be helped. But she needn't have worried with a mother like Carrie.

As they rounded the corner, a wonderland of twinkling silver and gold lined both sides of the drive, and the little cottage was decked with icicle lights and had a 'Happy Birthday' sign over the door.

They both stood speechless. She had expected to drive round the corner into pitch black. Her brain whirred.

"Happy Birthday! Wow - good of the owners to give us such a welcome!"

Gil, shocked from his lethargy, asked:

"Did you tell them when your birthday was?" He looked puzzled.

"Oh, no. They must have taken it off the hire forms." What a transparent lie.

How would he ever accept that! But he did - he was too bemused to do anything else.

"What a fantastic little cottage. It looks like a gingerbread house with the snow on its roof. Bet its real cozy."

He went to look through the window but Giulia grabbed his hand.

"Come on. They've done this for us. Let's explore a bit first."

She sighed with relief, and they wandered up the drive hand-in-hand like Hansel and Gretel, looking this way and that at the lights and their reflections twinkling on the virgin snow.

'What else did Carrie have up her sleeve?' Giulia pondered.

As they rounded the corner and the house came into view, Gil stumbled back against a tree, dumbstruck.

The house was decorated inside and out like a fairy-tale castle. The work they had done before had been doubled. There were icicles from every horizontal surface – real and artificial. The little snowman family had been arranged round a miniature tree and had carol sheets in stick hands. Someone had molded their mouths into 'O's.

The enormous tree Carrie had put up in the cathedral room stood to the left of the window, decorated to within an inch of its life. Its lights were flickering and glowing on the snow outside.

Giulia pulled a shell-shocked Gil to his feet and marched off to the house steps, curious herself to see what the interior brought. It didn't disappoint.

But the biggest shock of all came when they opened the door to the cathedral room. Around the huge ice sculpture of an angel was arranged a feast fit for a king. Whole salmon, salads, turkey and even some fries sitting on a table warmer. Giulia looked at her mother for a moment and when she smiled, ran into her arms.

"Well, today is my baby girl's birthday. I couldn't miss that."

Then the full fruit of Giulia's endeavors began arriving, singly and in twos and threes. First Nancy with two wide-eyed boys who looked around them in wonder, and nearly forgot Gil's existence. They'd travelled with the two girls in Liz's SUV.

Then, separately, Jeff and Todd with Mickey Stone and the other boys from the band India, who arrived in a people carrier with ice chains; Harry and David and the LA contingent: John and Suzy; Gloria came to see her Mr. Gil. And lastly came Giulia's own family – Larry, shaking snow from his hair, and his elfin wife Diana; and Tony with their big step-sisters Joanna and Jenny.

All good friends. People he loved Gil realized, and with surprise, friends who loved him in return.

As coats, hats and gloves were removed and the guests moved round the house, Carrie turned to Giulia and said in a loud voice.

"Damn and blast, Giulia Giordano! Get them into the big room. The ice sculpture's ruining the carpet."

"Who the hell's Giulia Giordano?" asked Davy Elliot in a voice which carried over all the chatter.

Everything was going better than Giulia could possibly have imagined. She wove through the crowd, chatting and talking to Gil's friends and relatives - the boys were wrapped round Gil's neck until he managed to pry their fingers free. Glasses were refilled, several semi-sober toasts made.

It had begun to snow again. Large soft flakes, which gathered on the outdoor plants and lawns.

Then Giulia realized Gil was missing. She half-ran round the house searching for him, desperately trying not to alert the guests something was wrong.

She found him at last sitting on the outside steps, a cigarette held in his hand, oblivious to the snow dusting his hair. He held her close and kissed her over and over.

"You are a miracle." Her heart swelled with happiness. "….. but this is too much, Giulia. I can't take it all in. I'm completely overwhelmed."

Harry had been observing them from the open doorway. He ran back inside.

"Dave……Davy! Car keys…pronto! Car keys." David tossed them to him without comment and continued downing his champagne. Great party, he thought, gazing around benignly.

"Giulia…. Cabin keys. NOW!", shouted Harry. They were in his hand in moments.

He ran down the drive as fast as his long legs would carry him and zoomed off in David's four-by-four. Giulia and Gil looked at each other. What the hell?

"There's a sitting room behind the door to the right of the hall. Its small and cozy. Why don't you have some quiet time? I understand it's all come as a shock," said Giulia to Gil.

He hoisted himself to his feet, shook off the snow which had collected in his hair and went to find the sitting-room.

It was a couple of hours before Harry returned.

"Where's Gil?" he asked Giulia.

"He's in the sitting room but last time I looked he was sleeping. Don't disturb him, Harry. I shouldn't have done this. He wasn't up to it."

Harry kissed her fondly on the forehead.

"You did exactly what was right. It was what he needed. Don't judge now - wait until morning."

Harry strode off to the sitting room, dragging David by the arm on the way past.

"C'mon, sot. We've work to do," he grinned.

In the cozy sitting room the fire in the log burner was glowing, and a single lamp alight. Harry grabbed a wooden chair from against the wall and jammed it under the door handle. He shook Gil awake.

"It's a little early," David said, "but we have a birthday gift for you."

Gil looked from one to the other, bleary-eyed.

"But first, you might need this." Harry took from his pocket a small parcel wrapped in a soft cloth and put it in Gil's hand.

Gil knew what it was immediately. It buzzed gently and when he pulled back the cloth the beautiful amethyst crystal sparkled in the firelight.

"How did you find this? It was supposed to be hidden away."

"A couple of weeks after you got it, the picture dropped off the wall and it fell out. I rewrapped it and put it back again. You were up on the mountain at the time and it didn't seem worth mentioning."

Gil was immediately infused with the belief that everything was going to be alright. Whatever happened would turn out okay. For a heartbeat the familiar, peaceful face of the monk Anukulah filled his mind.

He shuddered with the enormity of the relief. David grabbed him by the arm.

"Well thank God you remembered that," said David to Harry, "because if that came as a shock, this is going to be the full earthquake."

They were talking across him, and Gil's head was moving right and left trying to take it all in.

David pulled a folded sheet of paper from the back pocket of his jeans and handed it to Gil, who spent a few moments reading it, then pitched forward in a dead faint.

"What the fuck!" said David. "I didn't realize he needed it that much, or I'd have driven over last week when we first got it."

They hauled Gil back onto the sofa and gave him time to come round. From ashen his color had returned to near-normal as he rubbed the crystal between his hands.

"One of Dave's contacts – jazz guy – has set up a small independent. We bullied him into taking the album. That's your copy of the contract. We were waiting to get your reaction before we returned ours."

"Yeah…. All for one and one for all. You're not under any obligation. Throw it in the burner if you don't want it," shrugged Davy.

Chapter Sixty

The rest of the night was a series of vague impressions for Gil. He remembered chatting away happily with people, then in mid-sentence chuckling, and walking away. He had a feeling he'd done that more than once.

Harry had taken Giulia aside to explain. She flung both arms round his neck. Both laughed as they parted, moist-eyed.

"For a happy occasion, this is a frickin' wet one," he chuckled."

She kissed his cheek and ran off to drag Gil under the mistletoe.

Her wonder of a mother had thought of everything, and slowly, beginning with the children and their parents, the guests dispersed to a Riverside hotel.

As she and Gil waved the last of their guests off, Giulia whispered in his ear.

"Come on. You look as if you've been struck by lightning."

Once in the bedroom she'd created for them she said:

"Let's get some rest. We're only halfway through the celebrations – that was my birthday, we still have yours to go tomorrow...," she looked at her watch. "Oh, no - today. Well never mind. Later, when you've come round a bit."

He looked completely shattered.

"Oh shit! Please don't make me do that again. It'd kill me!"

"Good job I planned a quiet day, just the two of us, in front of the TV then?"

He sighed with relief and was sleeping like a baby within minutes.

It was six-fifty when Giulia woke him.

He didn't want to get up, but she was so insistent he put on the robe she tossed at him and followed her to the cathedral room.

In the doorway he stopped dead. He couldn't be seeing this. It was impossible.

The window wall – from left to right - looked out onto the mountains, obscured by darkness since their arrival.

Now the emerging sun rimed their snow-covered peaks with pink and gold. The heavens still held a scattering of stars. Before his eyes, the sun exploded over the horizon, turning the snow beneath to glittering drifts of silver-white.

He dream-walked to the window and placed his hand against the glass.

There was nothing he could say. He looked at Giulia, his soul shining in his eyes.

"Happy Birthday," she whispered, and dropped the keys to her gift into his palm.

Coming soon

Book Two of the 'Universal Link' Series

"The Twinkle in Pa's Eye"

Printed in Great Britain
by Amazon